W9-BHX-981

House Divided

A Novel

By Peter G. Pollak

ACKNOWLEDGEMENTS

I owe a debt of gratitude to a number of people who helped me at various points in the writing of this novel.

Hoping not to forget anyone, thanks go to Edward Beck, my expert on the Arab-Israeli conflict, to the members of the crime fiction Linked-Inn interest group who helped with firearms and explosives, and to Paul Joseph Wood on Naval careers.

Salvatore Scibona (author of *The End*) and Ann Mallen provided input on the opening chapters.

I'm grateful to critique partner Sonja Hutchinson and to Nathan Van Coops (author of *In Times Like These* and *The Chronothon*) whose insights and suggestions made this a better book.

Susan Lider, who is serving as publicist for *House Divided*, provided valuable input into the manuscript as well.

To the extent to which *House Divided* is free of grammatical and spelling errors as well as typos, my thanks go to Adele Brinkley's With Pen in Hand editorial service with an assist from Barbara Baird Sullivan who proofed an early version.

Jude Ferraro, my biggest fan, contributed in too many ways to cite.

Any remaining typos, grammatical, or other errors are fully my responsibility.

Once again I called on Kelly Mullen of *InVision Studios* for the cover design and once again I couldn't be more pleased with the result. Cover design is only one graphics area in which she is highly skilled.

The events of *House Divided* were conceived as a work of fiction. Let's hope they remain so. All characters, places, and events sprung from my imagination.

You can learn about my other novels as well as share you views on this book at *petergpollak.com*.

Peter G. Pollak

College Park, Maryland: Tuesday, March 13

Susan stood in her apartment doorway watching Sammy and Marisa walk down the stairs. A light on the second floor flickered and went out. She would have to call the landlord.

Susan hoped Marisa would obey Sammy's injunction against discussing their plans where she might be overheard. She suspected Marisa felt the need to assure him she was up to doing her part. Sammy had that effect on people; they wanted his approval.

Susan had felt that way at first. Now she wondered about some of the things he'd told her, but it was too late for second-guessing. Everything was ready, Sammy had told them at the end of their meeting. He just needed a few more items to be able to finish the bomb.

Susan hoped he'd get what he needed soon. She wanted what they were planning to be over. No matter what happened afterwards, she just wanted it to be over.

Peter G. Pollak

New York City: Thursday, March 15

"You did what?" Leonard Robbins asked his daughter, not sure he heard right due to the din in the Manhattan restaurant where he and his wife were celebrating Courtney's twentieth birthday.

"I said I joined Students for Palestinian Justice."

Leonard threw his hands into the air. "Why?"

"You're the one who taught me to root for the underdog."

"The Palestinians like to pretend they're the underdog, but don't ask them what they're doing with all the money they get from us, the United Nations, Qatar, and even from Israel."

"But, Dad, the Palestinians are not occupying Israeli territory."

"Courtney, you should know the history of that region better before--"

"Len, not now," Alison Robbins said, placing her hand on her husband's arm. "It's neither the time nor the place."

Leonard frowned, but deferred to his wife. "You're right. Sorry."

The silence that followed was not broken until three members of the restaurant wait-staff arrived, one with a candle in a large cupcake. Leonard detected a look of annoyance from his daughter, as if she thought this was another example of their treating her like a child. Yet, she couldn't help but smile when the waiter lit the candle and led a funky rendition of the happy birthday song.

Courtney puffed up her cheeks and blew out the candle to applause from diners at nearby tables.

Alison removed a small gift-wrapped package from her pocketbook and handed it across the table. "Happy twentieth."

Courtney slid the ribbon off the package and tore the wrapping paper off the box. It was a dark blue velvet jewelry store box. She extracted a set of four silver bracelets. "Mom, you shouldn't have."

"Those were the ones you wanted, right?" Alison asked.

Courtney nodded. She put them on and raised her arm to show them off.

Leonard waited a few seconds before he pulled an envelope out of his jacket pocket and handed it to her. "Just don't donate any of this to the Palestinians."

Courtney opened the envelope. "Thanks, Dad. In other words, they can have my body, but not my money?"

"When you put it that way, I'm not sure which is worse," Leonard said.

"Enough, you two," Alison said. She waved down the waiter. "We should be getting back to the hotel. I'm sure your father wants to go over his talk one more time."

"I do," Leonard said.

"You're not nervous, are you, Dad?"

He chuckled. "Hardly. Besides, you probably have some school work to do."

"Not on my birthday! Sue Philips is waiting for me. We're going out."

"Then we won't detain you any longer," Leonard said.

"Should I hail a cab?" Courtney asked.

"No need, dear," her mother replied. "We drove over in our van, but you can help your father maneuver his wheelchair out the front door while I pay the bill."

"How'd it go with your dad?"

Courtney Robbins turned around. It was Doreen Rupert, a tall brunette from her International Politics class. "Join us," she said, motioning for Doreen to pull up a chair.

"Doreen, this is my roommate Sue Philips. Sue, Doreen."

That morning Courtney had mentioned to Doreen that that her parents were coming to town to take her out to dinner.

"Lucky you," Doreen had ventured.

"I'm not so sure," Courtney replied.

"What do you mean?"

"My dad can be a little overbearing. He's always asking questions about every thing I do."

"Dads can get that way," Doreen said.

"Yours, too?"

"I wish mine came with a remote."

Courtney chuckled remembering Doreen's comment. She'd have to remember that one.

Courtney showed off her new bracelets when Doreen returned to their table. "I got these from my mom."

Doreen took a close look. "Nice."

"And a check from my dad."

"I'll drink to that," Doreen said.

"Now I can stay in the city for the summer."

"Dads are good for something," Sue said. "Mine is always ragging on me for my clothes and hair, but he pays the tuition on time."

Doreen saluted her with her drink. "There you go."

"On the other hand, my dad isn't happy about my joining the campus SPJ group," Courtney said.

"Your family's not Jewish, are they?" Doreen asked.

"It's not that. I guess he doesn't buy the idea that Israel is in the wrong."

"Did you explain?"

"My mom stopped the conversation."

Doreen raised her glass. "You survived!"

"No doubt he'll bring it up the next time we talk."

Doreen nodded. "Show him some of the pictures on SPJ website and ask him to read some of the stories about families forced to abandon houses they'd lived in for decades."

"Good suggestion. He can be so stubborn, but that's not going to stop me!"

"Good for you, Courtney. You're how old--twenty-one?"

"Just twenty."

Doreen shrugged her shoulders. "Still, you're your own person. You get to decide what you believe."

"Here, here," the roommate echoed.

Courtney downed the last of her margarita. "I still wish he trusted me more."

Two days later, Alison Robbins handed Leonard her cell phone. They were waiting for their van in the lobby of the Regency Hotel. Alison had called her daughter to let her know that they were driving back upstate.

"How did your talk go, Dad?"

"Fine. I told them what they didn't want to hear and they told me all the reasons I'm wrong."

"You always say people don't like to face the truth."

Leonard laughed. "Speaking of which we need to talk about the BDS movement. When are you coming up to Albany?"

"Never, since you put it that way."

"I fell into that one, didn't I?"

Alison reached for the phone. "Len. Please don't lecture her."

Leonard shrugged. "Okay, Court dear. Just promise me that you'll use that brain of yours to test out whatever bunk they try to sell you."

"Only if you do the same, Dad," Courtney replied.

Leonard was quiet on the three-hour ride back to Albany. He told himself not to worry about Courtney's having joined Students for Palestinian Justice. At some point she was bound to see through the group's moral failings, but he wondered if she had chosen that group because she knew he'd disapprove.

Is this just an 'I'm a grown up' game she's playing? The problem he wanted to tell her is people get hurt when not everyone is playing by the same set of rules.

Peter G. Pollak

Washington, D.C.: Tuesday, March 27

Assistant Director of the CIA, Alan Goldberg, came forward as Leonard Robbins was escorted into the conference room. "Lenny, glad you could make it. Any hassles out front? I told them to go easy on you."

Leonard and his wheelchair had been thoroughly searched before he was permitted to enter the White House. It was a humiliating experience, but one he had gotten used to. He angled his chair to the spot Goldberg had cleared for him.

"You're looking good, Lenny," Goldberg said. "Academia must be agreeing with you."

"And, you're looking--"

"I know--the same. My wife tells me I age one year for every two years she does. Drives her nuts. Can I get you anything? Tea, right? Martinez will be down shortly."

"Hot tea would be nice."

Goldberg motioned to the young woman standing near the back of the room. "How about a Danish?"

"No thanks. What's this about, Alan?"

"Let's wait for Martinez. She'll spell it out."

The door opened. Three people Leonard didn't know entered. Goldberg introduced them. The sole woman was Assistant Director of the FBI's Counterterrorism Division. Sally Peterson was short, blond, and looked like she practiced frowning. The older of the two men, Miles McLaughlin, was Deputy Director at the National Security Agency. McLaughlin had wavy white hair, glasses, and shook hands with Leonard as if they were old friends.

The third person was a deputy director at Homeland Security.

"Odell Sanders. Nice to meet you, professor."

Leonard thought the name sounded familiar. "Didn't you play football for the--"

"Dallas Cowboys? Sure did."

Before Leonard had a chance to ask Sanders about the Cowboys' most recent season, Assistant to the President for National Security Affairs Rosa Martinez burst into the room, followed by an entourage of assistants. She headed straight toward Leonard.

"Thank you for coming on such short notice, Professor Robbins," she said, offering her hand. "Let's get started. I don't have a lot of time this morning."

Martinez was even thinner in person than she appeared on TV, and the bags under her eyes made her look downright unhealthy. Leonard was aware of her accomplished background. She had all the right degrees and twenty plus years in the State Department.

One of Martinez' assistants extracted a set of documents from a briefcase and started passing them around the table. When one landed in front of him, Leonard was surprised to see a copy of the article he'd sent over to the CIA a week ago as per the agreement he'd signed when he retired that allowed them to review any manuscript he was submitting for publication.

The editor at *Foreign Affairs* had commissioned "Terrorism--The Next Frontier" after he'd attended Leonard's recent foreign policy speech. Leonard expected some pushback, but not being hauled to Washington in front of the President's National Security Advisor.

"We brought you here today, Professor Robbins, to talk to you about your article," Martinez said. "Simply put, we can't allow you to publish it as it stands."

"Why is that?"

"To start, any terrorist organization that wants to attack us could use it as a blueprint."

"If I may be so bold, that horse has already left the stable."

"In what sense, sir?"

"In the sense that there's nothing in my article that our enemies have not already figured out for themselves. They know the best way to generate isolationist sentiment in the U.S. is to bring the war onto our shores."

"Where's your proof of that?" Alan Goldberg asked, tapping his pen on the table.

Leonard pointed to the article in front of him "Did you read--"

"And what about the fact that new groups crop up every other month?" Rosa Martinez asked. "You're telling them where we're weakest."

Leonard took a deep breath. "Most of those groups are splinters or fronts for existing organizations. More importantly, only a state-sponsored organization with considerable resources at its disposal represents a threat to do serious damage here in the states."

"Al Qaida didn't have a state sponsor," Alan Goldberg interjected.

Leonard nodded. "True, but after nine-eleven we raised our security barriers to prevent likely terrorists from entering the U.S. The fact that Al Qaeda has been unable to penetrate our borders the past sixteen plus years is not for lack of trying."

"All that may be the case, Professor Robbins," Martinez said, regaining control of the meeting, "but from a policy viewpoint what you recommend--increased monitoring of emails and social media--would violate the civil rights of thousands of Americans."

"Which is why I wrote the article," Leonard said. "The American people need to be warned that we have not seen the end to terrorist attacks on our soil. Someone needs to let them know unless we revise our thinking about security, future attacks are likely to come from folks who might otherwise be considered 'red-blooded Americans.'"

Goldberg jumped in again. "But to suggest that a terrorist organization could recruit Americans to attack their own country, that's . . ."

"Crazy?" Leonard smiled. "I'm not offended, but you're making my point. If it's so unlikely, why stop me from printing my theories?"

"Because someone might read your article and decide it's worth a try," Martinez said. "We have our hands full as it is."

"I'll bet you ten bucks that it's already happening. There could be a dozen recruiters in this country right now looking for the next Tsarnaev brothers."

"You can't believe that, Lenny," Goldberg interjected.

"I do. You forget not so long ago a small group of Americans called the Weather Underground decided the best way to force us out of Vietnam was to blow up a few army-recruiting offices. It doesn't take a lot of zealots to do a lot of damage."

"Preposterous," Goldberg said, looking at Martinez for confirmation.

"That was a different time, Professor," Odell Sanders offered.

"It was, but conditions are ripe today for a similar scenario. I cited some examples in the paper."

"Based on what?" Martinez asked.

"Based on what is being taught in college classrooms these days. Students are told that this country is racist in its foundation, that it oppresses people all over the globe, and that we are endangering future life on this planet by our greed and disregard for the environment. After hearing that day after day, why is it so unlikely to suggest that a naïve young American or two will be tempted to take direct action to as the SDSers used to say 'wake up the American people?'"

Odell Sanders raised his hand. "Surely, you're not denying this country's history of slavery?"

"Of course not, but I object to statements from people like the Stanford professor who questioned the moral right of the United States to exist. Do you want me to read what he said? It's right here on page . . .seven, second paragraph." Leonard waited for the others to find the page. "And I quote 'based as it is on the ethnic cleansing of the indigenous peoples of North America and hundreds of years of slavery and structural racial discrimination.'"

"I don't see what's incorrect about that statement," Sanders ventured.

"Let's start with the fact that slavery pre-existed the founding of this country, so how can you blame the country for 'hundreds of years' of slavery? As far as structural racial discrimination is concerned, we outlawed the last remnants of that fifty years ago."

"Not without a fight!" Sanders said.

"Sure, a few fought to the bitter end, but the vast majority of Americans were for the civil rights legislation passed in '64 and '65. I'm not saying prejudice doesn't exist. I'm saying it's factually wrong to call this country 'racist.'"

NSA Martinez stood up. "This is a fascinating discussion, Professor Robbins, but I'm afraid our time is up. We've informed *Foreign Affairs* of our objections. If you'd like to revise your piece, we'll certainly take another look at it."

Leonard watched Martinez and her crew gather their papers and leave. The other three followed. Alan Goldberg accompanied Leonard to the van that would take him back to Reagan National for his flight home. "Sorry, Len. Just change a few words and it'll be fine."

Leonard didn't spend much time pondering what he'd been told at the meeting before deciding he would not revise the article. Everything he'd written was defensible. *The hell with them. If they can't stand to hear the truth from me, they'll have to find out some other way.*

He was not in a good mood as his flight descended over the State University at Albany campus into Albany International Airport. His greatest hope when leaving the CIA for academia was that he would have the opportunity to influence public policy. If he couldn't publish his views, why retain the academic credentials? Maybe it was time to move to someplace warm and write his memoir.

"Shit," he said out loud, startling the man in the seat next to him. "Sorry, I just had a terrible thought." *They'd probably kill my memoir, too.*

New York City: Thursday, April 12

Courtney Robbins' head felt like it was exploding. She and Doreen had just heard a Palestinian woman who called herself Tarab Abdul Hadi rant on and on about the need for Americans to be more aggressive in support of the Palestinian people.

Erik Greene, one of the leaders of the NYU boycott Israel group Students for Palestinian Justice, had invited Courtney to meet Hadi. He had pulled Courtney aside at a SPJ party in his apartment. An NYU law school student, Erik was short, had curly brown hair, and wore thick glasses. After some small talk he asked her how committed she was to the SPJ cause.

"Very much," she replied, not sure what he was asking.

"I'm glad to hear that. There's someone I'd like you to meet--a Palestinian freedom fighter. She can tell you what Israel is doing to her people from personal experience. Would you be interested in meeting her?"

"Sure," Courtney said.

"Good. Doreen will let you know when the meeting will take place."

"I can give you my cell," Courtney volunteered.

"Unh, uh," Eric said. "That's not safe. Please don't tell anyone else. Don't mention it in an email or on your cell. We can't take any chances the authorities will try to stop her from telling her story."

"What would they do?"

"Probably put her in a detention camp and then deport her."

"For what?"

"Exercising her right to free speech."

"Really?" Courtney asked.

"I can document some examples if you need evidence," Erik said.

"No, I believe you."

For the next few days Courtney could think of little else. Maybe the woman could verify some of the things Courtney heard at SPJ meetings. That way she'd have ammunition to use when she and her dad had it out.

Thursday Doreen showed up at her dorm room just as Courtney was beginning to think about dinner. "If you want to meet the freedom fighter, we have to go now."

After walking a few blocks, Doreen turned into an alley and knocked on the side door of a white van that was parked out of sight of the main street.

Erik Greene opened the door. "Hurry. We're late."

Doreen got in first. Courtney exchanged greetings with two people she knew vaguely from SPJ meetings.

"It's about a forty minute ride, folks," Erik told them. "Hang tight."

When Erik finally let them out, they were in an alley behind a brick apartment building with a rickety fire escape and laundry hanging from the top floor. He shepherded them into the building through a street level entrance into an unlit hall and then up two flights of stairs into a sparsely furnished apartment.

A thin woman with long black hair was sitting in a chair far from the windows talking to two men. Courtney was surprised how young the woman looked. She wore jeans and a long purple top.

Erik did the introductions. He let it be known that Tarab Abdul Hadi wasn't the woman's real name. "It's a name she's adopted for this mission to honor a famous female Palestinian activist," he stated.

Erik didn't introduce either of the men. One looked similar to the woman—dark with furtive eyes; the other was stocky, balding, and dressed like a typical graduate student with a button-down shirt and khakis. They were told the latter would translate if she needed help.

The young woman hammered out her message in a meandering hour-long presentation. She condemned Israelis as colonialists and racists. Only raising the price of their occupation would convince them to withdraw from the West Bank, East Jerusalem, and the other Palestinian territories.

"Our struggle against the Zionists is reaching the final stage," she said in conclusion. "We are near to victory. With your help we can retake our homeland."

Courtney was surprised that no one had objected to her suggestion that martyrdom was necessary to win the war, but then again, no one questioned anything the woman said. Courtney wasn't sure how she felt about any of it. She'd never met anyone who was so committed to a cause that she'd kill or be killed to defend it.

At the end of the presentation, without inviting questions, Erik restated the importance of doing even more to bring the Palestinians' cause to the general public. Courtney wanted to ask him what he had in mind, but he told them they had to leave, and they would discuss it at the next SPJ meeting.

"What did you think?" Doreen asked as they walked back to the subway after the van let them out near 116th Street.

"She was pretty militant."

"You'd be too if you had to put up with what she's had to suffer," Doreen stated.

"There's always another side to every story."

"Come on, Courtney. Is that your father talking? You're a big girl now. You've got to decide who's telling the truth and who's covering up."

Courtney nodded. She felt bad for the Palestinian woman and for the women and children living in refugee camps. "At least it seems as if the BDS movement is growing."

Doreen stopped walking. "We can't count on what people are doing someplace else. As Erik said, we have to do our part to convince the American people to support the Palestinians and not the Israelis."

Courtney truly hoped Israel would withdraw from the territories, but what would happen if they didn't? Would there be more fighting like 2014 when over twenty-five hundred Palestinians had died?

Washington, D.C.: Friday, April 13

Ben Hartman was glad the day was almost over. It had been a long week and he was tired of Friday the thirteenth jokes. One woman brought stuffed black cats to work, which she surreptitiously moved to different people's desks during the day. Another woman made a black cat out of black paper and hung it from the top of her door, the meaning of which Ben didn't want to know. Friday the thirteenth is a pagan thing he kept telling his office mates, but no one listened. They were having too much fun, pretending to consign each other to seven years of bad luck for walking past a black cat without throwing salt over your shoulders or some such maneuver.

It had been a hectic week. As PR director for the American Israel Association, Ben had multiple responsibilities for the events that would take place the following week in celebration of the seventieth anniversary of Israel's founding. He'd issued numerous press releases for the past two months announcing various events, arranged for media interviews, and harassed AIA staffers responsible for each of the venues to confirm that everything that needed to be done for each event was in place.

As he scanned his planning document for the twentieth time that day, he found no empty check boxes signifying there were tasks he needed to perform before going home to celebrate Shabbat with his wife and their four-year-old son. Next week would be hectic, but he was fairly confident that things would come off smoothly.

As the clock inched toward closing time, Ben cleaned up his desk and packed things to take home-- his empty lunch bag, the Daniel Silva novel he was reading during lunch breaks when he had the luxury of actually taking a lunch break, and the latest issue of *Commentary* in hopes he would be able to delve into them over the weekend.

His phone buzzed just as he was retrieving his overcoat from the rack in the corner of his office.

"Ben. Are you expecting a package?"

It was Tanika at the front desk.

"Not today. Who's it from?"

He heard Tanika repeat his question to someone in the lobby.

"It appears to be from your printer."

Ben was expecting some handouts for Wednesday's press conference, but not until Monday. The printer must have gotten them done earlier than promised.

"It's okay," Ben said. "I'm leaving, but you can sign for them and leave them in the mail room."

"Okay, Ben. Have a nice weekend."

Ben hung up the phone and went back to get his trench coat. He put it on and retrieved the things he planned to take home that were sitting on the chair next to his desk.

Whenever he thought back on what happened next, all he could remember was the floor's erupting. His initial thought was an earthquake had hit the building. Things happened too fast for a second thought.

Albany, New York: The Same Day

"Leonard, come quickly. You've got to hear this," Alison called Leonard from the family living room. She was turning up the sound on the big-screen TV when he wheeled into the room.

"I repeat," the announcer was saying. "An explosion has been reported within the hour at the H Street headquarters of the American Israel Association, the largest and most influential pro-Israel lobbying organization in the U.S."

The screen showed a file photo of the location.

"We have crews on the way," the announcer said. "Damage is reported to be extensive. Emergency crews and police and fire services are on their way. We do not have any details at the moment as to casualties, although it would be a miracle after such a large explosion if no one was injured or killed."

Alison looked at her husband. He was shaking his head. She went over and rubbed the back of his neck knowing that was where he got tense. "What do you think?" she asked.

"If I had to guess, I'd say it was a bomb."

"Damn! Are you sure?"

"I hope I'm wrong."

"We are getting our first live images," the announcer stated.

The camera panned the outside of what had been a modern D.C. office building. The entrance way was now a mad sculptor's collage of steel and concrete. Cars sat at odd angles to the street making it difficult for emergency vehicles to get close. Behind the reporter, stretcher carriers were trying to make their way through the debris.

"It's amazing it didn't happen before now," Leonard said.

"Why? AIA must have the best security money can buy."

"There's no such thing as fool-proof security, and it doesn't take much to do that kind of damage."

"Who do you think is behind it?"

"It's too soon to speculate. It could be a crazy anti-Semite or it could be a terrorist organization. Let's see what people are saying on the Web."

Alison followed Leonard back to his study and his multiple computer screens.

"What is President Wheatfield going to do?" she asked as he opened various news websites.

Leonard shrugged. "I've no idea. Her national security advisor told me not one month ago that nothing like this could happen. Will this change their minds? Who knows?"

When Alison finally turned off the TV, the death total had reached seven, five of whom were AIA employees. The number injured was double that, including people who'd been on the street on foot or in cars.

Within hours the media reported pro-Palestinian groups praising the bombing. Their statements were eerily similar: the U.S. was learning what their support for Israel was costing. They all forecast more bombings until the U.S. withdrew its support for Israel or until Israel withdrew from the West Bank, Golan Heights, and East Jerusalem.

Delmar, New York: Sunday, April 15

Leonard wheeled himself to his place at the dining room table where his wife had laid out the *Albany Times Union* and the *New York Times*.

"How was your workout?"

"Tiring," he replied. Although he would never regain the use of his legs, his doctors painted a scary picture for him should he not maintain a regular conditioning regime. As a result, exercise equipment designed for paraplegics had been installed in a spare bedroom, including a resistance pool that had been purchased with insurance money.

Leonard's daily routine consisted of upper body strengthening, followed by thirty to forty-five minutes in the resistance pool. The official report blamed the accident in a suburb of Caracas on a drunken truck driver. To this day, Leonard was convinced he'd been targeted by leftist guerillas.

Sunday's newspaper coverage focused on the basics of the D.C. bombing--who, what and when. The *Washington Post* and *New York Times* provided local coverage supplementing reports from the Associated Press, but twenty-four hours had not been enough time for much information to be generated.

The opinion columns and editorials speculated on who was behind the bombing and whether U.S. administrations past and current had done enough to prevent such acts.

"Learn anything?" Alison asked when she got up to clear the breakfast plates.

"Nothing new. Most people don't realize that investigating a bombing is a very arduous process. It can be weeks before they learn what materials were used, how the bomb was detonated and so forth."

"So what did the editorial writers say?"

"That the government of Israel is to blame for not negotiating with the Palestinians."

"Really?"

"That's been the liberal establishment's position for the past decade or more. Nothing is going to shake them from that conclusion."

"That's unfortunate. By the way, did you read your email this morning?" Alison asked.

"Not yet. Anything important?"

"Courtney emailed she's going south with a couple of her roommates over spring break."

"Not to some boycott Israel conference, I hope."

Alison frowned. "You have to let her work these things out for herself, Len."

"Why can't she work on things that normal twenty-year-old girls have to work on, like having too many boyfriends or saving some endangered species?"

Alison shook her head. "She's probably into those too."

"Great. Is she still majoring in psychology or is she switching to Boycott, Divestment and Sanction Israel studies?"

Alison sighed. "That's not even funny."

"Sorry. And this summer, does she have any plans?"

"You know her plans, Len. She's staying in the city to take two courses so she can graduate with her class."

"I did know that, didn't I?"

"Speaking of summer plans," Alison said, "I'm going to put a couple of hours in the garden to get it ready for spring planting. Buzz me when you get hungry for lunch."

As he wheeled himself into his study, Leonard paused before logging into his network. The D.C. bombing seemed to confirm his analysis of a new direction in international terrorism. It also rendered his *Foreign Policy* article moot. The question was should he spend any time putting together an opinion piece on what should be done. He could probably find a newspaper that would print it if the CIA reviewed it quickly and gave him permission. He decided to write the article and see what happened.

He checked his email. Courtney's email reminded him that even more important than whether the administration would allow him to voice his opinion was his relationship with his daughter. Once they had been like a wrestling tag team, managing crises together as she emerged from her fairy princess years into and out of a tomboy stage through the trying high school years with boys and self-esteem taking precedence.

Until recently, Courtney had come to him whenever she was troubled. Now, a junior at NYU, they talked less and less and when they did talk, it seemed she had changed teams and they were rivals instead of teammates.

He hoped it was only a phase, a necessary gaining of independence, "becoming her own person," as Alison put it. Such experiments, however, could go awry. Unlike the past when she was a teenager and could be sheltered or rescued, the consequences of actions taken in her early twenties could be life-changing.

He made a note to call her later that day. During her freshman year they'd talked every Sunday night after watching *60 Minutes*, he and Alison in their living room, Courtney in her dorm, but when she returned to school as a sophomore, she announced she didn't want to feel bound by those weekly calls. "I'll call when I get a chance," she told them. "After all, we can always email."

Email wasn't the same thing as hearing someone's voice on the phone. Maybe she'd be home that evening. Maybe she'd open up to him. He could always hope.

Albany, New York: Monday, April 16

Alison drove Leonard to the Rockefeller College campus in mid-town Albany in time for his eleven o'clock meeting with a student. She had packed a dinner, which he planned to eat in his office, because he taught a seven to nine evening class.

He was in the middle of going over the student's paper when his phone buzzed.

"Professor Robbins, I apologize for interrupting. You have a call from the office of the National Security Advisor. Should I put it through?"

Leonard held the receiver to his chest. "Mark, I've got to take this call. Can you give me a minute?"

"Sure, Professor Robbins." The student left the office.

"Okay, put the call through."

Leonard listened to background music for a several minutes, trying not to be annoyed about the interruption. Finally someone picked up the line.

"Professor Robbins, this is Aaron Hayes, assistant to National Security Advisor Rosa Martinez. How are you today?"

Leonard remembered Hayes from his recent White House visit. "Fine. How can I assist you?"

"President Wheatfield is assembling a group of political and academic terrorism experts at the White House Wednesday for a discussion of this recent bombing. She would like you to be present."

"Fine," Leonard said. "Give me the details."

"Please stay on the line. Someone from our staff will make the travel arrangements."

Another command performance! Leonard wondered whether they were ready to listen to him now or whether he'd hear more explanations that showed the president's top people still hadn't grasped what they were up against.

Washington, D.C.: Wednesday, April 18

At ten after three Wednesday afternoon, everyone in the large conference room except Leonard Robbins rose to their feet as President Gloria Wheatfield, the first female president in U.S. history, entered the room. Before she arrived, Leonard had enjoyed a brief conversation with one of his former instructors, K.T. Alcorn, professor of International Politics at Georgetown.

"What do you think of Wheatfield?" Alcorn asked in a hushed voice.

"I didn't vote for her, but she's been a pleasant surprise," Leonard replied. A compromise candidate who was chosen when the two top Democrat candidates came out of the primaries neck and neck, Wheatfield edged her Republican opponent by distancing herself from the unpopular policies of previous Democratic administrations. She campaigned on reforming the Affordable Care Act to enable businesses to control healthcare costs and promised to increase the military budget, both of which she accomplished in her first months in office.

"Wheatfield is the anti-Hillary," Alcorn said.

"Meaning?"

"She's tough in public and easy going in private. Clinton is the opposite."

Wheatfield gained her spurs as governor of Illinois, a state that had become almost ungovernable due to political divisions and underlying economic distress. Her qualifications included running a manufacturing company that had been founded by her great-grandfather before moving on to manage the city of Cicero. She left both in better condition than when she arrived.

Wheatfield called the meeting to order and asked people to introduce themselves. In addition to Vice President Harold Lee and NSA Rosa Martinez, top officials were present from the Justice Department, the FBI, the CIA, the National Security Agency, the U.S. Attorney's Office, the Defense Department, and Homeland Security. Four academics in addition to Professor Alcorn and Leonard had been invited. The majority and minority leaders of both houses of Congress were present as were the top ranking Democrat and Republican on each of the Homeland Security committees. President Wheatfield made the number at the table an even twenty-four. A large number of staffers hugged the walls.

"We're here today to discuss the implications of the explosion that took place last Friday," President Wheatfield stated after the introductions. "The FBI informs me that it was caused by an incendiary device that was the equivalent of one half ton of TNT. This was not some homemade bomb set off by a disgruntled employee or garden-variety malcontent. We have received messages claiming responsibility, including groups with names like *Out of Palestine* and *Boycotts and Bombs*. They state that the bombing will continue until Israel ends its occupation of Palestinian territories.

"We absolutely cannot have these things happen in this country--in particular in our nation's capital. I've asked you to come here today to talk about what we should do. How do we find out who's behind this bombing, and how do we make sure they are not able to fulfill their promise?"

"What do we know about the person who carried the bomb into the building?" Leonard asked, figuring they ought to get right to the point.

The President turned to the Director of the FBI. "Director Shortell."

Everett Shortell could have passed for J. Edgar Hoover's double were it not for the fact that his ancestors had been born in Africa. He had loose jowls and a bulging midsection. "We believe the bomb was brought into the building by a former student at the University of Maryland. We're waiting for forensic confirmation before we release the name to the public."

"What do we know about this person?" President Wheatfield asked.

"Very little. She was a Caucasian female, aged twenty-two, originally from Maryland's Eastern Shore. She does not have a criminal record nor does she show up in our terrorist database."

"A woman. That's not good," stated Professor Alcorn.

"No, it's not," Director Shortell responded.

"I'm sure I speak for my colleagues, Madame President," Leonard said, "in saying that we'd like to help you figure out how something like this could have taken place and how to prevent its ever happening again. We just don't have enough information."

"I'm aware of that, Professor Robbins," President Wheatfield stated. "I'm also aware that you've written that the next phase of terrorism will involve the use of American citizens. It appears you were correct. What do you recommend we do?"

Leonard cleared his throat. "If what I predicted has indeed come to pass, there is no easy solution. Instead of sending agents to do the job themselves, our enemies have agents in this country searching for Americans who are willing to engage in what the Weather Underground used to call 'direct action.'"

"A week ago I would not have thought that possible," President Wheatfield admitted, "but now I'm not so sure."

"Here's a question," Alcorn said. "Was it a suicide bombing?"

"We don't know," Director Shortell stated.

"If you're asking me," Leonard said, "I don't think so. I hope things have not reached a point where a naïve, young American can be convinced to die for someone else's cause. It's likely that the bomb maker exploded the device to get rid of someone who could connect him to the bombing. Of course, it's also possible the woman set the bomb off accidently--perhaps when she started a timing mechanism--or the bomb could have exploded because of a mistake in its construction."

"Where does that leave us?" Wheatfield asked the room.

Leonard raised his hand. "The problem we face is that we can no longer confine our close monitoring to persons of Middle Eastern descent who are of the Muslim faith."

"Nor can we give in to the terrorists," President Wheatfield stated. "What should we do?"

Leonard glanced over at Rosa Martinez. "My recommendations can be found in the paper your administration quashed. I wrote that our past failures have not been due to a lack of know-how or lack of resources. They have been failures of leadership. In the past, we haven't been sufficiently committed to stopping terrorists in part because we didn't want to believe they could do what they've done and in part because agency jealousies interfered with the flow of information necessary for leadership to make informed decisions."

"Assume we are fully committed this time," President Wheatfield said, "then what?"

"Then we make sure everyone knows finding who was behind the bombing and preventing them from striking again is a top priority."

"It can't be that simple, can it?" Wheatfield asked.

"The previous administration did tremendous damage in my opinion by preventing the FBI and other agencies from educating their people about the jihadist ideology that drives our enemy."

"We've taken steps to correct that problem," Rosa Martinez stated.

"I'm glad to hear that," Leonard said, "but the barn door was left open too long. As a result I'm afraid we've made it too easy for the enemy to infiltrate our country with jihadists like the one who persuaded that young woman to commit an act which cost her life."

"There's no doubt that we screwed up in the past," President Wheatfield said. "This is a new administration and I'm not going to repeat our past mistakes."

She waited to see if there were any dissenters. "What will it take, Professor Robbins, in your opinion to get the job done?"

"It won't be easy and some people will suffer from sore toes along the way--"

"I assume you mean feet will have to be stepped on," President Wheatfield stated.

Leonard nodded. "Feet will have to be stepped on, noses will have to be tweaked, and arms will have to be twisted to overcome the whole nine yards of resistance that people like to put in the way of committing to a mission. I'll go so far as to say certain laws will have to be ignored and those who ignore them will have to know they will not be hauled into court."

"That's not going to happen, Professor."

Leonard turned to see who had spoken. It was David Gross, a Democrat from Indiana and chairman of the House Committee on Homeland Security. "We're a nation of laws, and we're going to have to solve this problem without trashing the Constitution and the laws of the land."

"That's not what I'm advocating, Sir. The President has wartime powers, and we are at war. It's time Congress recognized that fact. In my humble opinion, if we don't respond as if we were at war, we'll be burying more Americans in the months to come."

"You paint a dark picture, Professor Robbins," President Wheatfield stated.

"It does not come easy for me to do so. Despite being confined to this wheelchair for the past nine years, my wife and friends will attest that I have an optimistic disposition. However, when it comes to terrorism and the safety of the American people, we cannot afford to be naïve. I'm telling you what I fear to be the case while hoping that I'm dead wrong."

The room was silent for ten seconds. Then a number of people began speaking at once. The discussion went on for another hour before President Wheatfield announced that time was up. "I want to thank everyone for their time and insights. America will not allow terrorists to operate on our soil with impunity. We will do all in our power to stop them. I promise you that."

Leonard was invited to accompany the other professors to NSA Martinez' office where she met with each of them separately for a brief period of time.

"President Wheatfield appreciates your coming today," Martinez began, "but I'm not sure she's ready to follow your recommendations."

"I'm ready to cooperate in whatever way I can," Leonard said.

Martinez shook Leonard's hand as he exited her office. "I imagine we'll be talking."

Alison picked Leonard up at the Albany airport with the family van that had been outfitted with a lift for Leonard's wheelchair. "How did it go?"

"I was impressed by President Wheatfield. I think she wants to do the right thing. She won't find it easy, however. She'll face resistance from her own party in Congress and from the bureaucrats in the agencies, each wanting to preserve their autonomy."

"I guess I can't ask you any specifics, but did you learn anything that supports your theory?"

"Yes and no. It'll be days before the bomb and forensics teams finish, but it appears a female American college student was recruited to carry an explosive device into AIA headquarters."

"A woman! That's terrible."

"I'm not surprised. From my study of the Weather Underground I've come to believe that women make better fanatics than men."

"Gee, thanks."

"I know, just what you wanted to hear."

"Explain."

"In general, women care more deeply about issues than men, which makes them susceptible to appeals to drastic action. Men care about accomplishments-- trophies. Women care about ordinary people."

"But to give up your life. I don't get it."

"They don't think they might die. They think people will wake up and see things the way they do."

"It wasn't a suicide, was it?"

"I don't think so. It can't be ruled out, but it's more likely that the person who assembled the bomb wanted to eliminate the one person who could identify him."

"The poor dear," Alison said as she turned onto the highway that would take them to their home.

Life resumed its normal pace in the Robbins household during the next few days. No formal announcements were made about the case. Leonard followed blog and website discussions looking for insights into the bombing. Over the weekend, rumors cropped up about the bomber being a woman. Then comments started appearing about a missing former University of Maryland undergraduate. The next day, the FBI issued a statement identifying Marisa Anderson of College Park, Maryland as wanted for questioning in connection with the bombing.

"That's who they think carried the bomb into the building," Leonard explained to Alison over Sunday night dinner.

"So, why not come out and say it?"

"This is the proper way. They're probably still going through the bombsite sorting out DNA. It's still possible she had nothing to do with it."

"But there must be a connection for them to issue that statement."

"They're not saying. They may have found something in her apartment or from having talked to some of her friends that suggests she was involved. We'll know more in a few days."

———

Albany: Monday, April 23

Leonard had just opened the door to his Rockefeller College office in the old Teachers College building in mid-town Albany when the department secretary buzzed his phone. "It's the White House for you, Professor Robbins."

Leonard picked up the call. "Hold for NSA Martinez."

"Professor Robbins. It's Rosa Martinez."

"Good morning, Ms. Martinez. How can I help you today?"

"President Wheatfield would like you to make another visit to the nation's capitol."

"Another meeting?"

"Yes, but this one will be with just you, me, and the president."

"What's the subject?"

"She'd like to explain in person. Can we get you down here first thing tomorrow?"

Leonard hesitated for only a second. While it was not fair to the college or to his students for him to be disappearing every other week, the national situation was too crucial to let such considerations override. This meeting might be his last opportunity to convince President Wheatfield to take an aggressive approach to stop this latest round of domestic terrorism. "I'll be there."

Peter G. Pollak

Washington, D.C.: Tuesday, April 24

Leonard's third visit to the White House in just over a month's time didn't diminish the thoroughness of the search procedure before he was admitted into the building. He was escorted to a reception area outside the oval office where he was told the meeting would start momentarily, but it was twenty minutes before Rosa Martinez showed up and another twenty before they were admitted.

President Wheatfield came around her desk to greet them while an aide made room for Leonard's wheelchair.

"I'm sure you're wondering why I asked you here today," Wheatfield began once they were settled--she in the large leather chair with the Presidential icon, Martinez on the couch opposite Leonard.

"With bated breath," Leonard replied.

After a brief smile, Gloria Wheatfield's naturally serious demeanor returned. "I've decided this situation cannot be handled--to use your words--by doing business the way we've always done business. The points you made the other day about the dysfunction of our agency structure were largely correct. Existing inter-agency groups, like the Domestic Terror Task Force, failed to foresee this possibility; therefore, I can't count on them to fix the problem.

"Normally, I'd add another duty to Rosa's job description, but I've given her enough to require any normal person to function without sleep, and frankly I don't think any of her deputies are up to the job. The person I want to help our country fix this problem is you."

"Me? That's very flattering, Madam President, but--"

"Hear me out. Here's my plan. I am going to create a new counterterrorism task force and I'd like you to head it."

"I don't know what to say," Leonard stated, feeling more than a little shocked.

"Let me be clear. Task force is not quite the right word for what I have in mind."

"You've got my attention."

"What we need is both answers and results. We need the task force that will find out who was behind the AIA bombing, root them out, and expose them."

"In other words, search and destroy," Leonard said.

"Exactly. Tell me what you need to do the job. I'll do everything within my power to give it to you and to see that you have free reign to get the job done."

"But won't that just be duplicating what the FBI, NSA, Homeland, and the rest already do?"

"Those agencies will still be your boots on the ground. They've got the people and the resources, but they lack proper supervision and fail to play nice with each other. That's where you come in."

"Sounds intriguing," Leonard said.

"Each agency will have a representative on your task force and I'll require them to report to you on a daily basis. You'll have the authority to require them to shift priorities or engage in monitoring a group you think is dangerous. Maybe--just maybe--we'll be able to chop our enemy off at the knees before they strike again."

"I'm with you, Madam President, but I want to be clear. If I'm put in charge, I'll need the authority to take steps that some will object to."

"I've discussed that topic with Rosa here. I can't give you carte blanche authority, and I want you to promise that you'll only use extra-legal measures if absolutely necessary."

"I promise."

"We'll need that in writing, Professor," Rosa stated.

"Sure," Leonard said.

Wheatfield leaned forward. "Here's what we have in mind. We'll introduce you as the executive director of a White House Terrorism Study Group and put a bunch of academics and a couple of members of Congress on the board, but that will just be for show. We'll keep them out of your hair while you--to use your words--search and destroy."

The President paused to see if Leonard was following. He nodded to show that he was.

"The one thing I ask," Wheatfield said, "is that you report to Rosa on a regular basis. Further, if you run into a situation where you feel you need cover, you're to contact Rosa. She'll be available to you twenty-four seven and I'm available to her twenty-four seven. How does that sound?"

Leonard nodded again. "That sounds ideal."

Wheatfield stood up and offered her hand. "Rosa's office will take care of whatever you need. Welcome aboard, Professor. Rosa will find you a desk where you can work the rest of the day. If you can give her a wish list by the end of the day, we'll let you go back home to pack a suitcase."

Leonard accepted her handshake. "I'm honored that you would offer this position to me, Madam President. I want to see whoever is behind this bombing stopped. I accept your offer."

Back in her office, Rosa Martinez motioned for Leonard to pull up to her desk. "Before you get started, I thought you and I should spend a minute going over a few items."

"Certainly," Leonard said.

"Gloria Wheatfield doesn't want to be remembered as the president on whose watch the terrorists had a field day, but she also doesn't want to have her reputation impugned because she let a cannon loose and innocent Americans were falsely accused or worse."

Leonard nodded. "Makes sense."

"I know you have certain ideas about how we need to go about fixing this mess, and that's why she wants you to head the project, but we still need to function as a team. Keeping me in the loop is going to be crucial to your success. I'll get you what you need, but I'll also tell you if you're about to cross a line that cannot be crossed. Am I being clear enough?"

"Perfectly," Leonard stated.

"Good. Let's say we chat Friday afternoons each week before you head back up to Albany, assuming you're going to go back to Albany on weekends."

"All this has happened so quickly, I haven't given it any thought, but a weekly conversation on Fridays. I have no problem with that."

"Excellent. Here's Juanita. She'll show you to a desk where you can get started and get you some lunch."

By late afternoon, Leonard filled up several pages of a yellow pad with notes about things he thought he'd need to run the task force, starting with the names of two key people he wanted on his team. He hated to call attention to his disability, but couldn't ignore the fact that he would need help if he was to spend any time by himself in D.C. His list in that regard included a van with a lift, drivers, and a hotel that could accommodate his need to exercise.

Next he dialed his wife.

"What did the president want?" she asked right off the bat.

"She wants me to find out who's behind the bombing and to blow up their network. Pun intended."

"Wow! Did you accept?"

"I wanted to check with you first, but--"

"You know I'd say do what you need to do."

"Thanks, hon."

"Do you start right away?"

"I do--although I'm flying home tonight while they line up those I want on the task force. If they get enough of the team on board by Friday, I'll come back then to start the ball rolling. The administrators at Rockefeller are not going to be happy, but when the president calls . . ."

"They'll understand."

"Also, Alison. I want you on my team."

"Me? Isn't that asking for problems?

"How so?"

"Morale issues, for one. Having the boss' wife around hinders team building. Plus, how can I contribute?"

"You know how to run field teams. I want you on that side of the operation."

"Len, I appreciate the offer, but I'm not sure it's wise for me or for us. Let's talk about it when you get home."

"Okay. Think it over. I'll be on the seven o'clock flight. Can you meet me?"

"Of course, dear. See you then."

After she picked him up at the airport, Leonard was surprised when Alison bypassed the highway that would take them home and drove to Wolf Road, one of the busiest commercial streets in the Capital District. "Where are we going?"

"You'll see."

Minutes later she pulled into the parking lot at Reel Seafood, one of their favorite Albany restaurants because the food was excellent and they accommodated Leonard's wheelchair without fuss.

"You're so smart," Leonard said.

Alison smiled. "Don't stop."

"You knew I'd be hungry by the time the flight got in. Stopping here was smart, but I'll bet you also knew we really couldn't have a discussion in a public place about you coming to work on the task force."

Alison just smiled.

"So rather than waste a moment to get away from what we're facing, let's just enjoy this dinner. We may not have the chance to do it again for a while."

Later that evening, while sharing a Courvoisier, Alison started the conversation she knew Leonard wanted to have.

"Tell me why you think you need me, Len?"

"Simple. I can trust you."

"And you can't trust the others? You're in big trouble if that's the case."

"It's not so much that I can't trust them. In terms of loyalty and dedication, of course, I can, but I can't always trust them to do the right thing."

"What specific job would you want me to do?"

"At some point we'll need to track down and monitor certain individuals. That's when I'd like you to come on board. Given your FBI training and general savvy about people, I know you'll get the job done."

"So, you don't need me at the start?"

"I'd like to have you there as another pair of eyes and ears, but if you have some reason for not joining us until I need you, I'll listen."

"There's what I mentioned earlier. I don't want to interfere with your people coalescing into a team, which can happen when a boss's spouse is around, but there's another, bigger reason."

"Your past?"

She nodded. "I did bust out of the FBI and I'm not sure I'd be welcomed or, as you put it, be trusted by the members of your team."

"That's one of the reasons I thought you should come on board. You weren't treated fairly at the time. Now's the chance to show them what they lost."

"That's not important to me. I know I did the right thing. I still think it was wrong for them to pressure me into resigning, but I don't feel the need to prove them wrong. What's past is past."

"I understand."

"If you said you needed me with you in D.C. to help you manage personally, then I'd drop everything. You know I put our marriage first and that means taking care of each other in ways the other can't."

"I am a little worried about how I'll manage. I asked them to put me up in a hotel that has a handicap accessible swimming pool as well as a van and drivers, but you do so many little things that make a difference."

"You'll be fine, although you may need to find a physical therapist down there for a few months."

"In any case, it'll be nice to come home on weekends for a little TLC."

"It'll be my pleasure."

"Okay. Let's leave it this way. You stay here and take care of your clients, but if and when we need to run our own surveillance operation, I'm going to want you to join our team."

Alison got up and kissed Leonard on the mouth. "Sealed with a kiss."

New York City: Same Day

"Doing anything tonight?" Doreen asked Courtney after their Wednesday morning International Politics class.

"What do you have in mind?" Courtney asked.

"Want to meet for a coffee around ten?"

"Why not? The usual place?"

"Works for me."

The rest of the day Courtney wondered what Doreen wanted to talk to her about. When the time came, she picked a table in the back of their favorite coffee shop and was nursing a chai latte with her psych textbook open in front of her when Doreen showed up with a guy she recognized from their International Politics class.

"Hi. You know Dick, don't you? I ran into him on the street and asked him if he'd like to join us."

Courtney blushed. She had noticed him although she didn't know his name. He was good looking, clean shaven, and dressed casually, but not sloppily like some guys. He also lacked any visible tattoos--another plus to Courtney. "I don't think we've ever been introduced."

"Well, then, Dick Hogan meet Courtney Robbins; Courtney Robbins meet Dick Hogan."

"Hi," Courtney said.

"Hi," he responded with a friendly smile. "Want anything? I'm getting a coffee."

"I'm good," Courtney replied lifting up her cup.

"Get me a coffee, black," Doreen said, reaching for her purse.

"It's on me," Dick said, walking toward the counter.

"I thought you'd be glad I grabbed him," Doreen said in a low voice as she sat down.

"What's that supposed to mean?"

"I've seen the way you look at him in class," Doreen said smiling.

"I'm that obvious, huh?" Courtney said, blushing again.

"Don't worry about it. He seems like a nice guy."

Dick returned with two coffees. "So how's the studying?"

Courtney frowned. "I have no idea why I decided to major in psychology."

"Not your thing, huh?" Dick asked.

"I like the courses and all, but I just can't figure out what I'd do with it. I don't want to become a psychologist. What's your major?"

"History, an equally useless subject when it comes to getting a job, unless you want to teach, of course."

"You'd probably make a great teacher," Courtney offered.

"Thanks," he said, blushing.

Doreen turned to Courtney. "I heard you're not going to participate in the leafleting tomorrow."

So that's it, Courtney thought. "Passing out eviction notices--that doesn't do it for me."

"Why not? It's a way to educate students about what happens to ordinary people in the occupied territories, and we need all the bodies we can get."

"Didn't the group get in a lot of trouble for doing that a few years ago?"

"From what I was told they only hit Palladium, which the administration thought was chosen because a lot of Jewish students lived there," Doreen replied. "This time if enough volunteers show up we're going to leaflet all twenty-three dorms. That way they can't accuse us of targeting Jewish students."

Courtney shook her head. "I still think it's going to turn off more people than it will persuade."

"How's that?"

"For one, Jewish students will still get the notice."

"What's wrong with that?" Doreen asked. "Maybe they'll wake up and see what's really going on."

"Just because someone is Jewish doesn't mean they're pro-Israel. Erik Greene and his wife are Jewish aren't they?"

"Just Erik, I think," Doreen said, "but the point is to let everyone know what it feels like to be told you have to leave the home you've lived in for decades."

"I'm just not sure it will accomplish what you think it will. What do you think, Dick?"

Dick seemed startled at being brought into the discussion. "Eviction notices are pretty far out, I agree," he said after a moment, "but I guess I'd have to go along with the group's decision unless I had a strong principled reason not to."

"Thank you, Dick," Doreen said.

He smiled self-consciously. Courtney liked that.

"Dick, why don't you join us tomorrow?" Doreen suggested.

"What time?"

"We're meeting at four outside Kimmel."

Dick took a moment to answer. "I guess I can do it."

Doreen smiled. "Great. As Dick said, it comes down to what it means to be part of a group. If everyone made up their own mind about everything, we'd never get anything done."

Courtney wasn't sure. "I suppose."

"The bottom line is are we going to do something to help the Palestinians or not?"

"I'll think about it," Courtney said. "It's late, and I've still got some reading to do. Maybe I'll see you guys tomorrow."

"Which way you heading?" Dick asked.

"Downtown."

"Me, too."

"Great, I could use the company."

They walked a few blocks in silence. "That Doreen seems pretty committed," Dick ventured.

Courtney nodded.

"If she comes on a little heavy, it's probably because she cares so much about what's happening over there."

"I care, too," Courtney said. "I didn't realize when I joined the group that I was agreeing to go along with everything they do."

"You don't, of course," Dick said. "I respect your right to make up your own mind."

"Thank you. I may come, but I haven't decided yet."

"I understand."

They stopped outside her dorm. "Nice to meet you," Courtney said.

"You, too. Maybe we could catch a movie someday?"

"Sure," Courtney said, hoping Dick couldn't see her blushing. "I'd like that."

New York City: Thursday, April 26

The next day, despite still being uncertain about whether it was the right thing to do, Courtney showed up for the NYU SPJ eviction action, hoping she'd see Dick Hogan.

He was there and greeted her with a warm smile. "I'm glad you came."

"I'm still not sure about this, but . . ."

"What's the worst that can happen?" he asked.

"Good question."

She was surprised that Erik Greene was not there. Instead Miguel from the group's steering committee and another guy she didn't know gave out instructions. She was handed a stack of flyers made up to look like eviction notices. She was to distribute the flyers to each room on floors six through ten at Gramercy Green--a high-rise dorm on Third Avenue. She was glad it was not Lafayette Hall, the dorm she lived in. "Come back here when you're finished," Miguel told everyone. "We may ask you to do a second dorm."

She read over the flyer in case someone asked her questions about it. The notice stated in small print at the bottom that it was not a real eviction notice, but by the time anyone read the disclaimer the impact of the heading--Eviction Notice--printed in large bold letters would have had its effect.

Courtney took a bus to Gramercy Green with two other SPJ members who'd been assigned that dorm. She entered the building and rode the elevator up to the sixth floor. The plan was to slide a flyer under the door of each residence room.

She was on the eighth floor when a group of female students came out of the stairwell and accosted her.

"What's going on? What's this all about?" a short girl with curly hair demanded, holding one of Courtney's flyers in her hand.

"Who authorized this?" a girl who had to be over six feet tall asked standing in the middle of the hall so Courtney couldn't get by.

"It's an educational leaflet," Courtney said. She tried to say more, but they didn't seem to be interested in listening, as several girls questioned her at once.

"You need a permit to leaflet in the dorms," the tall girl told Courtney. "So, get your butt out of here before we call security."

"Okay, but please read the leaflet," Courtney said as she backed up toward the elevator.

"We're going with you to make sure you leave," one of the girls said. Three of them got in the elevator with her and stared at her all the way down as if she were some kind of zombie.

Courtney wasn't sure what she should do when she got to the street, still feeling upset as a result of being challenged. She decided to wait to see if the others had a similar experience.

"Over here," she called when she saw one of the SPJ leafleters exit the building.

"How'd it go?" the girl asked.

"Not so good," Courtney admitted. "I got booted out of the building and didn't even finish the eighth floor."

"Really, booted out by whom?"

"Some of the girls. They told me we needed a permit."

———

"No one said anything about that to me."

"The one who said it sounded like she knew what she was talking about," Courtney said.

"Anyway, you tried. I didn't have any problems other than having to see a bunch of guys in their skivvies. Let's wait for Melody and then head back."

When they got back to Washington Square, Miguel approached them. "How'd it go?"

"I was tossed out of the building," Courtney replied. "They told me we needed to get a permit in order to leaflet."

"Technically, that's true," Miguel said. "We didn't bother applying for one because we knew they'd turn us down."

"You might have warned us," Courtney said.

"Chill out. You got hassled. That's nothing compared to what Palestinians in the occupied territories face on a daily basis."

Courtney looked around to see if anyone else heard her being reprimanded.

The other group leader came over. "We need someone at Palladium. Can you do that?"

Courtney shook her head. "I've had it."

She looked around for Dick Hogan, but didn't see him. She thought about waiting until he returned, but decided against doing so. Instead, she headed over to Broadway to catch a bus back to her dorm where she expected to find an eviction notice shoved under her door.

Peter G. Pollak

Washington, D.C.: Friday April 27

Leonard Robbins wheeled himself into the assigned conference room at FBI headquarters, the location of the first meeting of DEFEAT--the name a White House PR person imposed on the President's new counterterrorism task force. They were meeting there because the office space Leonard had requested would not be ready for them until Monday.

Leonard was pleased that the two former CIA colleagues he'd asked for were present. Meir Epstein was an expert in Islamic terrorism. A few years younger than Leonard, Meir retired after being diagnosed with prostate cancer. He'd undergone treatment and had been declared cancer-free. Pavel Zavarov, who was a native of Russia, was a terrorism expert who had served with Leonard during two of his overseas assignments. He too had retired early for health reasons; untreated eczema growing up had matured into severe arthritis. Leonard shook hands with each man and thanked them for coming.

"Let's go around the room and introduce ourselves," Leonard said when everyone had settled around the conference table. "I suppose everyone knows who I am, but I'll go first anyway. My name is Leonard Robbins. Three years ago, I retired from the CIA and am now a professor of international affairs at the Nelson A. Rockefeller College of Government Policy in Albany, New York. I'm also a graduate of the U.S. Naval Academy.

"President Wheatfield asked me to head this task force as a result of the bomb that was set off here in Washington two weeks ago. Our job is to pool the resources of all of the relevant federal agencies, figure out who was responsible, and make sure they can't hit us again."

Leonard took the floor again after having each person identify himself. "Thank you all for coming today. Another team member, Larry Burnside, who will be our IT security expert, is at work in Herndon laying in the network and computer hardware in our new offices. My wife, Alison Robbins, a former FBI agent, may also be joining us later on in the project. Additional specialists will be added to the team as needed.

"We won't have a receptionist as such, but we will have an office manager who has FBI clearance to handle personnel matters, travel arrangement, office supplies, and the like. He or she will be on board early next week as well.

"Let's begin. Our mission is to find out who bombed the AIA building and to destroy their operation. Not disrupt or hinder, but destroy as in remove those individuals responsible from the playing field and call to account any foreign government or organization that played a role. Are you with me thus far?"

He paused to see if anyone had a question. Seeing no one did he moved on.

"Some of you are here as representatives of your agencies. Who you choose as the permanent member of the task force is your agency's choice. If you want to assign someone else after today's meeting, that's fine. I just ask that whoever you send next week stay with us until the job is done.

"At some point in the investigation we will need the resources of each of the agencies present at the table today. We need the investigatory capabilities of the FBI, the CIA's ability to monitor our overseas enemies, National Security Agency's data gathering and analysis capabilities, and Homeland Security's access to immigration information and ties to local governments across the country.

"The key to success is communications. I'll expect each agency to bring pertinent information to the task force, and I'll see to it that each of your agencies have access to any and all information we acquire.

"The hardest part of the liaison's job may be to channel the task force's perspective to those in your agency doing the job on the ground." He turned to face Sally Peterson, who was in attendance representing the FBI. "For example, if we conclude that the FBI is not monitoring a group that we believe needs to be monitored, Ms. Peterson, you, or the person you assign to the task force, will need to shepherd that recommendation through channels so that it gets taken care of quickly and without pushback.

"If anyone has problem with that, you'll have to take it up with President Wheatfield."

"No objections in principle, Professor," said Homeland's Odell Sanders. "We'll have to see how it works in practice."

"Agreed," Leonard said. "I'm open to refinements as we move forward.

"Starting Monday, The DEFEAT task force will be based in Herndon, Virginia. I'll meet with each person to go over individual assignments after your security briefing that will include login procedures to our network computers. Any questions?"

Leonard waited ten seconds. "Seeing none, I'd like to turn the meeting over to Ed O'Reilly. He's going to brief us on the latest information the FBI has on the bombing."

O'Reilly thanked Leonard and pushed a button on a control device that lowered a screen at the end of the room. People moved their chairs to be able to see the screen. The first image was a college yearbook picture of Marisa Anderson.

"Here's what we know thus far. On the screen is the University of Maryland freshman photo of the young woman who matches the image we retrieved from video footage taken on the street outside AIA headquarters. At approximately ten minutes to three in the afternoon on Friday the thirteenth of April, Anderson entered the AIA building on H Street wearing a messenger service uniform and carrying a toaster-sized package wrapped in brown paper. Video footage shows her walking directly to the receptionist's desk, and announcing that she had a package for someone who works at AIA.

"Apparently the package was addressed to a real person on the AIA staff because video footage shows the receptionist calling someone in the building. Seconds later, the receptionist signed the messenger's tablet with her finger and handed it back to the messenger. The messenger then touched the tablet screen, which is what we believe touched off the explosion.

"The video camera inside the building was a casualty of the bomb so we can only construct what happened next from forensic sources. That work continues, but we believe that the messenger was thrown backwards into the glass window behind her, breaking the window and killing her instantly. What remains of her body was mingled with that of a woman who had been sitting in a chair in front of the window. That person has been identified as a D.C. resident by the name of Judy Jacobs. Jacobs was apparently waiting on a friend who works at AIA.

"The receptionist, whose name was Tanika Brown, was killed instantly, as were three additional employees. One of them was killed along with his wife as they were walking past the receptionist's desk at the moment of the explosion.

"More than a dozen people were injured including some who were either walking by the building or in vehicles that were passing by. Additional AIA staffers who were in the building at the time of the explosion suffered injuries, several serious. The present total is seven fatalities and fourteen injuries. Damage to the building was considerable. Repair estimates are in the millions of dollars. Do you want me to go into our analysis of the bomb itself?"

"Is the bomb team finished?"

"No."

"Then let's leave that discussion for the moment and come back to it if we have time later today or next week," Leonard stated. "What I'd like to have you go over next is what we know about the woman who delivered the bomb. How were you able to identify her?"

O'Reilly advanced the image on the screen to an image showing an enlargement of the messenger's face. "We were able to retrieve video footage of AIA headquarters taken from a street cam which provided us with an image of our suspect. We put the images out on social media and it didn't take long before we got hits identifying Anderson.

"We found her address in College Park, as well as a cell phone number and an auto registration. We put out a bulletin on the car, which we found parked in the back of the College Park metro station lot. It contained a pocketbook with her wallet, twenty-four dollars in bills and some loose change, her college ID, a credit card, but no keys or cellphone.

"After obtaining a search warrant, we entered Anderson's apartment Saturday evening around nine thirty. The next series of images I'll show you are from the apartment."

O'Reilly gave those in the room a few seconds to study each of six images.

"You can see that there is evidence of the apartment having been tossed."

"That's the condition you found it in when you got there?" Leonard asked.

"That's correct," O'Reilly answered. "It appears that someone got there ahead of us. Presumably, they entered with a key because the door was locked and the lock had not been tampered with or damaged. That person or persons searched the apartment thoroughly. As you can see, the bedding was stripped off the bed, dresser drawers pulled open, and clothes were dumped on the floor. Same with the desk drawers."

"What about a computer?" Leonard asked.

"Missing," O'Reilly answered. "There's an outline where the computer must have been sitting on the desk. Whoever searched her apartment must have taken it."

"Did neighbors notice anything?" Leonard asked.

"Unfortunately, no. Our guess is that the apartment was entered the evening of the day the bomb went off."

"What do you think they were they looking for?" CIA Deputy Director Alan Goldberg asked.

"Our guess is that they wanted to make sure there was nothing in the apartment that connected Anderson to the person or persons who supplied her with the package."

"Will we have access to your final report?" Leonard asked.

"Absolutely. A draft has already been circulated to top officials at the agency. I believe Ms. Peterson has seen a copy."

"I have," Peterson said.

"Here's a question," Meir Epstein said. "Is there any evidence that this Anderson knew what was in the package?"

"That is an important question," O'Reilly replied, "but to this point in our investigation we can't answer it definitively either way. It's entirely possible she was duped into thinking she was delivering something innocuous--copies of signed petitions for example. Killing her might have been the intent of her handlers to prevent her from identifying them."

"I don't believe she expected to die," Sally Peterson stated.

"Explain," Leonard said.

"I only had time to skim your report, but I noticed some things that suggest she expected to return to her apartment after delivering the package. For example, if she knew she was going to die, she would have done certain things like clean out her medicine cabinet and bedside table. The report indicates you found condoms, a vibrator, and other indications of an active sex life. No woman expecting to die would leave those kind of things around to embarrass her family."

"Good point," Leonard said. "She might have known the package contained a bomb, but believed it would not go off until she had left the area. The other possibility is, as Agent O'Reilly suggests, that it had been programmed to go off immediately in order to remove the carrier. At this point, we're just speculating. Do you have anything else you want to share today, Agent O'Reilly?"

"One item. We couldn't find her cellphone either in the car or the apartment. We've tried to trace it, but thus far no luck."

"You're checking with the carrier, I assume," Leonard said.

O'Reilly nodded. "We expect them to get back to us in a day or two with all the numbers she called or received calls from over the past year."

"What's next?"

"We're doing the usual gathering of information about her from the University. We're also trying to identify her friends, people she hung out with, and, of course, we've talked to her parents."

"Anything there?" Leonard asked.

"The parents are divorced. The mother lives on the Eastern Shore. As you can imagine, her daughter's death hit her hard, but she shed no light on what her daughter was doing in D.C. on the thirteenth. Our agents in Miami, Florida, have been to see her father. He is extremely angry. He blames the University for not protecting her. He also claims she couldn't have known she was carrying a bomb in the package and she did not intend to die."

"One more question," Leonard said. "Have you come across any evidence that Ms. Anderson would have been capable of constructing the bomb herself?"

"None. She was studying sociology and had last taken chemistry in high school. There was nothing in the apartment that suggests the bomb was made there. No trace elements of the explosive. Nothing."

"Thank you," Leonard said. "As you are aware, the purpose of this task force is to find those responsible for the bombing. From what you've told us, my guess is that that someone recruited Ms. Anderson and supplied her with the bomb. Whether or not she knew she was carrying a bomb remains to be seen.

"Our job is to find the recruiter, uncover those behind him--"

"Or her," Sally Peterson said.

"Or her," Leonard said, nodding in Peterson's direction.

"I know you'll keep the task force apprised of any and all developments, Agent O'Reilly. We will do the same as we commence our own investigation. Ms. Peterson, as the representative of the FBI, do you see any problems that we need to address here and now with regard to the protocol of exchanging information with your investigators?"

"None," Peterson replied. "You'll have our complete cooperation."

"Great. Next I'd like to focus on the messages claiming responsibility, but let's do that after lunch."

Leonard and Meir were waiting for Pavel to join them in the cafeteria when he returned from a cigarette break.

"What's the plan?" Pavel asked when he placed his tray on the table and sat down.

Leonard put down his sandwich. "You and Meir are going to be my eyes and ears as well as my legs. There'll be daily briefings, which you guys will run if I'm not in the office or tied up. Unless I've completely lost touch with the way things work in the federal government, you'll have to have your bullshit detectors at full ready. Anytime you smell a rat, your job will be to track it down and bring it out into the open."

"Easier said than done," Pavel stated.

"That's true, but you know what to look for. Every agency has its divisions, its jealousies, its interpersonal animosities, and its managers who have climbed beyond their level of competency. We've seen too many examples where bureaucratic inefficiency cost lives."

"As in nine-eleven, Iraq, and Afghanistan just to mention a few minor fuck-ups," Meir said.

"Exactly," Leonard said. "George Bush got bad info because of bureaucratic inertia and weak agency leaders. As a result, the right questions weren't asked and when staffers came across valuable info, they didn't know how to use it."

Meir nodded his agreement. "I'd even go so far to say that nine-eleven was totally preventable."

"And the price we paid for what we came away with in both Afghanistan and Iraq is a tragedy," Pavel ventured.

Leonard took a sip of his iced tea. "While the FBI and other agencies work on the AIA bombing, we need to figure out what they're not paying attention to."

"No small order!" said Meir. "What's the division of labor?"

"Pavel, I assume you have connections in places that the CIA doesn't. See if anyone in your network knows anything about recruiter agents being sent into the U.S. You should also keep a close watch on what the CIA sends over to make sure they're not holding out on us.

"Meir, you'll focus stateside. Let's try to figure out who the FBI is not watching who needs to be watched and where their network is weak. I'll have enough to do running the show so I won't be able to look at everything as it comes in. You guys will have to monitor the data flow and bring anything to me that doesn't pass the smell test."

"That's okay by me," Pavel said, "as long as I get to break some heads when we find the people behind that bombing."

Leonard chuckled. Pavel was always threatening to break heads despite the fact that he probably couldn't lick a ninety-pound girl in a fair fight. Besides his arthritis and cigarette habit, Pavel hadn't exercised since grade school and loved rich, spicy food.

Meir raised a finger to get them back on point. "Whoever planned this must have more than one agent on the ground."

"That's right," Pavel said. "You always send in extras in case a couple go rogue or get caught."

Leonard nodded. "While the Bureau focuses on finding whoever recruited this Anderson woman to do the D.C. job, we'll focus on finding the rest of their organization."

"What about the bomb?" Pavel asked.

"What about it?" Leonard asked.

"Surely they didn't bring the material into the country with them."

"You're right. They're probably trained to use a number of possible methods of obtaining the materials and constructing a device capable of causing death and destruction. We've done a good job making it harder for the average person to access the necessary ingredients used in most bombs of this type, but it's still possible to do so without a red flag being raised. Someone would just have to get a job at any number of places--a hardware store, chemistry lab, or research facility. We'll leave that side to the FBI. These guys won't make a bomb until they've found a carrier. We'll focus on finding the recruiters before they find their next carrier."

Peter G. Pollak

Albany: Sunday, April 29

It was past eleven. Alison Robbins told Leonard he ought to go to bed since he had to get up early the next day to catch his flight to D.C. "I'll stay up until I hear from Courtney."

"That's assuming she'll call as promised."

"I'm sure she will, Len."

They'd been calling and emailing their daughter ever since they heard the news about the leafleting incident at NYU. Courtney texted a short note early Sunday morning. "I'm okay. Will call tonight," it read.

After Leonard wheeled himself into the bedroom, Alison snuggled into one of the large chairs in their living room with their home phone on the armrest and the novel her book club was reading that month. If Courtney didn't call that evening, Leonard had suggested she drive or take the train down to the city the next day to confront Courtney in person. Alison hoped that wouldn't be necessary. Fortunately, she and Leonard didn't have to have that conversation, as the phone rang a little before midnight.

"Hi, Mom. How's it going?"

"We're fine. What about you?"

"Everything is fine."

"That's not the impression we got from the news."

"You mean about the leafleting? The administration was pissed. They called some of the group's leaders on the carpet, but I don't think it'll go too bad for them."

"We're not worried about what they do to the leaders. We're worried about what could happen to you."

"Nothing. Really. It's okay.

"I hope you're right. Your father and I would like to know what role you played in it."

"I was one of the people distributing the flyers. I wasn't going to, but at the last minute I took a stack and tried to distribute them."

"What do you mean you tried?"

"Some of the students in the dorm I was assigned confronted me and said I should leave, so I did. End of story."

"I don't blame them for getting upset. I don't see the point of eviction notices."

"It's what some Palestinians have been subjected to by the Israeli government."

"So two wrongs make a right?"

"They're not real notices. It says that right on the flyer."

Alison was getting frustrated. Courtney seemed to be taking the whole thing too lightly. "Your father would say the eviction business is taken out of context. The Israelis are not evicting people because they're mean and hate the Palestinians. They do it because they're trying to root out terrorists and provide for security of law-abiding people."

"Don't those Palestinians have any rights--like more than twenty-four hours to remove their belongings from a house their family has occupied for decades?"

"But did your leafleting accomplish what you set out to do? I read most students ignored the leaflets because they'd heard about the group's doing the same thing four years ago, and the article said your group didn't have a permit to leaflet in the dorms. Were you aware of that?"

"The leaders told us that the administration wouldn't have given us permission."

"So they just went ahead? That's disturbs me because it suggests if they don't like some other rules, they'll violate those too."

"Can we talk about something else, Mom?"

"Fine, but next time don't make us wait three days until we hear from you. We were concerned about your well-being."

"I know, but I just didn't want to be lectured to, speaking of which, where's Dad? He usually doesn't let us talk for this long before wanting to get in on the conversation."

"He went to bed already. He has to get up early tomorrow to catch an early plane to D.C."

"It seems like he's down there a lot."

"He's not really happy about the travel, but he's been appointed to a joint White House task force and he couldn't say no."

"When were you guys going to tell me?"

"They expect the announcement sometime this week."

"Is it about terrorism?"

"I'm afraid it is. Everyone's up in arms since that explosion in D.C."

"Did they ever figure out who was behind it?"

"They think they know who brought the bomb into the building, but it's not known whether she meant to die in the blast."

"She! It was a woman?"

"Yes, Courtney. A student from the University of Maryland."

"Where was she from--Palestine?"

"Nope. Red-blooded American."

"Yikes."

"That's what's so disturbing about it," Alison said.

"Do they know who's behind it?"

"Several groups claimed responsibility. Your dad says they do that so the government doesn't know who to go after. Most of the groups don't exist. They just make up the names to confuse us."

"Tell him I'm sorry I didn't get a chance to talk to him and that I love him."

"Will do, Court. Try to stay out of trouble."

"Talk to you next week, Mom."

Herndon, Virginia: Monday April 30

Leonard's driver left him off near the elevators and then went to park the van that had been assigned to the task force to transport Leonard around D.C.

"Where to?" the driver asked when he came back to help Leonard up the ramp to the basement level elevators of the nondescript office building located a few miles from Dulles International in Herndon, Virginia.

"Top floor," Leonard instructed. When the elevator door opened, a wiry thin man with a Marine length haircut and a white shirt with a red, white, and blue tie who looked to be in his late thirties stood up from behind a reception desk. "Welcome, Professor Robbins. I'm Ed Morgan. Justice sent me. Larry Burnside asked me to show you around and then deposit you in his office where he'll get you set up on our systems."

Leonard followed Morgan through the keypad-locked entrance to the main part of the office, promising him that Burnside would assign him a passcode to that entrance as part of his orientation.

"We have the entire floor as you requested," Morgan said.

"Good," Leonard replied. "I didn't want to share space with some rogue software hackers."

Morgan laughed. "As you can see, the main part of the floor is taken up by the 'bullpen.' There are two rows of seven cubicles each. If you tell me who you want assigned to which cubicle, I'll let them know as they arrive."

"Let me think about that as you show me around."

A wide aisle had been left unencumbered by furniture or other obstacles between the windows and the cubicles to allow Leonard access to all parts of the office.

"The conference center you asked for is at the far end of the floor," Morgan stated, leading Leonard in that direction.

Morgan pointed to the row of large monitors mounted on both sides of the room. "This space is equipped with the latest in conferencing technology, and it can be divided in half in case two groups need to conference at the same time."

Leonard spent a few seconds studying the conference area and then followed Morgan down the inside row of cubicles. A floor to ceiling wall had been installed from the conference room halfway back to the front of the floor.

"On the other side of this wall is a hall leading to the combined restroom and locker room area," Morgan explained. "Next to the locker room is where we go to eat lunch or relax."

Leonard wheeled around the corner to inspect that part of the office. The space along the outer wall had been divided into a break area with a couch and easy chairs and a kitchenette with appliances on a counter that Leonard couldn't reach. He decided against mentioning anything now.

"And here we have the IT rooms," Morgan said, pointing to the label on the closed door, "but before I bring you in to Larry, let me take you to your office."

Leonard followed Morgan into a large corner office that had been fitted up for his use.

"Someone knows their stuff," Leonard said as he wheeled himself into the room.

"Indeed. They must have known that most desks are too tall to access from a wheelchair," Morgan said.

"The main problem is getting the wheelchair under the desk," Leonard said.

An oval conference table occupied one corner of the room. Leonard was pleased to see that it was the right height for him to use, as were the two long worktables on which sat a row of TV and computer monitors.

"They've even set it up so you can adjust the curtains and shades electronically," Morgan said. He demonstrated by using a push button control panel to open and close the curtains that separated Leonard's office from the rest of the floor and then to adjust the window covering to the outside.

"Very nice," Leonard admitted.

"Ready for Mr. Burnside?"

"I am. Good job, Ed. I think we're going to get along just fine."

Leonard spent the next hour with Larry Burnside while Burnside's assistant Betty Liu went through the same orientation procedure with Meir Epstein--the first task force member to arrive after Leonard.

Burnside took a set of fingerprints for the elevator. "I've already printed your drivers. They'll bring you up most of the time, but just to be on the safe side, I want you in the system as well."

Burnside took Leonard into the corner office where they set up his login and password for a variety of systems, including the communications system that would enable Leonard to use voice commands to make out of the office phone calls as well as contact members of the team whether they were in the office or out. The same login-password combination allowed him total access to the office network.

When they were finished, Ed Morgan came back to ask Leonard about cubicle assignments.

"I want Meir Epstein across from my office and Pavel Zavarov next to him opposite the IT room. Save the next one in that row for the NSA rep. Other than that, let each person decide where he or she wants to sit."

"What about reserving one for you?" Morgan asked.

"Good thinking. I may want to work out there at times. Put me in the middle one on the outside."

The rest of the day was spent meeting reps from the various agencies one on one. Pavel Zavarov showed up at eleven just ahead of the FBI rep Gary Mackey. Like Leonard, the latter was physically handicapped. He had only limited use of his right arm as a result of being wounded in a shoot-out with a white supremacy group more than a dozen years ago. His superiors at the Bureau rated him high in every area from intelligence to attitude to reliability.

Midday came and went but they still had not heard from the National Security Agency, making Leonard nervous. He was counting on NSA's potential to uncover enemy communications and wanted to get their rep started.

He knew the first week would be slow, but he planned on beginning each day with a debriefing session at which time each person would be expected to report any new developments from the previous day. He also planned to take a few minutes at the end of each morning session to set priorities for that day.

Leonard gave each person the same pitch. "If each of us stays focused on our unique species of trees," he told them, "a picture of the forest will eventually emerge."

New York City: The Same Day

Doreen was waiting for Courtney outside the International Politics classroom. "You okay?"

"Sure, why not?" Courtney replied, peaking into the classroom to see if the previous class had left.

"I heard you had some problems in the dorm they sent you to."

"You could say that. I ran into a posse. They told me to get out of their building unless I had a permit, which I didn't have."

"Well, it's a credit to you that you came through. It's important for others to see that when you're committed to a cause, you can't just pick and choose when it's convenient to show up."

Courtney stopped on the sidewalk and turned to face Doreen. "It wasn't a question of it being convenient. I had doubts about the whole idea and what I had to deal with confirmed that I was right."

Doreen wet her lips. "Look, Courtney, most people are apathetic. They don't want to know that unpleasant things are going on in the world or that they have an opportunity to do something to help out those who are less fortunate than they are. Our job is to make it difficult for them to be complacent."

"Next time, I hope the leaders pick an action that doesn't turn so many people off."

Doreen frowned. She seemed about to say something, but followed Courtney to their normal seats. "To change the subject," Doreen said after they had sat down, "have you decided whether you're staying in the city this summer?"

Courtney opened her notebook and got out two pens. "I've got to take two classes this summer in order to graduate next spring, so yes."

"Are you still looking for an apartment?"

Courtney nodded. "Unfortunately, I haven't found anything I like that's affordable."

"I've got to find a new place to live, too. Do you think we could share?"

"Sure, why not," Courtney said. "I've been looking mainly at studios, but if you want to room together, that gives us more options."

"I've already got a job this summer, so I'll be able to split the costs."

"Where?"

"Emily Greene got me a job at the law firm where she works in the city. It's just clerical--copying and junk like that--but it pays pretty good."

"Nice. Let's talk after class about looking for a place."

On Friday Doreen came up to Courtney after class. "I told Erik you wanted to meet with him," she said passing Courtney a piece of paper folded into a two-inch square.

Meet me at 4:30 at the coffee shop on the corner of Fifth Avenue and East 8th Street.

Courtney stuffed the note in her jeans. "Okay. I've got it."

"Good," Doreen said. "Keep in mind he's got exams, too."

"I know," Courtney replied. "I won't keep him long."

Courtney waited over a half an hour at the coffee shop before Erik Greene appeared. He seemed friendly enough in greeting her, but Courtney caught him looking around the room. *Is he nervous?*

"Doreen said you wanted to talk to me."

"I did. Thanks for taking the time. You're probably supposed to be studying for your law exams."

"That's okay. I needed to get some fresh air and a decent cup of coffee. I've been reduced to drinking instant lately."

"Been there, done that."

Erik surveyed the room once more. "So, what's up?"

"I just had some questions about where things are going with the Students for Palestinian Justice group."

"Ask away."

"About that eviction demo the other week, it bothered me that we weren't told we might get in trouble for not having permits."

Erik nodded. "We realized the administration might sanction us but decided it was worth it. We didn't think they'd hassle more than a few of the leaders, and so far they haven't."

"But what if the group loses its charter?"

"That wouldn't be the worst thing that could happen. It would show students whose side the administration is on, and we can function fine even if we can't use university buildings to meet in."

Courtney sighed. "But didn't the action turned off a lot of students?"

"I wouldn't say 'a lot.' Some reacted negatively, but it's a price we were willing to pay to educate the apathetic majority. The next time we have a speaker or some other event, more students will be likely to pay attention to us."

Courtney thought about that for a second.

"Is that it?" Erik asked.

"Well, actually I was wondering about what happened in D.C. You know, the bombing?"

"What about it?"

"Was that woman--Tarab Abdul Hadi--involved?"

"Why would you think that?"

"Because of the kinds of things she was saying."

Erik looked around the room and then leaned forward. "She wouldn't tell the likes of me if she was."

Courtney nodded. That made sense.

"Was there anything else?" Erik asked.

"Not really."

Erik sat back in the chair. "I thought you might ask me how I could support the Palestinians since I'm Jewish."

"I did wonder about it, but it's none of my business."

"I'll tell you anyway," Erik said, looking around the room again for a few seconds. "My father used to say founding the state of Israel was the worse thing that could have happened to the Jewish people."

"Why?"

"He said as long as we're spread out all over the globe, we can't be wiped out, but by most Jews moving to Israel, we're all in one place. All it would take is one bomb."

"So what does that have to do--"

"I think he has a point, which is why I'd rather see a secure Palestinian state with Arabs and Jews living side by side."

"So, is that why you want to pressure Israel to withdraw from the territories?"

"I see it as a step they need to take to come to the realization a separate Jewish state is not viable. It's also forced them into creating an apartheid state."

"My dad says that's a false analogy."

"He's entitled to his opinion. What do you think?"

Courtney frowned. "I guess I'm on the fence. I don't like a lot of what's being done in the occupied territories, but I'm not sure that it's the same thing as South Africa."

"What they do is a form of racial profiling. If you're a Palestinian, you're automatically a suspect--guilty until proven innocent. Most people know what apartheid means. When we say *apartheid* they get the picture."

Courtney thought about that for a second.

"Don't get caught up in terminology, Courtney. Focus on the big picture. Something needs to be done to help the Palestinians. That's why the BSD movement was formed."

"But what if Israel won't get out of the Palestinian territories? What if they keep building new settlements in East Jerusalem and on the West Bank?"

Erik looked around the room again. "The best thing you can do right now is keep working to educate the apathetic and the uninformed. That's doing really valuable work."

"It's hard to be patient. I can't imagine what it's like for the people who live there."

"You're right, but we have to take our cues from them. Anything you do is a help."

"Okay, but keep me in mind for those next steps."

Erik smiled. "Sure, Courtney. You're one of our group's rising stars."

As she walked back to her dorm, Courtney thought over what Erik had said. It was all so complicated.

Peter G. Pollak

Herndon: Friday, May 4

As he flew home Friday afternoon at the end of the task force's first week, Leonard tried not to be annoyed that not much had been accomplished. Each person had been tied up for half a day with IT having their fingerprints taken for the elevator, getting set up with computer log-ins and passwords, going over emergency contact protocols, and more.

What also slowed things down was that it took a day or more for some of the agencies to send over their permanent liaisons. The liaison Leonard wanted to talk to the most was the analyst from the National Security Agency, although that person--one Ekaterina Stepanova--did not arrive until Thursday morning, which meant Leonard didn't get to "orient" her until that afternoon.

According to the papers NSA sent over with Stepanova, she was a thirty-seven year old Russian refugee who had defected ten years ago at a computer conference her government had sent her to attend. The U.S. government allowed her to stay when she proved Russia had sent her to place a bug in the conference computers so they could spy on the U.S.

Despite her severe physical appearance--she had the thin body of a smoker, Stepanova was handsome in the way of certain Russian women--especially when she didn't think anyone was looking at her.

After Leonard explained the task force's mission, he asked Stepanova what she felt she could contribute.

"What do you want me to contribute?" she replied.

"Initially, I want you to find any communications that might shed light on the D.C. bombing, starting with communications that might identify who knew about it in advance. That means phone calls, emails, and text messages to and from the alleged bomber or about the bombing."

"You need a court order to do that," Stepanova informed him.

"I'm aware there are protocols for getting approvals for certain kinds of data collections that may include getting a court order. If we have to stop and get the proper documentation for every search we need you to do, we're never going to catch these terrorists."

Leonard studied Stepanova's reaction, which was to sit there impassively. As a result, he decided to restate the critical importance of their mission.

"This task force has blanket permission from the President of the United States to do whatever it takes to catch those responsible for that bombing. Your job is to use all the resources at your agency's disposal to help us accomplish that. Is that understood?"

"I understand what you want," she replied, "but I can lose my job and go to jail if I do something without proper authorization."

"Let me assure you that you will not lose your job or go to jail based on what I ask you to do, but we still don't seem to be on the same page. What instructions were you given when your agency told you to report here?"

"I was told on Monday to finish up the assignment I was working on and to be prepared to start on a new assignment by the end of the week. Yesterday they told me to report here, but no one said anything about what the job entailed."

Leonard sighed. "We'll get that cleared up. Meanwhile, have you talked with Larry Burnside about creating a hookup into your agency's computer system?"

"I told him I don't have the authority for such a thing."

Leonard rubbed his face with both hands. "This is just ducky. We'll have to get that straightened out too."

"What should I do then?"

"At this point, I want you to assume that you are going to be given permission to do the data searches by accessing your agency's network. Until that is in place, can you write the routines or whatever you call it that will pull out the data we're looking for?"

Stepanova gave Leonard a slight nod in response. "I can try, but you need to tell me what you want me to find."

"I'll write down the information in as concrete terms as I can and have it ready for you tomorrow morning," Leonard said. "Meanwhile, you might introduce yourself to some of the other members of the team so you know who's who."

She looked at him like he'd just asked her to walk on a bed of nails.

Leonard was doubly frustrated by Stepanova's attitude. Because her agency had not told her the nature of the job, it might be days before he could convince her to follow his instructions. He wondered if she had been sent over because someone at NSA wanted to get her out of his hair or worse to make life difficult for his team.

Leonard knew he would have to deal with the matter of court approval. He just didn't think it would handicap them from the get-go. That meant moving up on his to-do list the task of talking to the legal folks at the Justice Department. First thing Friday morning he asked Justice to send someone over on Monday to discuss procedures to obtain authorization for task force activities.

During the week, whenever he had a minute, Leonard tried to stay on top of the FBI's investigation. Agent O'Reilly gave a briefing from the bureau's D.C. office Wednesday morning that Leonard was able to join in on.

"Our immediate focus," O'Reilly reported, "is trying to find people at the University of Maryland who can help us understand Marisa Anderson's role in the bombing.

"Here's what we know. Anderson moved into her apartment last fall. Until then, she had been living in a dorm with two female students. She spent the summer living with her mother in Ocean City where she worked as a waitress at a couple of restaurants. We're tracking down some of the wait staff who worked with her to see if they can offer any insights into where her head was at the time and who she was hanging out with."

"You've talked to the mother, right?" Leonard asked over the network.

"The mother hasn't been much help. It seems Marisa didn't confide in her, and after she moved back to College Park in the fall, they mainly emailed."

"You're working on getting those emails, right?"

"We are. That may take a few more days," O'Reilly said.

"What about bank records and Internet sites visited?"

"We're leaving no stones unturned," O'Reilly replied.

"Were the roommates helpful?" Leonard asked.

"One graduated last May. She said she was not particularly close to Marisa, but she did tell us Marisa's boyfriend dumped her mid-semester. We're tracking him down. In terms of her studies, Anderson told this roommate that she wasn't sure she could afford to return to school in the fall."

"That might be an opening," Leonard said.

"We're looking into it, of course," O'Reilly said.

"What about the other roommate--you said there were two?"

"Correct. The other one told us she moved in with some other girls over the summer since she was staying on campus. Marisa contacted her about living together in the fall, but she told Marisa said she was happy with her current situation."

"Did she add anything about Anderson's mental condition or hint of any interest in the middle-east conflict?" Leonard asked.

"No, but she suggested Anderson was the kind of person who ran hot and cold. She got into meditation for a while, Meyers told us. Then she got interested in climate change and made her roommates recycle everything from junk mail to toilet paper centers."

"What's on tap for today?"

"Today we're talking to the instructors in the classes she took last year and the ones she was taking in the fall before she dropped out, and we're continuing to identify and track down other people she was friends with."

The FBI's reports the rest of the week did not add much to what was already known. Anderson had taken out a loan in September to pay part of her tuition, but she withdrew from school and took a second part-time waitressing job after her father failed to come through with a check that was due the first of November that she needed in order to pay her rent and living expenses.

Conversations with the faculty did not yield any concrete leads, O'Reilly reported on Friday, although they still had several instructors left to interview.

Peter G. Pollak

Herndon: Monday, May 7

"Phone call for you, Professor Robbins. It's the Justice Department."

"Put it through," Leonard responded.

"Hello, Professor Robbins. My name is Joel Bray. I've been assigned as liaison to your task force. I was planning to come by this afternoon as you requested, but the message we received said you wanted me to call first."

"That's correct, Mr. Bray. I have a question for you. If I ask you to get authorization to put a wire tap on an individual's phone, is that something you can authorize yourself or would you have to get approval of someone else in the department."

"For a wire tap, I'd have to get an approval first."

"From whom?"

"The head of my unit."

"Name and title?"

"Of--?"

"The person who is the head of your unit."

"Paul Grier, Assistant Attorney General."

"Please tell Mr. Grier I would like him to come in your place. Tell him I'll be here until ten this evening, and I'd like him to call my office when he's on his way so we can buzz him in."

"I'm not sure Mr. Grier will want to do that, sir. He asked me to be--"

"Joel. I'm sorry to interrupt. Please convey my request to Mr. Grier. Tell him to call me if he has a problem."

Half an hour later, Leonard took Paul Grier's phone call.

"Professor Robbins. I don't understand--"

"Then let me explain, Mr. Grier. You assigned Mr. Joel Bray to the task force. I'm sure he's a very competent individual, but we're rejecting Mr. Bray. You're the person I need to meet with, and I need to see you today. I'll be here until ten this evening. Mr. Bray has the address."

"But--"

"Mr. Grier, when President Wheatfield asked me to head up this task force, she said I would have full cooperation from the executive agencies. Now, I don't want to explain to the president that I'm not getting the kind of cooperation I need from the Justice Department because she will have to call the Attorney General and guess who he will call. Are you getting the picture?"

There was a pause. "I'll be there as soon as I can."

"Excellent," Leonard stated. "I look forward to meeting you."

Leonard researched Paul Grier's background. He was a former law professor and had been with the Justice Department for nine plus years. As an assistant attorney general, he headed up the department's Office of Legal Counsel.

Grier arrived at the task force's Herndon office building at a quarter after seven. Meir Epstein buzzed him into the building and escorted him to Leonard's office.

Ten years younger than Leonard, Paul Grier was a thin man of medium build and a narrow face. He looked like he had just taken a seat in the dentist's chair and was waiting for the Novocain.

"Let me explain our mission here, Mr. Grier and then I'll tell you what we need from Justice. Do you see the pictures on the wall behind me?"

Grier nodded.

Leonard waited for a few seconds to allow Grier to study the photos. "Those are the seven people who died in the bombing on H Street a month ago. The one on the right end is Marisa Anderson. We are fairly certain that she carried the bomb into the building. What we don't know is whether she knew she was carrying a bomb, but we do not believe that she intended to die. As a result, we include her as one of the victims.

"Our mission, Mr. Grier, is not just to find out who recruited her and convinced her to carry out the mission, and who gave her the package that contained the bomb, but also to stop them from carrying their threat to kill more innocent people. To succeed in that mission, we are likely to need to employ a variety of surveillance techniques, including taping phone conversations, obtaining email and Internet usage records, plant listening devices in homes, cars, or places of work, and we may need to use satellite technology to spy on people. What I need from you is the legal cover to do that work."

"Professor. Joel Bray--"

"Joel Bray said he would have to get permission from you in order to do what I asked of him. That's not good enough. In the business of fighting terrorists, when we get a lead, we'll need to act right away without waiting for your representative to track you down to get the okay."

"But--"

"Let me finish, please."

Grier sighed and sat back in his chair.

"As I was saying, we won't have time to wait for the paperwork before we do what needs to be done. Your job is to give us legal cover so that none of the task force members have to worry about being hauled into court and so that neither Congress, the press, nor her political opponents can ever question President Wheatfield as to her judgment in forming this task force or appointing me to head it."

"That's not how things work, Professor."

"I understand where you are coming from, Mr. Grier, and under normal circumstances I'm with you all the way, but these are not normal circumstances. We're not dealing with a gang of thugs or a Wall Street Bernie Madoff. We're dealing with a terrorism operation that we believe originated in a foreign country--Iran most likely--and that operation almost certainly maintains a network of well-trained terrorists on American soil.

"In other words, Mr. Grier, we're at war."

Leonard paused to let that statement sink in. "To put it another way, what we're trying to do is prevent having to add more pictures of innocent victims to that wall. Do you have children, Mr. Grier?"

Grier gave a slight nod.

"Grandchildren?"

"Professor-- "

"I'll tell you what, Mr. Grier. I'll give you a choice. I can either call up President Wheatfield, and she'll call your boss and he can clarify whether my instructions here are to be followed, or if you rather, you can call the parents of the young man and his wife who just happened to be walking past the reception desk when the bomb went off or call the fiancé of the young woman who was sitting in the lobby. You can ask them what you should do."

Again, Leonard paused for a few seconds. "Either way, I'm asking you to make sure the paperwork authorizes what we need to do is in order, even if our request arrives after we've instituted the surveillance procedure. Your turn."

Paul Grier, whose face had reddened considerably, took a deep breath. "I'll see that your requests are handled expeditiously so that you can do your job, Professor Robbins."

"Thank you, sir. I look forward to the day when I can call you up to let you know the task force will no longer need your services."

"I look forward to that day as well," Grier said. He stood up and after taking a second to look at the photos on the back wall of Leonard's office turned and left the room.

After seeing Paul Grier to the elevator, Meir Epstein returned to Leonard's office. "How'd that go?"

"Believe it or not, I don't like to be a hard ass," Leonard said, "but sometimes I don't have any choice."

"I hear you."

"There's one thing I didn't consider when I took this job that weighs heavily on me right now."

"What's that?" Meir asked.

Leonard who had been looking out the window, turned back to face his long-time friend. "It's on me if we fail to stop these people."

"No, Len. You're wrong. It's on all of us."

"Thanks, Meir. Let's get something to eat."

By the time his day-shift driver, Frank Johnson, helped Leonard out of the agency van at his hotel, Meir Epstein had secured a table at the hotel restaurant, moved a chair out of the way to accommodate Leonard's wheelchair, and ordered a first round of drinks.

"Do you want to invite your driver to join us?" Meir asked.

"I did," Leonard replied, "but he said he's already eaten, and his shift is over at ten."

"You've got someone available twenty-four seven?"

"I do. It feels like overkill right now, but if we get a call at three a.m. that a bomb has exploded someplace, I won't want to have to wait for someone to come pick me up."

"Makes sense. Here's our waiter. Know what you want?"

After the two of them ordered, Leonard inquired after Meir's family. "How does Rachel feel about your coming out of retirement?"

"Mixed, I guess," Meir answered. "She's probably happy to have me out of the house, but unhappy about my erratic schedule."

"Just like old times."

"Exactly."

"And the kids?"

"Great, except they're not kids anymore. Our son is working for a start up--a software company. He doesn't make much, but he's got owners' shares so if they are successful, he'll do well. His wife works too. So they're able to make ends meet."

"And Marcia?"

"She's pregnant again."

"Congratulations."

"Rachel has got her fingers crossed that they'll have a girl this time."

"It's her third, right?"

"Right. The oldest will be five in a few weeks. The youngest turned three two months ago."

"Wonderful."

"How about you, Len? Is Alison happy about the move to Albany and what about Courtney? She's in college now, right?"

"Alison and I have adjusted to Albany. It's not D.C., but neither is it Cairo or Manila. We found a house that accommodates my needs. I moved my Endless Pool and exercise equipment into a spare bedroom."

"Nice, and Alison?"

"Alison is still working as a personal coach. The pool of potential customers in the Albany area is much smaller, of course, than it was here in D.C., but she's picked up some new clients and she still works with three CEOs down here. She flies down once a month, sees all three over a two-day period."

"Good for her. And Courtney?"

"Not so good--at least in my opinion."

"What seems to be the problem?"

Leonard took a sip of wine. "It's hard to define. To me she's going through a rebellious stage that some go through when they're much younger."

"What does Alison think about it?"

"She thinks it's normal for people her age to try things out."

"What is she doing that worries you?"

"Changing majors for one, and now she's gotten involved in the NYU boycott Israel group. I'm very unhappy about that."

"I would be too."

Leonard nodded. "For you, it would be much worse."

"Believe it or not, some American Jews think Israel took over the Palestinians' homeland."

"That shocks me!"

Meir nodded.

Leonard took another sip of his wine. "I don't want to censor Courtney's thinking or tell her she has to see things the way I do. That would be arrogant. I just don't like to see her being used."

Meir nodded his agreement. "That is tough."

"She'll figure it out, I'm sure, but at the moment it's a subject we can't talk about or she changes the subject."

Leonard signaled the waiter for their check. "I just wish she'd hurry and get into something else like saving whales or falling head over heels for some boy."

Meir laughed. "Be careful what you wish for."

Herndon: Friday May 11

The second week of the official operation of the counterterrorism task force saw some progress in learning who Marisa Anderson was or who had recruited her to deliver the bomb to AIA's D.C. headquarters.

The FBI ran down a University of Maryland student named Josh Meadows who had dated Marisa Anderson during her sophomore and junior years. A senior chemistry major, Meadows reported he'd gotten involved with someone else about midway through their junior year and hadn't gone out with Anderson since. He said he saw her on campus once in a while and had talked to her in the fall before she dropped out of school.

Agent O'Reilly played the tape of their interview with Meadows at their briefing session on Wednesday morning.

"How did she seem the last time you talked to her?" the interviewing agent asked Meadows.

"At first, she made out like everything was okay, but then she admitted she would have to drop out of school if her father didn't come through with the money he'd promised."

"How did she feel about that?"

"She was pretty pissed. She was looking forward to getting her degree so she could get a job and move out of her mother's home."

"She didn't get along with her mother?"

"She told me her mother was always broke, drank too much, and could get nasty."

"Were you surprised to learn that she had died in the D.C. bombing?"

"Of course, man. I couldn't believe it. I thought it had to be someone else with the same name."

"Why?"

"I know she could get into her causes, but becoming a suicide bomber--that wasn't Marisa."

"What about the movement to boycott Israel? Did she ever talk to you about it?"

"You know, I did see her one day on campus passing out some flyers. I took one from her, but I was on my way to a class so we didn't get a chance to talk about it."

"Do you have a copy of that flyer?"

"I doubt it. I read it over, but I'm not into politics, so I didn't go to the meeting."

"What can you remember about the flyer?"

"As I recall, it was announcing some kind of meeting about boycotting Israel. They had a speaker coming to the campus, I believe. Other than that I don't recall the details."

After watching the interview, Leonard had a few questions for Agent O'Reilly. "Did you follow up on the meeting?"

"We're in the process of doing so. We should have the details by tomorrow."

The next day the FBI detailed what they'd learned about the boycott meeting. The speaker, who had been sponsored by the University of Maryland chapter of Students for Palestinian Justice, was a University of Toronto professor famous for her books attacking economic globalization. O'Reilly uploaded the articles and photos on the event from the University newspaper.

_____

"That may be when Anderson was recruited," Leonard said. "The question is how did she graduate from boycotts to bombs?"

"Keep in mind, Professor, we still don't know whether she was aware of what was in the package," O'Reilly stated.

"You're right, but it's clear she was motivated enough to participate in whatever scheme she thought she had signed up for. A key question is whether other members of the SPJ group knew about or were involved in planning the bombing."

"None of the members we've talked to claim they had any prior knowledge of the bombing," O'Reilly said. "Several condemned it. Further, there's no indication from Anderson's life up to that point that she could do something like this on her own."

"That suggests someone outside of the group recruited her and convinced her to play the role of package deliverer. How are you coming in identifying who that might have been?"

O'Reilly scanned through his stack of papers. "No leads at this point. The newspaper said more than one hundred students attended that meeting. It will be a matter of sheer luck if we can find someone who saw her talking with someone who later checks out as a possible recruiter."

As of Friday, the FBI had failed to find out anything more about who might have recruited Anderson.

Pavel spent the week touching base with his network of contacts without uncovering any information that shed light on the bombing. Meir, along with FBI liaison Gary Mackey, reviewed the FBI's surveillance programs that were in place to identify potential terrorist threats. On Friday, he spent an hour and a half with Leonard reporting his findings.

"They're running a pretty thin operation, wouldn't you say?" Leonard asked after Meir concluded his presentation.

"No doubt," Meir replied. "They don't have the manpower to monitor every possible group whose leanings suggest sympathy for Iran, Al Qaeda, and the rest of the terrorist world."

"What can we do to get deeper into that world?" Leonard asked.

"I think Pavel is still our best bet. He has the network."

Leonard nodded his agreement.

"How are we coming with straightening out the situation with NSA?" Meir asked.

"We're making progress. I had a long talk with Miles McLaughlin. He said he understood what I was after and would work on making it happen. I didn't hear back from him until Thursday. The bottom line is that they can give Stepanova limited access from here, but for more advanced searches including access to data held by AT&T, Google, and the rest of the network operators, she'll have to do that at NSA headquarters."

"How do you feel about that?" Meir asked.

"I'm not happy, of course, but for the moment it's better than nothing. I had her start working on getting emails, Internet histories, and the like for Marisa Anderson from the campus ISP. It turns out since she's dead, we don't have to go to court to get the records. If we want to pursue someone we find through that data, however, we will have to get a judge's signature. Fortunately, Justice seems to be willing to give us immediate approval for any requests and get the necessary signatures after the fact."

"Good. Is Stepanova on board with that arrangement?"

―――――

"She's a hard one to read."

"Pavel may be able to help."

"I noticed that they seem to take their cigarette breaks at the same time," Leonard said.

"I thought you'd asked him to do that."

"Nope. He's just being Pavel."

Meir laughed. "Anything else?"

"That's where we are. Slow but steady may not win the race, but you can only push the bureaucracy so hard before you start slowing yourself down."

Peter G. Pollak

Herndon: Thursday, May 17

A break-through came the following week when FBI Agent O'Reilly texted Leonard on Wednesday that they had identified a person who may have been Marisa Anderson's recruiter and handler. "Details in the morning."

Leonard found it hard to sleep that night. He worried whether the lead was already cold. Had the person left the country or perhaps gone to another city to replicate what he'd pulled off in D.C.? In the middle of the night he got up and wrote down on a yellow pad the steps that they would need to take if in fact they had a solid lead. Then he overslept and missed out on his morning swim.

The entire office gathered around the large wall screen in the conference room as Agent O'Reilly called in from the Bureau's Fourth Street Washington offices.

"Here's the story," he began. "We asked the University to notify each department, division, and what have you to report any unexplained absences dating from the bombing. Yesterday, we heard from the unit that manages the on-campus computer network. They set up students' emails, provide networks for academic departments, manage the servers around campus, and so forth.

"One of their employees--a male by the name of Sammy Haddad--has not shown up for work since the day of the bombing, nor have they been able to contact him. He doesn't answer emails, and the cell phone number he gave them is a non-working number.

"I sent an agent to the address he gave the university as his residence. It turns out he wasn't living there. A guy who also works for the computer unit told us that Haddad asked him if he could have his university mail sent there.

"When we asked what excuse Haddad gave for wanting to use that as his mailing address, he told us Haddad claimed the mail where he was living in D.C. was often stolen by people looking for money."

"Did he tell this person where in D.C. he was living?" Leonard asked.

"An apartment in Southeast, but Haddad didn't give the co-worker the exact address."

"How long had he been working for the University?"

"He was hired a year ago March."

"Thirteen months. Does the rest of his identity check out--his social security number and whatever else the University had on him?"

"None of it is real," O'Reilly replied. "The social belongs to a deceased person. We're checking the school and work references this morning, but I'm confident we'll find they're phony."

"Did they have his finger prints or a photo?"

"No finger prints, but there is a photo which was taken for his ID badge. I'll send it over to you later this morning. We're using it to put out a BOLO."

"Other than the fact that this person has disappeared and his personal information is fictitious, do you have any evidence of a connection to Marisa Anderson?" Leonard asked.

"Not at this time. Unless we get lucky with the guy's photo, he's going to be hard to find."

"Another avenue to explore is where he got his phony social."

"I might be able to shed some light on that," Pavel Zavarov said.

"Let's hear it." Leonard said.

"The Russian mob specializes in producing identity documents--for the right price, of course. He may have gotten his papers from them."

"Okay, Pavel. Check it out and let us know what you find. O'Reilly, good work. Keep us posted."

The FBI was unable to generate any further information about the missing computer technician until Friday afternoon. Leonard was about to sign off and head for the airport to fly back to Albany for the weekend when O'Reilly buzzed him.

"We've got something," O'Reilly said when Leonard picked up. "We found a student who had a conversation with Sammy Haddad. He told us Haddad seemed to be testing his interest in going beyond getting students to endorse the boycott."

"Excellent. That's the link we were looking for. What did you learn about the recruiter?"

"The student, whose name is Marcus Flowers, said he attended the meeting that Anderson was leafleting for. Flowers said he asked the speaker during question and answer time if she thought the petitioning effort would be sufficient to produce the results they were after. He said her response to his question was ambiguous and as a result he told her they needed to engage in civil disobedience. Afterwards several students came up and spoke with Flowers about his comments."

"Interesting," Leonard commented. "Is that when Haddad approached him?"

"No. He showed up at Flowers' dorm suite the following week claiming that someone in that unit had complained about wireless reception on their floor. Then while supposedly checking out the network, he started a conversation with Flowers by mentioning he'd heard his question and comments at the SPJ meeting."

"Do you have Flowers on tape?"

"No. He would not agree to having our conversation taped."

"Okay. So how did he describe his conversation with Haddad?"

"Let me read from my notes. Haddad said he agreed with Flowers that getting people to sign a petition endorsing the boycott was not going to be enough and asked Flowers what kind of actions did he think would work. Flowers said based on his reading about the American Civil Rights movement, he believed they will have to engage in civil disobedience in order to get the attention of world opinion.

"He said Haddad asked him if he'd be willing to attend a meeting of some people to discuss other forms of action on the issue. Flowers told him that while he sympathized with the Palestinian cause, it wasn't his fight and that he only said the things he said so that those who did care would consider alternatives to petitioning."

"How did Haddad react?"

"Apparently he didn't like that response. Flowers said Haddad told him it was hypocritical to advocate something you were not willing to do yourself. Flowers said he disagreed and then not wanting the conversation to continue told Haddad he had to get back to his studies."

"And did Haddad contact him again?"

"Apparently not."

"Good work. The next step is finding someone who can tie Haddad to Anderson. Also, any results from the BOLO?"

"None yet, but you know those things can hit at any time."

"Understood. Talk to you next week."

Peter G. Pollak

United Airlines Flight 5182: Monday, May 21

Leonard was half way to D.C. on an early afternoon flight from Albany when his phone buzzed, interrupting his reading.

"Explosion in Arizona," the text message read.

He stared at the message, knowing he couldn't call back because cell-phone use was still prohibited on commercial flights. The best he could do was text his ETA to the office and hope each person knew what he or she was supposed to do in this kind of situation.

He had been delayed leaving Albany by a visit to his ophthalmologist, who informed him that the spots floating in his left eye were normal for a person his age and that his mind would adjust to them eventually.

It was good to hear that the condition probably wouldn't get worse, but Leonard hoped the part about his brain adjusting would happen soon because the condition, which had started the previous week, was extremely annoying. When the spots first appeared, he kept closing his eyes in hopes that they would disappear, but they didn't. He wondered whether something serious was happening to his body and thought about having his driver take him to the emergency room, but experiencing no other symptoms, he decided to call his ophthalmologist who eased his concerns about the condition being life-threatening and set up the appointment.

Leonard wondered if additional health problems were a cost of his taking the task force assignment.

Working long hours at the DEFEAT office upset the schedule he'd set up for himself when he moved to Albany, a routine designed to achieve a balance between work, leisure, and exercise. The latter was crucial, according to his doctors, to postpone long-term debilitating effects of his spinal cord injury.

Although the hotel where the White House had put him up had a handicap-accessible swimming pool, Leonard knew he needed to do a better job of making use of it. Only by getting into the pool by 6 a.m. was he able to get in a modest amount of exercise, shower, get dressed, eat breakfast, and be ready for his driver at half past eight.

He had already cheated more than once after staying late at the office by sleeping late, but then he had to put up with a guilty feeling the rest of the day.

Leonard got Meir on the line as soon as the flight hit the tarmac. "Talk to me."

"A bomb went off approximately one hour ago in the district office of Representative Steven Trent, a Democrat from Tucson. No confirmed numbers of injured or dead. No one has claimed credit."

"That's Gabrielle Gifford's old district, right?"

"It is."

"Was Trent in the office?"

"Apparently not, but the FBI hasn't said where he is."

"Okay. Rodolfo should be outside security with my van. I'll be there shortly. I'll want to know as much as you can find out about the explosion and if it was a bombing, why anyone might want to hit Congressman Trent."

Everyone present in the task force's office was either on the phone or banging away on their keyboards as Leonard wheeled to the desk in the middle of the bullpen area where he worked when he didn't need the privacy of his corner office.

Meir Epstein was on his feet as soon as he saw Leonard enter the room. He sat down in the chair next to Leonard's desk as Leonard logged into the network.

"What do we know?" Leonard asked.

"Nothing much really. There are casualties, although at this point no one's saying how many."

"What about Trent?"

"He's in D.C."

"Still no claim?"

"Not that I've heard."

"Okay. Listen up everyone," Leonard said loudly.

Meir stood up to make sure everyone was paying attention. "Someone get Larry and Betty."

Leonard waited for Larry Burnside and Betty Liu, the IT team, to emerge out of their lair and for office manager Ed Morgan to come into the bullpen area from his desk in reception.

"Each of you should know what you're supposed to be doing in this kind of situation," Leonard began, "and I'm sure you're already doing it. Come see me if you have any questions. Feed anything you come across--no matter how insignificant--onto the network. If you are confident you've come up with something major, such as someone taking credit for the bombing or a possibly related incident, call it out.

"We need to know whether this explosion was a bomb or perhaps a natural gas leak or some similar occurrence. If it was a bomb, we need to know who the target was, and, of course, we need to know who is responsible."

Team members went back to the assignments Leonard had given them during their individual orientations. The agency liaisons were monitoring information coming into their separate agencies.

Leonard reviewed his assignment list to make sure everyone was on task. Russell Knowles, the CIA rep, was checking overseas noise, Betty Liu, Larry Burnside's assistant, was monitoring network and cable news TV channels, while Justice Terrorism Division rep Carole Jean Hall was responsible for monitoring the online reports issued by the Associated Press and national print media. NSA analyst Ekaterina Stepanova was supposed to be running searches on keywords related to the event to capture Internet traffic. Worried that she might not be on task, Leonard asked Pavel to check up on her.

First on the scene and therefore the agency most likely to produce vital information about the incident was the Tucson FBI office. Gary Mackey, the team's FBI liaison, was the person likely to be providing most of that morning's intel.

As per usual in events such as this one, the FBI did not make any announcements until they were certain the bombsite was free of explosives.

When the FBI announced a press conference at two p.m. Arizona time, everyone in the office gathered in the conference room to watch.

"This is a preliminary statement," the local FBI bureau chief stated after introducing himself to the press corps. "We want to get information out as quickly as possible in hopes that people will come forward to help us find the person or persons responsible for today's event.

"This is what we know. At approximately eight forty-five this morning, an explosive device was detonated in the regional office of Congressman Steven Trent. There are four confirmed dead. Two persons have been taken to ASU Medical with serious, but not life-threatening, injuries; two people were treated for injuries on the scene that did not require hospitalization.

"The names of the deceased and injured will not be revealed until their families have been contacted.

"We will not be discussing what kind of explosive was used at this time. Please don't ask me any questions about that.

"We have not received any messages or phone calls from the person or persons responsible for this heinous act. We are appealing to the citizens of this region to come forward if you have any information that might lead to the apprehension of those responsible.

"That's the end of my statement. I'll take a few questions."

Not surprisingly the media tried to get the bureau chief to provide information he didn't have or couldn't reveal. After ten minutes, he called the press conference to a close and stated they would hold another briefing as soon as they had new information to share.

Leonard addressed his team. "Comments? Observations? Questions?"

"What are we getting on the bomb?" Meir asked Gary Mackey.

Mackey stood up. "It seems to have been a crude device--definitely something home-made. It was set off in the reception area and all of the people who were in that area are confirmed dead."

"Where were the ones who were injured?" Meir asked.

"Both were in the next room," Mackey replied.

"Who were the victims?" Leonard asked.

Mackey consulted his notes. "The victims are the office receptionist by the name of Quanita Navarro, aged twenty-six, Michael Frederickson, age twenty, a student intern from Arizona University, a local citizen by the name of Nelson Rullison, age unknown, who had an appointment with the Congressman's local manager, and another staff person, a Phyllis Russo, age thirty-four."

"It doesn't sound like any of those people delivered the bomb to that office," Leonard stated.

"That's our belief as well."

"Who was this Rullison, Gary?"

Mackey, who had sat down, got back up. "He was employed by the Arizona State Farm Bureau. According to Congressman Trent's Washington office, he was there to talk about water rights."

"Not likely to be our carrier," Meir stated.

"What about the student?"

"We're still gathering data on him," Mackey said. "He might have been the one."

"Does Tucson feel like a repeat of the AIA bombing?" Leonard asked the group. "Any opinions?"

"Too early to say," Russell Knowles ventured.

Several agreed.

"Depends on the student," Meir suggested. "He might be affiliated with Students for Palestinian Justice or some other radical group."

"Okay. Let's stay at it."

Later that afternoon the FBI's report came back on the student. He was, in their terms, "squeaky-clean"--no radical affiliations or sentiments were found tying him to SPJ or any other radical group.

The team stayed at the office late that evening, but after listening to the FBI's second press conference, at which time they revealed the names of the victims to the public, they were still in the dark. It was past eleven when Leonard told them all to go home. "This is likely to take a while to sort out. I'll see you in the morning."

He had texted Alison that he'd call her when he had a minute and almost forgot to do so. After taking off his clothes and brushing his teeth, he wheeled over to his desk where his cell phone was charging.

"Hi, Hon," Alison answered. "Rough day?"

"It was, and if you've been watching the news, we barely know more than you do."

"Have any first impressions?"

"It doesn't feel like the work of the person behind the D.C. bombing," Leonard replied. "Doesn't mean it wasn't, but none of those who died look good for being the carrier."

"Still there's a sick mf out there someplace. I hope they catch him quick."

"Okay, dear. I'm exhausted. Talk to you tomorrow."

"Try to get some exercise tomorrow."

"I will Ali. I promise."

Peter G. Pollak

Herndon: Thursday, May 24

As the data rolled in on the Tucson blast, the DEFEAT task force focused on finding any hint of a connection to the April thirteenth D.C. bombing. They held daily briefings to share what they'd learned the day before and worked late hours.

Forensic analysis confirmed that the blast was caused by a crudely assembled explosive that was most likely set off when someone--the logical candidate was the receptionist--opened the box that contained the device.

Gary Mackey began the Thursday morning briefing. "From what we've pieced together, we believe someone delivered a package to Congressman Trent's office late Friday afternoon addressed to Quanita Navarro after she had left for the day. When she came in Monday morning, she must have believed the box, which apparently was addressed to her, was a present. Her birthday would have been yesterday. We know all this because we talked to the staff person who received the package and because the two women who were wounded told us Navarro called them into the reception area to watch her open it. Two of the staffers who had been injured had been delayed joining the rest, which saved their lives."

"So it looks as if someone had it in for the receptionist?" Leonard asked.

"It appears that way," Mackey replied. "None of the commercial delivery services have any record of making a delivery to Congressman Trent's office Friday afternoon. It's possible the package was delivered by someone impersonating a delivery person, similar to the *modus operandi* of the AIA bombing."

"That's interesting, but why would a terrorist organization--if that's who did this--target Congressman Trent's receptionist?" Leonard asked.

Mackey shrugged. "That's a good question."

"It's unlikely they were trying to influence Trent himself," Meir Epstein said. "He's a freshman in Congress, which means he has very little power or influence."

"Does anyone know if Trent has ever made a statement on any issue, domestic or foreign, that would make him a target?" Leonard asked, looking around the room.

"We have checked through his records pretty thoroughly, Len," Epstein replied, "but can't find anything that would make him a terrorism target."

"So what's the motive? Why the receptionist?"

The answer to that question came in later in the day.

"The Tucson FBI has a theory," Mackey informed the group. It turns out that the receptionist had recently broken up with a boyfriend to go out with a new suitor. Her sister, who lives near Phoenix, told us she'd had a phone conversation with Quanita Sunday morning during which her sister raved about her new boyfriend. Navarro told her sister that she was breaking up with the man she'd been dating for about a year because she learned he was involved in drug trafficking."

"Has the Bureau tracked down either of the boyfriends?" Leonard asked.

"They found the new boyfriend in Tucson. He seemed genuinely devastated, and gave our agents no cause to suspect that he was the one who sent her the bomb. We haven't been able to find the old boyfriend, however. He was probably an illegal. Some residents in the neighborhood where he reputedly lived said they knew who he was, but no one would give us an exact address or even tell us his real name. They knew him by one of several nicknames, including "El Sobrino," which means "the nephew." One person said he'd gone back to Mexico several weeks ago, but could offer no proof of that. We suspect people are covering for this El Sobrino out of fear."

"But does killing an ex-girlfriend with a bomb fit any profile in your system?"

Mackey shook his head. "It doesn't, and to have used a courier to deliver the package also seems unique."

"Anything else?" Leonard asked.

"We're working with DEA and Homeland Security to try to identify this El Sobrino."

"What about the Mexican authorities?"

"That's being pursued," Sheila Stewart, the team's rep from Homeland Security stated. "I'll keep you posted."

"Okay, good. Let's keep a close eye on this case as more evidence comes in, but unless someone can find some connection to our anti-Israel terrorists, we'll go back to focusing on finding the guy who induced Marisa Anderson to carry that package into the AIA offices."

Leonard didn't look forward to his Friday afternoon conversation that week with Rosa Martinez. The task force had finished its fourth week in operation and thus far had added nothing of great value to the D.C. investigation or advanced their overall charge.

Martinez seemed satisfied, however, that they had concluded there was no connection between the bombing in D.C. and the one in Tucson.

"If someone's targeting members of Congress, all hell's going to break loose," she stated. "So now what?"

"Yesterday we went back over everything we know about the D.C. bombing," Leonard replied. "We're still following the angle that this Sammy Haddad recruited Marisa Anderson as a result of her having been involved in the campus Students for Palestinian Justice group. We're going to put some pressure on the group's faculty supporters to help us find anyone who might have seen Haddad with Anderson."

"Okay. Keep me posted," Martinez stated, ending the conversation.

Delmar, New York: Monday, May 28

Leonard lifted his glass. "To the start of summer."

The people sitting around the picnic table in the Robbins' backyard joined in.

"I hear it's going to be warmer than last year," said Art Polanski, a widower and faculty member at the Rockefeller College of Public Affairs.

"Not too warm, I hope," Leonard replied. "Hot weather and wheelchairs are not compatible."

"Sorry, I never thought of that," Polanski stated.

"It's okay. Except on weekends, I'll be in my air-conditioned hotel, my air-conditioned van, and my air-conditioned office."

Polanski laughed.

Leonard tried to get Courtney's attention. "Speaking of air-conditioning, Court, I hope your new apartment has that modern convenience."

"Say what?" asked Courtney, who had been talking with a high school friend who came to the Memorial Day barbeque at the Robbins with her mother and her mother's boyfriend.

"I asked if your apartment has air-conditioning," Leonard said, smiling to let her know he was not being critical.

"Oh, I seem to remember seeing a couple of units in the windows."

"Better check them out before the hot weather arrives."

"I will, Dad. We're not moving into a slum, you know."

"Your mother will be the judge of that," Leonard replied.

Alison looked up from her conversation with Mindy's mother, a divorced social worker who had brought her latest boyfriend to the celebration. "Given what they are charging for rent . . ."

"That's true," Leonard said.

"Did you ever live in the city?" the boyfriend asked Leonard.

"Never had the pleasure, you?"

"I did, for about a year and a half, when I still thought I had acting talent. Tried out for plenty of plays, but never got hired. I might have stayed longer, but I wasn't much good at waiting tables, either."

That comment brought chuckles from the others. The boyfriend smiled and got up to get himself another beer from the cooler. Courtney took advantage of the moment to drag her friend into the house.

"How's the task force of yours coming?" Professor Polanski asked.

"We've barely been together a month," Leonard replied. "It takes that long just to get up to speed."

"Tell me about it. I was on a federal committee once. It took three phone calls--this was before email--to order lunch."

"Technology has made things like that somewhat easier, but we still run into bureaucratic roadblocks."

Polanski accepted a bowl of corn chips from Alison, put some on his plate, and passed it along to Leonard. "So, do you think there'll be more bombings like the one in D.C.?"

Leonard took some chips and set the bowl down on the table "It wouldn't shock me. That's what each of the groups that claimed responsibility promised."

"Can't you trace where those statements came from?"

"That's not as easy as you might think," Leonard said. "Everyone these days is pretty sophisticated about disguising the location of the server where their messages originate."

"Seems like the hackers are always one step ahead despite all the money we pour into NSA," Polanski said.

Leonard nodded.

"So what were they after?" the boyfriend asked, having retrieved his beer and pulled his chair to where he could join in the men's conversation.

"Who's that?" Leonard asked.

"The ones who bombed that Jewish group."

"They want Israel to turn the entire region over to their rule."

"That's all, eh?" the boyfriend said. "But doesn't Israel bring this kind of event on itself?"

"How's that?" Leonard and Polanski asked simultaneously.

"Look at the numbers. During the last conflict, the Israelis killed more than thirty Palestinians for every one of their people who died."

Polanski deferred to Leonard for the response. "That wasn't for lack of trying on Hamas' part. The Israelis have better weaponry and better intelligence."

"That's what I mean," the boyfriend said. "It's kind of unfair."

Leonard sighed. "So you mean if someone smaller and weaker than you challenges you to fight and you beat him up, it's your fault?"

"Well, if you put it in those terms."

"It is unfair to the Palestinians in one sense," Leonard said. "Hamas gets humanitarian aid from the U.S., the United Nations, and even from Israel, but instead of using the money to build schools, hospitals, and housing for their people, they pay young men to be soldiers and build tunnels so they can attack Israeli civilians."

"That's right," added Polanski. "When Israel warns they're about to bomb a building, Hamas tells women and children to go up on the roof."

"I guess that shows how little the Palestinians value human life," the boyfriend mumbled.

"I don't know about that," Leonard said "but I do know one reason they send civilians into harm's way is because Israel uses drones to identify the source of rocket fire, but they'll often call off their attack if they see civilians near a military target."

"Jeesh, but tell me this," the boyfriend said. "Why is it that so many Palestinian civilians are killed?"

"Art, you want to answer him?" Leonard asked.

"Go ahead," Polanksi replied. "You're the expert."

"I don't know that it takes an expert to explain. The casualty figures come from Hamas. They label everyone a civilian to make it look like Israel's targeting civilians. An analysis of the body count, however, suggests that a disproportionate number of dead are men between the age of eighteen and thirty-five--Hamas soldiers in other words."

"So what you're saying is that they're lying about the civilian count?" the boyfriend asked.

Leonard spooned some salsa over his chips. "The reason they report the dead the way they do is to try to make Israel look like the bad guys in the public opinion war."

"I guess they fooled me," the boyfriend admitted.

———

"And plenty of others," Leonard said.

"Mindy and I are going out, Dad," Courtney said two hours later as their guests were leaving. "I probably won't be awake when you leave in the morning."

"That's fine, Honey. Sleep late."

"I probably won't see you until summer school is over."

"I understand. I'm sure you'll have a good summer."

"Right, but I'll be studying mostly."

"Glad to hear it. No time for leafleting dorms."

"Dad, it's time to let that one go."

"Come here. Give us a hug."

Courtney gave Leonard a hug and a kiss. "Bye."

"And don't forget to call once in a while."

Peter G. Pollak

College Park, Maryland: Wednesday, May 30

Accompanied by Justice Department liaison Carole Jean Hall, Leonard wheeled into a conference room in the main administration building at the University of Maryland for their eleven a.m. appointment. Leonard picked Hall because she looked the part--she dressed like a business leader and could make even the most confident male feel inferior.

The women, who had been conferring at the far end of the room, continued talking for thirty seconds before coming forward to introduce themselves. From her photo on the University of Maryland website, Leonard recognized Mary Francis Waterson, associate professor of American Studies and a member of the board of directors of the American Studies Association, a professional association that several years previous endorsed the anti-Israel Boycott, Divestment and Sanctions movement. She looked to be in her late forties, wore her hair short, and was dressed casually with black slacks and a short-sleeved cream-colored top.

The second woman introduced herself as Elizabeth Foster, the university's Vice President for Student Affairs. Foster was taller than Waterson and wore a light blue suit with a yellow blouse.

Waterson had not made it easy for the task force to get the appointment. Only when informed by Aaron Hayes from Rosa Martinez' office that the task force had subpoena power did she agree to the meeting.

"I'm on a tight schedule this morning, Professor Robbins," Waterson said. "I was assured this meeting would be brief."

Not willing to be provoked, Leonard thanked Waterson for making time for them in her schedule. "We would not have requested this meeting if we didn't think the subject warranted your direct involvement."

Waterson seemed taken aback. "What's it about?"

"We need your help finding the person or persons who masterminded last month's D.C. bombing," Leonard replied. "Our investigation strongly suggests that Marisa Anderson, the former University of Maryland student who died in the bombing, was recruited as a result of her membership in the campus Students for Palestinian Justice."

"I don't see what that has to do with me," Waterson stated.

Leonard handed Waterson a blow-up of Sammy Haddad's id photo. "Do you recognize this individual?"

"No, I don't," Waterson replied, handing the photo back to Leonard.

"Please take a closer look," Leonard said offering the photo back to Waterson. "This is the individual we believe recruited Marisa Anderson."

"I'm sorry, I don't recognize him."

"We know he tried to recruit at least one other student who attended a SPJ meeting last fall."

"Sorry. Is that all?"

"No, SPJ members identified you as an advisor to the group. As such, we'd like your assistance in finding anyone who might have seen this man with Marisa Anderson or who knows anything about him."

"I'm not their faculty advisor; therefore don't see how I can help you."

"Who is the faculty advisor?"

"Not every group has a faculty advisor," Dean Foster stated. "I can find out if SPJ has one and let you know who it is."

"So are we done here?" Waterson asked.

"Whether you're the official advisor or not, your name keeps coming up," Leonard said. "That suggests that you could help us find out if anyone had seen this Haddad at any of the SPJ meetings and help us find other students he might have tried to recruit or who had seen him with Marisa Anderson."

Dean Foster took a step forward. "The FBI has already been on campus interviewing people. If Professor Waterson says she can't help, she can't help."

"I'll try to be clearer," Leonard stated. "Some of the students we interviewed view Professor Waterson as the member of the university faculty most sympathetic to the Palestinians' cause. More than one student reports having spent time in Professor Waterson's office discussing the issue."

"Okay," Foster said, "But--"

"Let me finish, please. Professor Waterson is likely to know how to contact the group's leaders and she may know other members of the faculty who support the boycott movement who may be able to identify students we should talk to. She may also know people who work in non-academic positions, like this Sammy Haddad did, who may have information that would be useful. We are asking her to provide us the names of anyone she knows who may have information that can help us find the man who contributed to the death of your former student."

"It sounds like you're trying to suppress student involvement in the issue, not find terrorists," Waterson stated.

"I don't know why you would get that impression," Leonard replied. "The Constitution protects your right to voice your opinions. It does not however allow you to harbor terrorists or criminals."

"Harbor is a pretty strong word, Professor Robbins," Dean Foster interjected. "Are you suggesting that someone on this campus is knowingly protecting a terrorist?"

"Not at all," Leonard said, "but a terrorist plot was generated on this campus and one of your students died as a result. Further, we found one other student who Sammy Haddad tried to recruit, and there may be more, which is the point of this meeting. We would like Professor Waterson's help in finding any other students who can help us catch Haddad and prevent him from killing more innocent people."

Waterson looked over at Dean Foster.

"I'm sure Professor Waterson wants to cooperate," Dean Foster said. "Give us some time to sort out a few administrative questions. Someone from my office will be in touch."

"Please do that quickly. Every day this man is on the loose puts lives at risk."

Thursday morning, office manager Ed Morgan intercepted Leonard as he wheeled himself off the elevator after having had lunch at a nearby restaurant with Meir and Pavel. "Dean Foster of the University of Maryland called for you. Here's her number," he said, handing Leonard a phone message slip.

Leonard called Foster back immediately.

"I've got a name for you," Foster said when she came on the line.

"Okay," Leonard replied, not happy that they were only providing them with one name, but willing to take anything at that point.

———

"Susan Gazzola," Foster said. "She's a junior American Studies Major. Professor Waterson is her faculty advisor. She says Gazzola may be one of the boycott group's leaders."

"Do you have her contact information?"

"I do. Ready?"

Leonard took down the information and thanked Dean Foster for her assistance. Next he buzzed Gary Mackey. "I've got a name and contact information of a UM student who may be able to help us. Can you get someone there this afternoon?"

Peter G. Pollak

College Park: Friday, June 1

Although she had been lurking by the bank of payphones in the campus center for twenty minutes, Susan Gazzola did not expect any of them to ring. As a result, when one started ringing she had to scurry to answer it before someone else did.

"Hello."

"Susan?"

"Sammy, is that you?"

"Yes, it's me. How are you, Susan?"

"Oh, I'm okay, I guess. I mean no one's talked to me yet."

"Assume that they will. You know what to say, right?"

"I . . ." Susan caught herself before saying 'I guess so.' Sammy told her she needed to give decisive, confident answers. "Yes, I do."

"Good. Remember what I told you about spitting out your answers like you don't have to think about them."

"Yes, I remember."

"Good. When you hesitate it suggests you're making up your answer."

"When are you coming back, Sammy?"

"Not for a while, Susan. I told you I have to wait until things cool down."

"They ran your picture in *The Diamondback*."

"Have you got the paper there? Read what it says."

"Sorry. I left it in my room."

"Then tell me what you remember."

"It said you are wanted for questioning by the FBI in the matter of the explosion in Washington, D.C."

"Don't worry. They won't find me."

"They say Sammy Haddad's not your real name."

"I told you that, Susan. Don't you remember?"

"No."

"You've got to do a better job of paying attention, then."

"I'm sorry."

"It's okay. I can't afford to use my real name. That would result in their being able to use people who care about me against me."

"I understand."

"When they show you my picture, it's okay to say you might have seen someone who looks like me on the campus."

"Okay."

"Keep in mind they can't make you testify against yourself. Just tell them what we discussed and you'll be fine."

"I hope so, Sammy, because I don't want to go to prison."

"You won't, Susan. Don't worry. I've got to go now. I'll call you in two weeks the same time."

"Sammy."

"What Susan?"

"Why did she have to die?"

"I am as upset about that as you. She must have done something to set the bomb off, but there's nothing we can do now except wait for things to quiet down."

"Okay, Sammy. I miss you."

"Me too. I'll talk to you in two weeks."

———

Susan was sweating by the time she reached her apartment. She opened the door, went into the kitchen, poured herself a glass of cold water, and sat down at her kitchen table.

Just then there was a knock on the apartment door.

"Come in," she called, thinking it was Martha, her next-door neighbor. Martha liked to gossip and at the moment Susan badly wanted some company. Instead of her neighbor, however, two people she didn't know came into the apartment: a tall man with a large head and thin hair and a short, stocky blond woman, both in professional dress.

Oh, no!

"Susan Gazzola?" asked the man.

"Yes," she said, barely getting the word out.

"I'm Herman Schlosser and this is Andrea Watson. We're with the FBI." They showed her their badges. "We'd like to ask you a few questions."

Not now! She was still upset about the phone call with Sammy. He said he would call her every week at the same time on a rotating group of payphones around the campus, but she had waited fruitlessly before that day. She meant to ask him why he hadn't called her those times, but she was so happy that he called this week that she forgot.

She knew the FBI would eventually want to talk to her because she was active in the SPJ group.

"I just got in and I'm kind of busy right now," Susan said.

"This will only take a few minutes."

Susan shrugged. Maybe it wouldn't be so bad. She'd rehearsed her answers often enough.

The agent named Herman, who reminded Susan a little of a TV character from a show she used to watch when she was little, handed her a blow up photo of Sammy's ID. "Susan, do you know this man?"

She shook her head. "Nope."

"Are you sure, because we've talked to a number of students who recall seeing you and him together in the Student Union."

That's where they met the first few times until Sammy told her he needed to meet during off hours off campus so that he wouldn't get in trouble with his boss.

"Are they sure? He doesn't look familiar to me."

"Susan, you need to think very carefully before you answer our questions because you may already be in a great deal of trouble. If you start lying to us, your problems are only going to get worse."

"Why are you threatening me?" she demanded. She burst into tears and had to get up and get the tissue box she kept in her bathroom.

"Susan." It was the woman who was talking. "We're just trying to help you. You probably didn't know what you were getting into, but we have very good reason to believe that this man convinced Marisa Anderson to carry that bomb into the offices of the American Israel Association."

Susan sobbed. She wanted to say that she didn't know Marisa Anderson, but the words would not come out. Then she began talking in spurts. She admitted she knew Marisa and then confessed she knew Sammy as well. More than an hour later she'd told the agents everything--how Sammy had courted her and praised her for being so smart and brave and told her she was pretty when she knew she wasn't and how he introduced her to Marisa and how the three of them planned to place a bomb at the AIA headquarters and how she was supposed to call to warn them so no one would get hurt, but the bomb must have gone off accidently. Everything. She told them everything.

Peter G. Pollak

Herndon: Monday, June 4

"Thoughts?" Leonard asked his team at the end of the FBI's briefing on Susan Gazzola's confession.

"Where did this Haddad guy come from and how was he able to operate without calling attention to himself?" Meir Epstein asked.

Leonard nodded. "Good questions. Anyone?"

"Let's start with the fake ID. That should have been flagged," Carole Jean Hall stated.

"Ekaterina, shouldn't NSA's systems be catching these?" Leonard asked.

"That's Social Security's jurisdiction, not ours."

"Figures," Leonard mumbled. "Gary, has the Bureau talked to Social Security about Haddad?"

"We have," the team's FBI liaison replied. "He used a legitimate number for a recently deceased person named Samuel Haddad. They admit that should have been caught, but their system isn't perfect. It's not easy keeping track of nearly three hundred million living people plus everyone who's died since the system began seventy-five years ago."

Leonard scowled. "What else do we know about this guy that can help us track him down?"

"He's supposed to call Gazzola again a week from Friday," Mackey offered. "If he does, we'll be able to track where he's calling from."

"Good. Is Gazzola willing to play along?"

"She is. We told her doing so will help her when she is sentenced for her part in the bombing."

"What's she facing by the way?" Leonard asked.

"Depends on what they end up charging her with," Mackey replied. "Life without parole would be my guess."

"This Gazzola woman doesn't have a background that suggests either a grudge against Jews or a tendency to violence," Leonard said. "Yet this man convinced her of the need to deliver a bomb to the offices of a Jewish organization."

"That pretty much confirms your theory, Len, that there are people who can be convinced to do just about anything."

"She claims he told her there would be no loss of life," Carole Jean stated.

"Which teaches us how skilled this Sammy Haddad is," Leonard said. "That means he's going to be difficult to find and stop, particularly if Social Security and NSA can't do a better job flagging false id's."

"To what extent do you think Haddad is operating on his own versus having been trained and sent here by our enemies?" Meir asked.

"Another excellent question," Leonard stated. "Anyone got any thoughts?"

Gary Mackey jumped in first. "According to everyone we interviewed, he spoke English without an accent. That suggests he was born here or came here when he was quite young."

"Good point. Anyone else?"

"Nothing he did required outside assistance," Pavel Zavarov pointed out.

"Yes and no," Leonard said. "Being able to conceive and pull off such a sophisticated operation, and then to escape without leaving a trace suggests there's a deep organization behind him. To do all that on one's own without help or guidance would be extremely difficult."

"And if there's an organization, it's likely there's more than one Sammy Haddad out there," Meir said.

"Exactly," Leonard said. "At this point we need to assume he was not acting alone. If we find out differently, fine, but until then, we have to operate as if there are other Sammy Haddad's in the process of recruiting bomb carriers. It's our job to find them."

"How do we do that?" Sheila Stewart, the Homeland Security rep, asked.

Leonard took in a deep breath and let it out slowly. "In the past terrorist organizations focused on recruiting Muslims living in the U.S. They've learned, however, that we're watching Muslim groups and mosques very closely, which makes that route more precarious. That's why I foresaw that they'd look elsewhere to find their bomb carriers."

"Like campus BDS groups," Meir said.

Leonard nodded. "That's where they found Marisa Anderson and Susan Gazzola, and I believe that's where we have to look if we're going to find Haddad and his fellow recruiters."

"How do we do that?" Carole Jean Hall of Justice asked.

"Gary, does the FBI have enough agents to monitor every community and college BDS group?"

"Not even close," Mackey replied. "We're lucky if we have three dozen agents who fit in terms of age and appearance. How many chapters of that group are there?"

"More than one hundred," Leonard replied. "There's another way--top down. We go to the faculty organizations that have endorsed the boycott movement and convince them to help us get the word out to the student population."

"Given the way that professor at the University of Maryland responded, that's going to be a tough sell," Carole Jean Hall said.

"You're right," Leonard said, "but we have to make the effort. To start, let's get as much information on both the student and faculty organizations as we can. If the student group has any kind of national officers, we'll approach them as well. I think we can make a convincing argument that it will only hurt their cause if they allow terrorists to use their meetings to recruit bomb carriers."

"Unless some of the student leaders are in on the plot," Meir stated.

Leonard nodded. "That's possible, but unlikely. Even if they are, they can't admit it publicly. They'll have to go along with us."

"What about religious organizations?" Meir asked.

"Several have backed boycott resolutions," Leonard said. "We'll send teams to talk to them also."

"I've got a list already started," Meir said.

"Excellent. Okay, people, time to get cracking. I want to set up meetings with the officers of the American Studies Association, the Asian-American Studies Association, and any other academic or religious group that has endorsed a boycott resolution. We'll need two or three teams to hit each group over the next few weeks--particularly at the colleges since the spring semester is over and people have dispersed for the summer. I'll pick the teams by Monday and decide who meets with which group."

New York City: Monday, June 11

Courtney and a tall, young woman Alison assumed must be her new roommate were sitting on the steps outside the apartment building when Alison pulled up in the family van. Alison saw that they had wisely placed two chairs on the street, reserving the space so Alison could park the van.

"Mom, meet Doreen," Courtney said after Alison maneuvered into the space. "Doreen, meet my mother."

"Nice to meet you, Doreen. I hope you're both feeling strong today because I brought a lot of stuff for your apartment."

The three women unloaded furniture and boxes for the next hour. Alison had packed the clothes Courtney had emailed her she needed for the summer, as well as bedding, curtains, and a few kitchen appliances. She also brought the desk chair from Courtney's bedroom, two folding chairs, and food items, including packaged rice mixes and pasta sauces.

It was Doreen who cautioned them against accepting the offer of a skinny guy of indeterminate age who labeled himself a "good Samaritan" by offering to watch the van while they dragged things into the house.

"Mrs. Robbins, you'd better stay here while Courtney and I take the first trip," Doreen said.

After they'd managed to get everything upstairs without anything being stolen, including Alison's pocket book, which she almost left in the unlocked van, they worked for another hour and a half sorting and storing things, and then hanging the curtains in Courtney's bedroom.

"I'm beat and starved," Alison told the girls after she determined the curtains she'd just hung were even. "Let me take you gals out for dinner."

Neither girl objected.

"I think you've lucked out on your place," Alison told them while they were waiting for their dinners at a neighborhood Mexican restaurant, "although I'm not sure about the neighborhood."

"There are a lot worse, believe me," Doreen said.

"Just be careful at night," Alison told them.

"We will, Mom," Courtney said. "Don't worry."

Alison had decided against talking about the Students for Palestinian Justice group, but Doreen brought it up while they were waiting for desserts.

"Courtney says you were concerned about her getting into trouble over the leafleting business. You needn't have worried. The administration knows it would backfire if they tried to suspend every student who participated."

"What about your mom, Doreen? Wasn't she worried when she heard about it?"

"My mom's dead, Mrs. Robbins."

"Oh, I'm sorry, Doreen. I didn't know."

"She died when I was eleven. Cancer. I lived with my grandmother for a while until she died, then moved in with an aunt until I started college. I'm on my own now."

"And your dad?"

"I didn't see him for years, and then he showed up without warning when I was in high school. Now I see him once or twice a year."

"That's good," Alison offered.

———

"I guess, but mostly he tells me how I'm going to end up like my mother."

"What about your aunt--do you get any support from her?"

"My aunt has her hands full with her own kids. I call her once in a while to tell her I'm okay."

Alison nodded. *This girl has had a tough life*, she thought. Normally she resisted applying psychological explanations for someone's involvement in radical movements, but in this case that notion seemed to fit. "I'm sure your aunt appreciates knowing you're okay."

Doreen gave Alison a thin smile. "My grandmother left me a little money. So, I'm okay for the moment."

"Still not having any parents at such a young age. That couldn't have been easy."

Alison noted that Doreen turned to Courtney as if she wanted her roommate to change the subject, so she decided to do so herself. "So how are your classes coming, Courtney?"

They talked about school for the rest of the meal. Then Alison walked the girls back to their apartment where she helped out for another hour before deciding it was time to go to the college friend's apartment where she was spending the night. "Doreen, I hope you'll come up to Albany with Courtney at the end of the semester. We've got a fun week planned. We'll go to Tanglewood to hear the Boston Philharmonic, do some shopping in Saratoga, and barbeque in the backyard."

"Thank you for inviting me, Mrs. Robbins," Doreen said. "I'm not sure my job comes with a week off."

"Maybe just for the weekend then. We'll take care of the train ticket and everything else."

Doreen smiled shyly. "That would be nice."

Alison gave Courtney a hug and a kiss and gave Doreen a hug, which seemed to shock her at first. *That girl needs some TLC.* She vowed to include Doreen as often as possible whenever she and Leonard came to the city or Courtney came up to Delmar. She was already thinking about Thanksgiving as she got into the van and headed to her friend's apartment.

New York City: Thursday June 14

Leonard Robbins had two reasons for being the one meeting with the president of the five thousand-member American Studies Association in person. Luisa Castillo was a professor at NYU, which meant he could take his daughter out to dinner and have a father-daughter conversation.

As was the case in his obtaining a meeting with Mary Francis Waterson at the University of Maryland, the task force had to exert considerable pressure to get Professor Castillo to accept the meeting. With Meir Epstein and the CIA's task force rep Russell Knowles handling the meeting with the Association for Asian American Studies, Leonard chose Sheila Stewart, Homeland Security's rep on the task force, to accompany him to New York. A short, heavy-set woman, Stewart didn't look imposing, but she had a mind like a steel-trap and a memory for all things political.

Professor Castillo brought three people to the meeting: Paula Nazare, ASA's executive director, Adam Tan, an associate professor in the American Studies Department, and Neil Mason, a representative from the NYU faculty senate.

"Thank you all for making the time to meet with us today," Leonard began. "Although our primary goal was to talk with Professor Castillo, we're happy to know others are interested in helping us."

"That remains to be seen," Professor Tan said, looking at Castillo for support.

"What kind of help are you looking for?" Castillo asked.

"Preventing a repeat of the recent bombing in Washington, D.C.," Leonard stated. "We believe that Marisa Anderson, the young woman who died in the bombing at the H Street headquarters of the American Israel Association, was recruited as a result of her association with the Students for Palestinian Justice group on the campus of the University of Maryland."

"Then you should be talking to the administration at the University of Maryland, not us," Professor Tan said.

"They are cooperating with the investigation," Leonard said. "The reason I'm here is we believe there are other terrorist recruiters in the U.S. who are trolling boycott Israel groups to identify possible bomb carriers."

"I still don't see how this involves the American Studies Association," Professor Castillo said. "I spoke with Mary Waterson who says you practically accused her of harboring terrorists."

Leonard shook his head. "I simply pointed out the negative consequences of ignoring the possibility that lending support for the boycott movement has provided cover for these recruiters."

"That's a pretty big leap," Professor Mason interjected.

"Be that as it may, Professor Mason, since the ASA endorsed the movement to boycott Israeli academic institutions, I would have to assume that many ASA members are in contact with the SPJ leaders on their campuses. We would like Professor Castillo to ask her members to issue a statement on each campus asking students to contact the FBI if they are approached by anyone who proposes taking any form of action other than peaceful protest."

"It sounds like you're trying to suppress the student organization, not find terrorists," Professor Castillo stated.

"That's what Professor Waterson suggested, but that's not the case," Leonard replied. "What objection do you have to warning students who may be exploited in a manner that could prove fatal, to report anyone who talks to them about committing acts of violence?"

"Isn't that the responsibility of each institution rather than individual faculty members?" Neil Mason asked before Professor Castillo could answer.

"We would like every college in the country to issue the same warning," Leonard said, "but students have a way of ignoring authority figures. They may be more inclined to listen to faculty they admire. That's why we would like Professor Castillo to ask her members to get involved in our effort to identify the terrorists."

"What evidence do you have that there are recruiters as you call them in the U.S.?" Mason asked.

"In the case of Marisa Anderson, the primary evidence that she did not act alone is that there is nothing in her background that suggests she would be capable of assembling the bomb that killed her and six others.

"Someone made the bomb and gave it to her to deliver and, while we don't know whether she knew there was a bomb in the package she was delivering to AIA headquarters, we do know she wasn't there to get help with a school paper since she was wearing the uniform of a non-existent delivery service which she'd rented from a costume store and modified to look more authentic."

"And evidence that there is more than one of these recruiters?" Professor Tan asked.

"The fact that whoever built the bomb is still on the loose is reason enough to be concerned," Leonard stated. "Evidence of others takes us into areas of the investigation I'm not at liberty to discuss. We did, however, receive statements from groups who claimed to have been behind the D.C. bombing who asserted that they do not intend to stop until they get what they're after. The fact that they are targeting American college students they meet at boycott meetings is why we're asking Professor Castillo and her association to help us."

"Be that as it may," Professor Castillo said, "what you're asking is not something that my association is set up to do. We're an academic professional organization--"

"I'm aware of the nature of your organization, Professor Castillo," Leonard said, interrupting, "but when your group stepped outside the academic sphere to get involved in the boycott movement, you gave legitimacy and support to those who use terrorism to bring about their goals. You ought to consider the possibility that your group's resolution has already contributed to the death and injury of innocent by-standers and has put the lives of others at stake."

Castillo's stood up. "That's preposterous and I resent your suggesting such a thing. Again, I must assume your real goal is to suppress the right of American citizens to protest Israel's apartheid policies. As far as I'm concerned this meeting is over."

Leonard shook his head. "Professor Castillo. I can understand that it's very disturbing to consider the possibility that your group's actions have consequences in the real world, but our only goal here is to stop the terrorists."

———

"It seems that you've both had your say," Neil Mason said. "Therefore, I suggest we adjourn this meeting."

"Fine," Leonard said. "I would urge you, Professor Castillo, to inform the members of your executive committee of my request."

"I can't promise you that I'll do that, but I will think it over," she replied.

Leonard and Sheila Stewart retreated to a coffee shop near NYU for lunch. Courtney had agreed to meet him for dinner, which gave Leonard a few hours to kill.

"How do you think that went?" Leonard asked.

"It depends on your goal, Professor Robbins. I think you made your point, but I'm not sure if Luisa Castillo is going to cooperate."

Leonard nodded. "I'm afraid you're right. Perhaps I should have let you do the talking."

Stewart gave him a sympathetic smile. "There's a fine line between convincing someone they need to do something and putting them on the defensive, yet I think the things you said needed saying."

"It amazes me that associations like the American Studies Association fail to recognize the implications of their crossing the line from the academic to the political," Leonard admitted.

"It wasn't always that way?" Stewart asked.

"No. Until the 'sixties, academic associations shied away from taking positions on non-academic matters. The Vietnam War hit too close to home for many of them to ignore and gave them license to pass resolutions on a panoply of non-academic matters."

"It's funny how Vietnam keeps coming up forty years after we left there."

"You're right. That war divided the country and we continued to be divided over what lessons should be learned from it."

"I've heard people say we should never get into a war without a clear mission. Is that based on Vietnam?"

"In part, yes, but of course, presidents don't always have all the information they should and as a result they sometimes make what turn out to be bad decisions.

"Are you referring to Iraq? Do you believe it was a mistake to go in there?" Stewart asked.

"That's a good example because George Bush decided to risk a great deal on what turned out to be weak grounds. Yet something needed to be done about Saddam. He was a butcher!"

"But what did we gain in the end?"

"President Bush made another mistake when he declared victory before it was clear that we'd achieved our goal. Then President Obama made an even bigger mistake in announcing a pullout date. That told our enemies all they had to do was wait us out. That decision gave birth to ISIS."

Sheila held out her glass when the waitress came by with ice-tea refills. "It's tough being the world's only superpower. We can't go around intervening in every conflict, but if we never intervene no one will ever take us seriously."

"Well put, Sheila. We have to pick and choose when to use force. The threat level has to justify the response. Communism was certainly a big threat given how aggressively Russia rushed in to control Eastern Europe after World War Two and then tried to export their ideology to the third world."

"Which is why we went into Vietnam."

"Correct, but we came up short on the intel side there as well. To start, we failed to appreciate the strength of nationalism and as a result ignored the long-standing hostility between the Vietnamese and the Chinese. The domino theory ignored the desire of local peoples to be free of colonialism. By bailing out the French, we made Vietnam dependent on Russia and to third world peoples our intervention made us look like the European colonialists."

"It wouldn't have been good to let them join the communist block."

"Looking back on it, I think we over-estimated the power of communist ideology and acted as if we didn't believe that our system of free enterprise, the rule of law, and democratic philosophy would prevail without military intervention."

"What about today? Jihadist Islam seems to be unstoppable. Isn't it a greater threat than communism was?"

"I'm inclined to agree with you, Sheila. In Russia, communism failed to produce the utopian socialist world Marx and his successors promised. The common man realized he was being fed a package of lies and withheld his efforts, which meant everything the Soviet Union produced was flawed."

"How's that different than Islam?"

"Religions have the advantage over secular ideologies because even when the real world fails to conform to the world their leaders paint, people are reluctant to break with the religion. This is all part of God's plan, they tell themselves. He's testing us, they say."

"So, how do we defeat them?"

"First, we need leaders who are not afraid to have enemies. President Obama took the absolutely wrong approach by apologizing for our past policies. That encouraged the jihadists to believe the U.S. wouldn't stand up to them."

"Don't we have to demand that people everywhere adhere to universal standards of behavior?"

"For countries that's true, but how can you impose standards on what religious leaders tell their followers?"

"Can't countries pass laws against religious based attacks on private citizens?"

"Of course, but law enforcement has to be diligent in enforcing the laws. They have to make it clear that they won't tolerate religious based attacks and they have to put law-breakers in jail."

"So, do you see the D.C. bombing as being part of a religious campaign?"

"Absolutely. A stated goal of the group behind the bombing is to weaken U.S. support for Israel. Israel is a Western outpost on the edge of what the Jihadists believe to be their world. If they take over Israel, they will turn their attention to taking over Europe. Then we in the U.S. would be looking at what we would have been facing had we not intervened in World War Two: enemies coming at us from both the west and the east."

"We can't let that happen."

"You're exactly right. In any case, we'd better head over to the FBI office. Gary Mackey set it up so that we can work there this afternoon. Then, I'm meeting my daughter for dinner at seven."

As he waited for Courtney to show up at the restaurant, Leonard reminded himself of his wife's admonition to avoid lecturing to their daughter. "If she thinks you're judging her, she'll clam up," Alison told him when he spoke with her on his way to the restaurant.

___

When Courtney arrived, Leonard kept the conversation light until they'd ordered, and then asked her how summer school was coming.

"So far, so good," Courtney replied.

"Remind me what courses you're taking."

"Two psych courses--Motivation and Volition and Environmental Psychology."

"So you're sticking with psychology as a major? Mom said you were thinking about switching. To what?"

Courtney nodded. "Polisci, but it's too late. Changing majors would be too complicated. I would have had to stay another full year to be able to get in all the classes I would have had to take."

"You've done pretty well in psychology, right? Mostly A's and B's as I recall."

She nodded.

"That's all grad schools care about."

"I'm not sure I want to go to grad school."

Leonard sipped some water. He had resisted ordering a glass of wine given that Courtney wouldn't be able to join him. "I'm not saying that's your only option, but if you do decide to do that at some point, I think you'll get accepted."

She shrugged.

"So, how's your new place working out? Are you all settled in?"

"It's getting there. Mom brought me some curtains and kitchen things on Monday."

"I thought the apartment was furnished."

"Semi-furnished. The bed's decent and the couch in the living room is new. I guess the previous tenants ruined the one that had been there."

"But surely the place came with curtains?"

"It did, but the ones in my bedroom smelled like cigarette smoke."

Leonard took a bite of the fresh Italian bread. "This is good. Try some."

"It's not on my diet," Courtney replied.

"How's your new roommate working out?"

"Fine. She took a job for the summer, so I don't see her much during the week, but we do things together on weekends."

The conversation lulled after their meals were delivered.

"Yours okay?" Leonard asked after a few minutes.

Courtney nodded, as she wiped her chin from the drippings of her spaghetti and clam sauce. "Very good."

"Mine, too.

When Leonard finished his baked tilapia, he decided he'd waited long enough before getting into one of the topics he wanted to confront Courtney about. "Any further repercussions from that leafleting incident?"

"I haven't heard anything new," Courtney answered.

"That could have been serious. You could have been suspended."

Courtney frowned. "Not really. Erik Greene--"

"Who's he?"

"One of the group's leaders. He said they knew the administration wouldn't go after the people distributing the flyers. There must have been more than three dozen of us."

"But before you do anything like that, don't you think you should ask yourself how you'd feel if someone did that to you?"

"It was an educational exercise, Dad, and it said very clearly at the bottom that it was not a real eviction notice."

"You don't have to be defensive," Leonard said. "I'm just saying that's a standard one ought to apply before participating in any such activity."

"Is that what you guys do at the CIA," Courtney said, "ask yourselves how your enemies are going to feel when a drone rocket smashes into their home and kills their wives and children?"

Leonard sighed. "There's a big difference between how one treats one's fellow students and how the government acts when dealing with its enemies, but, as a matter of fact, we do consider how our actions will impact our allies and others before we act."

"Now who's being defensive!"

"Courtney, that's rude."

"Okay, Dad. New subject."

"Dessert?" their waiter asked offering desert menus.

"Not for me," Leonard said. "Court?"

She shook her head.

"I guess not," Leonard told the waiter, "but I'd like some hot tea. Do you have Earl Grey?"

"I'll look."

"You ought to try green tea, Dad. It's better for you."

"Supposedly."

Courtney turned her hands palm upwards--a gesture that Leonard recognized as something he often did when someone didn't appear to be getting the gist of what he was saying.

"We've got some green tea at home," Leonard said. "I'll give it another try."

Courtney smiled at him.

"By the way, Court, did you know that the president of the Palestinian Authority has been against the boycott movement from the start?"

"They told us that," Courtney replied.

"How did they explain it?"

"They said it had to do with internal Palestinian politics, and we have a right to form our own opinion on the matter."

"But do you still think it's the right approach to bringing about a fair settlement of the differences between Israel and the Palestinians?"

She nodded her head.

"You know that I disagree."

"I know, Dad."

"Do you want to hear why?"

"Do I have to?"

"Of course not, and maybe this isn't the time for that discussion, but I hope you'll consider the possibility that the people behind the boycott movement are not giving you the whole story."

Courtney didn't say anything. Leonard knew he should probably stop there. "For example, it's very likely that the person who armed the University of Maryland woman with the bomb that killed her and four others recruited her at an SPJ meeting."

That information seemed to get Courtney's attention.

"And there may be recruiters lurking around SPJ meetings at other campuses looking for naïve students who they can convince to bomb a Jewish organization or government building."

"I've heard the opposite," Courtney said.

"What do you mean?"

"That it's the Israelis who are behind the bombing. They want people to blame the Palestinians to take the attention away from the occupied territories."

"That's totally nuts, Courtney. They'd never do such a thing."

"How do you know, Dad?"

"I just know. Don't listen to junk like that. It's disinformation--a way to confuse people."

"Okay, Dad."

Leonard studied his daughter who all of a sudden seemed to find her chair uncomfortable. He knew it was no use saying anything more at that moment. "Are you sure you don't want dessert?"

"I'd better go, Dad."

"Okay, Court."

"Thanks for dinner."

"You don't have to wait," Leonard said waving at their waiter for the check.

"I don't mind. I'll wait for your van with you."

"Thanks, Court. That would be nice."

Alison Robbins met Leonard at the airport the next morning after his short flight from LaGuardia. He was looking forward to a quiet weekend, including some quality time with his wife. She asked him about his dinner with Courtney when he called her the previous night after returning to his hotel.

"It went okay," Leonard told her.

"By okay, I assume that means neither of you disrupted the other diners?"

Leonard laughed. "We were good neighbors. No food was thrown."

Len filled Alison in on the details during the ride from the airport. It was a warm June Saturday. People were out and about, purchasing plants and seeds for their gardens, mowing their lawns on their tractor mowers, or just out enjoying the sunshine.

At one in the afternoon, Alison called Leonard into the kitchen from his office for lunch.

"Everything quiet?" she asked.

"At the moment, but I'm worried that the terrorists will strike again before we get a solid lead on either the AIA bomb maker or one of his colleagues."

"I take it the guy you're after has disappeared?"

"Totally, which suggests he knew where he was going to go long before he set off the bomb, which in turn suggests a fairly deep and sophisticated organization."

"I don't like the sound of that."

"Me neither," Leonard stated. "Me neither."

Herndon: Friday, June 22

Leonard had his driver swing by his hotel on their way to the airport so he could pick up the birthday present he'd purchased for Alison, but had forgotten to pack that morning in his rush to get to the office. The doorman had barely let him through the front door when his cell phone buzzed with a text message from Ed Morgan. "Explosion in Chicago." He looked at his watch. It was four-forty-seven, which would be three-forty-seven Chicago time.

Leonard wheeled to the side of the hotel lobby, which was buzzing with people, and called the office.

"What happened?" Leonard asked when FBI liaison Mackey picked up the line.

"We're just getting the details now, but apparently an explosion occurred a little over an hour ago at the offices of the Jewish Federation in downtown Chicago."

"Any casualties?"

"Unknown."

"Okay. I'll tap into the network from my room here and follow the reports as they come in. Can you put Ed Morgan on the line?"

Leonard asked Morgan to see if he could change his reservation. "Send me out on the last flight if they have space."

He then phoned his driver to let him know about the schedule change and while waiting for the elevator called Alison to let her know what was going on. "Ed's trying to book me on the 9:50 flight, but I may have to stay here over the weekend. I should know shortly."

For the next hour, he waited for details to come in. At a quarter to seven, Gary Mackey posted a note on the network saying he had information to share. Leonard instructed him to open a voice line. "What are you hearing?"

"Everything's still very sketchy. They're saying it's extremely likely that the explosion was caused by a bomb--not by a gas leak or some similar cause. There were casualties, but we don't have a count at this time."

"Anyone taking credit?"

"Not so far," Mackey replied.

"Okay, keep us informed."

Learning that the explosion in Chicago had been caused by a bomb convinced Leonard to stay in D.C. over the weekend. He called Alison to tell her he wouldn't be coming home, and then had Ed Morgan cancel his reservation.

Around nine o'clock Betty Liu, who was monitoring the Chicago news media, notified the team that WBBM, a Chicago TV station, was about to make an announcement about the bombing. "Put it on the network," Leonard instructed.

"We have new information about the explosion at the offices of the Jewish Federation of Chicago," a male announcer stated. "We received a fax to this station from a group calling itself American Front for the Liberation of Palestine, which is taking credit for the explosion.

"The FBI has asked us not to read the statement on the air in its entirety, but we are allowed to summarize it. According to the statement, the group wants Israel to agree to their three demands which are as follows: one: withdraw from the occupied territories, two: grant the right of return of all Palestinians, and three: grant equal rights to Arabs inside Israel. The group is calling on the Wheatfield administration to pressure Israel to comply with these demands or additional locations in this country will be targeted.

"I repeat, we received a statement faxed to our studios just a few minutes ago from a group that calls itself American Front for the Liberation of Palestine that is taking credit for a bomb that exploded late this afternoon at the downtown headquarters of the Jewish Federation.

"The FBI has informed us that there have been fatalities as a result of the explosion, but they are not releasing details at this time. Stay tuned for more breaking news as it happens and all the day's news at 6 and 11--"

"It's them," Leonard said out loud in his hotel room knowing that no one could hear him. He didn't need to share that thought as undoubtedly others had the same reaction. "Anyone ever hear of that group?" he typed.

"We've seen similar names," Meir Epstein texted back, "but not that exact wording."

Leonard informed the team he needed them back in the office the next morning at 9 a.m. "We'll assess the situation then."

By the time he was ready to unplug for the night, Leonard was convinced that the Chicago bombing was connected to the one in Washington. Although official confirmation would have to wait until the FBI's forensic and bomb teams had a chance to do their jobs, his team would act on the assumption that the same group was behind both bombings.

The fact that both targets were Jewish organizations was a major concern. It echoed the kind of events that had been taking place in Europe recently--from the infamous hostage taking incidents in 2015 to attacks on individual Jews on the street by gangs of thugs, shouting anti-Israeli and anti-Semitic slogans.

These attacks meant that Jewish organizations in the United States would have to re-double their security measures and that local police authorities would have to add such targets to the sites they were already monitoring, stretching even thinner already over-stretched resources. It also meant his task force would have to work that much harder to expose those responsible for the bombings, or opponents in Congress and in the agencies would begin to question whether they were helping or hindering the nation's counterterror efforts.

Herndon: Saturday June 23

At nine the next morning the eleven permanent members of the DEFEAT task force assembled in the conference room--most with coffee mugs in hand to stoke their mental energies after having stayed up late the night before. Leonard wheeled into the room amid the noise of TV monitors and heated conversations. "Okay, folks. Let's settle down. Someone mute the TVs, please."

He waited while people grabbed chairs. "Fatalities still at four?" he asked, looking to Gary Mackey.

Mackey nodded his head.

"Injuries?

"Six, two critical."

"No video, right?"

Mackey shook his head. "Nothing from the street; nothing on the inside."

"That's a shame. It means it's going to be difficult to reconstruct what happened."

"It'll be more than a week before we issue a preliminary report," Mackey stated.

Leonard sighed. "This has the same look and feel of D.C. Anyone disagree?"

No one did.

"Someone delivered that bomb," Meir Epstein said. "The question is, did that someone die in the blast?"

Leonard turned to their FBI rep. "Gary?"

"Too soon to tell. Our agent in charge is on the local media asking anyone who has any knowledge about the bombing to come forward. We'll get dozens of calls, but rarely anything helpful. Occasionally, we'll get lucky, but who knows in this case."

"Then there's not much for us to do," Leonard stated, "except to continue to focus on the big picture. Who's behind the bombings? What's their next target? How can we uncover their network? Ekaterina, I need you to look for communications that suggest someone knew this was about to take place, look for anyone revealing knowledge that hasn't been released to the public, and look for someone suggesting where they'll strike next. Everyone else, cover all the bases and share what you find. Let's get cracking."

Nothing new popped up the rest of the morning. The names of three of the victims were revealed shortly after one p.m. Chicago time. All three were Federation employees. The identity of the fourth victim was unknown.

Because the Chicago Federation did not have video surveillance of its entrance or lobby, the FBI had no images of the fourth person. Leonard assumed that person's identity would be determined sooner or later either through data taken from the remains of the body or more likely by someone reporting a missing person, but that could take days. He picked up the phone in his office and dialed Gary Mackey's extension.

"What's up?" Mackey answered.

"Let's assume it's the same group that bombed the American Israel Association. That means your local office should get some agents over to DePaul, the University of Chicago, and any other college in the region with chapters of Students for Palestinian Justice."

"They're stretched thin right now. I'm not sure when they might get to that."

"Then Washington needs to send in reinforcements. The longer we wait, the colder the trail will be when we find it."

"Are you certain the carrier was a student?"

"I can't be positive. He or she could have come from some other group, but I assume you're already monitoring Islamic militants in the Chicago region, correct?"

"We are."

"If it doesn't look like any of them were involved, I think we have to look into the possibility that someone recruited a student to do the job."

"I'm surprised after all the news coverage of the AIA bombing that any student would fall for the same deal as the last one," Mackey said.

"True, but that doesn't mean it didn't happen."

"You'd like me to contact the director?"

"Please. Tell him I'd be glad to explain over the phone or in person."

"I'll give him a call and let you know what he says."

Leonard didn't doubt that the Director of the FBI resented being told how to do his job, although he didn't say so outright when he got Leonard on the phone.

"I'll take it under advisement," Everett Shortell said after Leonard laid out the rationale for focusing on SPJ groups.

Leonard didn't see any point in arguing. As soon as he hung up the phone, however, he asked DEFEAT office manager Ed Morgan to get Rosa Martinez on the line.

"I wanted to give you a heads up concerning Chicago," Leonard stated when he finally got Martinez on the phone almost four hours after Morgan placed the initial request.

"I'm listening," the President's National Security Advisor replied.

"There's every indication the same people who bombed the AIA building are behind the Chicago bombing. Like D.C., they chose Friday afternoon to deliver the package just as the Federation was about to close for the Jewish Sabbath. Also, it seems that the bomb exploded when the receptionist signed for it."

"Suicide?"

"I don't think so, although I have no basis for saying so other than my feeling that the person recruited to the job was probably under the impression what happened in D.C. was an accident and that he or she would deliver the package and be outside when it exploded."

"Any leads?" Martinez asked.

"The FBI is doing forensics and bomb analysis, but that can take days if not weeks. We need to move fast to find the identity of the carrier and discover how he or she was recruited. To delay invites more bombings. I've recommended that the FBI put pressure on the students involved in the Students for Palestinian Justice chapters at colleges within one hundred miles of central Chicago. Unfortunately, Director Shortell doesn't seem inclined to follow my advice."

"You've spoken with him?"

"Yesterday."

"Okay. Let me see what I can do."

"Thank you, Rosa. I may be wrong, but if they can pull off two such attacks, what's to prevent them from picking another location next week and another the week after that?"

"I get your point," she replied. "I'll see what I can do."

Herndon: Sunday, June 24

"I feel bad about not being there," Leonard said after wishing his wife a happy birthday.

"Why? You did the right thing staying in D.C."

"Who have you heard from?"

"My mother, my brother, and, believe it or not, Courtney."

"Courtney up before noon on a Sunday! Wonders never cease."

Alison laughed.

"Did she have anything interesting to say?"

"Summer school started. She likes her instructors. It's hot. That's about it."

"Nothing new on the SPJ front?"

"Not that she mentioned."

"Good. Listen, I'd like your opinion on something. You know what happened here strongly suggests the terrorists are targeting members of Students for Palestinian Justice."

"So their recruiting the University of Maryland students was part of their game plan?"

"That's how I see it."

"What's your question?"

"I keep thinking about Courtney's involvement in the NYU group. Should I send someone to the city to talk to her? Maybe she's seen or heard something that could be useful."

"Len, don't you think she'd come to you if she had?"

Leonard hesitated. "I suppose so."

"Give her a little credit."

"I guess you're right. By the way, I bought you a present, but you'll have to wait until Friday to open it," Leonard said.

"Are you going to keep me in suspense?"

"You bet."

"You've got a PT appointment this week, right?"

"I do--Tuesday afternoon."

"Try not to miss it."

"I won't. Love you."

"Love you, too."

Herndon: Tuesday, June 26

Leonard noticed Meir Epstein lurking around his closed office door and motioned for him to come inside.

"What's going on, Meir?"

"I thought you might like to talk about it."

"Talk about what?" Leonard asked.

"About whatever is bothering you."

"It's that obvious, huh?"

Meir shrugged his shoulders. "I know your tells."

Leonard smiled. "It's Martinez. She promised on Saturday to put some pressure on Everett Shortell to send some agents to Chicago to work the college campuses, but either she hasn't talked to him yet or he hasn't complied. Meanwhile, the trail is getting colder and colder."

"She's supposed to have our backs."

"She's always maintained her distance, maybe so she won't get wet if we step in any puddles--"

"But that doesn't help us with the immediate problem, does it?"

Leonard shook his head. "Any suggestions?"

Meir paced the office for a minute, stopped, and raised a finger. "One."

"Shoot."

"The media."

"Spell it out."

"Get the Chicago press looking in that direction. That would force the FBI's hand."

"Brilliant," Leonard said. "Find someone at the *Trib*, the *Sun Times*, or maybe one of the TV stations who seems to be following this story."

"I'm on it."

The next morning Meir called out to Leonard as he was wheeling himself into his office. "Check the *Sun Times*' website."

Leonard logged in, opened a browser, and scanned the headlines in the center column. Nothing. He scrolled further. *Bomber may have been recruited at local college.* "Found it," he called out. The piece was written by *Sun Times* columnist Virginia Russo.

> *The person who delivered the bomb that killed four, injured six, and caused four million dollars in damage to the building owned by the Jewish Federation of Chicago may have been a student at one of the area colleges according to federal sources.*
>
> *Terrorists recruited a member of the University of Maryland Students for Palestinian Justice to deliver the bomb that killed her and four others in Washington, D.C. earlier this year, our source told us, and they may have done the same here in Chicago.*

"Found it. That's perfect," Leonard yelled out to Meir.

Meir came into his office. "One of the TV stations has already picked up on it as have two radio stations."

"Excellent. By the way, why did you choose the *Sun Times*? Aren't they the smaller of the dailies?"

"Much smaller. They don't even print a daily paper anymore."

"I guess I read that someplace."

———

"But they're hungrier than the *Trib*. I felt if I talked to the right person, we'd get quicker results."

"Perfect. Now, let's see if it does its job."

Wednesday afternoon, Gary Mackey informed Leonard that the FBI was sending a dozen agents from nearby offices to assist in a screening process of college SPJ chapters in the region--looking for possible connections to the Chicago Federation bombing.

Mackey said the head of the Chicago bureau warned him that finding students with useful information was not going to be easy because the colleges were on summer schedules.

Leonard smirked. "Making excuses before they even start? Even if the student leaders are not on campus at the moment, your guys ought to be able to find out where they live and interview them. Most no doubt live in the Chicago region."

Now that the problem of the Chicago FBI's not focusing on the college SPJ groups was resolved, Leonard was ready to resume his focus on what they could learn from the event. He called his team together late that afternoon to focus the task force's efforts. "Logic tells me Sammy Haddad was not behind this bombing, or if he was, he had help on the ground prior to arriving in Chicago."

"How do you figure?" Carole Jean Hall asked.

"There wasn't enough time for him to travel to Chicago, pick out a target, screen for, indoctrinate, and train a carrier--which could take weeks, and then pull off the operation."

Meir picked up on his line of thought. "What you're saying is unless someone was already there and had done the preliminary work, the only way this Haddad could be involved would be if he came in at the last minute."

"Perhaps just to build the bomb," Leonard said.

"Makes sense," Meir said.

"Which means we've got to continue to try to track down Haddad while at the same time try to identify the other person or persons involved in the Chicago bombing. Someone is bound to report a missing person any day now, but until that happens, we've got to put on our thinking caps. There's got to be some aspect of these bombings that we're not focusing on."

"Too bad Haddad never tried again to get in touch with Gazzola?" Meir stated.

"He must have suspected she would spill the beans once the FBI cornered her."

"I agree. From what I've seen of her, I wouldn't have trusted her either," Pavel Zavarov said.

"The FBI is still monitoring those pay phones, but so far no calls from Haddad," Gary Mackey said.

Leonard raised his hands to cut off the discussion. "We still have to find him. Let's get on it, people."

Gary Mackey came into his office as Leonard was gathering his personal belongings to be driven back to his hotel. "We've got something."

Leonard wheeled himself into the bullpen to his personal station and logged in. "Agents have just finished interviewing a DePaul University student by the name of Mark Cheslock," Mackey stated. "They've got it on tape and will play it for us when they get back to the office, but here's the gist of the story. Cheslock is one of the SPJ leaders at DePaul. He says about two months ago a student from the University of Chicago invited him to meet a Palestinian woman who was touring the country talking about conditions on the West Bank and--"

"Is this the first time we've heard about this woman?" Leonard asked.

"Affirmative," Gary stated.

"Go ahead. Sorry to interrupt."

"No problem. Cheslock went to that meeting. The woman was quite charismatic--his term. She put the onus on the students in attendance to do something more dramatic than gather signatures. At the meeting, a man Cheslock described as looking Middle Eastern called for actions that would punish Chicago's Jews for having financed the occupation of Palestine."

"Question," Leonard asked. "Was this person someone traveling with the woman or local?"

"He didn't know," Gary answered.

"Okay. Keep going."

"Here's what's interesting. Cheslock said the Chicago Federation was mentioned as one possible target and he got the distinct impression they were talking about something more than picketing."

"Did he give up any names or contact information for any of the others who were at the meeting?"

"He gave us the names of the two he knew who were also DePaul students. He wasn't sure, but assumed the rest were enrolled at the University of Chicago or Loyola. He also said it was made clear at the beginning of the meeting that no one was to use their real name. He agreed to give us physical descriptions for each person as best he remembers what they looked like."

"Excellent. This could be our big break. Let us know when we can watch the interview tape," Leonard said, "oh, and check to see if anyone else knows anything else about this Palestinian woman."

Peter G. Pollak

Herndon: Friday June 29

A message was waiting for Leonard when he arrived at the office Friday morning. "NSA Martinez wants to hear from you as soon as you cross the threshold," Ed Morgan informed him.

Leonard smiled. He expected some kind of reaction. "This should be interesting," he told Morgan, as he wheeled into the bullpen. Instead of rushing to his office to call Martinez, he rolled around the full circumference of the floor wishing each person a good day and discussing whatever they were working on.

Thirty minutes later he pulled himself behind his desk and buzzed Morgan. "Okay. Call her for me, please."

Martinez picked up faster than usual. "Don't you ever do that to me again," she said without a greeting. "And don't play smart with me by saying 'Do what?' You know what I'm talking about. I told you when you came on board that we had to work together as a team, and that does not mean going behind someone's back. That means you come to me straight if you've got a problem. Got it?"

Leonard didn't see any point in arguing with Martinez. "Got it."

"I'll talk to you later today at our regular time."

Leonard smiled. *The next time I ask you for something maybe you won't sit on it.*

Ten minutes later he was in the conference room ready for the morning's briefing.

"It looks like we've identified the bomb carrier," Gary Mackey announced. "A University of Chicago student by the name of Philip Logan, who was enrolled in summer school, has not been seen for several days. His parents called the school when they couldn't reach him."

"Any details?" Leonard asked.

"His computer and cellphone are missing," Mackey replied. "We've requested the cell data from his carrier and we're getting a court order to retrieve the computer data from his backup service. We also got hair samples from a brush which we can use to match the DNA collected at the bomb site."

"Now we're getting someplace," Leonard said.

The FBI report convinced Leonard that Logan was their man. Members of the University of Chicago SPJ group who knew him stated that he seemed consumed by the topic and was always speaking up for taking more militant action both on and off campus.

"This Logan seems to have been just what a terrorist recruiter would be looking for," Leonard said, after gathering the team into his office later that day. "Any leads on his handler?" he asked Gary Mackey.

"We're not sure. A couple of members of the group told us that Logan was often seen with two guys who didn't appear to be University students, but since the meetings were open to the public, no one questioned them. No one we talked to thus far can give us their names."

"Did you get physical descriptions?"

"Yes, our artist is working with some of the students to come up with images we can circulate."

"Did your agents show Haddad's photo around?" Meir asked.

"They did. No matches."

———

"Damn," Leonard said. "That's too bad."

"You're right," Meir said. "Even if Haddad came on board to give them the bomb, it means the terrorists have more than one recruiter looking for bomb carriers."

"Precisely. Let's see if the BOLO's we put out turns up anything."

In addition to the immediate questions Leonard didn't want to lose sight of the new information they had uncovered from the DePaul student. He tasked Pavel and Homeland Security's Sheila Stewart with researching the possibility that a female Palestinian was traveling across the country meeting with student groups.

"There are lots of questions to pursue," Leonard told them. "Is she here legally? Where has she been? I don't need to spell out all the questions we need answers to. You both know what to do."

Over the next days individuals found avenues to pursue without hitting paydirt. Pavel suggested that the CIA might have Palestinian contacts who could tell them what they might know. Leonard told him to pursue it. Sheila Stewart contacted the immigration division of Homeland Security to see if her agency had any information based on the description of the Palestinian woman provided by the DePaul student, but came up empty.

Still Leonard felt encouraged. Although they had not been able to prevent the loss of more innocent lives and they still seemed to be two steps behind the terrorists, the pattern was becoming clear. They just needed to pick up the pace and get ahead of the terrorists before they struck again.

Peter G. Pollak

Herndon: Thursday, July 5

It took the better part of a week for the FBI to track down the associates of the University of Chicago student who had died in the June twenty-second bombing. Using conferencing software a Chicago FBI agent briefed the DEFEAT task force on the results of their investigation.

"Based on leads generated by fellow students we identified two individuals who were often seen with Philip Logan. Jesse Guerra and Aziz Nahos were taken in for questioning this past Sunday as potentially having aided in the bombing of the Jewish Federation building.

"Jesse Guerra, age twenty, is a native of Chicago. He just completed his first year at Harold Washington College, a division of the City Colleges of Chicago. He admitted that he accompanied Logan to SPJ meetings and activities on the University of Chicago campus.

"When we questioned him about the bombing, Guerra said he had no knowledge of it prior to the event. He claimed Logan hadn't been around much the last couple of months. He assumed Logan was busy with schoolwork. Guerra lives with his mother and four siblings in the Pilsen neighborhood on the lower west side. We searched their apartment, but found no materials or literature concerning the manufacturer of explosive devices. We did find, however, pamphlets attacking Israel's policies toward the Palestinians."

"What about our D.C. bomber?" Leonard asked.

"We showed him the photo, but Guerra claimed he had never seen or met him."

"How about the other guy?"

"Aziz Nahos, age twenty-four, is a native of Lebanon who was in the United States on an expired student visa. He was enrolled at Harold Washington College for three semesters before dropping out fifteen months ago.

"Nahos also denied prior knowledge of Logan's plans although he said Logan once told him not to be surprised if something dramatic occurred in Chicago before the summer was out. When he asked what he meant, Logan told Nahos he couldn't tell him the details because it would put him in danger.

Nahos lived with two other illegal immigrants--all of whom have since been arrested and turned over to Immigration and Customs Enforcement (ICE) for processing."

"We asked both Guerra and Nahos for names of anyone else they attended SPJ events with. Together they came up with four names. We're just beginning to check those out."

"I've a question," Leonard stated. "How did these two come to ally themselves with Logan?"

"Interesting that you should ask," the agent answered. "We identified a professor at Harold Washington who seems to have made a practice of bringing disaffected students together. He is a tenured professor in the educational department by the name of Dmitris "Nick" Nicholson. Guerra and Nahos separately told us this Professor Nicholson introduced them to Logan."

"And how did Logan know this professor?"

"That we don't know at this point."

"Have you questioned Professor Nicholson?" Leonard asked.

"We visited him at Harold Washington early this week. He refused, however, to answer any questions other than give us his name and title. We will continue to investigate his involvement in events related to the bombing."

"What about Logan? Have you learned anything further?"

"We interviewed Logan's parents, siblings, former teachers, roommates, and several other individuals who knew him. If I may summarize, it appears that Logan harbored a hatred of Jews on the basis of readings he undertook while in high school. We found anti-Semitic literature in his bedroom at his home."

"What about the bomb? Do you think Logan manufactured it?"

"We did find literature on the manufacture of explosives at his home, but not in his dorm room, but did not find any traces of bomb making chemicals or materials in his dorm room or in his house, nor did we find evidence that the bomb was constructed in his house."

"Any ideas on where it might have been put together?" Leonard asked.

"We're still checking out some possibilities, starting by trying to figure out where the materials they used in the bomb might have been obtained."

Late Thursday afternoon, after hearing reports from each team member, Leonard summed up their situation. "Whoever recruited Philip Logan must have known about his political leanings," Leonard stated.

"That suggests the recruiter was on the campus on a regular basis, most likely either as a student or employee like Haddad," Meir said. "It had to be someone whose presence would not stand out."

"I agree," Leonard said, "and, if he or she were on campus and did contact Logan who was living in one of the dorms--"

"I think they call them residence halls," Meir pointed out.

"Sorry, you're right. If the recruiter contacted Logan on campus or at his residence hall, someone must have seen that person with Logan. It shouldn't be that hard to come up with an identification."

"Unfortunately since school is not in session, it's not going to be easy to find that needle in the haystack of students," Meir stated.

"Fine, but Meir, I'd like you to focus on doing whatever can be done given those circumstances to follow up on that possibility. See what the local FBI hasn't done and see that they do it. Go out there yourself if necessary.

"I'd also like someone to look into Professor Nicholson's background. Any volunteers?"

Russell Knowles raised his hand. "I'll do it."

"Thank you, Russell. The job's all yours."

"Meanwhile, the rest of us have two primary tasks to keep us busy--namely, finding Sammy Haddad and the Palestinian woman who is speaking to SPJ groups."

Leonard was about to dismiss the group when he decided to voice a question that had been nagging at him. "Also, someone needs to help me understand why we can't we figure out how these people communicate with each other. If we could, perhaps we could find out where they are planning their next attack."

"I have a thought about that," Pavel stated.

"Speak," Leonard said.

"In both cases, it seems that the bombs were set off by the bomb carrier from a tablet that had been signed by the receptionist."

Leonard sat up straighter in his wheelchair. "Ah hah. I see what you're getting at."

"You need to spell it out," Sheila Stewart said. "I'm not following."

"Here's what Pavel is saying: someone must have created an application for the tablet that looks enough like the ones the receptionists were familiar with having signed for other deliveries. That means the terrorists have someone in their organization capable of writing specialized apps."

"Or access to someone who writes apps," Pavel said.

Leonard nodded. "Point taken."

"Is that it?" Sheila asked.

"No. You explain, Pavel."

Pavel smiled. "There is a second aspect of this, which suggests their technical capabilities are very sophisticated--namely, the connection between the signature app and the detonation of the bombs. The first programming feature--creating a signature box--is relatively easy. Am I right, Larry?"

Larry Burnside nodded. "Any average college student could do that."

"What about the second feature?" Leonard asked. "Would that be more difficult, Larry?"

"Yes and no," Burnside said. "Setting off the bomb is fairly tricky, but doable. The aspect of what Pavel suggests that is most troubling is that NSA hasn't found the messages between the bomb and the devices that detonated it."

"I'm still in the dark," Sheila stated.

"Let me try," Burnside said. "In order to detonate the bomb a communications has to be sent from the tablet either directly to the bomb or to the person who then detonates the bomb. If those messages go through public networks, NSA ought to be able to find them, but so far they haven't done so."

"Okay," Sheila said. "I think I'm following."

"Good," Burnside said. "And, if we could find those communications we should be able to find the people behind the bombings."

"Clear now?" Leonard asked Sheila. She nodded.

"Good," he said. "Larry, I'd like you and Ekaterina to focus on that problem. Can the app be traced, either in terms of who programmed it or where it resides? Better yet, can we find out the next time someone downloads it? Pavel, great thinking! That's what we need to do, folks: ask questions that no one else is asking."

The next day Leonard called Rosa Martinez from the van that was taking him to the airport. "I think we're on the verge of a breakthrough."

"Good to hear after all this time. What have you discovered?"

For the first time since the task force had been put together, Leonard had looked forward to their Friday briefing. In general, he found Martinez difficult to read. He was not sure whether she agreed with President Wheatfield's having set up the task force or having chosen him to run it. She might have felt she should have been in charge or perhaps that the existing agencies should have been given a chance to solve the case.

Leonard was also conscious of the fact that his task force had not produced anything of real significance, and thanks to Leonard's penchant for going over agency heads whenever he felt the need, the task force undoubtedly had complicated the president's relationship with some of her top-level executives. Being able to tell Martinez that they beat the other agencies in generating a solid lead was very satisfying.

"I was right about the second bombing being tied into Students for Palestinian Justice," Leonard reported, "and although we're having a hard time identifying who recruited and armed the student who delivered the bomb, we feel we have a way to figure it all out."

"And what is that?" Martinez asked.

"The terrorists are using software that touches off the bombs. To do so, a digital message must be sent to the bomb causing it to detonate. If we can find those messages, it should lead back to whoever built the bomb and to their organization."

"Very interesting. I hope you're right."

The one part of that story Leonard didn't report that Friday was that so far they had not been successful either tracing where the tablet application originated or isolating the messages that touched off either of the bombings.

Larry Burnside was working with Ekaterina Stepanova to try to access the National Security Agency's systems to find the signals that touched off the bombs. "It's like looking for a needle in a million haystacks," was how Larry explained what they were up against minutes before Leonard called Martinez.

"How optimistic are you that it can be done?" Leonard had asked.

"In theory extremely," was his response, "but the practical is often more difficult than the theoretical."

When he hung up the phone from his conversation with Rosa Martinez, Leonard debated how much time to give Burnside and Stepanova to get the job done and what to do if they didn't succeed. His ruminations were interrupted when Pavel Zavarov popped into his office.

"Got a sec?"

"Sure," Leonard said, making a note on a sheet of paper so he could go back to the question he'd been pondering.

Pavel sat down. "I've been thinking. Maybe we need to bring in someone to help Larry and Ekaterina."

"Do you have someone in mind?"

"Panav Chaudry."

"Never heard of him," Leonard said.

"MIT? W3C?"

Leonard shook his head. "Enlighten me."

"Chaudry is one of the world's leading social media gurus."

"What's 'W3C'?"

"World Wide Web Consortium. They're the folks whose job it is to keep the Net open and fair."

"And you think this Chaudry can help us solve the problem of how these people are setting off the bombs?"

Pavel gave Leonard one of his sly smiles. "I'm almost positive. The problem is there must be dozens of people who want a piece of him at any time."

"Since you brought it up, your job is figuring out how we can have a conversation with him."

"Of course," Pavel said. "It'll be tough, but I have some ideas."

"I'll give you until Monday," Leonard said.

Herndon: Tuesday, July 10

Leonard buzzed Russell Knowles to come into his office to discuss his report on Dmitris "Nick" Nicholson, the Harold Washington College instructor who had seemingly played a role in radicalizing Philip Logan and other students.

"Good job," Leonard said when Knowles arrived holding up a copy of the report. Up to that point, Leonard had felt he hadn't been able to take advantage of Knowles' talents. It wasn't that Knowles didn't respond promptly or efficiently to information requests, getting what he could from the CIA bureaucracy that Leonard knew only too well was akin to drawing water from rocks, but he'd also had a hard time figuring out Knowles as a person.

Russell Knowles was in his late thirties. He was married with one child and had all the proper credentials: an undergraduate degree from Rice University and an MBA from Vanderbilt. After college, Knowles was hired by the Senate Committee on Homeland Security and Governmental Affairs at the request of the senior senator from Texas, the result of a family connection. Russell's father was an oil company executive and big contributor to the Texas Republican Party. From there Knowles moved to the CIA, not as an analyst or field representative, but on the management side, overseeing the people who crunch numbers for the agency's political appointees when it was time to justify requests for more money.

Initially, Leonard had not been happy about Knowles having been assigned to the task force. He would have preferred an analyst, but he decided not to send him back. He suspected someone--probably his old nemesis Alan Goldberg--had picked Knowles to try to get a rise out of him. Instead, Leonard decided to try to use Knowles' talents. He assigned him to manage the task force budget, but he had a problem finding other useful tasks to assign to Knowles. As a result, Leonard had been surprised when Knowles volunteered to research the Chicago-based college instructor, and he was pleased at what he came up with.

"I think you solved the puzzle about what motivated Nicholson to push these students into SPJ and other radical causes," Leonard said.

Knowles smiled. "His brother."

"Exactly." Knowles discovered that Dmitris Nicholson had an older brother who had been a member of the radical Weather Underground group in the 1970s. George Nicholson had died in a battle with police in the streets of Chicago. The family accused the police of killing their son. The police denied the claim, and no one was ever charged with the crime. Nicholson had been eleven years old at the time.

"But the question is what can we do about it?" Leonard asked.

"I consulted with Carole Jean and she's got some people at Justice looking into it," Knowles replied, "but their preliminary feedback is that we don't have anything to arrest him on and if he refuses to cooperate there's little we can do."

"You indicate that he was already known to the Chicago Police Department and the local FBI office, but he's been very careful not to put his own neck on the line."

"Exactly," Knowles said. "He gets his students to do so and lets them take the fall."

"Yet if he put Philip Logan together with the bomb maker, which is very likely, he's an accessory to murder."

"You're right, Professor Robbins, but we still don't know who assembled the bomb, and we don't have any proof that Nicholson made the connection."

"In any case, this was good work. We'll add it to our files on Chicago and see where it leads. Meanwhile, how are we doing with our budget?"

"We're actually spending less than projected."

"Excellent. One less reason for those who don't think we're needed to try to shut us down."

Russian-born Pavel Zavarov was the one who convinced Leonard to try a new place to eat dinner that night--the appropriately named *Russia House* in Herndon. The three former CIA agents didn't have a regular night when they ate out together, but they tried to do so at least once a week.

Leonard was looking forward to the dinnertime conversation. He wanted to test out some ideas he'd been thinking about. He waited until they ordered and then announced he had a question. "Ready, guys?"

The two had been discussing which restaurants in the D.C. area served the best caviar. Reluctantly, it seemed to Leonard, they readied themselves for company business.

"Is there some way to turn the fact that a second student member of Students for Palestinian Justice has paid with his life into an opportunity to catch the perpetrators?"

Neither Pavel nor Meir offered an immediate response, but Leonard persisted. "Maybe I'm not stating it very well. Try this: is there some way we can turn those tragedies into a means to catch those responsible?"

"We've already established that neither the FBI nor any other agency have enough people to monitor one hundred plus student organizations," Meir offered.

"Even if we did," Pavel said, "our enemy could just as easily change course and go back to using disaffected Muslims like the Tsarnaev brothers."

"Maybe," Leonard said, "but the point is we need help in spotting these recruiters."

"What makes it worse is we don't know how many are out there," Meir stated.

Leonard nodded. "Exactly. So, what do we do?"

Pavel made a 'you're asking me?' face. True, he was not one of the best people to look to for answers that involved American culture or politics. Despite the fact that he'd been living in the U.S. for more than twenty-five years, a lot of things passed him by––references to TV shows, the names of sports stars, and even the inner workings of the American political system.

Meir, on the other hand, was a crossword puzzler's dream. He knew the damnedest trivia and had close to a photographic memory. "I'm not sure she'd do it," Meir said after several moments of silence, "but what about asking President Wheatfield to issue a statement about the bombings asking the American people for help?"

Leonard had to think about that one. "That could be the answer, but––"

"But what if she says no?" Pavel interjected.

Meir raised his hand. "Here's another thought. Why can't Congress hold hearings on the bombing and invite you to speak?"

Leonard nodded. "I like that line of thinking better."

"What does it mean hold hearings?" Pavel asked.

"Congress invites people to give testimony on certain subjects. Depending on the topic, the press may cover the event."

"And they will do so just because you ask them?"

"The White House created our task force with Congress' blessing, which means we'll have to write up a nice wrap-up report for Congress. But Meir has a point. Getting President Wheatfield to put out a statement might be difficult because there are still so many unknowns. She'd be risking a great deal if she comes out and blames the wrong party or is so vague no one pays any attention, but if Congress held a hearing on the bombings and asked me to testify, that would give me a chance to tell people how they can help stop the terrorists. Meir, contact both Homeland Security committees tomorrow morning and urge them to schedule a joint hearing as soon as convenient."

That problem solved, Leonard focused on enjoying his meal. Even when he stuck to his daily exercise routine, he had to fight a tendency to gain weight around his middle. As a result, he knew he should do a better job watching his food intake both in terms of volume and meal choices. Most nights he limited himself to fish for his main course with a salad, but this evening he allowed himself the luxury of ordering the pate hors d'oeuvre along with a flounder main course.

They stuck to small talk topics while eating until Pavel changed the subject. "Meir, I've been meaning to ask you. How do you feel about this boycott and divestment movement?"

Meir put his fork down. "What do you mean?"

"I know you don't like it," Pavel said, "but help me out. What's so bad about speaking up for the Palestinians who live like we used to be in Russia, always afraid the police will come and arrest your father or your brother just because they need to blame someone for whatever crime took place?"

Meir frowned. "You're not comparing the Israeli police to the *politsiya*, are you?"

"No, no," Pavel replied. "But you know what I mean. There are bad guys on the Palestinian side, certainly, but what about the average person who's just trying to get by and raise a family?"

Leonard was surprised at the question, but was glad Pavel felt comfortable enough with Meir to ask it.

Before responding Meir pushed his dinner plate aside and emptied the second wine bottle equally into each of their glasses. "Look at it this way. Everyone agrees that this situation has gone on decades too long and a solution must be found whereby the Palestinians have some kind of legal autonomy. So, what's stopping them from reaching a settlement? Hamas, which controls Gaza and has a huge presence in the West Bank, doesn't just want autonomy in those territories. They want the end of Israel. They want it all for themselves and the Palestinian Authority is afraid to agree to a settlement because they fear they will be blamed for accepting less than the whole thing.

"As long as Hamas keeps attacking Israel whether with rockets or suicide bombers, the Israeli government must do whatever it can to protect its population. That's why daily life can be difficult for the Palestinian who just wants to raise his family."

"But they go too far sometimes, don't you think?" Pavel asked.

"Who goes too far?" Meir asked.

Pavel turned his palms up. "The Israelis."

"At times individual soldiers and private citizens have gone too far, and when they do so, they are punished, but let me bring this discussion back to your original question--what do I think about the BDS movement?"

"Okay. Good."

"First, it's naïve to think this is just about creating pressure on Israel to withdraw from the territories. Not only do the BDS's supporters fail to defend Israel's right to exist, but the second plank of their platform--right of return by all Palestinians--would essentially mean the end to Israel as a Jewish state. That's a non-starter. What does it mean when you have as a demand the destruction of your enemy?"

"I guess it means--"

Meir laughed. "That was a rhetorical question, Pavel. You don't have to answer it. I'm going to tell you what it means."

"Okay, sorry."

"It means you're not really about peace or protection or equality. Rather, you are operating as the propaganda arm for those doing the fighting."

"Then why do so many people support it?"

"Good question. You want to jump in, Professor?" Meir said, turning to Leonard.

Leonard shook his head. "You're doing just fine."

"Okay, I'll continue. There has been a pro-Palestinian Left in the West going back to the 1960s. American leftists consider the Palestinians oppressed peoples of Western Imperialism, by which they mean the European Jews who settled in Palestine even though many of the early settlers were socialists who tried to help the Arabs organize to upgrade their living conditions."

Pavel emptied his wine glass and wiped his mouth. "Then, how does U.S. policy fit in?"

"The Left views Israel as an oppressor nation--notwithstanding the fact that its neighbors have waged war against Israel since the day it became a nation, and because the U.S. has been a strong supporter from the beginning, it fits into their anti-US ideology. In Obama the Left finally had a president who broke with traditional support for Israel, giving Hamas and its ilk an opening which cost many lives."

Pavel thought about that for a second. "But how is it that the American Left is so strong?"

"Another good question," Meir said with a smile. "At the end of the Vietnam War, when they failed to bring about a revolution in the U.S., the Marxist Left set about entrenching themselves in American universities and left-leaning Protestant churches. From there, they launched a campaign tarring this country as racist, sexist, and the world's leading environmental destructor. Those teachings appeal to naïve young people as well as adults who know very little about world history, much less about the history of their own country, and *voila!*, you have fodder for the BDS movement."

Pavel nodded. "Very interesting. I don't know if I can ever understand you Americans."

Leonard and Meir both laughed.

"Join the club," Leonard said.

"Your turn," Meir said turning to his long-time colleague.

"There's not much more to say," Leonard said. "The BDS movement and its student arm is a smart strategic move on the part of those who want to milk the Palestinian situation for their own aims."

"I'm not following," Pavel said.

"Iran, for sure, and probably groups within Russia and China couldn't be happier to see the Middle East continue to be a powder keg."

Pavel nodded. "That is true. The Russians back the Palestinians because they feel it distracts the U.S. from what they are doing to regain their control over Eastern Europe."

Leonard motioned to their waiter to bring their check. "Good. So, you understand why they send money and weapons to Hezbollah and Hamas."

"Do you think they are behind these bombings, too?"

"Yes, and if I had to put my money on who is backing the recruiters I'd say it's a faction inside Iran."

"Like the Quds Force?"

"Exactly. They have the resources to back a campaign like this--one that requires money as well as operational sophistication."

Pavel sat with that for a while. "Maybe I can help. There is someone I should talk to."

"Who?" Leonard asked.

"A friend. Give me a couple of days. I'll let you know."

"In that case, shall we call it a day?" Leonard asked. "I don't know about you, but I could use a good night's uninterrupted sleep."

Peter G. Pollak

Herndon: Friday, July 13

When Leonard arrived at DEFEAT headquarters Friday morning, he was surprised to see a stranger sitting in one of the vacant cubicles his fingers flying over one of three keyboards like a fancy electric piano. Larry Burnside, looking like he hadn't slept at all the night before, introduced Leonard to MIT Professor and social media guru Panav Chaudry. Younger than Leonard imagined, Chaudry appeared to be shy, offering a limp handshake and then backing away as if in the presence of a superior.

Chaudry had agreed to give the task force forty-eight hours of his time after Pavel came up with a unique way of getting his attention. The clock had started the night before with his 11 p.m. arrival.

None of the initial ideas Pavel came up with to reach Chaudry had worked. He had contacted Chaudry's department chair at MIT, and when that approach failed, he escalated to the president, who confessed he had little sway of Chaudry's schedule or accessibility. The breakthrough came after Pavel contacted a social media guru at Google by the name of Simi Berman. Berman had studied with Chaudry when the latter was less well known. "He loves to solve puzzles," Berman told Pavel. "Present him with a challenging enough puzzle, and you'll hear from him."

The puzzle Pavel posted on a bulletin board that Berman assured him Chaudry monitored was the one their own experts didn't seem capable of solving: How do we find the messages that set off the bomb?

Several days after posting the puzzle, Pavel, Larry Burnside, and Ekaterina were going over dozens of entries. It was Burnside who realized Chaudry's submission was exactly what they had been looking for. "This is the one," he said standing up and stretching his sore back.

Pavel was surprised that Burnside made his choice quickly without knowing the name or affiliation of the submitter, but when it turned out to have been Chaudry's solution, he was thrilled. Then began the difficult matter of negotiating for Chaudry's direct participation in the project.

At first, Professor Chaudry didn't want to be involved in actually writing the search routine that he theorized would isolate the offending messages. "You guys do that," he told them. "You don't need me."

Naturally they came to Leonard to explain the problem. "I see what he wants us to do," Burnside said, "but it would take me weeks to write the routine, test it, etc."

"What about you, Ekaterina?" Leonard asked. "You should know how to do this."

She shook her head. "Too difficult. Maybe it doesn't work."

"It'll work, all right," Burnside said, "but how are we going to get it in place unless someone can convince Chaudry to at least get us started?"

"Pavel?" Leonard asked.

"He doesn't need the money or credentials," Pavel replied. "I'm not sure what would motivate him."

"I've an idea," Leonard said. "Give me his contact info and get the hell out of here, please."

———

It took Ed Morgan six hours to get Panav Chaudry on the phone, but not before he promised this would be the last time the task force would try to contact him.

"Professor Chaudry. Thank you for taking my call," Leonard stated when he got the elusive social media guru on the phone.

"What is it that you want from me?"

"It's what the country needs not what I want. How long would it take for you to write enough of the search routine so that someone else could finish it in less than a week?"

"Let me think. Fifteen hours--eighteen at most."

"Okay. NSA's top analysts say it can't be done in less than two weeks. Would you like the chance to prove them wrong?"

Leonard could almost hear the wheels turning in Professor Chaudry's head.

"I have to come down there?"

"We've a very quiet office."

"Yes, I need extreme quiet, certain foods and beverages, and a place to sleep in the office."

"We'll get you whatever you want."

"Okay. Book me on the last flight out of Boston tonight. I'll start as soon as I get there."

"It's a deal, Professor. The people of United States thank you."

Leonard kept tabs on the progress being made by the social media guru over the next two days--as much as Larry Burnside could gauge it and then convey to someone whose idea of programming was what was offered each night on TV.

"I thought he was going to leave last night," Leonard said to Burnside when the latter checked in Sunday morning.

"He decided to give us a few benchmarks. Said whoever took over might get lost otherwise. I've got him on an early afternoon flight back to Boston."

"Super. Boil it down for me so I can explain it to Rosa Martinez."

"Okay. I'll try," Burnside said. "The essence of the matter is that there are social media channels whose content is not being captured by the big ISPs and thus is not available to the National Security Agency."

"Channels?"

"Opportunities for people to communicate including chat rooms in games that people use to talk to each other during the play."

"Which enables the bad guys to do what?"

"If they have a code worked out, it enables them to communicate without being tagged; then, it allows them to initiate apps without going through the standard signaling pathways. For example, they could create an app where if one player does x and another player does y, a signal is sent to a device that makes it go boom!"

"Unbelievable. Can we find those signals?"

"In theory, yes, but first the routine has to be completed. Then it has to be tested, and then we have to figure out how to capture new games and channels. Otherwise, we'll be fishing in waters after the fish have moved upstream."

Leonard sighed. "In other words the light at the end of the tunnel is more like a pin-prick than a beacon."

"Something like that."

"You know what I'm going to say next."

Burnside laughed. "Keep me posted?"

"You got it."

Herndon: Thursday, July 19

Leonard, Pavel, and Meir were at their favorite table in the far back corner of Russia House, which was turning out to be their favorite guys-night-out restaurant.

"What do you have for me?" Leonard asked Pavel.

"My Israeli contact tells me Iran is running the show using agents they planted here years ago. He's also heard they smuggled a Palestinian or two into the country, and get this. He's relatively positive that the computer programming they are using was written by a Russian hacker group."

Meir Epstein set down his menu. "That would explain a lot."

"It would, and it means things are worse than we thought," Leonard said.

"How so?" Meir asked.

"In the sense that we're not up against a bunch of amateurs or rogue jihadists. If some group in Iran-- maybe even the Iranian government--is willing to pay Russian hackers, then our job just got a lot harder."

Just then the waiter came by. "Pate for you tonight, sir?"

"No, I don't think so," Leonard said. "I'll just have a salad and the fish special."

"How does he remember what I ordered last time?" Leonard asked when their waiter left with their orders.

"A local company started a business that helps restaurants track customer tastes," Pavel explained. "Neat, no?"

"Very neat."

"In any case, I thought you'd find my intel interesting," Pavel said.

"Of course. It helps to know what we're up against," Leonard said.

"But . . . ?"

"But knowing doesn't really tell us what we can do about it."

"I think it does," Pavel said. "Talk to Ekaterina. She knows these hacker types. Maybe she can figure out how they're sending messages and intercept them."

"Now that would be fantastic, but what are the odds she will say she can't?"

"Give her a chance," Pavel said. "She's actually a damn good analyst as well as an incredible programmer."

The next morning Leonard buzzed Larry Burnside. Larry came into his office looking like he'd been working all night. He needed a shave, and he was twitchier than normal.

"You look like hell," Leonard said.

"Thanks. Is that why you called me in here?"

"No. I wanted to find out how you're coming on the social media search routine."

"We're making progress. In fact, I think we're just about there."

"Good, because I've got another project I'd like to put Ekaterina on."

"What's that?"

"Pavel believes a Russian hacker group is helping the Iranians with the programming used in the bombings.

He says Ekaterina might be able to figure out which group is behind it and intercept their signals."

"That would be great if she could do it."

"What's she like to work with?" Leonard asked.

Larry uncrossed his left leg and then crossed it again. "I've worked with dozens of programmers and each is more eccentric than the last one, but she tops them all."

"In what way?"

"No matter what you ask her to do, she tells you she can't do it. Then if you insist that she try, she does it quicker and better than you thought possible."

"So, the key is not to let her attitude get the better of you?"

"Exactly. You're cheating yourself if you downgrade your request based on her initial reaction."

"Why do you think she's like that?"

"Who knows," Burnside confessed. "Maybe it's how she got out of having to work growing up."

"Or maybe she's afraid of failing," Leonard said. "In any case, when can I ask her to start on this new project?"

"Give me another twenty-four hours just to make sure I can finish up what she's been working on."

"Okay. You got it."

Larry stood up and started to leave the room.

"Oh, Larry. One sec."

Larry stopped and turned around.

"When you're finished, what will the search routine generate?"

"It will poll areas of social media that normal searches can't access. It will then trace the source of those messages, looking for patterns that can help us identify where they are sent from and possibly even who is sending them."

"Great. Let me know when it's turned on."

Leonard invited Ekaterina, Pavel, and Meir into his office the following Monday. Larry had texted him over the weekend that he and Ekaterina had finished the coding the social media search routine, and he would be able to do the testing and installation part of the process without her assistance. As a result, he wrote, Ekaterina is free to start on the search for the Russian hackers who were helping the Iranians.

"Pavel, tell Ekaterina what you learned."

"My source says a group in Iran hired Russian hackers to write the bomb delivery program."

Ekaterina arched her eyebrows, but didn't say anything.

"Pavel thought you might be able to figure out which group is involved and intercept their communications," Leonard stated.

Ekaterina looked at Pavel like he'd just suggested she should strip for the three of them.

"Is he right?" Leonard asked her.

"These groups are very good," she said. "Better than your NSA."

"So, there's no point even trying?" Leonard asked.

She shrugged. "I can try, but I can't promise you anything other than it will take many hours."

"You understand this may be the only way we'll know when they're planning another bombing," Leonard said.

She shrugged again. "If you say so."

"Even if it's a long shot, I'd like you to try to determine which group is working for the Iranians and then find a way to intercept those signals."

She looked at Pavel and then back to Leonard. "I try, but don't hold breath."

"Thanks. Just do your best," Leonard said.

"I'm not encouraged," Meir said after she left Leonard's office.

"She's that way," Pavel said. "She is, how you say modest, but she's very good. Maybe as good as the hackers."

"But there's only one of her," Meir pointed out.

"True," Pavel said, "but she knows many of those guys. She went to school with some of them and met others at conferences. She can hold her own."

"Let's hope so," Leonard said, "because we're running out of options."

Peter G. Pollak

New York City: Friday, July 27

Doreen tried not to feel annoyed. She had arrived at the Greenes' apartment at the appointed time, but was told she'd have to wait outside "for a minute." A minute turned out to be twenty before Emily Greene let her in without explanation. "The meeting will start in a few. Do you want anything to drink?"

Empty glasses, a half empty bowl of chips, and a musty smell in the living room suggested that there had been a meeting before the one she was arriving to participate in. Neither Erik nor any of the other members of the NYU SPJ steering committee she expected to find there were in sight.

"Just water with ice, please," Doreen answered. It was still muggy despite being past eight p.m.

Emily tried to engage her in small talk, but Doreen was more interested in discovering where everyone else was and what had gone on before she arrived.

The ostensible purpose of that night's meeting was to discuss plans for the fall. The SPJ chapter had grown considerably during the previous year, and although the leafleting episode had been a setback in the minds of some, Doreen knew Erik and the other chapter leaders were thinking about engaging in even more aggressive tactics in the fall. She, for one, was all for that.

Miguel Brizuela came out of a back bedroom, nodded at Doreen, and then disappeared into the bathroom. Seconds later, Erik, and someone she'd never seen before came into the kitchen.

"Doreen, this is Omar Mejbari. He's a research fellow at Columbia and informal advisor to our group. Omar, Doreen."

"Pleased to meet you," Omar said with a nod of his head.

The newcomer was stocky with a round face, shaved head, and penetrating eyes. She guessed he was in his thirties. If his name didn't make it clear, his accent and skin shading strongly suggested a Middle Eastern origin.

"We'll start in a minute," Erik told her. "Why don't you find a place in the living room?"

Doreen took her water glass into the living room and decided to sit on a cushion on the floor. All three men came and sat facing her. Doreen felt she was on trial. She hoped Emily would join her to even the odds, but she stayed in the kitchenette.

"Doreen," Erik said. "Before we talk about the fall, we have a question for you."

"For me?" Doreen asked. *What could this be about?*

"Do you know who Courtney Robbins' father is?"

"He's a professor of some kind up in Albany."

"Yes, he's that, but he's much more than that," Miguel said. "He's CIA."

Doreen was surprised. "I didn't know that." She knew Courtney and her parents had lived in the D.C. area for a number of years, but thought her father worked in international business since that is what Courtney said he taught.

"Worse, he's the head of a special White House task force on terrorism," Erik said.

Doreen blushed. They made it seem like she was responsible for having brought someone evil into the group. "I had no idea."

"That brings up the key question," Erik said. "Do you think Courtney is spying on us?"

———

"Courtney, spy on us? I don't know what to say. I mean--"

"She's pretty aggressive," Erik said. "Remember, she asked to meet with me a few months ago. She asked a lot of questions about our plans, about the movement as a whole."

"You're living with her now, right?" Miguel asked.

Doreen nodded.

"What kinds of things has she asked you about the group?"

"Like what?" Doreen asked.

"Like where we get our money, who are we in contact with, and what are plans are."

"She's never said a thing about money."

"What kinds of things do you two discuss?" Omar asked.

"The usual stuff--what to wear, shopping, school, boys . . ."

"Nothing about the group?" Mike demanded.

"Occasionally, but since we haven't been meeting for a couple of months, there hasn't been a lot to talk about, really."

"We want you to find out if her father told her to join the group to spy on us," Erik said.

"How am--?"

Omar held up his hand. "Find a way. Come back next Friday and report."

Doreen's head was spinning as she walked to the subway. They decided it was too late to discuss plans for the fall, although she noticed that Miguel and Omar stayed behind when she was leaving. *Maybe they don't trust me*, Doreen worried.

She tried to think about things Courtney had said or done to see if it seemed like she was gathering information for her father. If she was, she certainly had disguised it well. She seemed genuinely moved by the Palestinian's situation and, other than resisting helping on the eviction flyer activity, she'd partaken enthusiastically in the other SPJ activities. Doreen didn't think she'd missed a meeting since she'd joined last winter.

The bigger problem was how was she going to do what the steering committee wanted her to do. What questions could she ask that would reveal the answer they were looking for? If Courtney was spying on them, wouldn't she deny it? Doreen still hadn't decided what she was going to do when she reached their apartment. Fortunately, Courtney had already gone to bed. That meant Doreen had a little time to come up with a plan.

Washington, D.C.: Tuesday, July 31

Congressman David Gross (D-Maryland) opened the hearing almost on time. "Need I remind everyone that this joint Homeland Security committee hearing is being held initially today in a closed-door session, which means disclosure of any of the information presented here today is a violation of federal law. Staff members, pay attention. Violators of that law will be prosecuted.

"At the end of this session, we will open the doors to the public and permit press coverage of the second part of the hearing.

"Each member will have seven minutes for questions. I will begin, and then turn the questioning over to Congressman Herald Brown from the state of Indiana, who will be followed by Senator Stern from New York. If any other committee members arrive in the interim, they will have an opportunity to question Professor Robbins as well.

"Professor Robbins, thank you for your presence this morning. We asked you here to help us understand what progress is being made by the President's Task Force on Domestic Terrorism that was set up to investigate the April 13 bombing of the American Israel Association. Six weeks ago, a second Jewish organization was bombed--this one in Chicago.

"You've been operating since the beginning of May, Professor Robbins. My first question this morning is whether your task force has discovered who is behind these bombings.

Leonard leaned forward to speak into the microphone. "No, sir. We have not."

"Have you made any progress?"

"Yes, sir. We have."

"Please describe."

"In both cases, college students were recruited as bomb carriers. We have a lead on the person who recruited the University of Maryland student who died in the D.C. explosion, and we are close to breaking open the Chicago bombing."

"You say you have a lead on the person behind the D.C. bombing--is that correct?"

"We have a suspect. Law enforcement nationwide is on the lookout for this individual."

"What can you tell us about him?"

"We don't know his real name. He used an assumed name and false identification papers to obtain employment at the University of Maryland. From that post he was able to recruit two women to assist him in bombing AIA headquarters. One of the women died in the blast. The second has been indicted for her role in the bombing."

"That would be Susan Gazzola?"

"Correct."

"And she confirmed this man was behind the bombing?"

"That is correct."

"What was she able to tell you about the organization behind these bombings?"

"She claims she was not aware of any organizational presence. She thought she was involved with a sole individual and that it was his idea. She claims he drew up the plan and constructed the bomb."

"How did this Susan Gazzola justify getting involved in the bombing of a Jewish organization? Was there anything in her background that suggested she was likely to participate in this extreme a venture?"

"In terms of her background, no. She was a typical college student, although perhaps a little more naïve than most. Interestingly, Ms. Gazzola claims they did not intend for the bomb to explode. She claims the bomb maker, who went by the name of Sammy Haddad, at first said it only looked like a real bomb, but would not detonate. Later he told her it was real, but he would not detonate it."

"Did he account for the change?"

"She says he told her they had to deliver a real bomb in order for their warning to be taken seriously."

"So the plan was to deliver the bomb, but not detonate it. Is that what she claims?"

"Correct. She said Marisa Anderson was supposed to call her after she had left the package with the receptionist, and she was supposed to call in the warning. She produced the wording they had agreed she would use on the phone. I think she believed that was what would take place."

"Did this Gazzola say what the purpose of this fake bombing was?"

"She claims their goal was to warn AIA and other Jewish organizations of the consequences of continued support for Israel's policies with regard to the so-called occupied territories."

"Sounds like she must be incredibly naïve or a good liar."

Leonard nodded.

"I see my time is up," Congressman Gross said. "Congressman Brown."

Harold Brown, Republican Congressman from Indiana, leaned forward and tapped the microphone. "Good morning, Professor Robbins. Thank you for your time today. Professor, the task force was set up to investigate the explosion here in Washington on the thirteenth of April. Is that correct?"

Leonard nodded. "Yes, sir."

"Tell us, Professor Robbins, what you have learned thus far? Do you know why these people chose the headquarters of the American-Israel Association?"

"All of the groups that claimed responsibility offered similar reasoning, which was the bombing was a message to the American Jewish community to pressure Israel to end its occupation of the West Bank, the Golan Heights, and East Jerusalem."

"Why would these women take it upon themselves to participate in such a venture?"

"You're asking me to speculate?"

"I'm looking for an educated guess, Professor. You are known to be an expert of sorts on these matters. What would possess two American college students to do such a thing?"

"It appears as if the man behind the Washington bombing was very persuasive. He had Ms. Gazzola believing that he was attracted to her, and may have convinced Ms. Anderson of the same."

"In other words he romanced them. Is that what you're saying?"

"Apparently so, but I confess I find it hard to believe they would go along unless they had also been convinced by this individual that their cause was just."

"The cause of the Palestinians living in the so-called occupied territories?"

"Correct."

"I'm still unclear as to how this person who you say was an employee at the University of Maryland could convince these women to participate in such an event."

"I agree with you, Congressman Brown. We know that both women were active in the University of Maryland chapter of a national group called Students for Palestinian Justice. That group uses speakers, petition drives, websites, flyers, and similar techniques to convince people that Israel is an apartheid state and that the way to force Israel to alter its policies is to support the boycott, divestment, and sanctions movement."

Congressman Brown turned to say something to one of his aides and then turned back to Leonard. "Professor Robbins, are you saying that involvement in that group--Students for Palestinian Justice--paved the way for those women to engage in the bomb plot?"

Leonard nodded. "Apparently so, Congressman."

"And does that also describe in your opinion the reason a young University of Chicago student participated in a similar exercise resulting in four deaths including his own?"

"It does, Congressman Brown."

"One last question, Professor Robbins. If that is the case, shouldn't this Students for Palestinian Justice be outlawed and its leaders arrested as accomplices in these bombings?"

"That's for the U.S. Attorney's office to decide, Congressman, but I might point out that Students for Palestinian Justice does not advocate the use of violence. To the contrary, they claim to be using peaceful and legal means to bring about needed change. I don't believe as a matter of law that the students involved can be held accountable for the fact that someone is exploiting their hostility to Israel and by extension to the United States."

"You make a good point," Congressman Brown stated, "but then who does deserve the blame for the fact that nine innocent people are dead and this group,

Americans for the Liberation of Palestine, is still on the loose?"

"I would say that faculty members of academic associations like the American Studies Association deserve some of the blame," Leonard stated. "I am not challenging their right as individuals to exercise their constitutional rights of speech and association. When, however, an academic association takes a position on an international political matter, they have to recognize that one of the consequences is a blurring of the lines between academic inquiry and advocacy, which in turn makes students they teach vulnerable to being exploited for someone else's ends."

"Your time is up, Congressman Brown."

"Thank you, Mr. Chairman. I yield to the senior Senator from New York."

Joseph Stern, a Democrat and the senior senator from New York, tapped on the microphone in front of him. "Is this working?"

"It is, Senator."

"Excellent. Thank you, Congressman Brown, and thank you, Professor Robbins for your remarks here today and for your willingness to serve your country in the capacity of executive director of the president's counter-terrorism task force."

"It's my pleasure, Senator Stern."

"Professor Robbins, who is behind these bombings? Who are they, how did they get into this country, and how were they able to recruit American college students to carry the bombs into their targets' offices?"

"In my opinion, Senator, the lax policies of President Obama with regard to the danger of Muslim fundamentalism enabled our enemies to recruit, train, and deploy a cadre of individuals to carry out this campaign."

"Are they Palestinians, Iranians, disaffected Saudis--who?"

"Since we have not confirmed the identification of any of the members of this organization, it is impossible for me to identify them by country of origin. We might extrapolate from our knowledge of Al Qaeda, however. Al Qaeda was able to attract militants from various countries throughout the Middle East and Asia. Their hatred for the United States overcame national, ethnic, and even sectarian religious differences. That means the organization we're fighting could be made up of militants from more than one country."

"I see. Following up then, what do we need to do to catch those terrorists currently on American soil and to prevent others from replacing them?"

"Our team is focused on uncovering those currently in the U.S. before they kill any more innocent Americans. I believe we will be successful, although of course, I can't promise you a specific date. Once we've broken their network, we should be able to advise the president on what steps need to be taken to prevent others from taking their place."

"Godspeed, Professor. The final part of my question is this: how have these people been able to recruit Americans to do their dirty work?"

"That's a tough one, Senator. As I have previously stated, that job was made easier by the existence on more than one hundred college campuses of groups supporting the Palestinian cause. The foundation for that support is a cadre of instructors who champion groups who engage in behaviors that would not be tolerated in this country. For example, Judith Butler, who teaches at the University of California, is quoted as having said '. . . understanding Hamas/Hezbollah as social movements that are progressive, that are on the left, that are part of a global left, is extremely important.'

"When you have a body of students who have bought the distorted reality painted by faculty like Judith Butler and by the leaders of Students for Palestinian Justice, finding one or two who are willing to go beyond peaceful methods is not difficult."

Senator Stern shook his head. "I can't tell you how much that upsets me. It causes me to wonder what's going on in our institutions of higher learning that young Americans can be so easily manipulated into supporting our enemies."

"I agree, Senator Stern."

"Nevertheless, I see my time is up. I want to commend you, sir, on the work your task force has accomplished to date. All of us are impatient for results, but I know it is not an easy assignment the president has tasked you with. Godspeed."

An hour later, after the closed-door questioning was concluded and reporters and the public were allowed into the hearing room, Leonard was reminded by the chairman that he was still under oath and asked if he had a statement to read.

"I do, Mr. Chairman."

"You may read it."

Leonard read the statement his team had helped him prepare. He concluded with a strong appeal for the public to contact the FBI if they had encountered anyone promoting the idea of violent acts against Jewish organizations.

"Anyone engaged in calling for violence or actually engaging in acts of violence against any organization is in violation of federal law not to mention local and state law in the jurisdiction where they are living. We ask the public to assist the federal government in putting an end to these acts by revealing the identity and/or location of such individuals."

Peter G. Pollak

New York City: Friday, August 3

Doreen had been in a funk all week. At first, she tried to interpret Courtney's every glance or comment as evidence one way or the other. Afraid she'd tip her hand, she studiously avoided mention of SPJ's fall plans, despite the fact that Courtney asked her several times what was on the group's agenda.

The two rarely spent any time together during the week, which complicated her task. Doreen was usually gone by the time Courtney got up, and when Doreen got home from work, Courtney had usually returned to the campus to study in the library.

As a result when Friday came, Doreen dreaded going to the steering committee meeting. She stood outside the Greenes' apartment trying to think of a good excuse not to go in. If she said she didn't think Courtney was spying, they might produce evidence that she was and as a result suspect Doreen was helping her. Yet she couldn't say that Courtney was a spy because she had not one shred of proof.

Another thought had been gnawing at her all day. What would the steering committee do if it turned out Courtney was spying on them? She wasn't sure she wanted to know.

Finally she knocked on the door and went into the apartment. Before the start of the meeting Erik pulled her aside to tell her they'd discuss the "Courtney matter" after the regular meeting was over.

Two hours later, Doreen found herself in the living room again facing Erik, Miguel, and Omar. "What did you find out?" Erik asked her.

"If she's spying on us, she's fooled me because I can't see any evidence of it."

"Okay," Erik said. "That's not a problem. We have been talking about it and we have come up with a plan to find out if she is, but we need your help."

Doreen wasn't sure she liked the sound of that.

"We're going to test her," Miguel said.

Doreen couldn't imagine what they had in mind.

Erik looked at some notes on a sheet of paper. "We have come up with a plan involving three steps. The first two are designed to see how she reacts to certain situations. The third will be the final exam. By the end of the process, we'll know if she's a spy or actually on our side."

"What steps?" Doreen inquired.

Erik consulted the paper. "Here's the first one. Tell her that the steering committee welcomes her participation in next Friday's meeting when we're going over our plans for the fall. We'd like to see what she thinks since she voiced a concern about the eviction flyer."

"Okay," Doreen said, still not seeing what they had in mind.

"When she gets here Miguel is going to propose something juvenile--like sneaking into the Jewish Student Union's meeting room and plastering the walls with Free Palestine posters, which is not a bad idea by the way. But he'll come up with something even more outlandish than that."

Miguel looked like the cat that ate the family goldfish.

"Then I'll ask Courtney what she thinks of that suggestion. We hope whatever Miguel comes up with will be so off the wall that she speaks up against it. When she does, you're to back her up. Got it?"

Doreen nodded.

"Then, I'll call for a vote. We'll vote down Miguel's action. That will make her think we value her opinion."

Doreen nodded. "That seems relatively easy. What is the second step test?"

Just then Emily Greene came into the room with some fresh lemonade. After everyone was served, Doreen repeated her question.

"The second stage will be when the freshmen arrive later in the month," Erik said. "We'll ask her to sit at our recruitment table and sign up incoming freshmen to a group orientation session, and we'll ask her to talk at that meeting about why she supports the Palestinians."

"How is that a test?" Doreen asked.

"Here's how," Miguel said. "One of the reasons we want to involve her more is so you can see how that affects her relationship with her father. You told us he was upset when he learned she'd joined SPJ. That may have been part of their plan, an act in other words, but since you're living with her, you should be able to see how her increasing involvement in the group affects their relationship. For example, if they're in cahoots, then her father may protest her volunteering to speak, but that shouldn't bother Courtney too much since she knows it's not real. But if she's sincere and he chastises her for doing it, she'll feel genuinely upset and you should be able to tell."

"I'll have to think about that," Doreen said. "So, what's the third step--the final exam?"

"The third," Erik said, "will depend on how the first two go. Let's just say it'll prove for once and for all if she's really with us or against us."

Herndon: Wednesday, August 8

"Gary has news from Chicago," Leonard announced when everyone was assembled in the conference room for their Wednesday morning briefing.

"I heard from the Chicago bureau yesterday," Gary said. "They have convincing evidence that the man who coordinated the Jewish Federation bombing was an assistant soccer coach at the University of Chicago by the name of Rashid Saab.

"Saab, who is of Iranian descent, resigned a week after the Chicago bombing, and he seems to have dropped off the face of the earth. His apartment was searched, but we did not find anything incriminating since it had been cleaned and was already rented to new tenants."

"How was this Saab connected to Philip Logan?" Leonard asked.

"You recall Logan's tagalongs from Harold Washington gave us four names of people they had met through Logan and Nick Nicholson, the school of education instructor. One of them--a University of Chicago student named Edward Taylor--reported that he'd seen Logan twice on the campus with this Saab, which struck him as odd because Logan was not an athlete and had no logical ties to the soccer program.

"The break-through came when we searched Saab's office computer. He thought he erased the hard drive, but we shipped it down to D.C. where our tech team uncovered bomb-making instructions, which he apparently downloaded from an email.

"We couldn't trace the email, but the instructions match what we know about the materials used in the Chicago bombing."

"He vanished?" Leonard asked.

"It seems that way. He told the head coach that he was returning to Iran to play professional soccer, but we find no record of someone with that name on any flight to Iran. Of course, if he did make it back to Iran, we're out of luck."

"Did you find any connection to Nicholson?"

"Agents will be contacting Nicholson today to ask whether he knew Saab. First, however, they plan to question both Guerra and Nahos to see if they admit knowing Saab or if they ever saw Saab with Logan or Nicholson."

"Good work," Leonard said. "I'm surprised the local bureau hadn't checked out Saab before this."

"Turns out the University of Chicago didn't go through its normal hiring procedure. Saab was a last minute replacement for an assistant who took a job elsewhere and his paperwork was never completed, which is why no one at the Bureau was aware of his presence in the city."

"Typical," Leonard murmured. "Check out the guy Saab replaced. He may have been in on the deal."

"Good point," Mackey said. "I'll convey that suggestion to our Chicago bureau."

"The other question we need to ask is if instead of leaving the country, he moved to another city to take on a new identity and replicate his success."

"I think we'd better assume he has," Pavel said.

"Which means the Bureau needs to distribute any photos they have of this guy around the country," Meir

Epstein said. "He's probably going to lie low for a while, but eventually, when he thinks it's safe, he'll re-emerge and look for another victim."

Leonard nodded. "Unfortunately, Meir, you're probably correct. It makes me very angry to think there's nothing we can do to stop these guys. We need a break, g-damn it!"

Leonard noticed the room got very quiet. "Sorry, people. I'm not angry at you guys."

"I don't blame you, Professor," Russell Knowles said. "We're all a little more than pissed by how easy it seems for these guys to get away with this shit. Excuse my French."

"You're excused," Pavel said.

"It almost seems as if the country is asleep," Sheila Stewart said.

"No," Carole Jean Hall said. "They're not asleep. They've been lulled into this false belief that if you treat other people nice, they won't rob or kill you."

"Well said," Russell replied.

Leonard's angry feeling dissipated for a moment as he listened to members of his team express their feelings about their failure thus far to stop the bombings. That moment reminded him of his days on the Naval Academy football team. Navy had just been defeated by a team they thought they would beat easily. One of the seniors on the team got up on a bench in the locker room and yelled at them. "Stop whining," he said. "We deserved to get beat because we didn't take our opponent seriously. If we do that on the battlefield, we won't just lose a game. We'll lose lives." The team went undefeated the rest of that season.

Peter G. Pollak

New York City: Friday, August 10

"Are you sure they want me to come to tonight's meeting?" Courtney asked.

"They do," Doreen replied. "They're finalizing plans for the fall semester and since you had issues with some of the things they did last year, they wanted to get your reaction."

"Okay," Courtney said. "I guess I can come."

It was a typical summer evening in New York. A thunderstorm had rolled through late in the afternoon, cooling things down only slightly. Courtney found the wet streets, with water dripping from trees and steam rising off the pavement a reminder of why she loved living in New York.

The Greenes' apartment felt muggy despite window fans. Emily was ready with fresh lemonade and store-bought oatmeal and chocolate chip cookies.

Courtney knew all of the steering committee members except for one.

"This is Omar Mejbari," Erik said, introducing her to a middle-aged man of Middle-Eastern origins. "He's a research fellow at Columbia and an informal advisor to our group."

"Nice to meet you, Omar," Courtney replied.

Erik began the meeting by listing meeting dates and activities, all of which sounded pretty reasonable to Courtney. "What do people think?"

"Too tame," Miguel said. "We need something to get the year off on the right note, something that shows the student body our passion for this cause."

"Like what?" Erik asked.

"Like what if we plant stink bombs in the Jewish student organization's meeting room and plastered the walls with Free Palestine posters?"

"Stink bombs and posters?" Erik asked.

"Yeah," Miguel said. "Trash their room. Show them we mean business--"

"Wait," Erik said, cutting him off. "Let's see what other people think."

Erik called on her when Courtney raised her hand. "I feel just as passionately about what's going on as you do, Miguel, but that's not the way to go about showing it. It'll just turn people against us."

"No, it won't," Miguel said. "People will join us if we show we're not just a bunch of sissies--"

"Let her finish what she was saying," Erik said, interrupting Miguel again. "Courtney, go ahead."

Courtney gathered her thoughts. "I don't see how that helps the Palestinian people."

Miguel leaned forward. "It helps because we need to show our solidarity. They're fighting back. We need to be in fighting mode, too."

Courtney was starting to see red. "We're trying to win over public opinion, not fight a war."

"Doreen, what do you think?" Erik asked.

"I agree with Courtney," Doreen said. "Our job is to get students at NYU to pay attention and hear our arguments about why they should join us. I don't think trashing someone's room is a smart way to go about doing it."

"Anyone else have an opinion?" Erik asked.

"I kinda like it," Sheldon Floyd said. "It'll get people's attention."

After a few more minutes of discussion, Erik started passing out slips of paper. "It's time for a vote. Write down 'yes' if you're in favor of Miguel's idea or 'no' if you oppose it."

Courtney took the paper and searched for a pen in her pocket book. She wrote 'NO' in capital letters, folded the paper, and handed it back to Erik. She would have to think about whether she wanted to stay in the group if Miguel's idea passed.

Erik counted the votes. "Two in favor of Miguel's action resolution, six against. The motion fails. Any other suggestions for this fall's program?"

Courtney wished she knew that they were looking for suggestions. She might have come up with an idea or two, but she didn't feel confident enough to do so on the fly.

"We have one more topic to discuss tonight," Erik said after the fall agenda was approved without Miguel's stink bomb plan. "We need volunteers to help out during freshman orientation. Janice, you're in charge. What do you need?"

Janice Nelson, an overweight junior of mixed race parentage whom Courtney found fascinating, gathered her papers. "We're going to set up a table when the freshmen first come on campus to publicize an orientation session where we'll explain what our group is all about."

She passed around a clipboard. "I need everyone to sign up for two hour shifts at the table. Please sign up for at least one slot. I also need people who are willing to help me with the orientation meeting. If you're available to help at the meeting, please sign up on the third sheet with your contact information. I'll schedule a meeting in a couple of weeks to start planning for that event."

Courtney noticed that several people were staring at her when the clipboard was passed to her. Was this a test of her commitment? No matter. She did want to participate in the orientation. She signed up for two hour-slots on both days and to be part of Janice's orientation committee.

New York City: Sunday, August 12

"Are you sure you can't get the time off?" Courtney asked Doreen, cellphone in hand, about to make her weekly call to her parents. Doreen had not given any serious thought to going with Courtney to her parents' home when it first came up earlier in the summer, but given her SPJ assignment, she realized it might be a good way for her to observe Courtney's relationship with her father. Moreover, she was getting tired of being "copier girl" at the law firm where Emily Greene had gotten her a summer job. "I'll talk to my supervisor tomorrow. If she agrees to give me the week off, I'll come with you."

"That would be great. My father will have to keep his kid gloves on if you're there."

"What would he do, spank you?" Doreen asked.

Courtney laughed. "He's not that weird. He just believes strongly in things and hates it when family members disagree with him."

"I see where you get it from," Doreen said.

Courtney had started clearing the dishes, but stopped to react to Doreen's comment. "I know I can be stubborn. I am trying to be more reasonable these days."

"I was just kidding," Doreen said. "What about your mom--does she go along with your dad?"

"Sometimes, but she has ways of persuading him to see things her way that the rest of us don't."

Doreen got up and started to run the hot water in the kitchen sink. "What kind of clothes will I need--anything formal?"

"Oh, yes, we dress for dinner."

Doreen turned to look at Courtney who was grinning like the Cheshire cat. "Yeah, right."

The next day Doreen informed her supervisor that she would like the third week of August off. The woman, who had not seemed satisfied with anything Doreen had done all summer, was suddenly very friendly, assuring her that not only could she have the week off, but she hoped Doreen would be willing to work part-time in the fall. Doreen told her she'd think about it.

That night, when she told Courtney she had gotten the time, Courtney seemed genuinely relieved, which made Doreen feel stupid for ever having doubted her sincerity about the boycott Israel movement. The more she thought about it, the idea that she was spying on the group for her father seemed far-fetched. Doreen couldn't imagine they'd send one of their own to do the spying-- if they even thought spying was necessary.

In terms of spending a few days with Courtney's parents, Doreen was a little apprehensive. She liked Mrs. Robbins who seemed genuinely interested in her the one time they'd met, but as far as Mr. Robbins was concerned, she hoped Courtney was right, that her presence would discourage him from badgering either of them about their SPJ activities.

Herndon: Thursday, August 16

Gary Mackey was waiting for Leonard when he arrived Thursday morning. "Good morning, Professor. We've got something you'll want to take a look at."

Leonard wheeled into his office. "Come on in, Gary. What do you have?"

"Our San Francisco bureau got a call from an adjunct at San Francisco State University who read about the Congressional hearing and wanted to report on a conversation he had with a female student towards the end of the spring semester. The student complained an individual made her uncomfortable because of anti-Semitic remarks he made at a SPJ meeting."

"That's not good, but what's the connection to our mission?"

"When they interviewed the instructor, they learned the person was advocating militant actions against local Jewish organizations."

"Now that's a horse of a different color," Leonard said.

"I thought you might want to watch the video."

Leonard watched the forty-minute video interview with Dane Clark twice. Clark, who was the faculty advisor to the SFSU Students for Palestinian Justice Chapter, described being approached by a SPJ member by the name of Felicia Vargas, who told Clark she was disturbed by remarks made by a man she'd never seen before.

Vargas described the individual as being in his mid- to late twenties, of medium height, average build, tan complexion, and closely cropped hair. She said he tried to convince her that the SPJ group was not doing enough to support the Palestinians in the occupied territories. She told Professor Clark the man said they needed to hold the Jews of San Francisco accountable.

A team had been sent to interview Ms. Vargas.

"It's a match," Mackey called out from his cubicle later that day.

"Haddad?" someone asked.

"Look for yourself."

Leonard wheeled out to Gary's cubicle where others on the task force had gathered. They made room for him to get a closer look. Mackey's monitor displayed the University of Maryland employee ID photo side by side with an artist's rendition of the person Felicia Vargas had told Dane Clark about. The set of the eyes, the thin lips, and the narrow face were almost identical.

"That's him," Leonard agreed. "Gary, what are they doing to find him?"

"The usual stuff. They'll show his picture to other students in the group, to campus security, the local police department, and anyone else who might have seen this guy."

"Do you think he might have tried to get a job there?" Meir Epstein asked.

"Good point," Leonard said. "Gary, can you remind your people to check that angle?"

Mackey nodded. "Will do."

"Any other suggestions?" Leonard asked.

"San Francisco State is not the only school in San Francisco with an SPJ chapter," Meir said.

Leonard nodded. "Of course. They should check any college in a fifty-mile radius that has an SPJ chapter to see if Haddad was spotted there as well. Be sure to include Stanford, although my guess is that Haddad is more likely to approach students at a school like San Francisco State than Stanford."

"Why's that?" Meir asked.

"First, I don't think he would find it that easy getting a job at Stanford. They probably pay better than other schools, which means jobs there must be in much higher demand."

"Although I hear they have problems because there's so little low-income housing nearby," Meir said.

"True, but I don't see Haddad being able to hire on at Stanford with a phony ID, plus the students there are less likely to fall for his line. They are probably more independent-minded than students at other schools."

Meir nodded. "I see what you're saying."

"In any case, this could be the break we've been waiting for. Let's stay on it, people."

Peter G. Pollak

Delmar, New York: Friday August 17

Doreen tried to hide her nervousness when Courtney's mother picked them up in the family van at the Rensselaer Amtrak station. She tried not feeling guilty about her true motive for accepting the invitation and was worried about meeting Mr. Robbins.

"I hope you girls have talked about some things you'd like to do during your week off," Alison Robbins said once they were underway.

"Sleep," Courtney said from the front passenger seat.

"Oh dear. That's too bad," Mrs. Robbins said with a wry smile. "Reveille sounds at six am daily."

"Mom!" Courtney squealed. "Don't. Doreen will believe you."

Doreen enjoyed the mother-daughter give and take, although it reminded her what she lacked in her life.

"Okay, I'll be serious," Mrs. Robbins said. "So, Doreen, Mr. Robbins will be arriving later this evening and will stay through Monday morning. It'll just be us girls during the week. We can go shopping, eat out-- even go to the track if you're interested."

"What kind of track?" Doreen asked.

"The flat track in Saratoga. I'm not much for betting, but the horses are magnificent and the city itself is charming."

"Sounds like fun," Doreen said. She'd never been to a racetrack although her uncle was a regular patron of the New York City tracks. She couldn't remember him ever taking her aunt with him.

Doreen had forgotten that Courtney's father was wheelchair bound. On the train ride up to Albany, Courtney told her that he'd been in a traffic accident in some South American country, the result of which left him without use of his legs. Courtney explained that the house had been set up to make it easy for him to maneuver and stressed that Doreen shouldn't leave her shoes or other items where he might not see them.

Mr. Robbins seemed friendly enough when introduced to her later that day. Like his wife, he seemed genuinely interested in her, asking her during dinner about her family and current interests. She was glad that he avoided asking about her involvement in the boycott Israel movement. Maybe that would come later.

After helping Courtney and her mom clean up after dinner, Courtney dragged her up to her room where she showed Doreen her senior yearbook--she had only attended the local high school for one year--as well as photo albums of some of the places they'd visited when she was younger. Doreen found most of it boring, but tried not to let on.

"Okay. Enough about me," Courtney said after an hour. "What shall we do the rest of the evening--watch a movie, read? Nah, too boring! Why don't I call around and see if any of my friends are home?"

Doreen listened to Courtney make three phone calls before finding one of her high school friends who was at home.

"Mindy doesn't live far away. I'll ask my mom if we can use her car."

With Mrs. Robbins' approval, they drove a few blocks to where Courtney's friend Mindy lived. She seemed nice, but the two of them talked about a bunch of people Doreen didn't know and by the time they were back at the Robbins' house, Doreen was wondering if she'd made a big mistake by coming along with Courtney. The thought of spending five more days in Delmar, New York was beginning to feel like the worst vacation ever.

After breakfast the next morning, Mrs. Robbins invited the girls out to her garden. It turned out she had more in mind than pointing out her favorite flowers. She gave Courtney and Doreen a list of things they could do to earn their keep, starting with dead-heading the marigolds, watering a bed of flowers that seemed dry, and then picking lettuce, radishes, and cucumbers for a luncheon salad.

Standing in the middle of the backyard garden, Doreen got a better feel for the Robbins' house than she had the night before. She had noted the wheel-chair ramps leading up the front and back entrances. The house was larger and fancier than any Doreen had been in her whole life. Set back from the street on a large piece of property, more than half of the considerable backyard had been dedicated to Mrs. Robbins' flower and vegetable gardens. There was also a gazebo in the back of the yard, but no swimming pool. Courtney had promised they'd go swimming when it got hot.

"I didn't realize I had such a green thumb until I moved up here," Mrs. Robbins told Doreen as she pointed out which zucchini were ready for picking. "We didn't have room for vegetables where we lived in Northern Virginia."

Later, Courtney borrowed her mother's car again and drove the two of them around Delmar. "I really don't know much about the area," she confessed. "I only lived here one year before starting NYU. We've a few interesting stores locally. I'll park and we can walk around."

"What are you studying?" Mr. Robbins asked Doreen after they'd sat down for dinner, which consisted of chicken, a pasta salad, and squash from the garden that Mrs. Robbins cooked on their large gas grill. Doreen was excited to see a wine glass in front of her place setting. "American studies," she answered.

"And you'll be a senior, like Court?"

Doreen nodded.

Mr. Robbins opened a bottle of white wine that had been cooling in the refrigerator. He held the bottle over Doreen's glass. She nodded her consent. "So, what does one do with a degree in American Studies?"

Doreen blushed. "I'm not sure."

"There are lots of things you can do with it," Courtney said, coming to her defense.

Mr. Robbins filled Courtney's glass and his own, and then passed the bottle to his wife. "I just hate to see people spend all that time and money on subjects that do not help them find a career where they can support themselves."

"Ahem, Mr. R," Mrs. Robbins interjected, "didn't you major in history when you were an undergraduate?"

"I did," Mr. Robbins confessed, "but those were different times and since I was at the Naval Academy I knew what was in store for me for after I graduated."

"You graduated from the Naval Academy?" Doreen asked.

"I did . . . in 1977. I served ten years before getting out to go to graduate school."

"It's got to be hard for students to know what to study these days," Mrs. Robbins said, "what with the economy so unstable."

"All the more reason to make wise choices," Mr. Robbins said.

"What did you major in, Mrs. Robbins?" Doreen asked.

"I was something of a jock growing up. I wanted to go into sports medicine, but I got married when I was a junior and switched to business so that I could support my husband while he went to law school."

"I didn't know that, Mom," Courtney said after passing the pasta salad bowl to Doreen.

"Jack came from a farm family that wasn't able to contribute to his education. So he was driven to do anything that meant he wouldn't have to go back to his father's farm."

"But you went to law school, too, right?" Courtney asked.

"I did. When Jack graduated, I told him it was my turn, but he wanted to move to Kansas City where he was offered a job. He wanted me to have babies, not go back to school. I wasn't ready for that and so we split up."

"And we're glad you did," Mr. Robbins said with a broad smile.

Mrs. Robbins smiled. "Someone finish the vegetables," she said, offering the dish to Doreen.

"I'm full. Everything was delicious."

"I'm glad you liked it," Mrs. Robbins said, getting up to clear the table.

"Wait a sec, Honey," Mr. Robbins said. "Let's finish this discussion. Then I think it's the girls' turn to clean up."

Mrs. Robbins sat back down. "Doreen's our guest. I already put her to work in the garden."

Mr. Robbins smiled at Doreen. "I'm sure she won't mind helping, right?"

"I'm happy to help," Doreen said. It would not be like cleaning up after some big function--a job she'd held during high school for a local catering company.

"Tell the girls the rest of the story," Mr. Robbins said to his wife.

"There's not much to tell. I decided to apply to several law schools and chose Missouri because they were the first to accept me. After I graduated, I went to work for the FBI."

"Tell Doreen that story," Courtney said.

"The FBI sends recruiters around to the various law schools and even though I had no intention of applying, my roommate said I should sign up for an interview because it would be good practice."

Mr. Robbins poured himself the remains of the wine. "You'd intended to go back to Topeka and work in the state legislature, right?"

"I did, but I signed up for an interview and they offered me a job. Turns out they were starting to recruit more women in those days and they liked my background. I almost didn't take the job."

"Why?" Doreen asked.

"I was afraid, I guess, afraid of moving out of the Midwest, and I suppose, afraid of not succeeding. My mom talked me into it."

"Your mom knew you needed to spread your wings," Mr. Robbins said. "Again, Courtney and I are glad you did."

"But all this doesn't help Doreen find a job after she graduates," Mrs. Robbins said.

"Oh, I'll be fine," Doreen said, feeling slightly embarrassed to have the discussion focus back on her.

"You've avoided all the traditional female jobs," Mr. Robbins said, "such as nursing, teaching, and social work as well as the newest professions like graphic arts, but you must have an idea of what you enjoy doing?"

"I'm not much of a student, I'm afraid," Doreen said. "I guess I'll get a job in an office someplace and figure it out eventually."

"Of course," Mrs. Robbins said. "You're still young, and living in New York City you're sure to find lots of opportunities."

Mr. Robbins emptied his wine glass. "Courtney on the other hand . . ."

"I think it's time to clean up," Courtney said, standing up and beginning to gather the dirty dishes."

"You girls go ahead," Mrs. Robbins said. "I'm sure you want to get started on your evening of fun."

Doreen got up and started to help clear the table. She had asked Courtney earlier what they were going to do that evening. Courtney's answer had been pretty vague. She hoped it wouldn't be another night watching TV at Mindy's and talking about people she didn't know.

Peter G. Pollak

Delmar, New York: Sunday, August 19

It was raining when Doreen woke up Sunday morning. She was glad because she felt drained. She took a nap after lunch, and when she woke up the rain had stopped. She found Courtney and her father on the screen-in porch on the side of the house.

"Join us," Mr. Robbins said. "We're talking about serious stuff."

Doreen sat down on one of the deck chairs. Courtney had a pained look on her face.

"Courtney tells me she's been asked to give a talk to incoming freshmen to get them to join your pro-Palestinian group."

Doreen nodded, not knowing what to say.

"I pointed out that it's her senior year and therefore time to get serious with her studies."

"I'm getting A's on both of the courses I took this summer, Dad, and I'll help out the group if I want."

"Of course I can't stop you, but tell me what you're going to say to the incoming freshmen?"

Doreen thought Courtney was going to get up and leave, but perhaps because of Doreen's presence, she let out a sigh and answered her father's question. "I'm going to tell them why I joined the group."

"Which is why?" Mr. Robbins asked.

"Everyone pays so much attention to the Jews needing a homeland because of the Holocaust, but what about the Palestinians? You can't take someone else's land just because you need a home."

"I might agree with you, except that the concept of Palestinians being a distinct national group was invented nearly twenty years after Israel's independence. That's not to say there weren't Arabs living in what was called Palestine going back hundreds of years, but there were Jews living there all that time if not longer. Either way, the fact that their ancestors lived there doesn't give the Arabs the right to wage war on Israel."

He paused and looked first at Courtney and then at Doreen. Doreen tried to think of what to say when Mr. Robbins started in again.

"They might have more justification if Israel sought to drive them out of the country," he said, "but that was not the case. The Arabs who were living in what became Israel were victimized not by the Jews, but by Egypt, Syria, and Jordan, who attacked Israel the day it declared independence. That forced the new Israeli government to take defensive measures that cost some people their homes, but the majority left because they were told by their local leaders to get out of the way of the Arab countries' attacking armies.

"The bottom line is that the one point six million Christian and Muslim Arabs who live in Israel today have full rights of citizenship. They are largely integrated into the society and eighty percent of them reject Hamas and its terrorist brethren."

"What about the settlements in Palestinian lands?" Courtney asked, "and what about people who have been evicted from their homes?"

"Both good questions and worthy of being on the agenda for a peaceful settlement, but there isn't going to be any settlement as long as Hamas and Hezbollah continue to wage war against Israel."

"But our group does not advocate violence," Courtney said. "To the contrary, we're asking the world to put pressure on Israel to recognize the rights of the Palestinian people."

Mr. Robbins shook his finger at her. "Except that your group's demand that Palestinian refugees be allowed to return to their homes would result in the end of Israel as a Jewish state."

"How so, Professor Robbins?" Doreen asked.

"It's a matter of demographics and control. The obvious goal of this plank is to open the floodgates which would inundate Israel and eventually result in an Arab majority."

Courtney sighed, but didn't respond.

"Here's another question: Are you girls also putting pressure on the Palestinians to stop attacking Israel with rockets, mortars, and suicide bombers?"

"One question at a time, Dad!" Courtney said.

"Okay, sorry."

"And it's not fair for you to tell me what to believe. I'm twenty years old and have the right to form my own opinions."

"I couldn't agree more. You have the right to your own opinions, but when you become an adult you are obligated to defend your opinions if you want anyone to accept them as justified. I'm not telling you what to think. I'm asking you to justify your opinions with facts and logic."

Courtney stood up. "Always a better answer."

Mr. Robbins reached out for his daughter. "Courtney. Don't go away. Stay here and fight."

"I'm tired of fighting. Doreen and I were planning on driving up to Thatcher Park."

Mr. Robbins nodded. "Okay, girls," he said after a few seconds. "Go have some fun. I'm sorry if I'm being too hard on you."

"It's okay," Courtney mumbled. "Let's go, Doreen."

Peter G. Pollak

Herndon: Tuesday, August 21

Leonard and the rest of the task force team waited anxiously for news from the heavy search effort underway in San Francisco to try to find Sammy Haddad. As of Tuesday morning, none of the leads, which included reported sightings after the University of Maryland photo was shown on the local TV stations, had panned out. Haddad was either adept at remaining invisible or was no longer in the area.

Leonard was getting antsy. "I'm not getting a warm, fuzzy feeling about the direction this investigation is going," he told his team at the morning briefing. "I'm thinking we need to move out to San Francisco and take over management of the search."

"I don't think we can actually do that," Carole Jean Hall, the Justice Dept. rep stated.

Leonard thought about that. "Of course, we'd have to go through channels so as not to ruffle any feathers."

Pavel Zavarov frowned. "Feathers will be ruffled, boss, no matter what you do."

Leonard had to agree. "You're right, but if we accomplish our goal, if we find the bastard, that's a price I'm willing to pay."

"Let me play devil's advocate for a second," Gary Mackey said. "Why go out there? What can we do there that we can't do here?"

Leonard edged his wheelchair around to face the FBI liaison. "Fair question. It's probably only a matter of degree, but it's hard from here to get a sense of how the investigation is going. Perhaps the people out there don't understand how this guy operates. To me, the very fact of his being there means he is confident he can find a carrier, and I imagine there are a dozen or more Jewish organizations in the region he could target.

"Perhaps the reason they're not spotting him is that the conversation that student reported took place more than a month ago," Meir said.

Leonard picked up his tea mug. It was empty. "Which could mean he's preparing someone to deliver a bomb this afternoon or next week."

"Or, it could mean he's struck out and moved to another locale," Meir said.

"I can't believe he couldn't find one person in the entire San Francisco area to do his dirty work," Pavel said.

"Either way," Leonard said, "we know his MO and need to use that to our advantage. To start, we need to make a list of potential targets and warn them."

"Can't we do that from here?" Mackey inquired.

"Of course," Leonard replied. "Maybe not all of us have to go out there. Maybe only a couple of us should go so that we're not burdening the local bureau."

"That sounds better," Meir said. "I'll be glad to go if you want."

"I was thinking about going myself," Leonard said.

The room got quiet. Leonard was conscious of what everyone was probably thinking. "Look. I'm not going to go zipping around San Francisco in my wheelchair in search of this guy. Our job is insight and oversight. We can feed suggestions to the people with feet on the ground and make sure they're doing what needs to be done."

"It's your show," Carole Jean said.

Leonard cringed. He was the head of the task force, but he didn't want to abuse that fact or override the judgment of other task force members. "I'm going to think about it some more, but that's the direction I'm leaning. Please feel free to tell me why you think I should or should not go."

"You said maybe only a couple of us should go," Meir stated. "Who else are you thinking about taking?"

"I guess I haven't thought it through. I've got some work to do. I'll let you know as soon as I make a decision."

Leonard got Alison on the phone later that morning. She'd just returned from a meeting with a potential new client. That knowledge made what Leonard was about to ask even harder. He hadn't told her about San Francisco. Now he told her Haddad had been spotted.

"That's good, Len. You're getting close."

"We are, and for that reason I want to go out there to be closer to the investigation, and I want you to come with me."

She laughed. "No beating around the bush with you!"

Leonard chuckled. "You know how I get when I'm zeroed in on something."

"I do indeed. I've three questions: why do you need to go, why do you need me there, and when do we leave?"

Leonard laughed loud and long. "That's my gal. How about if I brief you on questions one and two when you get there? I'd like to leave first thing in the morning and get you booked for tomorrow as well."

"If that's what you need, Len."

"It is. The guy behind the D.C. bombing may be about to pull off another bombing, and we may be able to prevent it."

"That's good enough for me."

Leonard called Ed Morgan into his office as soon as he hung up with Alison. "I need your help, Ed. Get out your notepad."

Leonard spent the rest of the afternoon on the phone. He talked to Rosa Martinez who wasn't excited about the idea of his going out to San Francisco, but she agreed to go along with it after warning Leonard not to interfere with the FBI's investigation.

"I've no intention of interfering," Leonard assured her. "I want to be part of the team that catches this guy before he is able to launch another attack."

He knew he could not just show up and therefore had to talk to the FBI. Everett Shortell was on vacation in Africa, but he was able to connect with Sally Peterson who had been in on the formation of the task force and who helped him get authorization to insert himself into the search for Sammy Haddad.

The issue that took the longest to resolve and in fact had not been resolved at all when his plane took off from Dulles the next morning was including Alison on the Task Force, thus giving her security clearance to be in on any Bureau meeting that Leonard wished her to be in on--even if he wasn't present.

As a result of the delay in getting her security clearance, when Alison had to wait at their downtown San Francisco hotel while Leonard multitasked--getting himself up to speed with the search operation while simultaneously negotiating with Washington over Alison's status.

"I know how much you want Mrs. Robbins to be on your team," Sally Peterson told him, "but we've gotten into trouble in the past for breaking rules around here and there's tremendous resistance against doing so now."

"I understand," Leonard said. "All I want from you is your word that this will be resolved by tomorrow morning. That gives you until noon Washington time."

"I'll do my best, Professor Robbins."

"I know you will."

"I told you that was not your best idea," Alison told Leonard over a late dinner in the restaurant attached to their San Francisco hotel.

"I'm stubborn on issues related to my family," Leonard said, sipping from the Chardonnay he'd chosen from the wine list.

"I can testify to that."

"By the way you look ravishing," Leonard said.

"Flattery may work with me, but it will not get the FBI to love me."

Leonard chuckled. "I'm going to tell you what's going on, where we are, and what I need from you."

"I'd better stop drinking this wine," Alison said with a smile.

Leonard chuckled. "It's not that complicated. The key takeaway is that I think Haddad is still here in this region. If I'm right that means he's got a target picked out and has either latched onto someone to be the carrier or is still recruiting."

"How does he keep finding these dupes? Doesn't anyone read the paper or watch the news?"

"He might have had to change his approach. Who knows? The point is we've got to find him before he strikes."

"Which we're going to do how?"

"First, the team in Virginia has started creating a list of possible targets. They will warn them about accepting packages that have not been scrutinized and verified."

"What if instead of a student dressed as a delivery person, he uses a real delivery service?"

"We've thought of that and are notifying all of the delivery services in the area to be on the lookout for Haddad or for suspicious-looking packages labeled to a list of addresses that fit his likely target."

"Good."

"That's not a perfect prophylactic, however, because there are so many courier and delivery services--some very small--in the region. We can't be sure he hasn't found one that didn't get the warning."

"What do you want me to do?"

"Interview faculty and students at colleges that don't have active SPJ groups. The FBI says they've checked out schools that do have active groups. It's possible, however, that Haddad is focusing on students at the other dozen schools in the region."

"Like where?"

"City College, Golden Gate University. There are more than a half dozen that need to be visited."

"Where do I start?"

"We have a list of every faculty person in the country who signed the BDS boycott resolution, including some from local schools without SPJ chapters. Start with them."

"Let's hope my clearance goes through soon," Alison said.

"I'm confident it will happen today and I know you'll do a great job."

San Francisco: Friday, August 24

Alison had little to report when she returned to the headquarters of the San Francisco FBI bureau after her second day of interviewing faculty members who had endorsed the boycott Israel movement. She found Leonard sitting in front of a bank of computer monitors reading reports from FBI field agents on one screen while monitoring DEFEAT task force activity on another. A third screen displayed muted local news channels in four quadrants. "Back so soon?" he asked her.

"Faculty leave early on Fridays," she replied.

"So, what did you come up with?"

"The ones I was able to connect with at the private schools reject the idea that their students are involved in politics at any level while those at the public institutions claim to have so little direct contact with students that they have no idea what their students are up to."

"None gave you any leads to students?"

She shook her head. "And to tell the truth, I suspect both are wrong."

Leonard looked puzzled.

"I'll explain," Alison said. "The faculty members at the private schools who claim to know their students so well are probably mistaken and the ones at the public schools probably know more than they like to admit."

"What's their beef?" Leonard asked.

"The public school faculty?"

Leonard nodded.

"They claim they're so overworked they don't have time for student conferences and the like."

"Gotcha. Did you exhaust the list?"

Alison shook her head. "Some weren't there, and some wouldn't talk to me because they had meetings or student visiting hours. I'll start up again on Monday. How are things going here?"

"As good as can be expected. My team has been in touch with a number of Jewish organizations in the San Francisco region: the local federation, synagogues, and schools--even the Contemporary Jewish Museum on Mission Street. All have been warned and given instructions to follow in case someone shows up carrying a package that looks suspicious."

"What about the local law enforcement efforts to spot Haddad?"

"The San Francisco police have his photos and the local agents have put out the word to all their sources, but so far nothing."

"Did you have lunch?"

Leonard pointed to a sandwich wrapper in the trash container next to his desk.

"Do you need to stick around longer or can we head out?" Alison asked, looking at the clock. It was almost three and they had planned to drive up to Napa for the weekend. She was told the traffic north could get heavy on Friday afternoons and wanted to beat the rush.

"We can leave, although I'm nervous about being out of touch."

"The B&B told me they had good phone reception, and the people here will notify you if something turns up."

"Let's hope so. I've tried not to get in their way, but I've gotten vibes that they really didn't want another person looking over their shoulders."

"Understandably so."

"The van's outside?"

"Even police lots have handicap spots these days."

"Let's do it."

Leonard shut down the monitors and logged out. Alison started clearing a path for him to the elevators.

"Professor Robbins."

Someone was calling him from the back of the office. One of the agents was holding his hand in the air. He held a phone to his ear with the other. "You might want to hear this," he called.

"What's up?" he asked after wheeling himself over the agent's desk.

"It's the Jewish Community Center over on California Street. They say someone tried to deliver a package to their gift shop, but they refused to take it. Do you want to talk to them?"

"Absolutely." He wheeled himself back to the desk he'd been assigned to and picked up the phone.

"Hello, this is Leonard Robbins of the White House task force on domestic terrorism. Who am I speaking with?"

"This is Leah Hirschman, deputy director, at the Jewish Community Center of San Francisco. I was calling to report a delivery service attempted to deliver a package this afternoon just before our normal closing time."

Half an hour later, Leonard summarized Leah Hirschman's answers in a message to his team in Virginia. A delivery person dressed in the traditional uniform of the United Parcel Service had tried to deliver a box approximately one and a half feet square with a label from one of the regular vendors of products sold in the Jewish Community Center's gift shop. Because the gift shop had already closed for the weekend, the receptionist on duty informed the carrier that she couldn't accept it. The delivery person did not appear to be upset at her response, but told her he'd try again on Monday.

"It's possible that this was Sammy Haddad, but it doesn't sound like him," Leonard said. Alison was driving them in rush-hour traffic on U.S. 80 heading to Napa wine country where they had a reservation for two nights at a bed and breakfast. "The woman reported the label on the box was one she recognized, and the delivery person was in a brown UPS uniform. She couldn't see if his truck was outside, but he seemed to act like a normal delivery person."

"False alarm?"

"Probably. I suggested to the agent in charge that he send someone over there Monday morning. It's possible Haddad somehow infiltrated the vendor and shipped a bomb rather than Chanukah candles."

"It appears if the instructions your office devised are being followed," Alison said. "That could end up saving lives."

New York City: Same Day

"She had me fooled," Doreen said, sitting on the couch in the Greenes' apartment with Omar, Miguel, and Erik all leaning in close to hear her every word. "But the more I thought about it, the more I realized she has been putting on an act for my benefit."

Erik didn't look convinced. "Explain."

"If she had brushed it off or decided to come back to the city then and there, I might have believed her," Doreen said, "but she kept going on and on about how stubborn her father was and how much it upset her that he didn't respect her decisions. That's when I realized she was faking it. She and her father know I've been made a part of the steering committee for the coming year and he must want me to keep bringing her to our meetings so she can report back to him."

Everyone started speaking at once in reaction to Doreen's statement. Erik raised his hand. "We'll go ahead as planned. Let her talk at the freshman orientation. If she's faking it, let's take advantage of it by using her. Everyone agree?"

No one dissented.

"Then we move to the final exam?" Miguel asked, looking at Omar.

"Indeed," Omar replied.

"So, what is the final exam?" Doreen asked.

"We're going to--" Miguel started to say, but Omar gave him a look that caused him to stop mid-sentence.

"We're not ready to discuss that now," Omar said.

"Why not let me know what you're thinking?" Doreen asked.

"We will at the right time," Omar said.

"It's not that we don't trust you, Doreen," Erik said. "The fact that you're living with her means we can't let her get any sense of what we're planning."

"Do you think I'd tell her?" Doreen demanded.

"No, you're not understanding--"

"Then explain it to me please because I'm getting pissed."

"Doreen, calm yourself," Miguel said. "We trust you, but sometimes people give clues without meaning to. Spies can be very smart about how they get information. She might say something just to get your reaction; it's better for all concerned that you don't know."

Doreen wasn't entirely convinced, but she could see they weren't going to tell her no matter how much she pressed, and if she got really angry they might begin to suspect her motives.

The truth was she was eager for the final exam--whatever that entailed--to take place. She wanted to pay Courtney back for being a spy and for using her to get information that she was relaying to her father. She was just another privileged white girl who thinks her shit doesn't stink.

San Francisco: Monday, August 27

When he checked into FBI headquarters Monday morning, Leonard discovered that J. Robert Snyder, the agent in charge of the San Francisco bureau, had not sent anyone to the Jewish Community Center to make sure the expected delivery was legitimate. Leonard wheeled into his office.

"I agree that this is probably a false alarm," Leonard said after hearing the arguments against sending an agent to the JCC, "but even so, I think you should send someone. There's a remote possibility the guy we're after got a job with the vendor and put a bomb in that box, but equally important, if you send someone you're showing the community the FBI will go the last mile to protect them."

Snyder relented and called in one of his people. Leonard explained the situation and then put in a call to the JCC gift shop, asking to speak to the manager.

"This is Arlene Seigel. How can I help you?"

"Miss Seigel. This is Leonard Robbins at the San Francisco FBI. We have reason to believe a terrorist who targets Jewish organizations is in San Francisco. One of his tricks is to send a phony delivery person just before closing time. That's why we're sending an agent to your building this morning to make sure the package being delivered from your vendor is legitimate."

"What should we do?" Mrs. Seigel asked.

"Keep your doors closed until our agent arrives. Then follow his instructions."

Leonard wanted to watch the proceedings and was able to persuade Mrs. Seigel to launch Skype on a portable computer that she placed on the counter facing the front door.

As instructed, Mrs. Seigel kept the shop closed until the FBI agent arrived and explained the procedure they would employ to assure the package was safe.

At half past nine, a brown UPS delivery truck pulled up in front of the building. The delivery person entered the shop carrying a package that resembled the one described on Friday--approximately fifteen by twelve by eight with the label of a vendor the gift shop purchased items from.

"Good morning," Mrs. Seigel said as the man in a UPS uniform approached the counter. "Where's Henry?"

"He's on vacation this week, Ma'am."

"We've had some threats about packages," Arlene said, "so I'm going to let this gentleman from the FBI inspect the package before I sign for it."

The FBI agent, who had been standing off to the side, came forward with a wand that could detect chemical signatures of the most likely components of a home-made bomb. The UPS delivery person seemed unsettled by this development, but stayed put when the agent told him to do so.

"There seems to be some metal in the package, Ma'am. Is that in line with what you are expecting?"

Mrs. Seigel looked at the printout of her order. "Yes, there should be metal candlestick holders in that order."

"Still, we'll have to be careful when we open the box. Can I see some identification?" the agent asked the UPS man.

Leonard noted the man fumbling for his ID, but discounted the reaction, which would be expected from any normal person in that situation.

The agent wrote down the information and handed the badge back to the UPS carrier. "Everything looks to be in order. You may sign for the package," he told the manager.

The agent took the box outside to the bomb squad's truck where it was x-rayed and found not to contain any items that looked to be a bomb.

The agent then stayed while Mrs. Seigel removed everything from the box, including the candlestick holders, some dishes, and some decorative cloth table settings.

Leonard thanked her for cooperating, and she thanked Leonard and the agent for their concern. It was a false alarm Leonard wrote in his report, but if everyone takes the situation as seriously as the people at the JCC did, another disaster might be avoided.

No further leads had been generated over the weekend. As a result, Alison headed back out to interview college instructors while Leonard remained at FBI headquarters monitoring developments.

Alison phoned Leonard at noon. "I may have something," she stated.

"Shoot," Leonard said.

"I'm at City College in Ingleside. Professor Marian Irwin of the Journalism faculty says a student submitted an article in one of her classes about a SPJ meeting he attended at San Francisco State University. In the article the student quoted someone in the audience having called for 'direct action' in support of the Palestinians. I've got the name of the student, but the administration won't give me his contact information. They want a formal request from the FBI."

"I'll put you through to Agent Carpenter. He'll take it from there."

After getting the contact information for the student who had submitted the article on the SPJ meeting, the FBI interviewed him at his home. Andre Rivera, a first year student at City College, who lived with his parents in the Oceanview neighborhood, was understandably nervous. Even after the agents made it clear that he was not in any trouble personally, his mother tried to postpone the interview until her husband, a bus driver with the County Transportation Authority, got home from work.

Rivera admitted writing up the meeting for his journalism class. His description of the person he quoted calling for direct action matched that of Sammy Haddad. Later, he confirmed Haddad's identity from the photos.

When asked whether he agreed with Haddad's statements, Rivera admitted he found them intriguing, but claimed he had not done anything to follow up on that sentiment and he denied having had any further contact with Haddad.

This second confirmation that Sammy Haddad had been in San Francisco was both unsettling and encouraging. "We need to assume that Haddad has found a carrier and is in the process of preparing that person for the delivery," Leonard told Alison that evening.

"In other words we need to find him, fast?"

"We do."

"How?"

"Keep doing what we're doing. Tomorrow, I'd like you to go over to San Francisco State and search out faculty or students who were at that meeting. It's likely Haddad tried to recruit one or more of them. That could be the break we need."

San Francisco: Tuesday, August 28

Alison spent a frustrating Tuesday morning trying to find faculty or students at San Francisco State University who had been present at the SPJ meeting reported on by Andre Rivera. She struck out until late in the afternoon when she met a student reporter who had covered the event for the *Golden Gate Express*, at the student newspaper's office in the SFSU Humanities Building.

"Thank you for taking a few minutes to meet with me," Alison stated, after convincing the young woman to accompany her to the coffee shop in the Cesar Chavez Student Center.

Sandra Douglass was a pert, dark haired young woman who gave off an air of intense seriousness.

"We have reason to believe that the man who recruited the University of Maryland student who died in the bombing of the offices of a Jewish lobbying organization in Washington this past April is currently in San Francisco," Alison said. "We believe he's looking for someone--probably a woman--to help him bomb another Jewish organization."

"Why do you say he's looking for a woman?" Douglass asked.

"Part of his MO is to convince the woman he wants to help him that he is attracted to her."

"Can I take notes?" Douglass asked.

"Actually, an article by you in your newspaper warning people about this guy could be very helpful."

Douglass took a notepad out of her backpack. "I can't promise that our editor will agree, but I'll pitch the idea to her later today."

Alison opened her briefcase and took out the two photos they had of Haddad. "This is the suspect. Do you recall his being at the May meeting?"

"Definitely. He was one of the first people to speak up during the question period."

"What do you recall that he said?"

"I have my notes right here." She started scrolling through her notepad. "Here it is. He said the group should do more than get signatures on petitions. He said the Israelis have been able to ignore that kind of pressure thus far. The group could have a larger impact by doing something like picketing Jewish organizations. When someone asked him what that would do, he replied it would begin to make the connection between what's happening to the Palestine people and the Jewish lobby in this country."

"Anything else?"

"That's it basically," Douglass said. "After the meeting I tried to catch up with him to ask him some questions, but he refused to give his name to me and told me not to take his picture. He said it could cost him his job. I tried to get him to answer some other questions, but he ignored me and started talking with some other people."

"Do you recall who any of those people were?"

"The ones he was talking to?"

Alison nodded.

"I'd have to think about it, but off-hand, no."

"Please try to remember and call me right away if you do."

"Okay," Douglass said.

"Did you get anything else?"

—

"No--wait. I started to write--oh, now I remember." She scrolled through her notebook again. "Here it is. He also said governments only respond when the price is raised to a high enough level."

"Anything else?"

She shook her head.

"Did you ask him if he was a student?"

"Those meetings are open to anyone, but I always assume only students attend."

"Have you seen or talked to him since?"

She shook her head.

"And, you didn't take his picture?"

"I think I did when he was at the mic. I think I still have it on my cell." She scrolled through her pictures. She handed the cellphone to Alison. "I got two of him. They're from a distance, but that's the guy."

Alison took the phone and studied the two photos. "Great. Can you email these to me?"

"Sure. What's your email?"

Alison gave Douglass the business card that Leonard had Ed Morgan make up for her before he left D.C. "Send it to the address on the card, and if you hear from him or hear about him from someone else, please contact the local FBI bureau immediately. It could save innocent lives."

Alison was told to join Leonard and the agent in charge of the local bureau in the latter's office when she returned to the FBI building.

"Good job confirming Haddad's presence at that event," Leonard said with a smile.

Agent-in-Charge Snyder nodded his agreement.

"But we don't know if he's still here or has moved on," Alison said.

"That's true," Leonard replied, "but we do know he's agitating and looking for someone to do his dirty work. With your permission Agent Snyder, we'll stay in town another week and see if we can pin him down."

"Be my guest," Snyder replied.

New York City: Friday August 31

Doreen sat anxiously through a tedious afternoon steering committee meeting wondering if Erik and the others wanted her to stay afterwards to discuss Courtney. Janice reported on the freshmen recruiting effort and praised Courtney's presentation as well as that of several other members of the group. "It looks like we have about fifty new people we can count on for demonstrations," she said, concluding her report.

"Emily would like to talk to you for a minute," Erik told Doreen as the meeting broke up. That was their signal that she should stay for the second part of the meeting. Maybe she'd finally learn how they planned to prove that Courtney was a spy.

As in the past, Omar didn't arrive until the others had left. His participation in the group seemed to be limited to the Courtney matter.

After sitting and talking about nothing important with Emily for ten minutes, the guys indicated to Doreen that she should return to the living room.

"Have you finalized your plan for Courtney?" she asked.

"We have," Miguel replied. "We want you to invite her to a special steering committee meeting here a week from Sunday."

"Then what?"

"At that meeting we're going to tell her that some people are worried that she's a spy for her father and that we have set up a task for her to prove that she's really one of us."

"What's the task?" Doreen asked.

"You'll find out that night."

Doreen tried to remain calm. "Same reason as before?"

"Exactly," Erik said. "We can't take a chance that she'll discover that we suspect her. If you don't know what we're going to ask her to do until that night, she won't be able to figure it out either."

Doreen had no choice but to accept their judgment. She had to admit there was some logic to their thinking. During the previous week, Courtney had asked her if anything was wrong.

"Why do you ask?" Doreen had answered.

"It seems like you haven't been yourself since we returned from Albany."

"I guess it's because it's the start of our senior year," Doreen said, making up a lie. "We won't be students next year at this time. We'll have to have found real jobs and join the nine to five crowd commuting to and from work."

"I know what you mean," Courtney said. "It scares me, too."

Doreen had smiled and tried to be more cheerful the rest of the week while inside she was alternately searching for signs of Courtney's betrayal and feeling anxious about what the guys had planned.

San Francisco: Same Day

It was the start of Leonard's second week in San Francisco and, despite evidence that Sammy Haddad had arrived there not long after the Washington bombing, neither his team nor the FBI had any firm leads as to his current whereabouts. Leonard didn't think he'd moved to some other city. Why did he choose San Francisco in the first place? Some in the FBI suggested it was the random choice of a solo terrorist, but Leonard disagreed. San Francisco was chosen intentionally, which meant in all likelihood he was still there, working to bring off another bombing.

Alison, meanwhile, was trying to track down and interview students at San Francisco State University who had attended the SPJ meeting where Haddad had been spotted. She reported talking to a pair of female roommates who had met with Haddad after the event. They claimed they resisted his suggestion that they do something with him separate from the group. "I told him I'd only go along with actions the group decides to do," Lu Mu-yen, one of the students, told Alison. Her roommate in a separate interview said she took the same position. Neither had heard from him after that.

Friday morning over breakfast, Alison told Leonard that her interview list was down to half a dozen people. He sent her off to find them, encouraging her to remain positive. Maybe one of them would provide the key piece to the puzzle they needed to find where Haddad was hiding out.

Fridays made Leonard nervous. It seemed that terrorists chose Friday afternoons to deliver their bombs because people in Jewish organizations were focused on closing to get home to celebrate the Sabbath and they might not pay careful attention to a delivery person who showed up with an unexpected package.

Therefore, as he was concluding a conversation with Meir Epstein back in Virginia, he was not totally shocked when one of the agents in the San Francisco FBI's bureau did the equivalent of pulling the chain on a fire alarm. A quick glance at his watch caused his stomach to lurch. "Pick up your phones," someone called out.

"He'll kill me if he finds me," Leonard heard a woman say when he was patched into the conversation.

"Where are you?" the agent asked.

"I can't stay here. I have to keep moving."

"Where are you right now?"

"I'm in the Y. He took my cell phone."

"Which Y?" Silence. "Miss. Where are you?"

"He's outside. You've got to help--"

A horrendous sound echoed through the phone--a sound no one wants to hear, but everyone comprehends immediately. As pandemonium broke loose, Leonard did his best to stay out of the way, while trying to learn what had just taken place. It seemed like forever, but it was probably just a couple of minutes before the location of whatever had occurred was identified: Steuart Street off The Embarcadero near Pier 14 and Rincon Plaza.

"The Jewish Federation is on that street," someone called out.

Unfortunately, the phone connection to the caller was broken without their having learned her name or where she was calling from.

"At least she didn't take it into the Federation," Leonard overheard the agent who had been on the phone with the woman tell Agent-in-Charge Snyder.

"Say that again," Leonard requested, wheeling toward the two. "Take what?"

"She said she put a package she was supposed to deliver to the Federation in a trash receptacle because she thought it might contain a bomb," the agent stated.

After posting a quick note on the DEFEAT network, Leonard sat at his desk his anxiety level rising as he waited for details. Again, it seemed like forever, but finally reports started coming in from the San Francisco Police Department--the first agency to arrive on the scene.

They reported an explosion had occurred outside a small restaurant located next to the building that housed the Jewish Federation of San Francisco, causing unknown deaths and injuries as well as considerable damage in the area. Among the casualties were people who had been sitting at tables both outside and inside the restaurant and people who had been walking on the street and driving past that location. A dozen cars parked on Steuart near the restaurant were demolished or severely damaged.

One of the first FBI agents to reach the scene, having been briefed while he sped to Steuart Street, entered the Embarcadero YMCA and found a young woman sitting on the floor in the lobby holding on to her knees with both arms, tears pouring down her face. The agent quickly determined that she was the person who had called the bureau and took her into custody. Agent-in-Charge Snyder instructed him to bring her to FBI headquarters while other agents helped the rescue crews and started polling people in the area for clues to what had happened and who might have been involved.

"How long will it take to get her back here?" Leonard called out when he heard the woman had been placed in an FBI van.

"Twenty minutes," someone replied.

"A half hour is more like it," someone else said.

That's too long. Leonard wheeled into Agent Snyder's office where he and his top lieutenants were listening to reports come in and waiting for visual reports from the local TV news teams.

"I need to talk to her now," Leonard said when he got Snyder's attention.

Snyder looked at him as if he had forgotten who he was. "She'll be here in a few minutes."

"Meanwhile, the bomb-maker is getting away. We need to know what kind of vehicle he was driving and where he might be going."

Snyder frowned. He didn't look happy.

"I can patch him through," one of the lieutenants said quietly.

Snyder shrugged his shoulders. "Okay, I guess it won't hurt."

Seconds later the agent in the back seat of the van bringing the woman caller to FBI headquarters told Leonard he was handing her his phone.

"Miss. My name is Leonard Robbins. I've with the President's Task Force on Domestic Terrorism. We need to know what kind of vehicle the man who gave you the bomb is driving."

All he heard was sobs.

"Miss, this is terribly important. People died this morning, and he'll do it again unless we catch him today. What kind of car was he driving?"

"It's a van," Leonard heard in between her attempts to catch her breath.

"What kind? What color?"

"White."

"Was there any lettering on the sides or back?"

"Yes. It said . . . let me think . . . it said 'delivery service' . . . 'overnight delivery service.'"

"Do you know the license plate number?"

"No."

"Who was in the van?"

"George."

"Anyone else?"

"No."

"Describe George. What does he look like? What is he wearing?"

"Brown skin. Nice looking."

"And his clothes?"

"Black slacks and a black t-shirt."

"Okay. You did good." He put his hand over the phone. "Agent Snyder, can you put out an APB on a white van with the words 'overnight delivery service' on the sides."

Snyder nodded and one of his lieutenants left the room. "He's probably abandoned it by now."

"Maybe not," Leonard said. "He needs to be nearby to get the signal that someone had signed for the package so he can detonate the bomb, so he might have seen her leave the building and drop the package in the trash container."

"So you think he set off the bomb at that point?"

"Undoubtedly, but consider this scenario. He sees her deposit the package in the trash instead of deliver it to the Federation. He detonates the bomb, but he doesn't know if she survived the blast or not."

"I suppose it could have gone down that way," Snyder said. "What's your point?"

"He knows she can testify against him. He has to eliminate her."

"But we found her alive and unharmed."

"Which means he was probably close by when the first police cars arrived. He goes back to his van, but the street is blocked. Cop cars and ambulances are arriving from all directions. Traffic is going nowhere. That means he couldn't have gotten very far. We still have a chance to get him before he escapes."

Alison could tell something major had occurred. She had tried without success to reach Leonard after having spent a mostly fruitless day searching for students who had attended the SPJ forum at San Francisco State University. Then, just when she was about to give up, the final interview of the day yielded a breakthrough. She wanted to update Leonard right away. Instead she was told to hurry back to the office.

The interview that had generated the lead had been with a SFSU student by the name of Daniel Cox. Cox, who had been picked out of a photo of the event by a classmate, agreed to meet Alison at the local pizzeria where he worked shortly before his afternoon shift.

He recognized Haddad from the University of Maryland photo ID and confessed to having been mildly interested in what he had said in the question and answer portion of the May SPJ forum. He stated he left the event, however, without making contact.

When she asked if he had seen Haddad after that event, Cox's answer surprised Alison.

"I did see him a couple of weeks later when he came in here to eat," Cox stated.

"Did he recognize you?"

"Not at first. I was in the back when he placed his order. I thought it was him, so I took his order out to him."

"Did you say anything?"

—

Cox nodded. "We had a short conversation."

"Tell me how it went word for word as close as you can remember," Alison requested.

"I'll try. I started by saying something like 'How's it going?' When I stood there instead of leaving after having placed his order on the table, he looked up at me and said, 'Do I know you?' I said, 'No, but I recognize you from the SPJ forum at State.' Then I said something like 'You were saying we have to do more than just circulate petitions, right?' He nodded and asked me if I agreed with him. I said I did, and then he asked me if I was interested in being part of a group planning a direct action. I told him it depended on what he had in mind. He asked me for my phone and email and said he'd contact me."

"And did he contact you?"

"No," Cox replied. "I never heard from him or saw him again."

"Was there anything else you remember that might help us find him?"

"When he left I saw him walk across the street and go into an apartment building."

"Across the street here?" Alison asked.

"Do you want me to point it out to you?"

Minutes later, with photos and the address recorded on her tablet, Alison phoned Leonard at FBI headquarters only to be told he was unavailable but had left a message that she should return to the office ASAP.

Peter G. Pollak

San Francisco: The Same Day

When they brought in the woman caller, Leonard asked to be allowed into the observation room to watch the interview. Agent-in-Charge Snyder nodded his approval. He announced he was going to take the lead, but brought a female agent into the room with him.

"Loren, that's your name, right?" Snyder began.

She nodded.

"Loren what?"

"Hutchison."

"Okay, Loren. I know you've suffered from a terrible shock, but we need to ask you some questions."

The young woman looked to be around twenty or twenty-one. She was tall--maybe 5'8" or 5'9," had stringy blond hair and large eyes; her face was blotchy from crying. She was wearing striped slacks that seemed to belong to some kind of uniform and a tan sleeveless top. She didn't have a pocketbook or any identification on her when they picked her up.

"Tell us what you know about what happened today on Steuart Street."

"He told me to deliver the package to those people--the ones who are oppressing the Palestinians. I didn't believe him when he said it wasn't real."

"What wasn't real?"

The woman wiped her eyes. "What he put in the package?"

"What did it look like? Describe it for us."

"Two grey bags that he handled like they were fine china and lots of wires. I just knew it wasn't a fake."

"Why? What made you not believe him?"

"He hated them. I saw it in his eyes."

"Who did he hate?"

"Jews--all of them--not just those in Israel. One time he said they all deserved to die."

"Did he say why?"

She nodded. "It was because of what they had done to the Palestinians. He said they pushed them out of the land they had lived in for thousands of years."

"Did he say he was Palestinian? Did he tell you about his family?"

She shook her head.

The female agent showed her Sammy Haddad's photos. "Is this the man who gave you the bomb?"

She nodded. "That's George."

"You told the agent on the phone you feared he would kill you," Agent Snyder said. "Was he waiting for you someplace?"

"When he dropped me off, he said he was going to drive around the block and pick me up after I'd delivered the package."

"And he was driving a white van--"

"Yes."

"--with 'overnight delivery service' on both sides?"

She nodded.

"You don't happen to remember the license plate number?"

She shook her head.

"Where did you meet him?"

"At the student union."

"Where? At a college?"

"City."

"City College?"

———

She nodded her head.

"Do you know where he lives?"

"He never said."

"You met him at City College. How?"

"He sat down at my table and said he'd seen me at the forum at State."

"San Francisco State?"

The woman nodded. "I went to the forum. They were explaining about what's been happening to the Palestinians, how they had to live in refugee camps, and everything."

"So he said he saw you there?" the female agent asked.

She nodded.

"Then what?"

"He asked me what I thought."

When she arrived at FBI headquarters, Alison was told Leonard was in the observation room. "What's going on?" she asked the person in reception.

"You haven't heard?"

"Heard what?"

"There's been an explosion. They're interviewing some woman who claims she was given a bomb to leave at the Jewish Federation offices."

"The Jewish Federation--did she . . .?"

"No, but it went off nearby. At least five people are dead."

"Damn!"

The woman nodded. "Your husband said to join him in the observation room. I'll take you there."

When she entered the room, Alison gave Leonard a squeeze on the shoulder, and then sat down in an empty chair in the back of the room.

"I said it upset me to hear about things like that," the woman was saying. "It wasn't right for someone to push people out of their homes just because they wanted their land."

"Go on," the female interviewer said.

"He said he agreed with me and was I willing to do something to help the Palestinians. I said 'Yes'."

"Did he tell you his name?"

"He said it was George."

"No last name?"

She shook her head.

"Then what happened?"

"He said he'd come up with something the two of us could do together."

"I said I hoped it could wait until after exams, and he said it could. He gave me some things to read and said we should meet once a week."

"And did you?"

"Yes, except for the week I went home to visit my mom. Can I use the bathroom?"

While the woman was taken to the restroom, Agent Snyder came into the observation room.

"What do you think?" he asked Leonard.

"Same MO. He finds a woman who has a soft heart, and I don't apologize for saying it, a soft head. It's a miracle this woman didn't do what he told her."

"So how do we find him?" Snyder asked. "She doesn't seem to know where he was living."

"Push on her whether anyone else was involved. Did he mention any names or places? How did he travel to their meetings? Did they always meet near the college?"

Alison spoke up. "I may know where he knew people or might even having been living."

Leonard wheeled around. "Why didn't you say so?"

"I tried--"

"Never mind. What's the address?"

Alison handed him her tablet open to the screen showing the building with the street address of the building underneath.

"A student saw him go into that building."

"When?" Agent Snyder asked.

"He couldn't remember the exact date, but he said it was at least a month ago."

"Okay, we'll send some people over there," Snyder said, handing the tablet to one of the agents in the room. "You know the protocol."

"Be careful, he's dangerous" Leonard called out to the agent as he left the room.

"No shit," Snyder said as he followed his agent.

"Great work, Honey," Leonard said to Alison.

"Thanks. Fill me in on what happened today."

Leonard told Alison what he knew until the interview with Loren Hutchison resumed. Minutes later the questioning was interrupted once again when Hutchison's father arrived with a lawyer and demanded to see his daughter.

Leonard took the opportunity to excuse himself. Alison guessed he was heading to the men's room to empty his catheter bag. When he came out, he motioned to Alison to follow him back to his desk. "Can you fill in the team in Virginia?"

Alison sat in Leonard's desk chair and started to type a preliminary report that the DEFEAT team could access. She knew she was providing them third-hand information, and as a result stuck to the highlights. After writing what she knew, Alison paused to decide whether she had left anything important out, when a woman called out across the office.

"Attention," came a voice over the speakers in the observation room. "A white van with 'overnight delivery service' lettering on the sides has been spotted heading west on Mission."

San Francisco: The Same Day

Alison joined Leonard and other agents in a scramble to the desk of the agent who was monitoring the San Francisco police radio band. "Quiet, everyone," she yelled in response to people bombarding her with questions as she turned up the speaker's volume.

"This is Car 11. I am in pursuit of suspect in white Ford Econoline with 'overnight delivery service' on the sides, license plate seven, N, as in Nancy, eight, eight, zero, four, nine. Suspect is traveling west on Mission approaching the intersection of Mission and Freemont. Attention! Suspect is crossing into the incoming lane. He is proceeding through the intersection with the light against him. Suspect is back in proper lane proceeding west on Mission."

For a few seconds they listened to sirens and to officers in other patrol cars reporting in.

"Is that him? The guy you're after?" Alison asked Leonard.

Leonard shrugged. "Not sure. Let's hope so."

"This is Car 38. We are traveling east on Mission. Please advise."

Car 38 was interrupted. "This is Car 11. Suspect is turning onto First Street, heading south in the direction of the Bay Bridge entrance ramp."

"This is Car 61. I'm on Folsom heading east toward First. Please advise."

"Car 61, proceed to First Street. Block the intersection at First and Folsom. Be on the lookout for a white van license plate seven, N as in Nancy, eight, eight, zero, four, nine. Suspect may be armed."

"Roger that."

"Car 49 here. I'm on I-80 heading east. Please instruct."

"Car 49, set up a roadblock at Harrison and First to prevent suspect from entering I-80. Suspect is driving a white van license plate seven, N as in Nancy, eight, eight, zero, four, nine."

"This is Car 73. I'm right behind 49."

"Car 73, same instructions. Block access to I-80. Car 61, report in."

"Can someone get an overhead?" Leonard asked looking around at the other agents.

"The police helicopter should be in the air," one of the agents said running over to her desk.

"They're probably on the way," another agent told Leonard.

"Good," he replied. "You okay?" he asked Alison who was standing behind him.

"Fine," she said, although she realized she was holding her breath.

"This is Car 61. A white van is coming in our direction. Suspect is weaving from lane to lane."

"Car 61, try to intercept."

"Roger."

Alison heard what she thought might be gunfire.

"This is Car 61. We're taking fire from suspect . . . We have an officer down. I repeat officer down at the corner of Folsom and First."

"We need a medical unit ASAP. We have an officer down at intersection of Folsom and First. Units near South of Market district please respond."

"Medical unit three here. Report officer condition."

"Officer hit in upper torso. Bleeding heavily."

———

"Where's the suspect?" someone at headquarters asked.

"Got him," someone called out, turning a computer monitor around so that everyone who had gathered near the police radio could see.

The screen showed a distant image of San Francisco's South of Market neighborhood. It took a few seconds before the camera operating zeroed in on the van. It was trying to get by a line of cars on the one-way street. It appeared to be only seconds away from the I-80 ramp.

"Where's the blockade?" one of the agents asked. "If he gets onto I-80, this could be another O.J. Simpson."

"Why?" Alison asked.

"With all the traffic on the freeway at this time of day it is very difficult to stop a driver with a weapon who doesn't want to stop without endangering other drivers."

Alison saw the van veer back into the left lane causing a sedan to pull to the right into another car. The van clipped the sedan as it edged by.

Someone turned up the sound of the police helicopter. "This is Captain Little. All units report in."

"Car 11 here. We're in pursuit behind the van on First."

Alison saw two police cars right behind the van.

"Car 38 here. I'm behind 11."

"Car 70 reporting in. I'm at First and Harrison."

"Do not allow the suspect to enter I-80."

"Roger that."

"Car 49 here. We're exiting I-80 onto Fremont."

"Block I-80 ramp. Suspect is armed. Use caution."

"Car 73. I'm behind Car 49."

"This is Car 49. He sees me. He's stopping."

"All units. There are people on the streets. Be careful not to engage civilians."

The image from the police helicopter showed the white van had stopped in the middle of First Street about twenty-five or thirty yards from two police cars that were now blocking the I-80 ramp. Another car was preventing the van from turning onto Harrison.

The two cars that had been pursuing the suspect pulled to the side to deny him a retreat route, one blocked a possible escape route through the gas station on the southwest side of the street, the other car turned sideways stopping traffic on First. The suspect was now trapped between the pursuers and the blockade set up in front of the Expressway ramp.

"What's he going to do now?" someone in the FBI office asked.

For the moment, no one moved. The helicopter must have swerved because for a moment they lost track of the action on the street, then zoomed back overhead.

They heard the amplified voice from someone in the helicopter. "That's Captain Little," an agent in the office said.

"Driver in the white Ford Econoline license plate seven, N, eight, eight, zero, four nine. This is Captain Little of the San Francisco Police Department. Exit the van with your hands in the air, then get on the ground face down with your hands in plain sight."

"Look out," someone yelled. The sound of a rifle shot echoed through the various radios. Visual contact of the action on the street was broken as the helicopter swerved.

"He shot at the copter."

"Cap, are you hit?"

"Negative. Give us a second."

The copter camera recaptured the scene on the ground, but from a greater distance. Someone at ground level had activated a camera. Alison could see the barrel of a rifle out of the driver's side window.

Windows of the police cars in front of the van exploded as the sound of the rifle being fired and the glass being broken startled the people in the Bureau office.

"Anyone hurt?"

Another window exploded, this time, the windshield of the car blocking the highway ramp.

"Captain Little here. All units, return fire on my mark. Ready. One. Two. Three. Fire."

Alison saw a fusillade of bullets strike the van before she heard the sound. The driver returned fire.

"Officer down," someone yelled.

"Medic. We need a medic here."

"Where are you?"

"Medical unit five is on its way. Report condition and location."

"This is Officer Woodson. I think I can get a line on him from the north side of the street."

"Superficial wound to left shoulder."

"How long will it take for you to get in position?"

"A minute or two."

"Medical unit five here. We're on our way."

"Woodson, let me know when you're in position."

Alison looked for some sign of the suspect. From the helicopter camera she could see the SFPD officers using their cars as shields. Sirens continued to wail in the background. A medical unit was trying to advance down Harrison toward First.

She heard the sound of another rifle round. The windshield of the car blocking the gas station blew out.

"He's on the passenger side."

"Woodson. Where are you?"

"I'm in position. Where is he?"

"He's moved to the passenger side."

Alison was surprised to see the van move. It seemed like he was trying to turn around.

"This is Woodson. I don't see him."

"All units. Fire on my mark. One. Two. Three. Fire."

The van rocked at the impact.

"Can anyone see the driver?"

"Negative, Captain."

"Likewise."

The van sat still. A minute went by.

This time there was no response from the van.

"All units. One. Two. Three. Fire."

From the street level camera, Alison saw the van's windshield disappear in a puff of shattered glass. She waited for a response, but there was none.

"Should we go in, Cap?"

"Negative."

"Woodson, can you see him?"

"Negative, Cap."

"Driver of white van. Come out with your hands--"

An eardrum damaging sound followed by a fraction of a second the image of the van disappearing as if by magic.

In the millisecond before the image from both the helicopter and street cameras went blank, a white something coming towards her caused Alison to flinch as if that something would erupt through the monitor.

People later reported that the energy source of that image lifted cars off the ground more than fifty yards away in every direction. Vehicles close to the van flipped over as if they were bowling pins. The police vehicles at either end of the block bucked like wild horses encountering a snake and were driven backwards, pining three San Francisco police officers underneath their vehicles.

Alison was not the only one left in a state of shock as if she'd been there in person. The unexpectedness of that instant of visual assault affected everyone who had been watching at the San Francisco FBI bureau, resulting at first in complete silence before a pandemonium of voices rang out, each person coming to grips with what they'd just seen.

Although it would be weeks before the total picture of the physical damage and injuries that resulted from the force that caused that van to disappear was tallied, one fact was certain. The van and its driver were no more.

Peter G. Pollak

San Francisco: Sunday September 2

"Why do you need to be there this early?" Alison asked Leonard as she drove him to FBI headquarters.

He had not allowed her to persuade him to leave Friday night until after midnight, nor was she able to dissuade him from getting up at six a.m. both Saturday and Sunday to drive him back to the FBI's Golden Gate Avenue offices.

"It's my job to find evidence linking Haddad to a larger organization. The FBI won't be as tuned into that priority as I am and could overlook something that wraps up this entire case."

On Saturday, they learned that the agents who had been assigned to investigate the building Haddad had been seen entering had been diverted by the van chase and had never completed their assignment. Leonard reminded Agent Snyder that important evidence might be found there and as a result, another team was sent to that location.

The agents had not been able to track down the building owner until Saturday evening at which time, according to their interview notes, they learned that he'd seen a man who matched Haddad's photos around the building and when he confronted him, he'd been told he was staying with his cousin for a few days.

It turned out the person whose apartment Haddad told the landlord he was staying with denied anyone was staying with him or that he was related to Haddad. The FBI began checking out everyone else in the building and learned that a different tenant had moved out of the building on Thursday leaving no forwarding information. The FBI had obtained some partial fingerprints that thus far had not come up with any matches.

Leonard set up a Sunday morning video conference call with his team in Virginia to review the status of the investigation.

"It's almost certain," he began when he had everyone on the call, most of them from their homes, "that the man we know as Sammy Haddad was the driver of that van. The FBI is trying to confirm that now. We may have some fingerprints from an apartment where he lived for a while, but if they don't match anyone on their database, we're out of luck until we find out his real name or find something else with his fingerprints on them. Our priority here is to find places where he was staying and where he assembled the bombs. Larry, I need you and Ekaterina to search for any indication that he communicated his intentions to anyone else, whether by phone, email, social media, or what have you.

"Second in importance to nailing down the identity of the van driver is finding proof that he wasn't acting on his own."

"Does someone think he was acting alone?" Meir Epstein asked.

"That's the impression I've gotten from some of the agents here," Leonard said.

"What about Chicago?" Meir asked. "I don't see how he could have been involved in that bombing as well as the one in San Francisco."

"You're absolutely right," Leonard replied, "but we need hard evidence, including proof that he was communicating with others or evidence that points to someone other than Haddad being behind Chicago. At the moment, we have neither."

"So how do we proceed, boss?" Pavel Zavarov asked.

"I need each of you to work your channels. The media has already started circulating Haddad's photo. If he has family in the United States, we should be hearing from them any minute now."

Leonard was correct. Shortly after one San Francisco time, Gary Mackey called to inform him that the FBI office in Richmond, Virginia had received a call from a man claiming to be the adoptive father of the man known to them as Sammy Haddad.

"It turns out his real name was Sadegh Moradi," Mackey said. "Agents from the Richmond Bureau are on their way to interview the adoptive parents. We'll have a tape of that interview in a couple of hours assuming they consent to being recorded."

Leonard thanked Mackey and told him to let him know when he could view the interview tape or hear the report from the agents. "Now that we have his real name, perhaps we can discover how he got involved in this business. We also need proof that he wasn't acting alone," he texted his team.

While waiting for more details from Richmond, Leonard resumed talking to individual team members. He had just started talking to his IT expert Larry Burnside when word came in about Haddad's real name. After taking a minute to fill up his coffee mug and grab a sandwich off the tray in the break room, he called Burnside back.

"Larry. Talk to me about the status of our search capabilities. If Professor Chaudry's program is as good as he says it is, shouldn't we be able to find some communication from Sadegh Moradi concerning Friday's event?"

"I'm running the routine as we speak," Burnside said, "but it could take a while to go through the millions of lines of social media traffic. I'll let you know the second I get something."

"Thanks. Can you patch me over to Ekaterina? She's next on my list."

It took a couple of minutes, but he finally got through to the Russian data expert.

"How's your search for Russian hackers coming?" he asked.

"I narrowed search down to two groups, but I have to be careful not to slip up. If they know it's me, they will send someone to Washington to plant a bomb in my car."

"Are you serious?" Leonard asked.

"You don't know these people."

"I hear you, but we don't have a lot of time. If Professor Chaudry's search routine doesn't come up with something, it's going to be hard to prove this guy was working with others, and if we can't prove that, we are going to have a hard time finding the rest of the organization."

"I understand."

"Can you think of some other way this guy might have been communicating with the rest of his organization?"

"Other than what?"

"Other than the telephone, email, or social media."

"Of course."

"Of course?"

"Yes."

"Well, how then?"

"VDN."

"Which stands for?"

"Virtual data network."

Half an hour later, Leonard corralled Alison away from her assignment monitoring the aftermath of the San Francisco explosion.

"She's killing me," he said when she sat down at his desk, a worried look on her face.

"Who?"

"Ekaterina."

"What'd she do now?"

When he explained that the Russian NSA employee had neglected to bring up the possibility that Sadegh Moradi was communicating with his colleagues using a virtual data network, all Alison could do was offer her sympathy. "That's a typical programmer's personality. They are very literal and don't volunteer information."

Leonard sighed and started to pull out his hair when he remembered how little he had left. "There are days when I want to send her back to NSA, but Pavel keeps telling me she's good."

"Is there something going on between them?"

"It's possible. They're the only two smokers on the team. Half the time you're looking for them, they're outside taking a break."

"The next time you need her to do something, have Pavel ask her."

"I didn't realize running a team like this required a degree in preschool education!"

Alison laughed and gave his neck a squeeze. "Stay calm. It'll all work out."

Just as Leonard and Alison were ready to leave for the day, Agent Snyder, who had not come into the office until noon, buzzed for Leonard to come into his office.

"How much longer do you think you'll be hanging out here?" he inquired.

"I've been thinking about that. We'll probably head back tomorrow night if nothing new comes up. I'm counting on you to keep us apprised as your investigation goes forward."

"Next time, can you please find your guy before he starts building bombs?" Snyder asked, winking to show he was joking.

Leonard held up his right hand, his thumb a fraction of an inch away from his first finger. "We were this close."

"Close only counts in bocce," Snyder said.

On the way back to their hotel, Leonard announced that it was time for them to head home. "I don't think there's much more we can do here, and I'd like to get back to riding herd on my team. What about you? Do you want to come to D.C.?"

"Not particularly," Alison replied. "I've got clients I need to touch base with and we've neglected Courtney these past two weeks. She's been good about leaving messages, but I haven't talked to her for more than five minutes since she went back to the city."

"She's probably still pissed at me," Leonard said. "I seem to have a knack of saying the wrong thing to her."

"And this time you did it in front of her friend!"

Leonard sighed. He opened the water bottle that he'd brought from the FBI office and took a swallow. "Tell her I'm sorry."

"You should tell her yourself, Len."

"You're right. I've got to do it. Do you think it's too late to try her tonight?"

"It's before midnight in New York. She's probably awake. Let's call her as soon as we get to the hotel."

New York City: Same Day

"You go. I've got studying to do for tomorrow," Courtney said when Doreen reminded her that the SPJ steering committee asked her to come to that evening's special meeting.

"They really want you there," Doreen said, looking vaguely upset.

"I just don't feel like it, and it'll probably go late. I've got studying to do and my parents expect me to phone them before eleven."

"The meeting will be long over by then," Doreen said.

Courtney went back to her room. The matter was settled as far as she was concerned, but Doreen followed her.

"Courtney, please!"

Courtney turned. "I said I'm not going."

Doreen stamped her foot on the floor. "They're going to blame me for not bringing you."

"Do you want me to write you a note?" Courtney asked.

"What's that supposed to mean?"

"So they won't blame you."

Doreen's mouth fell open. "Courtney, I'm on the steering committee now. They expect me to get things done when I've been assigned them."

"No, and that's final." Courtney shut her room door harder than she intended. She stood there for a moment, expecting Doreen to start banging on it, but she heard her roommate walk away, swearing under her breath. A few minutes later she heard the door to their apartment slam shut.

"Your turn," Alison said, handing the phone over to Leonard.

Leonard took the phone. "Hi, Court. Things going well?"

"Good, Daddy. How was your vacation?"

"You heard about went on out here?"

"I could hardly miss it. It's all over the news."

"Sorry, I was trying to say our trip was mainly for work. The vacation part amounted to a weekend in wine country."

"Glad you got to do that at least. Is it true that the guy who built the bomb blew himself up?"

"We're waiting for forensics to confirm."

"Is your job over then?"

"Unfortunately, no. I'm convinced there are other members of his organization in this country searching for people they can convince to carry bombs into Jewish organizations."

"That's terrible."

"It is, but anyway, I'm heading back to D.C. while your mom gets to go back to her normal daily life."

"That's good, although I doubt few people would consider anything about your lives as normal."

"That's probably true. So, I wanted to apologize again for the way our conversation ended back in Delmar."

"That's okay, Dad. I thought about what you said, and I understand that it's because you care about me."

"Of course, I do. Along with your Mom, you're the most important person in my life. I just want you to avoid the nasty repercussions that can happen if you hang out with the wrong people."

"But you'll have to take my judgment that the people in SPJ are not wackos."

"I hope not."

"They're not. They just happen to care about the Palestinian people."

"I just wish they would be as critical of Hamas as they are of Israel."

"Okay, Dad. Talk to you soon."

"Take care, C."

When she heard the apartment door open a few hours later, Courtney was sitting at their kitchen table reading her psychology assignment. Doreen gave her a sheepish look as she came into the kitchen. "They said it was okay."

"Well, I'm glad because I really didn't want to go tonight. Some other night I'm sure it'll be fine. It doesn't mean I don't support the group."

"I understand. Can you come next Sunday . . . at seven thirty?"

Courtney thought about it for a minute. "Sure."

Peter G. Pollak

New York City: Same Day

Erik Greene tried to keep his emotions from running riot. For months he'd done everything he'd been asked to do and, as his reward, Omar Mejbari had just informed him that the leaders of the American branch of Popular Front for the Liberation of Palestine wanted him to participate in a meeting that night to decide how to handle Courtney Robbins. Telling Emily he'd be back later without providing any explanation--something he knew he'd hear about the next day, he followed Mejbari out to his Opel van.

"How do you like it?" Mejbari asked after Erik buckled himself in.

"Nice," Erik said, although he could not see what was so nice about an eight-year old beat up van.

"I got it cheap."

Erik smiled to show his appreciation. "Smart."

"When I came to this country, friends told me the best car to buy was a used delivery van."

"Why's that?"

"They said they are always well taken care of and cost little to buy. Plus cops don't give parking tickets to vans."

This one belched exhaust and sported tiny holes in the windshield, but none of that mattered as Erik tried to control his excitement about being included in deciding Courtney's final exam.

Before that night's steering committee meeting, Omar told him to table discussion of how to handle

Courtney Robbins. Doreen had tried to pin him down after the meeting. "Stop asking me," he told her. "You'll know when Courtney knows."

Mejbari had turned up Third Avenue. "Where are we going?" Erik asked.

Mejbari didn't answer. When he turned onto East 36th Street, Erik guessed they were going to someplace in Queens or perhaps Long Island. He knew better than to ask a second time.

Mejbari took the entrance to the Queens Midtown Tunnel and continued on the Long Island Expressway, driving somewhat slower than most drivers, although Erik wasn't sure if that was intentional or because the van couldn't go much over sixty.

Erik tried to pay attention as Mejbari exited the Expressway, merged onto the Brooklyn/Queens Expressway, and then exited right away. He was lost, but he supposed it didn't matter. Fifteen minutes later, Mejbari pulled into a parking space on the street in a neighborhood of well-kept town houses and apartment buildings.

"Out," Omar instructed.

He led Erik on foot for several blocks before stopping in front of a four-story apartment building. He pushed the buzzer of one of the apartments.

Erik was surprised when a person he recognized answered the door. It was Tarab Abdul Hadi's bodyguard. He and Mejbari exchanged greetings, but the man ignored Erik's presence, talking to Mejbari in a foreign language as he led them to the elevator.

The apartment was on the fourth floor. Erik was doubly surprised when he saw who was in the apartment. The Palestinian woman who called herself Tarab Abdul Hadi stood up to greet him.

––––

"Thank you for coming," she said in her thick accent. "I know it's late, but this is important."

"Thank you for asking me," he replied.

"Would you like some coffee?"

Erik noticed the aroma of strong coffee. He nodded.

Omar must have agreed to some other beverage because the bodyguard poured a reddish brown liquid into two small glasses and handed him one. The men clinked the glasses. Mejbari took a sip and offered appreciative-sounding noises.

After an older woman dressed in black with a shawl over her head brought him his coffee, Abdul Hadi motioned for Erik to sit in the sole easy chair in the living room. She and her bodyguard sat on the couch, while Omar pulled a wooden chair into the living room from a mismatched dining room set.

Erik looked around the room. There was little furniture. A small TV sat in the corner of the living room on the kind of fake wood TV stand you put together yourself. There were no pictures on the wall, no plants, or other signs that they had been there long.

He had to pee, but didn't want to delay the start of the meeting.

"Before we begin," Abdul Hadi said, looking over at her bodyguard. "I want to tell you my real name."

The bodyguard frowned, but looked away.

"My name is Manar Hajib and this is my brother-- Ali."

Erik saw the family resemblance. Both had narrow faces and broad foreheads with dark eyes and black hair. He wore a permanent scowl, but she had a look of vulnerability that made you empathize with her the moment you met her.

"I tell you this to show that we trust you. We bring you into our circle because we need your help with this important action."

"Thank you," Erik said. "I'll do my best."

"We need to show the United States government that their children are not immune from the consequences of their continued support of the Israelis. Tonight, we decide how we will proceed with Professor Robbins' daughter. What do you recommend?"

Erik was surprised by the question. Omar had always framed the discussion about Courtney Robbins. The last time they'd talked about it, Omar stated she must be asked to do something she would not do if she were a spy. When Miguel started making suggestions, Omar cut him off, saying they would not decide that evening. Erik took that to mean that Mejbari, not someone on the steering committee, would make the decision. Now they were asking for his opinion.

"Something that will embarrass her father," Erik suggested.

"Yes," Manar replied, "but what? Omar, what do you recommend?"

"Deliver a bomb," Omar replied as if stating what he wanted to eat for dinner.

"Where?" Manar asked.

Erik told himself to breathe.

"We have time to decide," Omar replied.

"Erik, do you agree?"

"Is that really necessary?" he asked. Manar looked disappointed in his question. "I mean. It depends on where. It has to be a worthy target."

Manar nodded. "I agree."

"Ali?" she said, turning to her brother.

He answered her in what Erik presumed was Arabic.

"I have to apologize for my brother," Manar said. "Ali is not confident to speak in English. He said the target doesn't really matter as long as she delivers them a bomb."

"What's to be gained?" Erik asked, hoping not to appear to be questioning Ali or Omar.

Manar looked at her brother, but answered herself. "If Professor Robbins' daughter delivers the bomb, he cannot continue with his task force. He will have to resign and others will think twice about taking his place."

Erik wanted time to think more about that, but had another question. "What if she refuses?"

"She won't. That we know," Manar said.

Erik decided not to challenge her statement. So they wanted to give Courtney a bomb to deliver to some location--most likely a major Jewish organization. He knew that the people who had delivered the bombs in D.C. and Chicago had died, and he'd learned from the TV coverage that the woman in San Francisco had refused to do so at the last minute although people had died when the bomb exploded outside the intended target.

Erik had also read about the man accused of supplying the bomb to her. He was of Iranian descent and had recruited the University of Maryland student who set off the first bomb. "Won't the likely targets be prepared . . . with security, I mean?"

Manar nodded. "Most likely. All we need is for her to get into the building. We will need you to visit some locations this week and tell us what kind of security they are using. I can't send Omar or Ali because the Jews will suspect them because of their brown skin."

He nodded. "I can do that. Will Courtney--I mean Professor Robbins' daughter--will she--"

"Will she die?" Manar said finishing his sentence. "What do you think? Should she die?"

"I don't think she should. She really supports your people, and it would make it hard for us to recruit new members."

Manar nodded as if contemplating his answer.

"Wouldn't it be worse for her father if she lives, but other people die in the blast?" Erik asked.

"Interesting," Manar stated. "If she dies, I suppose she becomes a martyr, but if she lives and is arrested, her family name is blackened. Omar, do you agree?"

Omar shrugged his broad shoulders. "Either way."

"Ali?"

Erik couldn't make out a word of Ali's response. He tried unsuccessfully to discover what her brother was saying by reading Manar's facial response, but she remained serious and impassive.

"Then it's settled. Ali will make the bomb. Erik, you will drive her to the location. Omar will accompany you. He will explain to her at the last minute why she must do as instructed."

"What about Doreen?" Erik asked.

"The other girl?"

Erik nodded.

"You can drop her off at one of the other locations with a box containing fliers or petitions or something harmless, unless you want her to carry a bomb, too?"

Erik shook his head. "She's been a good soldier."

"She would break," Omar said.

Erik was about to ask what he meant when he figured it out. She might turn on the group if threatened with jail time.

"You must pick the best location, Erik--one where the CIA agent's daughter can get into the building. We will find a uniform for her to wear."

"When?" Erik inquired. "Have you picked a date?"

"We are thinking the anniversary of nine-eleven," Manar answered

"That's not a good choice." Ali gave Erik a dirty look, but he ignored it. "They will have extra security everywhere that day."

She nodded. "Thank you, Erik. See Ali, it is good that we have Erik on our side."

"I would do it before nine-eleven," Erik said. "The eleventh is a Tuesday. They won't be expecting something a week from tomorrow, which is the tenth."

"Monday the tenth, it is," Manar said. "Our people honor you, Erik. You are a good person to help us."

Peter G. Pollak

Washington, D.C.: Wednesday, September 5

Rosa Martinez, the Assistant to the President for National Security, was waiting in the White House conference room when Leonard arrived. Also in the room were Aaron Hayes, Martinez' representative on Leonard's task force, as well as two people who had been involved from the beginning of the DEFEAT task force: Sally Peterson from the FBI and Odell Sanders from Homeland Security. Leonard didn't recognize the fifth person in the room. The man who introduced himself as Paul Hoffer informed Leonard he was sitting in for Miles McLaughlin who was out on medical leave. Hoffer, who looked to be in his mid-forties, made no attempt come around the table to shake Leonard's hand.

Leonard had not been surprised when Hayes had informed him on his arrival at the DEFEAT offices Tuesday morning straight from his red-eye flight from San Francisco that Martinez wanted to see him the following morning. He both expected and relished the opportunity to defend the work of his task force to a group of people who had not been particularly enthusiastic about President Wheatfield's decisions to set up an independent task force or to name Leonard its director.

"Thank you for joining us this morning, Professor Robbins," Martinez said after everyone was seated. "As you can imagine, we are anxious to get your take on where things stand after the events that transpired this past Friday in San Francisco."

Leonard took a sip of tea, put down his cup, and looked around the room. "Thank you, NSA Martinez, for inviting me. I look forward to answering your questions."

"My first question is what can you tell us about what happened in San Francisco beyond what the media has reported?"

"I can say with some assurance now that the man we first came in contact with when he sent a University of Maryland student to bomb the AIA headquarters found another willing recruit in San Francisco."

Leonard took another sip of the tea. "The woman who was supposed to deliver the bomb was apprehended at the scene and has been undergoing questioning over the past several days. She confirmed what we had begun to piece together from the previous bombings concerning the terrorists' modus operandi. Unfortunately, she claims not to know the bomb maker's real name or where he was living. Nor did she know whether he was acting as part of a group or on his own."

"Yet she went along right up to the last second with his plan to bomb the Federation?" Martinez asked.

"Sadegh Moradi--that's the name of the man we've been pursuing--told her it wasn't a real bomb. She believed him at first, but when she started to have doubts, she failed to call for help. Then, after he dropped her off in front of the Federation building, she panicked."

"And the man who blew himself up in the van was this Moradi?"

"We're ninety-nine percent positive it was Moradi. Yesterday the FBI discovered that he had been living with some Jordanian students in Oakland. They are testing his belongings for DNA and fingerprints."

"Is that the end of this whole bombing business?" Martinez asked.

"Not at all. We are fairly confident Moradi was not involved in the Chicago bombing, which means there is at least one other person out there, undoubtedly plotting future attacks on Jewish organizations."

"That's very disturbing," Martinez said. "I have some additional questions, but will pause here to allow others to ask their questions."

Leonard waited as Peterson, Sanders, and Hoffer took turns deferring to each other. Finally, it was decided Hoffer should go next.

"Professor Robbins. I've studied the record of your task force's use of our analyst Ms. Stepanova. Apparently, you've asked her to conduct searches of dubious legality, which concerns us greatly. Please explain why you see it necessary to engage in activity which, if it became public, could embarrass the current administration?"

"Thank you for bringing that up, Mr. Hoffer. In terms of the legality of our data searches, we obtained legal clearance from the Justice Department for all of our data probes that required such clearance. I can provide you with copies of those documents if you so desire. In terms of why we had to push the envelope, we have reason to believe that what appears to be the work of a sole terrorist is, in fact, part of a larger scheme whose goal is to weaken this country's commitment to Israel. Moradi and the others operating in the U.S. have the backing of an organization that provided them with custom software to detonate the bombs. We believe that Russian programmers wrote the software and that their work was paid for by Iran. Further, we believe the terrorist group is using communication channels that are not currently accessible to the National Security Agency. We had to write new search routines to try to intercept their communications."

"Has any of that paid off?" Martinez asked.

"It has. I learned yesterday upon my return from San Francisco that we found a post in a game room most likely from Moradi that identified Friday as the countdown date for his operation. We do not yet know the identity of the others in the game room, but my programming team tells me we are close to figuring that out."

"Do you have any proof that Iran and Russia are behind these bombings?" Odell Sanders asked.

"The suggestion that a group in the Iranian government was behind this came to us from a reliable source. They also told us to investigate the possibility that one of the Russian hacker groups that hires out its services to criminal organizations was paid to do the programming. Our NSA analyst--your Ms. Stepanova," Leonard said nodding to Hoffer, "says she has narrowed down her search to two hacker groups. In terms of whether Iran is involved, the more we learn about Sadegh Moradi, the more likely that seems."

"How so?" Martinez asked.

"Moradi was brought to live in the United States by his uncle when his parents died in a car crash in Iran. When he was sixteen, he travelled to Iran when his paternal grandfather was on his deathbed. Moradi stayed there for five months. That is probably when he was recruited by a radical group with the intent of turning him loose at some later date as a suicide bomber. Instead they found a better use for him--someone who could recruit willing bomb carriers."

"That's an interesting story, but where's the factual evidence," Sanders stated.

"The evidence may be largely circumstantial at this point, but the pieces of the puzzle are starting to fit together."

———

"Two questions, Professor Robbins?" Martinez said.

Leonard took a nibble of a pastry. "Shoot."

"First, how many of these recruiters remain?" she asked, pausing for Leonard to answer.

"We don't know."

"Best guess?"

"Fewer than six, I'd say. If there were more, we'd have already seen more bombings."

"Okay, next question. Why would Iran back this kind of venture?"

"That's easy. Iran has long supported Hamas and Hezbollah in their war on Israel. To them Israel represents an outpost of Western values in the Middle East, something the Ayatollahs hate. Because Israel has beaten back Hamas and Hezbollah in part using U.S. technology, Iran had to find new avenues to attack. The scheme they came up with was to use the naiveté of young Americans against us."

"Again, that's highly speculative," Sanders stated.

"Think of it this way. These bombings send several messages that help Iran's cause. First, they show America to be vulnerable; second, they show the world that some Americans support Israel's sworn enemy; third, they distract us from what they're doing in terms of building a nuclear arsenal and supporting terrorist groups. Should I go on?"

"That'll do," Martinez said. "Ms. Peterson, any questions?"

"Thank you," Peterson said. "I do have one. You and your wife went out to San Francisco when you learned someone had tried to recruit students to engage in some sort of action, correct?"

"We did."

"In so doing, you inserted yourself into the middle of a critical investigation, tying up resources at the local FBI office--"

"That's incorrect," Leonard stated. He took a deep breath to calm himself. "I tied up a desk and some computer equipment that no one else was using and perhaps used the Bureau's technical support team for about an hour. After that, I spoke up only when I had something useful to contribute. My wife, on the other hand, did an incredible job, proving that it was Haddad--or rather Moradi--who had tried to recruit the students. She even found where he'd been living for a while. If he'd scheduled his bombing a week later, I'm confident we would have caught him."

"But don't you think you could have played the same role by staying in your offices here in the District?"

"No, Ms. Peterson, I do not. I just pointed out how my wife in a matter of days found students who identified Moradi. The FBI was not looking where she was, and they may never have found him."

"Your wife was once an FBI agent, correct?" Peterson asked.

"She was."

"Wasn't she fired over an incident where she failed to obey a direct order? Yet you turned her loose in a crucial investigation where she might have made the wrong decision and cost lives including her own."

Leonard tried to calm himself down before he spoke. Rosa Martinez beat him to it. "Ms. Peterson, perhaps this is not--"

"No, I want to answer her," Leonard said. "Twenty two years ago, my wife was offered the choice of resigning or being busted back in rank. She chose to resign. Yet I would match her temperament, intelligence, savvy, and character against any agent in the whole damn FBI. That's why I gave her a job that needed those qualities, and she came through. As far as speculating about other scenarios, I see no point in that."

"Let's move on," Martinez said. "Deputy Sanders, any questions?"

"Thank you, NSA Martinez. I do have one general question. Your task force is costing taxpayers something in the neighborhood of thirty-five thousand dollars a week. Is that correct?"

"I believe so," Leonard replied.

"Despite being in business for three months, your group failed to stop two additional bombings, and all you have to show is a theory about who's behind the bombings. Do you think President Wheatfield and the American people have gotten their money's worth?"

"Thank you for that question, sir. Prior to the first bombing here in D.C., I posited a theory about what our enemies were considering and what we needed to do to stop them. The theory turned out to be correct. In terms of stopping them, we still have work to do, but we're very close. That doesn't mean I'm not cognizant of the toll taken by these madmen, and I promise you I will stay on the job until we stop them or until President Wheatfield tells me my services are no longer needed."

"And on that note, this meeting is adjourned," NSA Martinez said. "Professor Robbins, please stay another minute."

Leonard followed Rosa Martinez and Aaron Hayes into her office.

"As you can tell, Professor Robbins, your welcome here in Washington among the executive agencies is wearing thin. The President shares their concerns, but is willing to give you more time. I remind you of our initial agreement--that you would keep me informed so that I could help you navigate deep waters. I don't feel you've lived up to your end of the bargain in recent weeks. I understand things fall by the wayside in the heat of battle, but we need to go back to our original agreement."

"I apologize if I haven't kept you as informed over the past week or so as I should have. Things got a little hectic, and I felt going to San Francisco in person represented our best chance of catching our prime suspect."

"Apology accepted. Let's hope your software can lead us to any other agents operating on our soil so we can shut them down and declare a victory."

"If I had a glass of wine, I'd toast to that."

"Good. I'll let you get back to your office. Aaron, will you escort Professor Robbins to his van?"

"Be glad to," Hayes said. "Right this way."

"How do you think it went, Aaron?" Leonard asked while they were waiting for his van to be pulled around.

"I think you answered all of their questions," Hayes replied.

"But did they buy the answers?"

"It's hard for me to say. The next month or two should tell. If we can come up with something that proves your theory about the Iranians, or if we can find the person behind Chicago, that would pretty much prove the task force was necessary."

"Well said. See you back in Virginia."

Delmar, New York: Friday, September 7

Leonard looked forward to the weekend. He hoped being home would lessen the tension that had built up in his body since the sighting in San Francisco of the man who had recruited two University of Maryland students to bomb the American Israel Association. In particular, Leonard looked forward to swimming in his wave pool, eating Alison's cooking, and reading about the latest Broadway play, and which wines are in season, and then perusing the New York Times Book Review section for new releases.

His flight didn't leave Dulles until seven, but Friday nights were always hectic at the airport so he asked his driver to pick him up at five so that he would have enough time to grab an oversized pretzel or some other snack at the airport.

He was about to text Alison to confirm which flight he was coming in on, when Pavel Zavarov poked his head into his office. "Got a minute, boss?"

"Sure, Pavel. What's up?"

Ekaterina Stepanova followed Pavel into the office, her eyes focused on the floor as if she saw something of great significance in the carpet pattern.

After they'd sat down in front of Leonard's desk, Pavel motioned for Ekaterina to hand over the paper she'd been carrying. "Look at these posts that came up on Professor Chaudry's search routine."

Anniversary party still on schedule for Tuesday?

Yes

Has the location been chosen?

Yes

Messenger secured?

Not yet.

Don't fail me.

"Those were translated from Arabic," Pavel said.

"Taken from where?" Leonard asked.

"An online bridge game."

"Interesting. What do you think it means?" Leonard asked.

"What big anniversary is coming up?"

"That's obvious--nine-eleven."

"Precisely," Pavel said. "Someone is planning an action on the anniversary of Al Qaeda's attack."

"Do you agree, Ekaterina?"

Ekaterina seemed surprised to have been included in the conversation. "I only find information. I cannot tell you what it means."

Leonard blew out a breath. He had to stop wishing for something more from the woman. "Thank you for calling this to our attention. Please let me know if anything else shows up with these same game players."

The NSA analyst sat there for a second, but when Pavel turned to look at her, she seemed to get the message that she had been dismissed. She got up, mumbled something that was not English, and left the room.

———

Leonard buzzed for Meir Epstein to come into his office.

"I thought you were leaving," he said to Leonard when he arrived.

Leonard looked at the time. He still had a few minutes before his driver would pull his van up in front of the building. He handed Meir the papers. "Read those over and tell me what you think it means."

Meir studied the messages.

"They were taken from the chat area of an online game, and they were in Arabic," Leonard told Meir.

"That paints a different picture," Meir said, re-reading the messages. "The messenger part bothers me, but I'm not sure it's enough to raise an alarm."

"Pavel, do you agree?" Leonard asked.

"I don't like the sound of it," Pavel said. "This is not a normal party."

"Meir, would you notify the FBI that we're working on something that may be in the works for nine-eleven and that we'll let them know if we learn anything concrete?"

"Will do.

"Pavel, stay on top of this and make sure Ekaterina lets all of us know the minute any of these game players post something, no matter what they post, or if anything else turns up that sounds like the party being planned involves mayhem and destruction."

"Got it. You'll be in Albany?"

"Yes. You know how to reach me."

"Okay, boss. Hope you have a quiet weekend."

"Me, too."

Leonard Robbins woke up Saturday feeling more relaxed than he had in weeks. He didn't push himself to his goal of forty-five minutes in the wave pool, but when he wheeled himself up to the dining room table for breakfast, he felt like a new man.

As the day went on, he caught up with the magazines he subscribed to and the rest of the mail that had accumulated. He paid a few bills and checked every few minutes to see if anything new had come in from Professor Chaudry's system.

The lack of any additional discomforting communications being captured by their search system enabled him to enjoy Saturday night with Alison. They ate dinner at Caffe Italia, their favorite Italian restaurant in the Capital District even though it was not easily accessible for Leonard's wheelchair. The staff had to help Leonard out of the van and into the restaurant while Alison parked since the restaurant lacked its own parking lot. When they got home, they watched a three-week-old episode of a BBC detective series that Leonard had set up to tape.

The next morning, Leonard was greeted with a beep signifying something was up with his team. It was Pavel. The system had pulled up another exchange between the same two players.

Party message ready?

I'm working on it

Make it sweet

Will do

What about the messenger?

Same as before.

Should I be concerned?

It's under control

Leonard saw that Carole Jean Hall was logged into their network along with Pavel and Meir.

"What party message do they plan to deliver?" she messaged.

"And to whom?" Leonard wrote. "And who is the messenger?"

No one responded.

"What do you think 'make it sweet' means?" Leonard asked.

"There are multiple meanings of 'sweet,'" Carole Jean wrote, "but it doesn't feel like they're talking about food."

"You've seen the other messages these people posted about the party on an upcoming anniversary. Anyone disagree that this sounds ominous?"

"I agree. I don't like it," Pavel wrote.

"Me neither," Meir said. "I wonder if the message is a bomb, and the messenger is their term for the person we've been calling the carrier?"

"But if they haven't secured the messenger," Leonard wrote, "which seems strange given that they've already picked the date and location."

"I think we need more information," Carole Jean wrote.

"Pavel. Forward this to Gary Mackey and ask him to let the NYC FBI know that it could be the group we've been tracking," Leonard wrote.

"Will do," Pavel replied.

"There's not much more we can do other than remain alert. However, if anyone thinks they know what's going on get in touch with me ASAP."

Late Sunday afternoon, another beep on his smart phone signified to Leonard that another message had been detected.

Messenger status?

On the way

Good work. KMP.

"They're keeping things purposely vague," Meir suggested when Leonard asked the team to get online.

"I agree," Leonard said. "For example, where do they plan to hold this party?"

"It's got to be New York," Pavel said.

"Why?"

"Symbolic reasons. They are going to show the world they can hit New York any time they want."

"What do the rest of you feel?" Leonard asked.

"I tend to agree," Meir wrote.

"It could be," Carole Jean posted, "but it could also be Washington."

"Good point," Leonard responded. "Okay. Stay local."

Leonard fretted the rest of the day, fearing he was missing something. Alison reminded him they needed to call Courtney. She didn't answer her phone. They left a message that she could call up to eleven, although Leonard wasn't sure he'd be up that late.

As he brushed his teeth, Leonard pondered whether the messages they'd uncovered meant someone was planning something ominous. Other than the date, however, they knew nothing--not where, what, or when. If they were just planning a demonstration, why use game chat to communicate since demonstrations could be planned in the open? No, the party had to be an attack of some kind.

He rinsed his mouth, wheeled himself over to his bedside table where he'd left his cell phone, and punched in Pavel Zavarov's number.

"I think you're right," he said when Pavel answered. "They're up to something and we're not going to like it."

"Big Apple, right?"

"If I were a betting man, I'd say they're going to do something in New York."

"So what do we do?"

"If it's some other group, we're not going to be much help, and the FBI and New York City police are on their own, but if it's the group that we've been tracking, we know their MO. They convince some naïve college student to deliver a bomb to a building housing a major Jewish institution."

"So what do we do, boss?"

"Tomorrow morning we do the same thing we did in San Francisco. We make up a list of likely targets and contact them warning them to double their vigilance. We also warn the FBI and city police to focus on those locations."

"Okay."

"We've got to do one more thing. I want twenty-four hour monitoring of the game-room chat data. Can you and Ekaterina handle that, or do you need more help?"

"Let me ask her."

Leonard heard the sound of Pavel walking across the floor and then heard him talking to someone in Russian.

"She says we can do it," he said when he got back on the line.

"Okay. Call me immediately if anything else comes in."

"Will do, boss."

Leonard hadn't been asleep an hour when his phone woke him up. It took him a few seconds to get oriented and had to ask Pavel, who was on the other end, to repeat himself.

"The messenger has been secured."

"What was the exact wording?" Leonard asked.

"This time it was the second player who posted first. He wrote 'messenger secured.' The other person didn't respond for a few minutes, but then wrote 'leave before the party.'"

"Say that again!"

"Leave before the party," Pavel said articulating each word.

"Anything else?"

"The first person responded 'Praise be to Allah'."

"Thanks, Pavel. That confirms it in my mind. Instead of Washington, I'm going to New York tomorrow. Wake me again if anything else comes in."

Leonard filled Alison in Monday morning after booking a flight to LaGuardia and enlisting Aaron Hayes to contact the New York City FBI to arrange for someone to pick him up with a handicap van.

"Are you convinced it's the same group that this Moradi belonged to?" Alison asked.

"Not entirely, but why take chances? If it's some other group, we won't be much help, but if it's the group we've been chasing, we might be able to get there in time to stop them."

New York City: Sunday, September 9

"What's the topic?" Courtney asked as she sat down to eat the spaghetti dinner Doreen had prepared.

Doreen looked puzzled.

"For tonight's meeting?" Courtney clarified.

"Oh. They're thinking of adding a special event and wanted you to help out."

"What kind of event?"

"I don't know. It's something Miguel came up with."

"Not stink bombs, I hope."

Doreen laughed. "I think he's still pissed we voted him down."

"He should be."

"We don't have to leave until six thirty," Doreen said as she cleared the table.

"Good," Courtney said. "That gives me time to do the dishes and call my parents."

No one answered when Courtney called her parents' home number. They probably had gone out to dinner.

"It's me. I'm going out to a meeting. You know which group," she told the answering machine. "I'll try later if it's not too late when I get back."

Emily Greene greeted Courtney and Doreen at the door. "Come on in. We're waiting for Erik and Miguel to get back. They had to run an errand."

They followed her into the kitchen. Omar was sitting at the small kitchen table with a laptop in front of him.

"Something to drink?" Emily offered.

"Nothing for me," Doreen said.

"Water, please," Courtney said.

Emily ran the water from the tap and filled a glass. Courtney walked behind Omar to get it. "You're playing a game. I thought you were doing something serious."

Omar looked embarrassed.

"What game is it?"

"Bridge."

"I tried that a few times my freshman year. Too much memorizing. Are you playing it yourself or is it an online game?"

"Online."

Courtney leaned over to look at the screen. "How does it work?"

"You start a game and invite the others to join you."

"Neat. I see you can chat with them."

Omar nodded. Just then, the apartment door opened and Erik and Miguel came in, each carrying cardboard boxes with a quick-print label on the top.

Courtney watched Omar click on the chat box and start writing in a foreign language. No one ever said where he was from. "What language is that?"

Omar closed the laptop. "Time for the meeting."

Courtney thought it odd that he wouldn't tell her, but Erik was calling them into the living room for the start of the meeting. He greeted Courtney, but looked somewhat agitated or perhaps preoccupied. She hoped the meeting would not last long. The semester had gotten off to a rapid start, and she was already behind in her reading.

Courtney sat cross-legged on a pillow on the floor next to Doreen. Erik and Miguel occupied the couch. Omar sat in the large easy chair. Emily Greene, who normally didn't participate in steering committee meetings, had pulled in a chair from the kitchen.

"So, Courtney," Erik Greene began, "we're glad you agreed to join us tonight. Our group is growing, and we expect great things from it this coming year."

Courtney gave him an encouraging smile to let him know that was good news to her.

"Thing is we can't have someone from the group report on what we're doing to people outside the group, people who oppose what we're doing."

Courtney nodded. *What's this all about?*

Erik fidgeted with a piece of paper on the coffee table. "There's no easy way for me to say this, Courtney. So, I'll just come out and say it. Are you spying on us for your father?"

Courtney stared at Erik, waiting for his words to make sense. "What? Say that again."

"I said, are you spying on us."

"Spying? No, I'm not spying. Whatever gave you that idea?"

"Maybe the fact that your father heads up a task force which has gone after SPJ groups around the country." That came from Miguel.

Courtney stared at him in disbelief.

"The problem, Courtney, is that we don't know if you're lying or telling the truth," Erik said.

"So, you want me to do what--leave?"

"We'd prefer that you prove that you are really one of us," Erik said.

Courtney wiped the tears that suddenly appeared in her eyes. "Prove it? How? How am I supposed--"

"We have devised a test for you," Miguel said. "You can leave if that's your choice, but to me that would be a confession of guilt . . ."

Erik motioned for Miguel to stop talking. "We are going to give you the opportunity to prove that you're not a spy by doing a simple task."

Courtney looked at Doreen. "Did you know about this?"

Doreen mouthed the word no, but Courtney wasn't convinced. Maybe that's why she had tried so hard to get her to come to the meeting last Sunday.

Courtney tried to calm herself. "My father is against my being in this group. Doreen, tell them."

"That doesn't matter now," Erik said. "Are you willing to take the test to prove that you're not a spy?"

Courtney took a couple of deep breaths. "That depends. What kind of test are you talking about?"

"It doesn't work that way," Miguel said. "You either have to leave or take the test."

"How can I decide if you won't tell me what it is?"

"We can't, Courtney," Erik said.

"I'm not going to do something stupid like smoke bomb the Hillel offices."

Emily chuckled quietly, but she was the only one.

"It's not something designed to embarrass you," Erik said. "It's a task to test your level of commitment. That's all I can say."

Courtney's face was flushed, and her hands had formed fists in her lap. She wanted to get up and leave, but Miguel had just said they would see that as an admission of guilt.

"Okay. I'll do it as long as it's not one of Miguel's dumb ideas."

Miguel reddened. He looked like he wanted to say something, but choked it down.

———

Erik looked around the room as if to make sure the rest of the group was with him. "Okay, then. Here's what we need you to do. Be on the corner of West Fourth and Broadway tomorrow afternoon at 3:30 pm. Doreen, you too. You can be dressed just as you are now, but both of you must leave your cell phones in your apartment, or we'll have to confiscate them."

Courtney was confused. "You're not going to tell me what I have to do."

"Not until tomorrow," Erik said. "Don't spend a lot of time worrying about it. If you come prepared to do what we ask, everything will work out fine."

Courtney started to question Doreen on the way home, but Doreen stopped her.

"Don't ask me. I don't know what they have in mind. I tried to find out, but they refused to tell me."

"But you knew something was up!"

"I knew they wanted you to perform some kind of task, but they wouldn't tell me what it was so I couldn't spill the beans."

Courtney didn't believe her. *I thought we were friends,* she wanted to say, *but you betrayed me.*

Courtney went straight to bed when she got home. After she turned out her bedroom light, she remembered she was going to call her parents. Her father would probably be in bed. Did she feel like telling her mother what happened at the meeting? She wasn't sure. Her mother would be more accepting than her father, but she might worry what kind of task they would ask her to do.

Courtney thought about turning on the light and calling them, but decided not to. *This is something I'm going to handle myself.*

Peter G. Pollak

New York City: Monday, September 10

Monday morning, Courtney spent more time thinking about how she was going to ask Doreen to move out of their apartment than worrying about the task the SPJ leadership had planned for her. It wasn't until lunchtime that the task ahead of her began to gnaw at her insides. A dark thought came into her head. Her father had warned her about SPJ members being used to deliver bombs to Jewish organizations. Two had died and the third probably only lived because she dropped the bomb in a trash bin and ran.

They couldn't be planning to do that to her! Too many people, including Doreen, knew about it. Doreen might not have been totally honest with her, but she didn't think Doreen would go along with a bombing, much less having her killed in the process. If it had only been Miguel, she might have been more worried. She trusted Erik Greene, and what about Emily? She wouldn't go along with a bombing, would she?

After her last class, Courtney returned to her apartment to eat some lunch. She recalled that she was to leave her cell phone home. *Why,* she wondered as she attached her phone to its charger.

She dialed her mother's cell ten minutes before she needed to leave to meet Doreen. The call went into message mode.

"Mom, it's Courtney. Sorry about last night. I forgot to call when I got back from the meeting. Some people in the SPJ group think I'm spying on them for Dad. Isn't that nuts? They want me to prove that I'm not a mole. That's where I'm going now. I'll call you when it's over."

Doreen was waiting on the assigned street corner. She gave Courtney a thin smile. "It'll be okay."

Courtney nodded, but didn't smile back. *Whatever happens is on you, bitch!*

Erik appeared when he promised, driving in a beige rental van. He motioned them to get in the back. Doreen opened the back door. Omar was inside sitting facing a narrow table on which sat was some electronic equipment.

"Get in," Omar told them.

Doreen got in behind Courtney and closed the door.

"Where are we going?" Courtney asked.

"You'll see," Omar said.

Erik pulled the van back into traffic.

Alison Robbins checked her cell phone as she exited the office building where she'd just met with the CEO of a high-tech startup that had received an infusion of capital and as a result was moving into new quarters while trying to ramp up their sales effort. Alison had convinced the CEO that she needed a personal coach to help her manage the ever-growing demands on her time.

Alison saw that Courtney had left her a message on her cellphone. She stopped half way to her car to listen to the message. Not believing what she heard, she played it again.

Upset by the message, she hit Courtney's speed-dial, but the call went into voice mail. "Damn. Damn. Damn," she said out loud, scaring a woman who was walking towards the office building.

Alison knew she'd better call her husband. It might not be as bad as it sounded, and if they did something that made it look like they didn't trust Courtney, intervening could backfire. The message, however, sounded too serious to take a wait and see approach.

Leonard wasn't immediately available. She forwarded Courtney's message to his email, got into her car, opened all the windows, and waited for him to call back.

"I can't believe this is happening," Leonard said fifteen minutes later. "I'm up to my neck trying to prevent another violent attack, and my daughter is playing footsie with the very people who may be involved in what's being planned."

"What should we do?" Alison asked.

"We have to find her, but how? I can't imagine calling the college would help."

"What about Doreen?" Alison suggested.

"Do you have her number?"

"Hold on, I'll check."

Alison searched on Rupert in her cell's contact list. "Yes, I've got it."

"Good. Find out if she knows what's going on. Tell her it's imperative that we get through to Courtney right away."

"Okay. I'll call you right back."

The call to Doreen's number went into voice mail. "Damn! Her, too?"

She left a message for Doreen, and then texted Leonard when his phone line was busy.

"Do we know the names of anyone else in the SPJ group?" Leonard asked when he called her back.

"I don't," Alison replied.

"What about people in their apartment building?"

"I don't think they know any of them, but I have the rental agency's number at home."

"Where are you now?"

"Albany."

"Go home and call the rental agency. See if they'll send someone over there to see if the girls are okay."

"Okay. Will do."

Instead of stopping at the mall to look for a pair of fall shoes as she had planned, Alison drove home as fast as she could without putting herself in danger of getting a ticket. She found the rental agreement and called the rental agency. The person who answered the phone was not cooperative until she explained it was an FBI matter and not just the normal worried mother.

"Why not call the police?" the rental agent manager asked.

"Please do as I ask, sir," Alison replied.

Having accomplished that, she got Leonard on the phone. "They're sending someone to open the apartment."

"Good. I'm hesitant to forward Courtney's photo to the NYPD. They've got their hands full with nine-eleven anniversary activities. You wouldn't believe how many warnings and threats come into various offices and agencies."

"People are nuts, Len."

"You keep telling me that."

"They are. They're simply nuts."

"You're home?"

"Yes."

"Stay there. I'll get my team to probe social media for any messages relating to a SPJ trial. I'll call you when I hear something. Let me know if Courtney calls you."

"I can't stay here, Len, knowing she might have gotten herself into something that's way over her head."

"What are you going to do?"

"Come down to the city."

"That won't help. We've got professionals working on this--"

"I'm not a professional?"

"Of course you are, Hon, but--"

"I'm coming. Goodbye."

Peter G. Pollak

New York City: Same Day

Courtney studied the contents of the van. A narrow table had been secured to the driver's side of the van. Two computer monitors were mounted on the table to the front of the van, with a TV monitor and a DVD player set up near the back. More equipment with cables was stored under the table. Four boxes, each about the size of a toaster, and two large boxes with labels from a costume store were stacked near the front of the van. The back door windows had been covered with black paper, but Courtney could see where they were going through the window to the front section of the van.

After initial greetings, Omar turned to study his computer monitors. Courtney knew it was useless to try to get him to answer any questions. She sat next to Doreen on a bench that ran along the passenger side of the van, pondering what kind of test they had created for her that would prove her innocence.

She had to hold on with both hands in order not to be bounced off the wooden bench at every bump in the road, which made her stomach, which was already tied up in knots, even more jittery. She was glad she hadn't eaten more than a few nibbles from the salad she'd made for her lunch.

Courtney tried to keep track of where they were going. From where he'd picked them up on the corner of West Fourth Street and Broadway, Erik drove over to Third Avenue and headed uptown. Traffic moved slowly increasing Courtney's anxiety level.

Finally, Erik made a left turn off Third, but they ran into a red light. When the light changed, he pulled into a loading zone across Lexington. Leaving his lights flashing, Erik came around to the back of the van. Courtney thought he looked pale and harried, which made her even more nervous.

"Ready?" he asked her.

"I guess so," Courtney answered.

"Here's the story. You're both going to deliver copies of our boycott Israel petition to separate locations. Doreen, you're going to deliver them to the offices of the American Israel Association on Madison Avenue. Courtney, you're going to deliver your box to the Jewish Museum on Fifth Avenue.

"We have uniforms for each of you to put on so that you look like commercial delivery personnel. Otherwise, they probably won't let you into the building.

"Your goal is to present the petitions in a package addressed to the executive directors of each institution. All you need to do is deliver the package to a clerical person and get someone to sign for the package.

"Omar has designed a program that runs on a Dell tablet. You present the tablet to the receptionist. She signs it with her finger. You then hit submit, and at that point you've passed your test."

"Why am I being tested?" Doreen asked, her voice tight with tension.

"You're not. You're going first to show Courtney how easy it is. Then she'll do hers."

Doreen seemed satisfied, but Courtney was not. "I doubt they'll let me enter the museum without inspecting the package."

"Maybe so, maybe not," Erik said. "It is the harder of the two places to enter, but it can be done. You just have to act like this is a normal delivery, which in essence it is, and don't let their security people put you off."

"Where do we change?" Doreen asked.

"Right here. I'm going to check out the first location to make sure it's clear. Omar will keep his back turned. Here's yours, Courtney," he said handing a box to her, "and here's yours, Doreen."

Courtney opened the box. It contained a pair of brown slacks and shirt, a hat with a UPS logo on it and even brown leather shoes. "How did you know my sizes?"

Erik frowned. "Does that really matter now?"

"No, I guess not," Courtney admitted. "Can I see the petitions?"

"Sure," Erik said. Omar took a box off the top of the pile and opened it. Inside was a stack of petitions the NYU SPJ members had circulated calling for the boycott, divestment and sanctioning of Israel for its apartheid policies in East Jerusalem, the West Bank and the Golan Heights. "Those are the originals. We made two sets of copies and packaged them with proper UPS labels so they'll look official. Any questions?"

Courtney shook her head. "Let's get this over with."

Erik got out of the van, promising to return in ten minutes. Omar turned his back to them. Doreen slid down the bench to the end and turned her back to Courtney. Courtney turned her back to Omar and quickly removed her slacks and put on those from the box. She was putting the shoes on when there was a knock on the back of the van. "It's me, Erik. Can I come in?"

Doreen looked back to see that Courtney had finished changing and opened the door.

"Okay, Doreen. You're first."

Erik climbed into the van and gave her one of the boxes. "Here's the package for the American Israel Association. The address is on the package. It should be a piece of cake."

Doreen got out and headed up the street.

"I'll stand outside in case a cop comes along and I have to move the van," Erik said.

That left Courtney alone with Omar, who continued to study his monitors.

What they wanted her to do seemed simple enough, but thinking about it, Courtney wondered how it proved that she was not a spy. A spy would have no trouble doing what they'd asked. The only danger was that she'd be arrested for impersonating a UPS delivery person, assuming what was in the package were copies of their petition.

Doreen had taken the box, which was covered with brown wrapping paper, without inspecting it. How did she know what was really inside it? Courtney vowed not to let them give her one whose contents she had not inspected.

Doreen returned about fifteen minutes later. She got in the van and told Omar to keep his back to them as she started to change back into her street clothes.

"How'd it go?" Courtney asked.

"Piece of cake. They ran the box through some kind of metal detector, but when it didn't set off any alarms, they signed for it. That was that."

When she'd changed, Doreen knocked on the back door. Erik got in, and Doreen exited.

"Where are you going?" Courtney asked.

"I've got an appointment with my advisor at four thirty. I'll see you back at the apartment. You can tell me all about it."

"On to the next stop," Erik said, closing the back door.

Courtney thought about opening the door and telling them she wasn't going to do it, when she saw the lock mechanism turn. They were locking her in. She turned and saw Omar looking at her with what was not a friendly look.

"Don't try it," he said.

"Try what?"

"Try to leave. It's your turn now."

Courtney shriveled back against the side of the van, trying to remain composed. She wished Doreen had stayed with them.

She tried to pay attention to where they were going. If Erik was telling her the truth, they should be heading uptown toward Central Park. Indeed, Erik turned onto Madison Avenue. Courtney tried to remember where the Jewish Museum was located. She thought it was across from Central Park, but wasn't sure how far uptown.

Traffic was agonizingly slow. Omar seemed to be done with whatever he had been doing on the computer. He turned to face her, a haughty smirk on his face. She thought about screaming for help, but decided she was being childish. If all she had to do was deliver a box of petitions, she could do that. Then it would be over. At that moment, she realized she would not remain a member of SPJ. Any group that forced a member to prove him or herself was a group she didn't want to belong to.

She tried counting blocks, but soon lost track. After a while, they turned to the left. She recognized Central Park in front of them. When the light changed, they turned left onto Fifth Avenue. "There it is," Erik called from the front of the van. Courtney couldn't see because there were no side windows inside the van.

Erik turned again a few blocks later and pulled over. Again he left the van's flashers blinking. "I'm going to check out your target," he told her.

"Wait," Courtney yelled, but he had already closed and locked the back door.

It seemed like an eternity, but it was probably only ten minutes before Erik unlocked the back of the van and motioned to Omar. "Can you come out here for a sec?"

Omar didn't look happy to have to leave his computers unguarded, but swiveled his chair and got out of the van.

Courtney couldn't make out what was being said, but shortly the door opened and both men got in.

"Seems we've a problem," Erik said after both got in.

"What's that?" Courtney demanded.

"I forgot that the Jewish New Year begins tonight. The museum is closed for the entire week."

Courtney breathed a sigh of relief. "Let's try again next week."

"We can't do that," Erik said.

"And why's that?" Courtney demanded.

"You might warn them. Instead, we'll find another location and have you do it tomorrow."

"If you're targeting Jewish organizations, they'll all be closed."

"True. We'll just have to find an alternative location where you can deliver the package tomorrow morning."

Courtney didn't know what to say. Erik and Omar seemed to be stuck in the middle of their own stupid game. She felt better seeing their plans messed up.

"There's one more complication," Erik said.

"And what's that?"

"We can't let you go home tonight."

Leonard was losing his cool. His back ached, his hands were cramping from all the maneuvering involved in making his way from Albany to New York, going up and down ramps, squeezing through crowds of people, and getting on and off the plane. Worse, his catheter bag needed emptying. The FBI van had been delayed in reaching the airport, and traffic crawled all the way to Federal Plaza. It was almost two p.m. by the time he got settled in at the NYC FBI headquarters with access to the DEFEAT network. He had barely started to immerse himself into the data flow when Alison called to tell him about Courtney's phone message. That problem not only diverted his focus for a good hour, but it ended on a sour note with Alison announcing she was not taking his advice, but was on her way to the city.

While munching on a sandwich one of the agents had procured for him, he realized he'd been wrong. Alison's coming to New York was a good thing. He should stop trying to manage multiple crises by himself. He texted that sentiment to her, worried she wouldn't see the text until she got to the city. She was probably royally pissed. Why he questioned her judgment in the first place was beyond him.

That Courtney had gotten herself into a jam with the NYU SPJ group offered a different kind of worry for Leonard. What would they do to her if they thought she was spying on them for his task force? It hurt his head even to think about it. He hoped she was not so stubborn as to go along with some stupid scheme. Of course, given her desire to prove her independence, she might just do what they tell her.

On top of all that was the fact that the people at the NYC FBI office were not happy to have Leonard on board during what was clearly a time of heightened anxiety, as the minutes moved rapidly closer to the anniversary of Al Qaeda's September 11, 2001 attack.

The FBI was working closely with the New York City police department to monitor every phone call, email, and other data source that pointed to possible anti-government actions--no matter how obscure or unlikely the source.

Leonard recalled reading how a number of Islamic jihadists who had escaped the crackdown on their Islamic caliphate, had made their way to New York City and had formed alliances with ex-cons who had converted to Islam in America's prisons. Groups of these men had taken to the streets on past nine-elevens, harassing anyone who looked Jewish as well as challenging members of the NYPD with taunts or worse whenever they enjoyed an advantage of numbers.

Looking for someone planning an event that superseded such conflicts by an order of magnitude was like searching through the proverbial haystack. The FBI had their tools to try to identify the most dangerous situations, but Leonard was only looking for one such situation--the targeting of a Jewish institution by a group that was using sophisticated communications technology developed by Russian hackers and paid for by Iran to detonate their bombs.

When he arrived at their offices, one of the Bureau's deputies made it clear that they needed Leonard to stay out of the way. His being wheelchair-bound did not increase the deputy's desire to be accommodating, but Leonard was used to that kind of response. "I'm here for one reason and one reason only, Agent Collins," Leonard told the deputy. "We are tracing text messages that suggest a major event is being planned for tomorrow. I'll let you know the second we learn any details. Other than that I'm happy to comply with your request."

Leonard mapped out the remainder of the day. He texted DEFEAT office manager Ed Morgan to book him and his wife into the Regency Hotel and scheduled a team-wide conference call at 5 p.m., restating for at least the hundredth time since the formation of the task force that he should be notified if anyone came up with something that might be relevant to their search.

A few minutes later, he had another thought and buzzed Meir Epstein. "Courtney's in some kind of jam with the NYU SPJ group. Have someone who's not too busy delve into the inner workings of that chapter. Who are its leaders? What are their backgrounds? What kinds of things have they been up to? Who among the faculty might be working with them? That kind of thing."

"Will do," Meir replied. "You managing okay?"

"You know there's one benefit of being confined to a wheelchair," Leonard replied.

"What's that?"

"I can't go running around like a chicken with its head cut off."

Meir chuckled. "I'll get on this, but don't forget to breathe once in a while."

Pavel texted Leonard thirty minutes before their 1700 meeting. "The guys we've been monitoring just chatted again."

"What did they say?"

Pavel forwarded the posts.

Party update. 16:00.

Go ahead.

Unavoidable delay. Target closed.

Come back here.

On our way.

"What do you make of it?" Leonard asked Pavel.

"They stopped bothering to be cautious about what they're saying. They don't think we're monitoring them. Apparently, something prevented them from pulling off whatever they planned."

"But that doesn't help us figure out who or where they are."

"We'll keep after them, boss," Pavel said. "We're still meeting at five?

"Affirmative."

The five p.m. DEFEAT meeting resulted in no new information or ideas concerning the impending event, or how to stop it. Meir promised the report Leonard had asked for about the NYU SPJ group within the hour.

After the meeting, Leonard wheeled himself around the FBI office, first using the restroom, and then polling the agents on the floor about takeout options. A couple of women who were ordering sushi invited him to join in. He gladly accepted.

He nervously kept his phone next to him while he ate, expecting Alison's call any minute, praying that Courtney was home and was no worse for the wear.

New York City: Same Day

Alison drove straight through to Courtney's Manhattan apartment. Heavy traffic slowed her progress once she reached the outskirts of the city. She hadn't left her house in Delmar until nearly three, and it was after seven by the time she found a place to park near the girls' apartment building.

While sitting in traffic, she'd called Len to find out if he'd made any progress in tracking down their daughter. "Did you get my text?"

"Yes," Alison replied. "I'm glad you see it my way."

"I do. Since I'm busy trying to prevent a major event, it's good that you can focus on finding Courtney. I asked Meir to research the NYU group. I'll let you know if he comes up with anything relevant."

"Len, since you've other things to worry about, why don't you send me Meir's report as soon as you get it? I'll go through it and let you know if there's anything relevant."

"Point taken. I'll do that. By the way, the Regency is booked. Ed put us into a hotel over on Lexington. I'll send you the reservation info. I'll meet you there late tonight unless you want to come here."

"Okay, but I won't be able to sleep until I find her."

Standing at the entrance to Courtney's apartment building, Alison kicked herself metaphorically for not having gotten a key when they signed the lease. *We're paying the damn rent. I ought to have a key.* She kicked herself a second time, realizing how Courtney would have reacted to her demanding a key. Alison knew better than to do so at the time, but now she was stuck with the consequences.

The rental agency had checked the apartment earlier that day and had informed her that no one was there and nothing looked awry. She doubted they would be as cooperative if she had to call them again to let her in, but what were her options, other than sitting on the stoop and waiting for Courtney or Doreen to show up?

When someone came out of the building, Alison grabbed the door before it closed. She took the elevator up to Courtney's floor and knocked on the door to her unit. No answer. She knocked again a little louder. Still no answer.

I guess it's time to call the rental people, she told herself. She started to dial the number, but saw only one bar on the top of her phone. Something in the building must be blocking the signal.

Just as she got outside and started to make the call, she spotted Doreen Rupert coming up the street. *Thank goodness.*

Doreen didn't see Alison until she started up the front steps. She stopped, backed down, and started to run back in the direction she'd come.

"Doreen. Stop," Alison called. "Where are you going?"

Doreen turned back, hesitated, and then started running again. Alison took after her. Fortunately she was wearing more sensible footwear than the younger woman, who had on high heels. Alison also had the advantage of being in excellent physical condition. She caught up with Doreen in middle of the next block.

"All right. I give up," Doreen said, as Alison cornered her between two stairwells.

"What's gotten into you?" Alison demanded. She was breathing heavily, but Doreen was bent over, totally out of breath.

"I don't know. I didn't expect to see you--"

"That doesn't make any sense, Doreen. What's going on? Where's Courtney?"

Doreen panted trying to catch her breath. "She didn't tell you?"

"She told me something about the SPJ group thinking she was a spy."

"I told her not to use that excuse."

"What do you mean? Doreen, stop playing around here. This is serious."

"She made that up. She's with her boyfriend."

Alison couldn't believe her ears. "With her boyfriend? That's why she isn't answering her cell phone!"

Doreen nodded. "They're taking a few days off to explore each other's sexuality."

That didn't sound like Courtney at all. "Okay then, give me his phone number."

"His phone is off, too, Mrs. Robbins."

"Well, where does he live?"

"I don't know--uptown someplace."

"Judas Priest! You mean I drove all the way down here thinking she was in some kind of trouble and she's shacking up with a boyfriend!"

Doreen nodded, but then looked away.

"I don't buy it, Doreen. That's not like Courtney, and by the way, why haven't you been answering your cell phone?"

"I was in a rush and must have left it home."

Alison shook her head. This wasn't adding up.

"She told me you wouldn't understand," Doreen said. "That's why she made up that story about SPJ."

"What's his name--this boyfriend?"

"Dick. Dick . . . Harris. He's a senior."

"Is he in the SPJ group?"

Doreen nodded.

Alison studied the young woman. She was having a hard time believing the shacking up story, but she couldn't dismiss it out of hand and wasn't sure what to do next. She knew she wouldn't be able to get NYU to give out a student's address on the suspicion that he was sleeping with her daughter, not to mention it was unlikely she'd find anyone there at this time of night.

She decided to head over to FBI headquarters. "Okay, Doreen. I'll let you go, but if it turns out you're lying to me, and something happens to my daughter, I'm going to see that you're held responsible."

The pinched look on Doreen's face satisfied Alison that Courtney's roommate was having a hard time making light of her threat. She would have liked to drag Doreen with her to the FBI, but she didn't have the legal right to do so, and if it turned out Doreen was telling the truth, she could sue Alison for unlawful imprisonment.

Doreen turned as if to head back toward her apartment.

Alison secured Doreen by the arm. "I'm going back to the apartment with you."

When they got inside, Alison found Courtney's phone on the charger. She took it with her. There might be calls on it that would help track her down. She didn't know Courtney's password, but maybe someone at the FBI could figure out how to access her recent calls.

"No way," Courtney said. "Let me out of here."

Erik Greene had spent ten minutes trying to convince her that her staying with them overnight was necessary to assure the group that she was telling the truth. "You deal with her," he said to Omar, backing out of the van and locking the doors.

"Let me out of here," Courtney yelled.

"You're not leaving until we say you can," Omar said. He handed her a black bandana. "Put this on over your eyes."

"Not until you tell me where you're taking me," Courtney demanded, tears streaming down her face.

"Do as I say, or I'll put this sack over your head myself," he replied showing a black cloth bag.

Courtney took the bandana. She considered what would happen if she started screaming and banging on the side of the van, but it was already moving, and her voice would probably be lost in the normal street sounds. She worried what Omar would do to her if she started yelling for help. She tied the bandana loosely over her eyes after giving Omar the most hateful look she could manage.

"Tighter," Omar demanded.

She tightened it slightly, and had to grab onto the bench as the van swerved around the corner.

"You can remove the bandana now," Erik told her when the van finally came to a stop.

Courtney sat up and removed the bandana. Erik was sitting on his haunches just inside the back of the van. Omar was in his office chair, his usual smirk dominating his face.

She had sobbed the entire drive from Manhattan to their current location--wherever that was.

"Everything's going to be all right if you just follow our instructions," Erik said.

"Why are you doing this?" Courtney moaned.

"This is no time for a discussion," Omar said. "It's time to get out of the van into the apartment where you'll be spending the night."

"I want to go home. I don't care about your stupid test."

"It's too late for that," Omar said. "Now move."

Courtney sent as nasty a look as she could muster in Omar's direction.

"Courtney," Erik said, drawing her attention away from Omar. "The only way to get through this is to do what we ask you to do. If you do that, everything will be over by noon tomorrow."

Courtney wanted to believe him. She wanted to think this was an innocent request and not her worst nightmare--not what her father had been warning her about. "What do you want me to do?"

"Put the bandana back on. I'll guide you out of the van and into the apartment building. Once we're inside, you can take it off."

Courtney whimpered.

"Ready?"

She nodded and slid the tear-soaked bandana back over her head.

With Erik guiding her, they exited the van, walked up a short walk. "Three steps, now."

He led her into an elevator. She couldn't tell how many floors it ascended. When the elevator stopped he led her into an apartment. She heard the door close behind her.

"You can take it off now," he said.

Courtney removed the bandana and looked around. She was in a small, dark, sparsely furnished apartment.

"You remember Tarab Abdul Hadi?" Erik asked.

She recognized the woman she'd met several months ago at the SPJ meeting. She was sitting on a couch looking at Courtney with a serious look on her face. The man who had been introduced in the spring as Abdul Hadi's bodyguard was standing by the front window peeking out between the blinds. He glanced at her and then looked away after saying something under his breath in a language Courtney didn't recognize.

Erik guided her to a chair and motioned for her to sit. "You're going to spend the night here. Tomorrow, Omar and I will take you to a new location where you'll deliver the petitions. After that, I'll take you home."

"I want you to take me home now," Courtney said. "You can't keep me here against my will."

"Listen to me, young woman," the Palestinian woman said. "We are not playing a game here. You agreed to do something for us, and we insist that you do it."

"The building was closed. That wasn't my fault."

The woman said something to her bodyguard and then looked back at Courtney. "Enough of this. I will show you something that will change your mind. Bring the equipment up," she said to the bodyguard.

Courtney didn't understand the man's reply, but the woman interrupted him with a sharp word. As a result, he and Omar left the apartment.

Erik brought Courtney a glass of water.

"I need to use the bathroom," she told him.

"I will take you," the woman said, standing up. She led Courtney down a short corridor and pointed to the bathroom. Courtney entered it, and was shocked when the woman came in as well, closing the door behind her.

"Can I have a little privacy?" Courtney demanded.

"I'll turn my back."

Courtney did have to pee. She waited for the woman to turn her back and then used the toilet. Afterwards, she washed her face as well as her hands.

Looking at herself in the mirror, she started to cry again. "You're going to kill me, aren't you?"

"Stop acting like an infant," the woman said.

"I was on your side. My father--"

"Your father is our enemy. That makes you our enemy, but if you do what you are told, neither of you will suffer any harm. If you disobey . . ."

She didn't finish her sentence, but Courtney got the message. The woman escorted Courtney back into the living room and sat her down roughly in the chair. Omar and the bodyguard were in the adjoining room setting up some computer equipment.

Courtney realized it was futile to try to appeal to these people's sense of decency. They had a plan, and she was part of it. She tried to make eye contact with Erik, hoping he would see how crazy this all had become and help her get out of there, but he was helping the men and avoided looking at her.

The men announced they were ready. Erik and the woman guided Courtney to a straight-backed chair opposite the small portable TV that had been in the van.

"Begin," the woman told Omar.

He pushed a button on the DVD player and a blurry image appeared on the screen. Courtney thought about not watching, but then recognized her parents' neighborhood in Delmar. The image had been taken from the inside of a vehicle that was approaching her parents' block.

"What's going on?" she demanded. "Why are--"

"Silence!" Omar raised his arm as if to strike her with the backside of his hand.

There was no sound with the video.

The vehicle stopped across the street from her parents' house. The focus zoomed on the front of the house. The video must have been shot recently because her mother had had the shrubs in the front trimmed less than a month ago. "They got so overgrown I couldn't do it myself," she'd told Courtney.

She saw someone--a woman--cross in front of the van, heading toward her parents' house. She was carrying a package. Instead of going up to the front door and ringing it, however, she looked around, and then slid it under the wheelchair ramp that had been installed to enable Courtney's father to use the front door. The woman then came back to the van. It was the Palestinian woman.

The video ended.

"What's going on?" Courtney demanded. "What did you put there?"

"I'll tell you when you stop talking," the woman said.

Courtney repressed a scream. "Bitch."

The woman slapped her across the face. "I said quiet."

Courtney cowered in the chair. She kicked at the woman who stepped aside and raised her hand as if to slap Courtney again. Courtney gave her a defiant look.

The Palestinian looked like she could kill. "Do you care for your parents?"

That got Courtney's attention.

"I planted an explosive device under the wheelchair ramp," the woman said. "If you do not do what we demand, we will wait until your mother or father is on that ramp, and we will detonate it."

"You're a bunch of crazy murderers!" Courtney screamed. She jumped up, hoping to make it to the apartment door, but the bodyguard was ready. He grabbed her left shoulder with one arm and her head with the other and threw her back into the chair.

"Let me go," Courtney screamed, sliding off the seat onto the floor.

The woman stood over her, and slapped her on her back as Courtney held her arms up to protect her face. "Shut up, woman," she yelled. "*Suker khajic!*"

Sobbing, Courtney curled up on the floor to avoid further hits.

"Courtney, you're making this harder on yourself than necessary," she heard Erik over the voices of the other three, who were talking all at once.

"You're a traitor, Erik," Courtney mumbled, without lifting her head. "A traitor to your country."

New York City: Same Day

"I'm getting a very bad feeling about this," Leonard confessed as he heard Alison's report of her conversation with Doreen Rupert.

"She's lying, isn't she?"

"That's pretty obvious," Leonard replied.

"I agree," Alison said. "First of all, that doesn't sound like Courtney, and why make up a ridiculous excuse like that?"

"The whole thing sounds phony. Doreen is covering up something, and the fact that Courtney doesn't have her cellphone with her is a bad sign. Bring the phone down here so someone can try to access it. I'll get you some food, and we'll figure this out together. Meanwhile, I'm going to talk to the people here about having Doreen picked up."

"On what charge?"

"I'm not sure, but we'll think of something."

Leonard was still uncertain what steps were the proper ones to deal with the NYU SPJ mess when he got a text message from Meir Epstein. "Core report sent."

For a moment, Leonard thought about ignoring it. What could it contain that would help them figure out where Courtney was? Maybe names of some of the people they could contact, but wouldn't they lie to cover up whatever was going on. They might all have been told to use the boyfriend line.

He'd promised to forward it to Alison and did so.

Then a text message from Meir came through. "Call me."

Leonard picked up his cell and punched in Meir's number at DEFEAT headquarters.

"Someone dropped off a package at the New York City AIA office a few hours ago," Meir said. "It contained petitions collected by the NYU SPJ."

"What! You're kidding me."

"They ran the box through a metal detector and it came up clean."

"Any video?"

"Yes. I sent you a link."

"Hold on." Leonard opened the second attachment Meir had sent him, found the video link and clicked on it. The image showed people going in and out of the AIA offices on the third floor of 477 Madison Avenue in Manhattan. "What am I looking––hold on, I got it."

He saw a woman dressed in a UPS uniform get off the elevator and approach the front entrance. The camera angle was above her and her cap covered up her face, but Leonard recognized the woman by her narrow face and tall, thin body. It was Doreen Rupert!

"Meir, I know that woman. She's Courtney's roommate. She came up to Delmar with Courtney a few weekends ago. Earlier today, Courtney left us a message that the SPJ group was making her prove she wasn't spying on them for me. There has to be some kind of connection, but I'm not seeing it."

"I take it you haven't been able to reach Courtney?"

"No. They told her she had to leave her cellphone in her apartment. Alison confronted this Doreen less than an hour ago. She told Alison that Courtney was shacking up with her boyfriend, but Alison isn't buying it."

"That sounds very wrong, Len. Why would Courtney tell you she was going to have to do something to prove her loyalty, and then it's Doreen and not Courtney who delivers the package to AIA?"

"Unless Courtney was being asked to deliver a package to a second location," Leonard said.

"But we've heard nothing about a second delivery."

"If it were just petitions, then you might not, but then why would Doreen lie about Courtney's whereabouts?"

"Did you know tonight is the start of Rosh Hashanah?" Meir said.

"Damn. I forgot all about that. Shouldn't you be getting ready to go to services?"

"Under normal circumstances, yes, but I'll ask God to forgive me. Stopping these guys and saving lives takes precedence."

"If he won't forgive you, I will," Leonard said, trying to be humorous.

"Thanks, but the reason I bring it up is that most Jewish organizations are closed this week. I'm surprised that AIA was open today."

"Now, I get it. In other words, they might have tried to send Courtney to a second office, only to find it closed."

"Exactly."

"In which case what would they do--send her home and tell her they'd try again next week?"

"Unless the second package contained something other than petitions . . ."

"Shit," Leonard said. "That's gotta be it. They can't let her go home until she makes the delivery, but Courtney wouldn't deliver a package that she knew contained a bomb. She knows what happened to the other deliverers."

"And if she told them she wouldn't do it, then what?" Meir asked. "They couldn't just let her go because you'd be the first person she'd call."

Leonard placed his hand on his forehead. "This gets worse and worse. What do you think they'd do?"

"Off the top of my head," Meir said, "they'd probably hold her someplace and make her do the delivery tomorrow."

"But how could they make her do it against her will?"

"They must have something over her."

"What?"

"I don't know. It doesn't add up, but I can't think of any other explanation."

"Mr. Robbins. Your wife is here." It was the Bureau receptionist paging him.

"Meir, Alison just arrived here. I've got to tell her. Who's still there?"

"Me, Larry, Pavel, Ekaterina, and Ed Morgan. The rest have gone home."

"Okay. Fill them in. Give me thirty minutes. Then I want some ideas about how we're going to get Courtney out of this mess and prevent another deadly delivery."

Leonard offered Alison some of his leftover sushi, but she just stared at the food, unable to lift a piece to her mouth. She kept going over in her mind what Leonard had told her when she arrived at FBI headquarters. The group that had already caused the death and injury of more than three dozen people using college students to deliver bombs to Jewish institutions very likely had convinced their daughter to do the same tomorrow in New York City.

She just couldn't wrap her mind around the logic. It made no more sense to her than Courtney's shacking up with a boyfriend. Not that Courtney was disinterested in boys. Being her mother, Alison thought Courtney was attractive, but she knew her daughter was a little thin for some boys' liking, and since she was quite independent and worldly, some guys her age found her intimidating.

Having an independent streak, wanting to be her own person--Alison recognized those battles from her own years growing up. She had tried to be more understanding than her own mother had been. Her mother had raised Alison and her sister like she'd been raised, which meant they had been expected to wear dresses on holidays and refrain from physical contact with boys, other than holding hands as long as they were still living at home.

But being independent to the point of throwing in with a group of terrorist lunatics--that made no sense. Nor did Leonard's explanation that they must have something to hold over Courtney's head in order to have coerced her cooperation. She couldn't think of anything they could threaten her with that would make Courtney kill innocent people, much less put her own life in danger.

There had to be another explanation, which meant they had to find her and soon. Leonard was briefing the NYC FBI on the situation in their conference room. She agreed not to attend the briefing when the agent in charge expressed doubts about the propriety of the mother being in the room where various responses were being discussed.

Leonard started to object. "She's more than just Courtney's mother," he asserted, but Alison intervened.

"I'd rather not be in there," she told him.

Leonard tried to ease her mind by reporting that his entire task force was working on finding Courtney and the terrorists, but what could they do from Washington?

The terrorists were not amateurs. They had pulled off three bombings without more than one of their group having been identified, and he was dead and unable to rat on his colleagues. They knew how to avoid detection.

Nor was Alison cheered by the agent-in-charge's assurance that both the FBI and New York City Police Department would remain on full alert until the terrorists were captured and Courtney was freed. The city was too big. There were too many possible targets and too little time. The only good news was that the Jewish New Year had started that evening, which meant that offices of Jewish organizations were closed, most of them for the entire week.

There was always the possibility that they would try to bomb a synagogue, but Alison wanted to believe the terrorists would know that such an act would turn the public against them in a way that bombing an organization's offices had not.

Her one ray of hope was that they would bring in Doreen Rupert, and she would confess and help them find Courtney. The FBI and NYPD were looking for her now. She prayed that Doreen was at the girls' apartment and would be brought in shortly. Alison knew they'd never allow her to question Doreen, but she'd like to think that Doreen would be more likely to tell the truth if she thought Alison was going to be alone in a room with her. She clenched her fists at the thought of what she'd like to do to her, feeling not an iota of shame at her thoughts.

"Eat something."

It was Leonard. The meeting must be over.

"I'm not hungry. Now that everyone knows the situation, what's the plan?"

"We let everyone do their jobs, including the FBI, the NYPD, and my team back in D.C."

"So you expect me to just sit here while my daughter's life is hanging in the balance?"

Leonard put his hand on her arm. "Tell me what you want to do."

"You're the one who always knows what needs to be done. You tell me. You say I'm so capable--a trained FBI agent. So, tell me what should I do? Where should I go?"

Alison looked around, hoping no one noticed her outburst or the tears streaming down her face. She got up, ignoring Leonard pleas, and ran to the ladies room.

The agent in charge of the NYC FBI office asked Leonard to take his wife to wherever they were staying and let them do their jobs. "And that includes tomorrow," he said. "We'll contact you the moment we know anything."

Leonard started to argue, but gave up before the words came out of his mouth. He'd tell any parent that exact same thing were he in the reverse situation. He was out of it now. He'd done everything possible, and he'd failed. He'd failed to stop the terrorists, and worse, he failed to protect his own daughter.

While an agent helped him pack up his computer monitors and keyboards, Leonard made a last call to Virginia. Meir was on the phone, so Leonard asked for Pavel.

"Any news, boss?"

"Nothing. We're going to our hotel. We'll be there until this is all over."

"Okay. Everyone's working their tails off here. Gary came back in and Aaron Hayes offered to come in, but I told him to stay home. He'd just get in the way."

"That's fine. What's Ekaterina working on?"

"She put in the additional search terms and is monitoring the feed. Do you want me to ask her if she's got anything?"

"No, just tell everyone I appreciate all you guys have done--the extra hours, the weekends . . .We were so close."

"It's not over, boss," Pavel said. "We can still find them before anything happens."

"I know. It's just--well, I'll let you go."

"Wait a sec. Ekaterina wants to talk to you."

"What about? Are we doing something illegal?"

The second those words left his mouth, Leonard hoped Pavel hadn't heard him. Apparently he hadn't, because Ekaterina came on the phone.

"Professor Robbins."

"Yes, Ekaterina. How can I help you?"

"It's maybe I can help you."

"How?"

"I heard from the Russians. I wrote up a theoretical and told them the first to come up with the answer would earn $25,000 American."

"And they believed you?"

"I hope you will pay the winner, Professor. Otherwise, they are going to kill me."

"We'll see about the money, but what's the point here? Did you find out how they're communicating?"

"Oh, yes. That part was easy. The games. We already know that. The part I mean is how they set off the bombs."

"The bombs? You mean the communications from the tablet that detonates the bomb?"

"Yes, that. I ask the groups to present the most elegant method. I now have three ways to try."

"Great. That's wonderful, Ekaterina. Look, I've got to get my wife back to our hotel. You can fill me in tomorrow."

Peter G. Pollak

Queens, New York: Tuesday, September 11

"I take you to bathroom now," the Palestinian woman informed Courtney from the doorway of the bedroom where Courtney had spent a sleepless night, secured to the bed by a long bicycle chain and a wristband.

Courtney's prayers to be rescued had not been answered. Her parents must be out of their minds trying to find her, but Courtney feared they would not be able to do so before she was forced to deliver what she had no doubt was a bomb to some office where innocent people would die.

If she refused to deliver the package, they would explode the bomb planted under the ramp at her parents' home. Nor could she erase the realization that she would be among the victims of the bomb she was expected to deliver. How had it come to this? What could she do to stop it?

Erik Greene called out as the Palestinian was escorting Courtney back from the bathroom. "Can I bring her some coffee?"

The woman hesitated. "We're not making any more."

Erik lifted the mug in his hand. "There was some left."

The woman walked away leaving the door ajar. Courtney thought of trying to make a run for it, but hesitated, remembering the beatings she'd received both times she tried that. Before she could make up her mind,

Erik came into the room and closed the door behind him. "Drink some of this."

Courtney took the coffee, went over to the bed, and sat down. Her neck was stiff and sore from when the bodyguard jerked her back by her hair and her wrist was sore from when he slammed her to the floor when she tried to get away a second time.

"Did you get any sleep?"

"What do you care?"

"Courtney, you're making this harder on yourself than necessary."

"They're threatening to kill my parents. That must be easy where you come from!"

"They only threatened you because you wouldn't have listened to them otherwise. If you do as they say, nothing will happen to your parents . . . or to you."

"If you believe that, Erik, you're dumber than I thought."

Erik blanched. She was glad her insult stung.

"They're picking a new place for you to deliver the petitions," he said.

"I want to see the petitions before I deliver them."

"That's not up to me."

"Then you ask to inspect them."

"Okay, I'll ask. In any case, it will all be over in a few hours."

"Says you."

Erik seemed about to say something, but he just gave her a sad look and left the room, locking the door behind him.

Alison sat down on the edge of the bed. She had finally dozed off some time after three in the morning. When she woke up, Leonard was sitting at the hotel room desk his attention divided between his laptop, the hotel TV, which was turned to CNN, and his extra monitor. Sections of the *New York Times*, *Wall Street Journal*, and *Daily News* were strewn on the floor and coffee table.

She nibbled on a piece of dry toast from the breakfast tray Leonard must have ordered when she was in the shower. The coffee was hot, but at the moment whether her coffee was not or cold was of little import.

She couldn't stay in that room all morning waiting for news of her daughter's fate. It wasn't the room itself, although it wasn't the hotel where they usually stayed, which apparently was full. Leonard's office manager had booked them into the Lexington--an east side boutique hotel. The problem was she couldn't stand not doing anything. "I'm going to go for a walk," she announced.

"That's a good idea," Leonard said, turning to give her an encouraging smile.

Always the optimist! Except she knew he was just as sick inside with fear as she, if not more so. She knew the possibility of error, of failure. He did not. Even his injury, the result of an auto accident he believed had been engineered by an Argentinian leftist group, did not represent a failure on his part. It had been his agency's failure, not his.

Now, for perhaps the first time in his life, he was faced with having failed and with the knowledge that the consequences were not relatively inconsequential, but the loss of a part of himself that could not be replaced.

She wanted to help him, but she couldn't help herself. She was angry--so angry she had not said but a few words to him since they left the FBI offices the night before. She knew the anger was irrational. Even had he been gentler and more understanding with Courtney in recent months, even if she had not been so set on rebelling, their daughter might still be in mortal danger, but the anger was there, and the only way she knew how not to express it at that moment in a way that would hurt both of them was to leave the room.

She wasn't sure what she'd do once she got outside. It was a warm end of summer day--the eleventh of September. She might find a bookstore, purchase a syrupy romance, and then sit in a coffee shop until he called her either to tell her their daughter was safe or that she was dead.

For the tenth time that morning Leonard went over the list he'd created on a yellow pad of what they knew and didn't know. The key question was what would the terrorists do, given that all the Jewish organizations they might have targeted were closed for the Jewish New Year. They couldn't let Courtney go. Today was September 11 and they had to make a statement to the world. He figured they would send her to a new target-- perhaps one having to do with the nine-eleven celebrations--and ask her to deliver an innocently wrapped package with not-so-innocent contents.

Although he still couldn't understand why she'd go along with them, the best chance of stopping them was to figure out where they were taking her.

He was glad that Alison had gone out. He didn't know what to say to her that would ease her fear that their daughter was going to die that very day. He had told her the night before that his team, working with both the NYPD and the FBI, would stop them, but how could he in good conscience expect her to believe him when feelings of doubt were tearing his insides?

Yet, he couldn't shut off his computer and let his team and the law enforcement organizations do their jobs. Deep inside, he blamed himself for Courtney's being in this situation, which meant it was his responsibility to get her out of it.

He opened a conference call with his team at 0900. They were all there, even Aaron Hayes from Rosa Martinez' office.

"We don't have a minute to waste, folks," he began. "First priority is figuring out where they might attack."

"You saw the list we put together, Len," Meir said. "Can you think of any other sites?"

"I know. I saw it--more than forty possibilities. That's too many. We need to find something that tells us for certain which one they've chosen."

"There's been no noise in the game rooms," Pavel stated.

"Why not? Have they switched to some other communications channel?" Leonard asked.

"Possibly," Pavel replied, "but it's more likely that the people who were using the games to communicate before are together in the same place."

"That could be the case, but we have to keep monitoring the games anyway."

"Of course, boss."

"There might be another way."

It was Larry Burnside.

"What's that Larry?"

"Algorithmic probability."

"In English."

"A program that assigns probability for specific observations. We enter all the variables that we know, and it ranks the likelihood of their choosing each location."

"How long will that take?"

"Not sure. I'm not even sure we have enough data, but I thought it was worth mentioning."

"You don't need my permission to give it a try, Larry. If you think that it's the best use of your time, and it could yield results in time to make a difference, go for it."

Leonard concluded the meeting ten minutes later telling them he didn't want to keep them from doing their jobs. "Let me know if you see anything––no matter how insignificant it seems––that might tell us what their target is."

Pavel buzzed Leonard's phone only seconds after the meeting broke up. "What's up, Pavel?"

"Ekaterina said she told you about her find."

"Yes, although it comes a bit too late, don't you think?"

"Maybe not. She didn't think you understood what she was telling you."

"Possibly not. Explain it to me."

"It means not only can she identify the tablet that is being used to detonate the bomb as soon as they launch the program, but she can communicate with it."

"What! Holy shit. No, she didn't make that clear to me."

"I didn't think so. She tried––"

"That doesn't matter now. How much of a time gap would there be between when they initiate their program and when we know where it is?"

"It'll happen right away, boss. She's got her system set up to detect any use of that program. Then in seconds she can tell us where the party is that's running the program."

"That's great, but let me think. Knowing where they are when they launch the program might be too late for us to get someone to that location. Can she disarm it or shut it down?"

"She's working on that."

"So the answer at the moment is no."

Pavel didn't say anything.

"Thanks, Pavel," Leonard said. "Tell her I'm sorry I–
–"

"No need to apologize, boss. There's still time. We'll stop them."

"I wish I could be that optimistic."

"Don't lose faith, boss. It's not over yet."

Peter G. Pollak

Queens, New York: Same Day

The Palestinian woman opened the door and told Courtney it was time. "Put on the uniform," she said, pointing to the box on the floor.

Courtney hesitated. "Do you want I should get Omar and my brother to hold you while I put it on you?"

Courtney gave the woman a dirty look, but did as she was told. As she dressed, the woman told her she would be blindfolded again. "You must keep the blindfold on until you are told you can take it off. Then you will take the package to the office where we tell you and wait for them to sign for it. If you disobey, we will ring the doorbell on your parents' house. When someone answers, we will detonate the bomb I placed under the steps. Do you understand?"

"You don't have to keep telling me. I get it."

Alison fought down the urge to scream. She was wandering through *Barnes & Noble* looking for a novel that she thought she could read more than a page of when for some reason her eye caught the title: *Gender and the Political: Deconstructing the Female Terrorist.* Gathering herself, she stumbled out of the store and started walking again, now looking for a coffee shop where she could sit down. She looked inside a *Dunkin' Donuts,* but there were no empty tables. The next block offered a *Starbucks.* She stood in line, got a flavored coffee, and found an empty spot on a couch. The remains of a *New York Times* lay between her and an overweight man with stringy hair. He was slurping something noisily from a plastic cup with a company logo on it.

The newspaper barely kept her interest for five minutes. She put it aside and just watched the people. She couldn't sit still any longer. She didn't know where to go, but then her phone buzzed. She gasped, causing people to turn to see what had happened.

She pulled her phone out of her purse, but was afraid to check it. Was it over already? Was she dead?

She peeked. It was Doreen Rupert. *Thank God.*

She fumbled to answer the call while getting up and pushing her way through the line of people waiting to place their orders. "Doreen. Where are you?"

"I'm sorry, Mrs. Robbins. I just had to apologize. You were so nice to me--"

"Doreen, where's Courtney?"

"You haven't heard from her?"

"No, we've been looking everywhere. Is she with those people?"

Silence.

Alison walked toward the corner. "Doreen. You have to tell me."

She heard Doreen snivel. "I don't know where they are. She was just supposed to do the same thing I did yesterday, deliver some petitions to a museum."

"If it was a Jewish museum, they were closed for the Jewish New Year."

"Oh, I didn't--"

"Where are you? At the apartment?"

"No, I stopped by there a few minutes ago. She wasn't there and I don't think she came home last night."

"Then who has her? Where did they take her?"

"She was with Erik and Omar from the SPJ group. I don't know where they took her. Erik didn't come home last night either. I checked with Emily. She's pissed--"

"Wait. Go over it again. Tell me about yesterday."

"They picked the two of us up in a van yesterday afternoon like Courtney told you--to test her. They told me I had to do it first so she would see how easy it was."

"Where? Where did they take you?"

"To some midtown office building. The package had the name and address on it. I went in. They scanned the box with some kind of metal detector; when it passed, they signed for the package and that was that."

"Then what happened?"

"Erik told me to make an excuse to leave them. That's what I did. I was on my way home when you saw me."

"So Courtney was supposed to do the same thing at a museum?"

"Yes."

"But if the museum was closed, why is she missing?"

"I don't know, Mrs. Robbins."

Alison entered the lobby of the Lexington Hotel. She hesitated going into the elevator for fear the connection would be dropped. She sat down in an easy chair near the entrance. "You said they picked you up in a van. Did the van belong to one of the others?"

"No, it was a rental."

"How do you know?"

"It had the rental company's name on the side. Rent-Me Vans."

"What color? How big?"

"Off-white. I'm not sure how else to describe it."

"What is Omar's surname?"

"Mejari or something like that."

"Spell it."

"I don't know. I just heard him say it. I never saw it written."

"What about the other one--Erik?"

"Erik Greene with an 'e' on the end. I can give you his address and phone number."

"Wait a minute. I'll get something to write on."

After writing down Erik Greene's address, Alison asked Doreen to describe both men: height, build, hair color, and any other distinguishing characteristics she could remember. "Doreen. Please call the FBI and turn yourself in."

"I can't, Mrs. Robbins."

"Yes you can. It's the right thing to do."

"I'm afraid."

"Afraid of what, Doreen?"

"Your husband. If anything happens to Courtney, he'll kill me."

"Doreen, if anything happens to Courtney, that's the least of your worries."

At that, Alison hung up the phone and headed for the elevator.

"It's time to go," Manar said to Courtney. "Do you want Omar and Ali to carry you?" she asked when Courtney failed to stand up quickly enough.

Erik came over and helped her stand and walk to door of the apartment.

Manar shoved a rag in front of Courtney's face. "If I hear a peep out of you, this gag is going in your mouth."

Courtney tried to shy away from Manar, but Omar and Ali held her arms firmly. They walked her to the elevator. Manar rode down with them.

They walked Courtney to the van and told her to get in. When she hesitated, they shoved her roughly into the van and secured her to the bench with the wristband and chain from the bedroom.

―――

"Courtney," Erik said, squatting down next to her. "Pull yourself together. Do what you're being asked to do, and no one has to die today."

She looked away from him, not wanting to give him the satisfaction of having any influence on her behavior.

"I'm going to drive us to the location they've picked out. It'll all be over in a short while."

Forty-five minutes later Erik found a spot to park in an unloading zone on East Forty-Eighth. The target was the New York City office of Senator Joseph Stern, which was located on the twenty-third floor of 780 Third Avenue.

Erik got into the back of the van. Omar had brought up the picture of the Robbins' house in upstate New York. When Courtney refused to look, he grabbed her chin and twisted her head toward the monitor. "I can set off the bomb from here."

"You don't have to do that," Erik said. "She gets it."

Omar gave him a look of disgust.

"Are you ready?" Erik asked Courtney. "Just deliver the package, and all will be okay."

Courtney looked at him as if she couldn't believe he was still trying to feed her that line.

Erik knew it was a line and didn't blame Courtney for not buying it. He suspected that Omar intended to set off the bomb they had planted under the wheelchair ramp no matter what Courtney did. He also feared that it was very likely that Omar planned to detonate the bomb in the package the moment someone signed for it in Senator Stern's office, killing Courtney as previous bombs had killed students in Washington, D.C. and Chicago.

He had made a decision during the drive into the city to do whatever he could to prevent Omar from killing Courtney and her parents. He couldn't help but notice that morning that Manar and Ali were packing up while he and Omar were carrying the computer equipment down to the van. He overheard the word Canada mentioned more than once, although his knowledge of Arabic was not sufficient to decipher the exact nature of their plans or whether Omar would be joining them.

Erik couldn't believe he had gotten himself in so deep. His complicity in what they were about to do very likely meant spending the rest of his life in prison. Meanwhile, Manar and Ali Hajib would have made their way back to the West Bank where they'd be received as heroes.

None of that mattered at the moment, however. In order to stop the bomb from being delivered, Erik had to convince Courtney to get out of the van and enter the building at 780 Third Avenue.

He handed Courtney a packet of tissues while Omar opened the lock that chained her to the bench.

She refused to look at him, but took the tissues and blew her nose.

Omar had his headphones on and was talking to someone--probably Manar Hajib.

"Courtney, listen to me," Erik said softly, hoping Omar wasn't paying attention. "You have to take the package and go into that building before Omar runs out of patience. That's the only way to save your mother's life."

Courtney took a deep breath and gave him a slight nod.

"Hear me out. Once you're in the building, don't go up to the twenty-third floor," he said, giving her a knowing look.

She looked at him now as if beginning to understand that her fate was not yet sealed. He didn't know how she could trust him, but trusting him was her only chance to survive.

"Wait a few minutes, then bring it back here. Tell Omar they wouldn't let you take it up to the twenty-third floor."

Now she looked him in the eye. Erik prayed that she'd follow his instructions. Omar was off his phone, so he couldn't say anything more.

"Ready?"

Courtney wiped her eyes with her uniform sleeve and nodded.

"Omar, is the package ready?" Erik said loudly.

Omar handed Erik the package, which had been rewrapped with a label addressed to Senator Stern.

It was the first time Erik had handled the bomb. Manar Hajib had informed him they used an advanced liner box that normal x-rays would not penetrate. He doubted that, but, he unlocked the back door of the van, and got out.

"Did you look at it?" Courtney asked.

Erik offered her the package. "Yup, just petitions."

Courtney sighed and took it.

"You're doing great," he told Courtney, as if he were her father leaving her off at an overnight camp.

"Don't forget the tablet," Omar called out to him.

The tablet with the program Omar had showed Courtney how to use sat on the bench. Erik retrieved it and handed it to her. He straightened her UPS ID badge. It looked quite official, but then again he wouldn't know a real one from a forgery.

Courtney took the tablet. She looked resigned, but ready to do what had been demanded of her. That was all he could ask. He handed her the package and pointed her in the direction of Third Avenue. "It's the big building on the corner and don't forget to smile."

He watched her walk slowly to her destination . . . and his.

Leonard was surprised when Alison burst into the hotel room. He had just wheeled out of the bathroom and was contemplating pouring another cup of coffee, knowing that he should switch to something less acidic like the banana that came with their room service breakfast.

"I just talked to Doreen," she said sitting down on the bed and took off her shoes. "She admitted the boyfriend thing was a lie."

"That's big of her. Did she reveal anything else useful?"

"Yes. They had her drop off some petitions yesterday. Apparently, whoever she gave them to didn't think it was anything unusual and didn't report it."

"We found out. She delivered them to the AIA's New York office, but we don't know why they had her do that."

"She told me it was supposed to show Courtney how easy a task they'd set for her."

"Then how does she explain Courtney's disappearance?"

"She said they told her to go home, but she overheard them say they were taking Courtney to some museum."

"Probably The Jewish Museum on Fifth Avenue, which was closed. That is why they kept her overnight. We already know all that. Did she tell you anything that might help us identify where they are?"

"She told me the names of the two people who were running the show, gave me descriptions of both and the address of one," she said, handing Leonard the piece of paper where she'd written down everything Doreen knew about Erik Greene and the man named Omar.

Leonard took the paper. "I'll get this to the FBI right away."

"She also said they were driving a beige rental van with a Rent-Me logo on the side."

"That's not going to help us much if we don't know their target!"

"I know, Len, but I thought you'd want to know--"

"You did good. Come here. Give us a hug."

Leonard got his hug. It wasn't the warmest he'd ever received from his wife of twenty-one years, but given the circumstances, he was thankful.

While Alison headed for the bathroom, Leonard entered the data about the men who had his daughter into his computer and transmitted it to his team as well as to the FBI. He turned to look at his wife when she returned. She looked more together than she had any time in the last twenty-four hours. He wished he could say that about himself.

Courtney stumbled towards the huge office building that dominated the corner trying to make sense of what Erik had told her. Don't go in the building? Come back and tell them they wouldn't let her in? Would Omar believe that? Would he use her failure as an excuse to kill her mother with the bomb under the wheelchair ramp?

She entered the building. The address on the label read Office of U.S. Senator Joseph Stern, twenty-third floor. She approached the bank of elevators even though the last thing she wanted to do was take the package to that office.

If she had to die to protect her parents, she would be the only one. She wasn't going to allow those people to kill anyone else. She looked around for directions to the rest rooms. Not seeing any she straightened her back and went over to the desk in the lobby. "Where's the lady's room?"

The woman at the desk, who was also answering phone calls, gave Courtney a quick look over. "Mezzanine floor. The pass code is 0780."

Courtney thanked the woman and made her way to the escalators. Getting off, she saw the sign for the rest rooms and used the pass code to enter the lady's room.

She sighed. It was empty. She put the package down on the floor in the stall farthest from the entrance and went back to the entrance. She went outside and stood by the door to prevent anyone from entering.

A beep startled her. It was the tablet she'd stuck in the pocket of the uniform. Omar must be looking for her.

Leonard's phone buzzed. It was Larry Burnside. Larry had texted him in the middle of the night that he'd obtained a version of a probability algorithm that could handle the data they wanted to throw at it. Now his message said he was ready to discuss the results.

Leonard put the phone on speaker. "What'd you come up with?"

"There was one location that scored much higher than all the others we entered into the program."

"And that was?"

"Senator Stern's New York City office."

"Which is where?

"780 Third Avenue, twenty-third floor."

"That's right around the corner," Alison said.

"Good work, Larry. I'll contact the Bureau."

"I'll go," Alison said. She sat down on the bed and started to put her shoes back on.

"Ali, it may not be--"

"Where's your gun?"

"What?"

"I know you brought one," Alison said. "Where is it?"

"Ali--"

"Leonard. The gun."

"My briefcase," Leonard said, pointing to the closet.

She opened the briefcase and removed his .40 caliber Sig Sauer and two magazines. She shoved the gun into the back of her pants and put a magazine in each of her pockets.

Leonard wanted to say something but saw the determined look on her face and kept quiet.

She gave him a quick nod, and then left the room without closing the door.

She'd forgotten her FBI badge. Leonard grabbed it and wheeled out into the hall. She was just getting on the elevator. "Wait! Your badge."

She turned, hesitated, and then came back. "Thanks," she said, taking the badge. She patted him on his arm, turned, and headed back to the elevator.

Leonard wheeled himself back into the hotel room. Maybe Alison's going after Courtney was for the best, but then what if she arrived too late? Would she ever forgive him? Would it ruin their marriage, leaving each of them bereft of the anchor that the other had served these past twenty-one years?

Worse, what if both of them died in the bomb blast? Leonard clenched his fists at the thought and wanted to scream.

Stop it. Nothing has happened yet. At that moment, he hated his useless legs. He could get himself outside, but then what? He'd just be in the way. No, he was tied to his computer screens and his cell phone. His chance of

New York City: Same Day

Erik got back in the van and sat on the bench behind Omar so that he could see what the Palestinian was doing. Everything on his main screen was in Arabic. On the second, smaller screen, he recognized a live shot of the Robbins' house in upstate New York.

"So what happens now?" he asked.

"We wait for the signal that the package has been signed for. Then, kaboom!"

"After Courtney is out of the building, right!"

Omar turned to face Erik. "She has to die; otherwise, you go to prison. Do you want to kill her yourself or let me do it?"

Erik felt a pain in the middle of his chest. "When this first came up you told me the bombs were not real, that they were just to scare people."

Omar shrugged, and then turned back to his computers. "I do what I am told."

"What about the one at her parents' house?"

"I will send a signal to their doorbell. When someone answers, I push this button," he said pointing to a device attached to the computer. "Kaboom!"

At that moment Erik wanted some deity to appear and stop the madness, but he didn't believe in deities, especially not the one that had let his great grandparents die in a German concentration camp. What could he do? Omar was twice his size and Erik had spied a gun in Omar's overnight bag, which now sat under the computer bench.

He also couldn't do anything about the electrical power. Omar's equipment ran off a battery pack that had enough power to run twice as many devices.

If Courtney failed to deliver the bomb and brought it back to the van, Omar wouldn't explode it, but he still might detonate the bomb at the Robbins' house.

Erik opened the back of the van. "I'm going up front," he told Omar. "We'll need to leave here pretty quickly when it goes off."

Omar nodded. Erik went up front, started the engine and pulled into traffic. What if they weren't there when Courtney came back? That was the best he could come up with--get far enough away so that maybe the detonator wouldn't work.

Alison hurried out of the hotel entrance. A beige Rent-Me rental van was in a line of trucks and cars waiting for the Third Avenue traffic light to change. Was it them? She started running. She caught up with the van and crossed in front of it. The driver was a youngish-looking man with curly hair and glasses. Erik Greene?

The driver didn't pay any attention to her until she stepped to the driver's side and called to him through the open window. "Turn off the engine and get out the vehicle with your hands over your head."

When he hesitated, she aimed the Sig Sauer at his head. This time he did as instructed, turning off the engine and stumbling over his own feet as he got out of the van.

"Turn around and put your hands on the side of the van," she told him, shoving him against the van. "What's your name?"

He started to turn his head, but Alison held it back with the pistol. "Your name, goddammit!"

"Erik. Erik Greene."

"Where's my daughter? Where's Courtney Robbins?"

"In the building," he said, nodding toward the large building behind him. "The package, it . . . it contains a bomb."

"Damn you to hell! Where's Omar? Where's your partner?"

"Inside," he said nodding towards the van.

She heard someone call out. "Erik, where are you? What are you doing?"

"That's him," Erik said.

"Is he armed?" Alison demanded.

Erik nodded.

"Erik, you shit. Answer me," the voice inside the van said, louder this time.

"Tell him there's a problem with traffic."

"We're stuck in traffic," Erik yelled. The light had changed; horns blared from the cars they were blocking.

"Will he come out if you ask him?" Alison asked.

Erik shook his head. "I don't think so."

She had to get inside the van. "Stay there."

"He's got the detonator," Erik warned her.

Holding the gun on Erik, she opened the driver's side door and peered in. There was a small window separating the cab from the back of the van. She might be able to take out Omar through the window, but he might detonate the bomb if he saw her first.

She got back out. "I want you to open the back door."

"It's locked."

"Where's the key?"

"On the key ring in the ignition."

Alison extracted the keys from the ignition.

Omar was yelling louder. "Erik, what's going on? Talk to me, you *bokhesh*!"

Alison tossed the keys to Erik and motioned for him to move to the back of the van. "Open the back door. Tell him to come out. Tell him you need his help."

"Put the gun down, lady."

Two uniformed police officers were approaching from the direction of the office building, their weapons drawn.

"I'm FBI," she called over her shoulder. "Cover the front of the van."

They hesitated. She flashed the badge, which she had clipped to her belt. "Do it," she yelled. They looked at each other, but complied.

Alison moved into position behind a *FedEx* Drop Box where she could see the back of the van. "Now, Erik. Open the lock. Tell him to come out."

Erik sidled over to the back of the van, put the key in the door lock, and turned it. "Omar, come out. I need to show you--"

Erik flew backwards. His head bounced as his body landed on the street. Blood oozed from his chest. The crack, crack, crack of Omar's pistol reverberated off the tall buildings.

"Damn," Alison said. She thought to call an ambulance, but there wasn't time. She had to get Omar before he detonated the bomb.

Erik had managed to open one of the back doors to the van, but she couldn't see the shooter.

"You, in the van," she yelled, crouching as low behind the *FedEx* box as she could. "This is the FBI. You're surrounded. Come out with your arms in the air."

In response, Omar fired three more rounds. The last one slammed into the *FedEx* box.

That was too close. She held her breath, fearing the blast that would indicate her daughter was dead. Nothing. Maybe there was still time.

Alison looked around. Pedestrians had cleared the area and the vehicles behind the rental van were empty. She saw two new uniformed city police officers coming from the direction of the office building, walking slowly, their guns drawn.

Alison flashed her FBI badge and motioned them to her side. "We've got a terrorist holed up inside the van. I want you and your colleagues to distract him by shooting out the front windshield on my signal."

"Lady. Why don't we wait for--"

"There's no time. The guy in the van has a detonator to a bomb that was taken into the building . . . to Senator Stern's office."

"Go ahead," the older of the two told his partner. "I'll help the lady."

Alison wasn't about to argue. "Get in position to fire into the van," she told the cop. "When I open the door, don't hesitate."

"Be careful, ma'am," the cop said.

Alison waited until the city cop had positioned himself behind an abandoned pickup truck, then crawled on the ground toward the back of the van. She heard sirens. Help was on the way, but she couldn't wait. Every second counted.

Stopping a few yards from the back of the van, she motioned to the cops in front to fire at the front of the van. They complied. She waited a few seconds, before motioning for them to stop. She waited to see if Omar would fire back. Nothing. Maybe they got him.

With the Sig tucked in her pants, she crawled to the unlocked back door, grabbed the door from the bottom, gave it a yank, and dove fully prone back onto the sidewalk.

The sound of gunfire boomed through the area. The shooting seemed to go on forever, but then it stopped.

Had the city cop got Omar? Maybe he'd been hit. She couldn't call out for fear of giving away her position.

Before she could react, an arm reached out of the van, grabbed the door handle, and pulled it closed. *Damn!*

Praying that the Sig's 12-capacity magazine was fully loaded, she got into a crouch, and holding the gun in both hands, frog-stepped toward the front of the van firing round after round into the side of the van until the magazine was ejected indicating all twelve cartridges have been expended.

There was no return fire.

Alison loaded and racked the second magazine.

"I think you got him, lady," someone called out. It had to be the cop in the back.

The crack of bullets exiting the side of the van she had fired into belied that conclusion. Why hadn't Omar detonated the bomb? Maybe he was waiting for an indication that it had been delivered. She couldn't wait a second longer. He had to be terminated.

Alison crept to where the three uniformed officers had positioned themselves behind a delivery truck. "The person in the van has a detonator to a bomb inside Senator Stern's office," she told them. "We have to take him out. Take cover on the other side," she said pointing to the far side of the van, "Then fire three rounds on my mark."

The men hesitated, but moved cautiously, eventually taking whatever protected positions they could. She hoped the cop in the back would stay where he was in case Omar tried to get out the back.

preventing what was going to happen had come and gone. Now Courtney's fate was in someone else's hands.

"Fire," she called out to the three city officers.

They complied. She waited a few seconds to see if Omar would fire back. Quiet.

Alison crept to the driver's side door, opened it, and climbed in. With the Sig at the ready she peeked through the small smudged window.

She could only see the head and feet of a large man who was crouched down under the window with his arms covering his head, a gun in his left hand.

Now, she told herself. She fired the Sig twice through the window, grazing the top of the man's head and hitting his arm.

The man fell to the floor and raised a bleeding gun arm in her direction. Alison didn't hesitate. She triggered the semi-automatic three times as she'd been taught-- two shots to the chest, one to the head, then dove away from the window and rolled out of the driver's seat onto the ground.

You got him, she told herself, but she needed to be sure. She counted to ten, climbed back into the driver's seat, and looked through the broken window. Omar lay on the van floor, the gun a foot away from his left hand. She couldn't detect any movement.

Alison leaned back in the driver's seat and let out the breath she'd been holding who knew how long.

"I got him," she called out. "I got the son-of-a-bitch!"

Peter G. Pollak

New York City: Same Day

Leonard was sitting in front of his computer screen, trying not to feel sorry for himself for being totally helpless at one of the most critical moments in his life. His cell buzzed. It was Pavel again, calling from Virginia.

He almost didn't answer it. What if it was already too late? Finally, he touched the screen. "I'm here."

"She did it, boss. She did it."

"Who did what?"

"Ekaterina. She broke the connection."

Leonard leaned back in his wheelchair. Tears came to his eyes. He didn't know what to say. "Pavel, I love you. Thank you. That's the best news I've heard . . . ever."

"I've got even better news, boss."

"Okay, I'm listening."

"She's texting with the person who was carrying the tablet."

"That's my daughter. Where is she?"

"Apparently, she took the package she was supposed to deliver to Senator Stern's office into the ladies room on the mezzanine floor after warning people to leave the area."

"But, it didn't--"

"Go off? No. We told her to leave the bomb in the middle of the room and get out of the building."

Whew. Leonard wiped his eyes.

"Hold on. Here's Gary. He's got more."

"Professor Robbins?"

"I'm here, Gary."

"In terms of your daughter, she's safe and we've got a bomb squad minutes away from the building. They're making their way through the traffic."

"Thank God."

"But that's not all. Minutes ago a woman identifying herself as an FBI agent, with the help of several New York City police officers took down two suspected terrorists in a rental van in the middle of East Forty-Eighth Street between Lexington and Third."

"Oh, my God. She got them?"

"One is in critical condition, the other is D.O.A."

"Gary, you don't know how good . . ."

Leonard wasn't able to finish the sentence. He managed to hit the mute icon on his phone before bursting into tears.

"Here's Daddy." Courtney jumped up and ran toward her father, who had been waiting for his wife and daughter at the New York City police headquarters, put her arms around his neck, and squeezed. "I'm so sorry, Daddy," she said through her tears.

"All that matters is that you're safe," Leonard Robbins replied, unable for the second time that day to hold back his own tears.

He caught his wife's eye as she too came to greet him. For a second, he could have sworn he saw in her face a future with the two of them sitting in their Arizona desert backyard, enjoying Sunday night phone calls from their adventurous, but never again reckless daughter.

New York City: Thursday, September 13

It was late in the afternoon before Leonard logged into the task force network. He, Courtney, and Alison had spent what was left of Tuesday and most of Wednesday being debriefed by the FBI and NYC Police Department before they were released--him with a warning that his gun was not legal in New York State, and Alison with a mixture of criticisms and commendations.

In terms of Leonard's gun, the mayor of New York City, with the blessing of the governor, instructed the police department not to confiscate it as long as Leonard promised not to bring it back to the city in the future.

Alison's having represented herself as an FBI agent when in fact she lacked the proper credentials presented a more difficult issue to contend with. The badge she'd been given in San Francisco was only for temporary use--not full reinstatement--and even that had expired. The NYC Police Department, whose men had followed her instructions, seemed unwilling to let that fact slip by until FBI Director Shortell personally contacted the Police Commissioner to inform him that she had not been lying. She had indeed been a federal agent at the time of the incident, having been granted that status on September first. The paperwork was a little slow making its way through the system he stated. From that moment on, the department offered nothing but praise to Alison for having taken out two terrorists in the middle of an attempted bombing.

Thursday morning Courtney withdrew from NYU. On the drive back to Albany, she talked about transferring once she had a chance to decide whether to continue to major in psychology. Both parents thought that was a fine idea even though it meant some added expenses on their part.

Doreen Rupert, Miguel Brizuela, Emily Greene, and the other members of the NYU SPJ steering committee had been brought in for questioning. Doreen and Miguel had been arrested on the spot and were awaiting arraignment. The others were released pending further investigation into what they called Courtney Robbins' final exam.

Erik Greene remained in critical condition. If he lived, Courtney's testimony might mitigate the time he would have to spend in prison.

The Students for Palestinian Justice chapter at NYU lost their charter over the objections of Luisa Castillo and other faculty members who were endorsers of the movement to boycott Israel. They argued unsuccessfully that the incident involving Courtney was the work of a minority and that the administration had no right to suppress legitimate protest.

The best news came Thursday while they were in their van, heading back home. Manar and Ali Hajib had been arrested attempting to cross into Canada using phony passports.

Leonard asked each of the members of the DEFEAT team to be available for a brief conference call the next morning at nine a.m.

"I don't think I have enough words in my vocabulary to express my gratitude to each one of you for the work you did, not just these past few days, but during the entire length of the task force," Leonard told the DEFEAT team Friday morning.

"As you know, we have cracked key elements of this operation which should enable us to find the person behind the Chicago bombing as well as identify all the other agents and fellow travelers in their network.

"It's possible that we can shut down the task force in a few weeks' time and let the FBI and other agencies do their jobs."

He paused to allow the cheers to die down.

"We're only kidding, boss." That was Pavel. "I, for one, won't be happy to go back to pretending I'm just a retired bartender who escaped Russia before the collapse of communism."

Leonard chuckled. "I'm sure a certain NSA analyst would be very happy if you greeted her with a mixed drink at the end of her long days on the keyboard."

"I'll haven't a clue what you're talking about," Pavel said, barely repressing a laugh.

"In any case, I'll be back there on Monday," Leonard said. "Take the rest of the week off."

He heard laughs and cheers.

"I'd like to talk privately to Ekaterina and then to Meir. Again, folks, thank you from the bottom of my heart. You're the greatest."

"We did good, boss?"

"You did great, Ekaterina. I can't tell you how grateful I am. You prevented them from detonating the bomb, saving who knows how many lives, including my daughter's."

"I'm glad. Larry helped, too."

"I know he did. Everyone did great. I hope your agency knows what they've got. Is Meir there?"

Seconds later his old CIA friend came on the line. "You okay, boss?"

"Hey enough with this boss stuff!"

"You mean only Pavel gets to call you that?"

"And now Ekaterina. She has earned the right to call me anything she wants."

"You should have heard the noise when she cut the connection. Everyone was running around here hugging everyone else. If we had any champagne in the fridge, it'd be all over the walls and floor."

"Well, tell everyone I'll order some for next week."

"I'll bet even NSA Martinez won't object."

"Speaking of whom, I'd better call her, but first, I don't know how to thank you, Meir. I couldn't have done it without you."

"I'm glad I was able to help, but I'm going to need a month to catch up on the sleep I lost."

"Don't worry, no more task force appointments for me."

"Okay. See you next week."

"You too, Meir and by the way, Happy New Year!"

Delmar, New York: Sunday, September 16

Leonard Robbins watched his daughter come out on the deck of the Delmar house with a tray of drinks. "A scotch on the rocks for you, Dad, white wine for mom, and a diet soda for me."

She passed the drinks around and sat down. "I'm ready to listen."

"School's back in session?" Alison asked while sipping on her wine.

"It's okay, Mom," Courtney said.

"I'll go easy on her," Leonard said.

"That'll be a first," Alison said with a smile.

Leonard laughed. "Hey, no fair."

"Joining SPJ seemed like the right thing to do at the time, but Dad was right all along," Courtney said. "They had all this documentation on how the Palestinians had been deprived of their homes and how Israel treated non-Jewish residents of their country like second class citizens, and on and on."

"The story is always more complex than either side wants to present it," Leonard said, "but when you take sides you have to know a lot more about whose side you're taking. In the case of the BDS movement, it's ninety-five percent propaganda on a small bed of fact."

"Like when they say they're not tied into terrorists?"

"Exactly. The BDS people want to rationalize what happened. They want to blame a minority of extremists without admitting that terrorism is endemic to Islamic theology. Once you believe yours is the only true religion and that God wants you to convert the entire world to your belief system, it's a short step to adopting the use of force as the necessary and proper means to that end."

"I still feel bad for what the Palestinian people have had to go through."

"That's fine, but you should also recognize that they didn't have to become refugees. The Arab population living in that region could have had their own country seventy years ago, but it would have meant living next to a Jewish state, and they weren't ready to accept that then and they don't seem to be willing to do so now."

"Their history books describe it differently, Dad."

Leonard picked up a paperback from the table next to his wheelchair and handed it to Courtney. "Speaking of which I've got a book for you to read."

Courtney looked it over. "It's pretty thick."

Leonard laughed. "But you've got plenty of time on your hands, right?"

"I guess so, but can't you summarize it for me?"

"Only if you promise to read it."

Courtney nodded.

"The title speaks for itself. 'From Time Immemorial, The Origins of the Arab-Jewish Conflict Over Palestine.'"

"Who's the author?" Alison asked.

"Joan Peters. She passed away a few years ago, but she spent seven years researching the topic, and even though the book came out in the 1980s, it's still the best book on the origins of the conflict."

"Okay, Dad. I'll read it."

"Good. It will help you deal with the BDS demand that the Arab refugees from 1948 deserve the right of return to their land in Israel."

"Maybe I'll read it too," Alison said.

"You should," Leonard said. "In the final analysis, one side rejected the authority of the United Nations to grant the Jewish people their own country and they continue to deny Israel's right to exist seventy years later. The other side grants full citizenship for all residents without regard to religion, just like we do here in the U.S. Furthermore, Israel stands for what we stand for--the rule of law, the rights of the individual, and democracy. If we let them get overrun, what does that say about us?"

"It sounds so simple when you say it, Daddy."

"It is and it isn't. That's why when you're done with that book, I've got three or four more you can read."

Courtney finished her soda. "Maybe I'll just worry about myself for a while."

"Taking some time after what you've been through is a good idea," Leonard said, "but the day will come when you're asked to take sides on some other issue. Learn from this experience. It's not taking sides that's wrong, it's letting someone else do your thinking for you that got you into trouble."

"And on that note, it's time to come inside and help me get dinner on the table," Alison said.

Leonard nodded. "I'll make the salad."

"You always make the salad, Daddy," Courtney said. "I want to do that tonight."

"Fine with me. I'll set the table. That okay, Mrs. R?"

"As long as you don't break any dishes, Mr. R."

-30-

Afterword

It was not my goal in writing *House Divided* to cover all of the innumerable angles of the Arab-Israeli conflict. Despite its flaws, Joan Peters' *From Time Immemorial* is a good starting point for anyone interested in learning the historical origins of the conflict. Another more academic study to look at is Anita Shapira's *Land and Power: The Zionist Resort to Force* (1999). However, like Leonard Robbins' advice to his daughter, you, dear reader, are encouraged to do your own research and form your own opinion.